ヴァッサロード

VOLUME 1
CREATED BY NANAE CHRONO

HAMBURG // LONDON // LOS ANGELES // TOKYO

Vassalord Vol.1
Created by Nanae Chrono

Translation - Alexis Kirsch
English Adaptation - Jennifer Keating
Copy Editor - Shannon Waters
Retouch and Lettering - Star Print Brokers
Production Artist - Michael Paolilli
Graphic Designer - Jennifer Carbajal

Editor - Lillian Diaz-Przybyl
Digital Imaging Manager - Chris Buford
Pre-Production Supervisor - Lucas Rivera
Art Director - Al-Insan Lashley
Managing Editor - Vy Nguyen
Creative Director - Anne Marie Horne
Editor-in-Chief - Rob Tokar
Publisher - Mike Kiley
President and C.O.O. - John Parker
C.E.O. and Chief Creative Officer - Stu Levy

A  Manga

TOKYOPOP Inc.
5900 Wilshire Blvd. Suite 2000
Los Angeles, CA 90036

E-mail: info@TOKYOPOP.com
Come visit us online at www.TOKYOPOP.com

ISBN: 978-1-4278-0614-7

First TOKYOPOP printing: July 2008
10 9 8 7 6 5 4 3 2 1
Printed in the USA

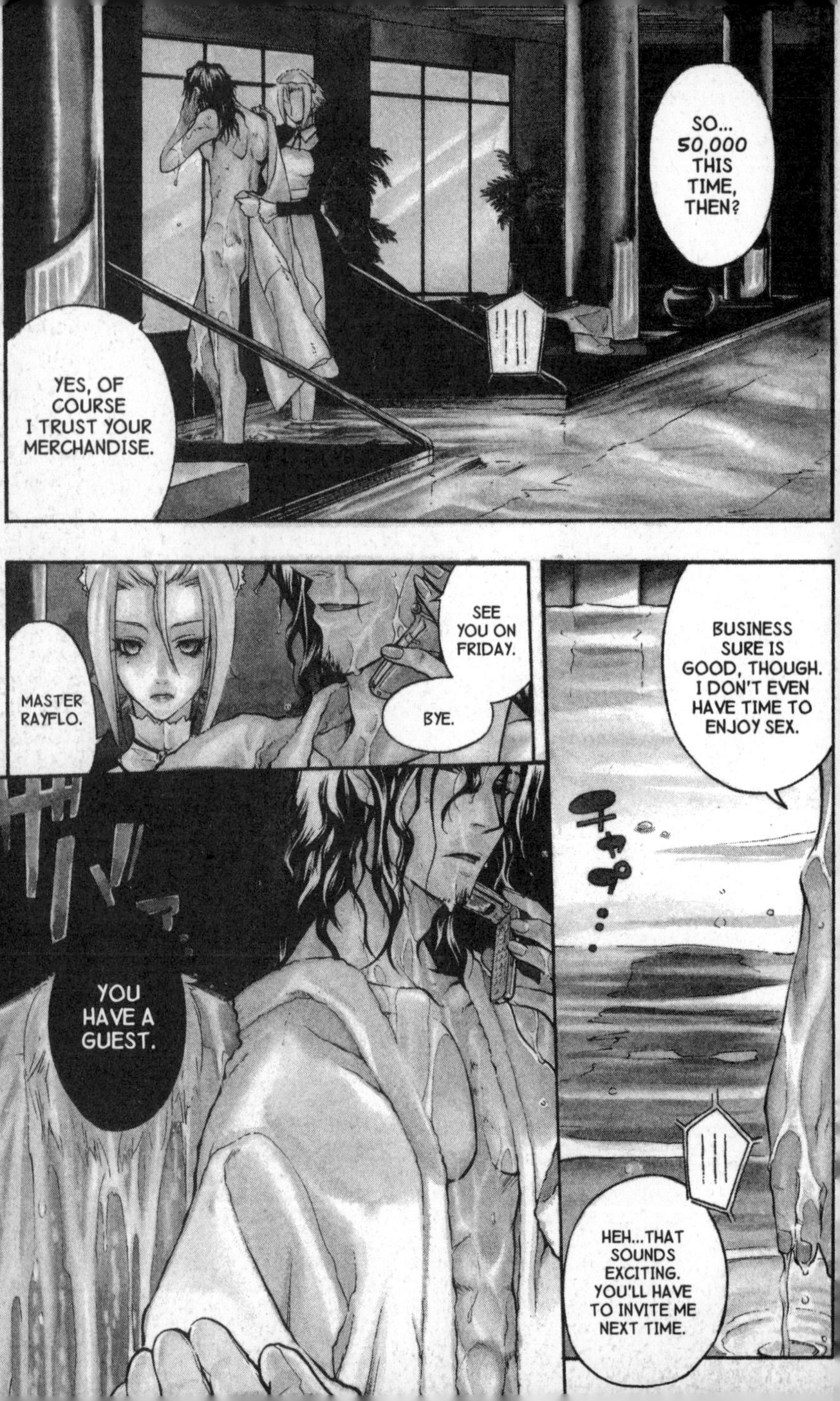
SO... 50,000 THIS TIME, THEN?
YES, OF COURSE I TRUST YOUR MERCHANDISE.
BUSINESS SURE IS GOOD, THOUGH. I DON'T EVEN HAVE TIME TO ENJOY SEX.
チャプ…
HEH...THAT SOUNDS EXCITING. YOU'LL HAVE TO INVITE ME NEXT TIME.
SEE YOU ON FRIDAY.
BYE.
MASTER RAYFLO.
YOU HAVE A GUEST.

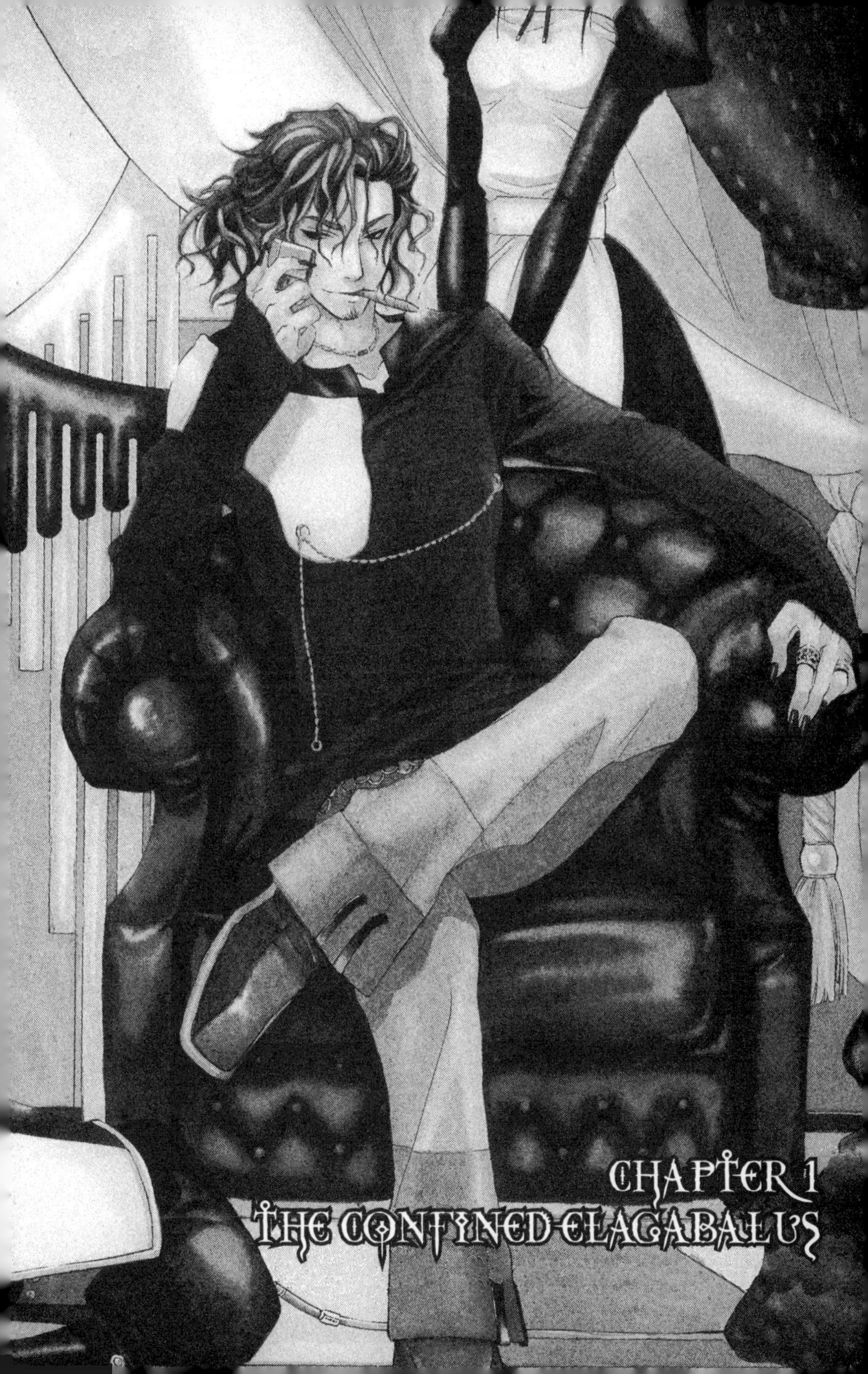
CHAPTER 1
THE CONFINED ELAGABALUS

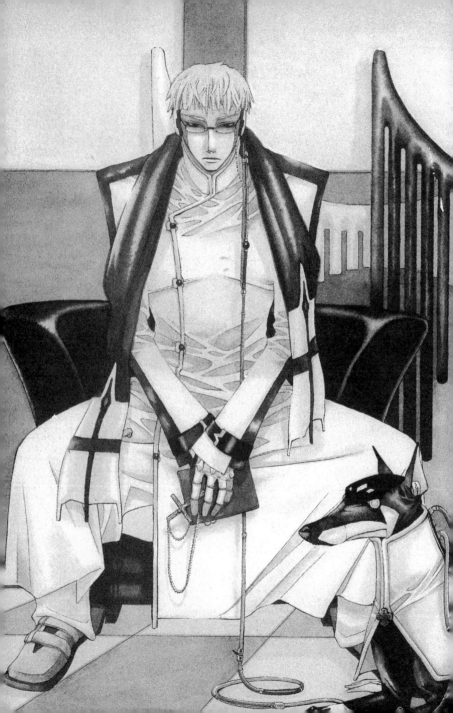

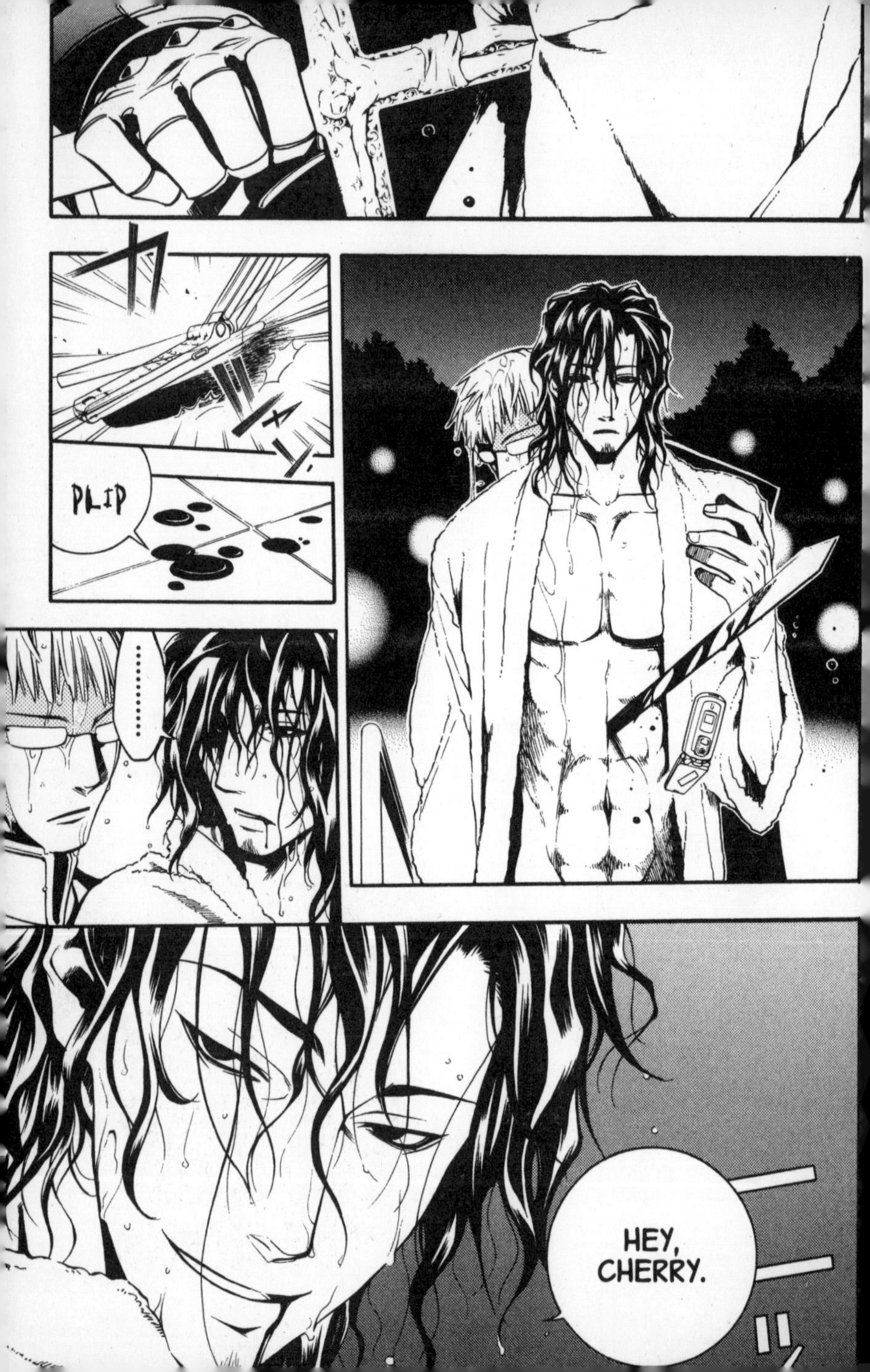
PLIP
......
HEY, CHERRY.

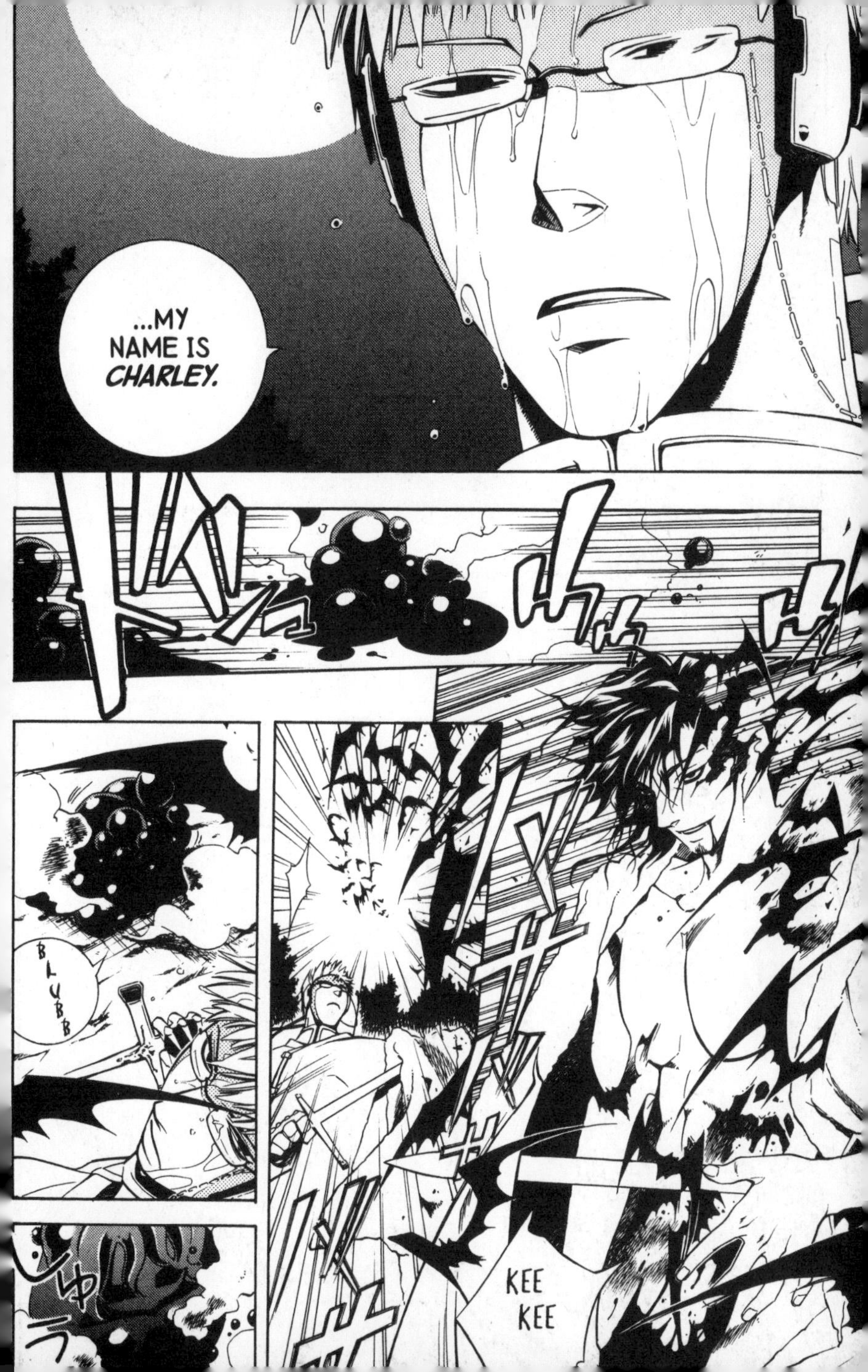
...MY NAME IS CHARLEY.
KEE KEE
BLUBB

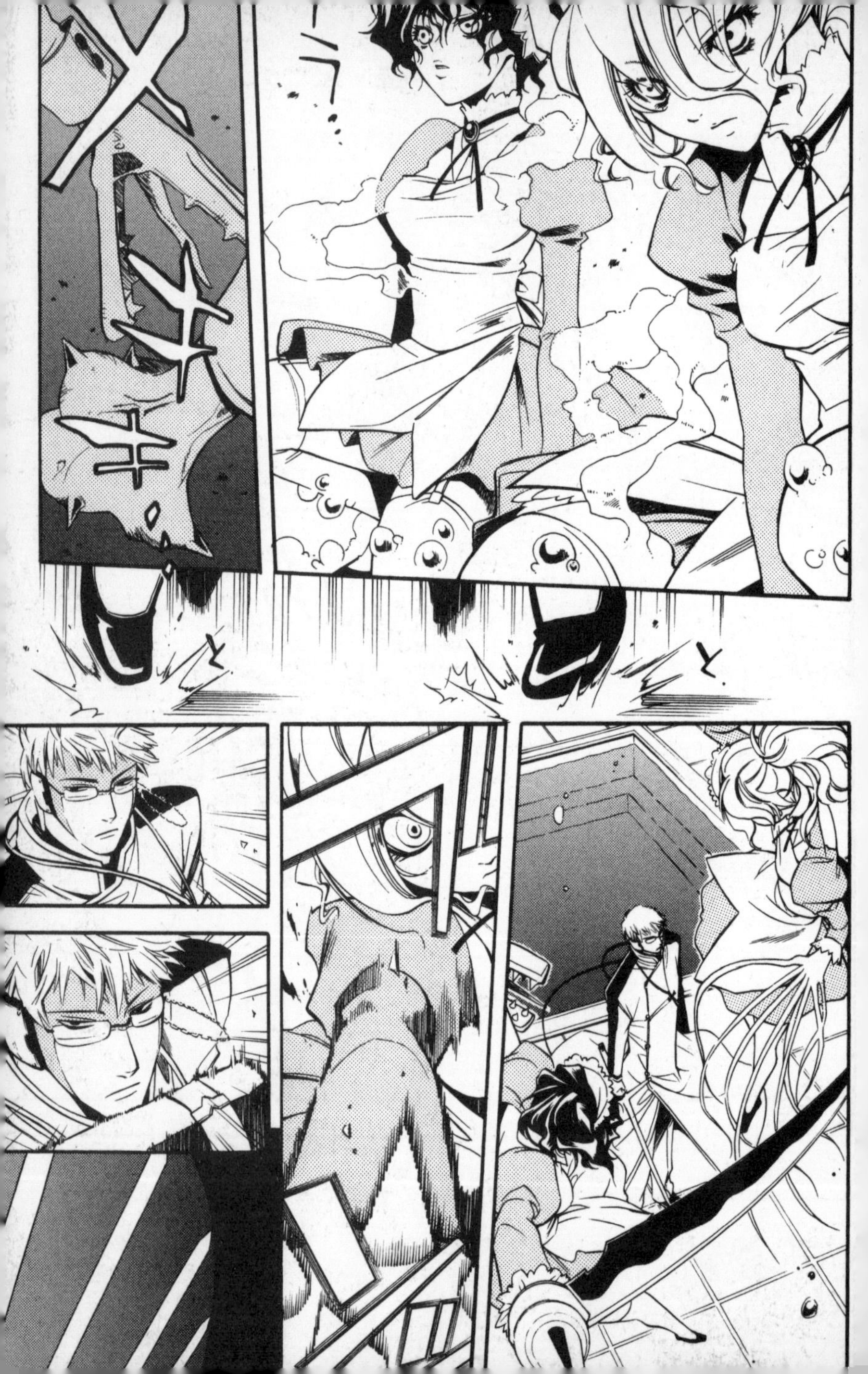

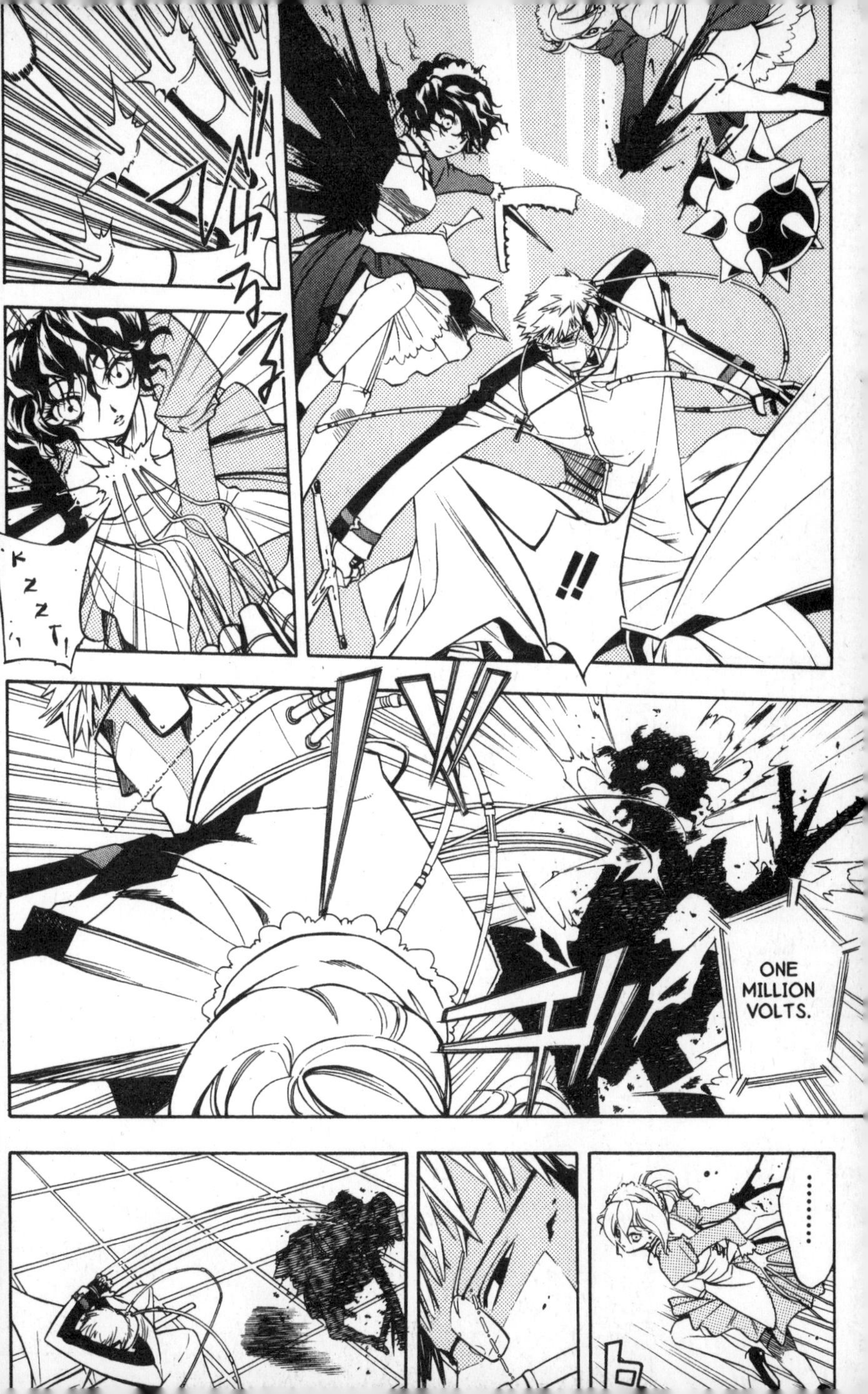

!!
KZZT!
ONE MILLION VOLTS.
......

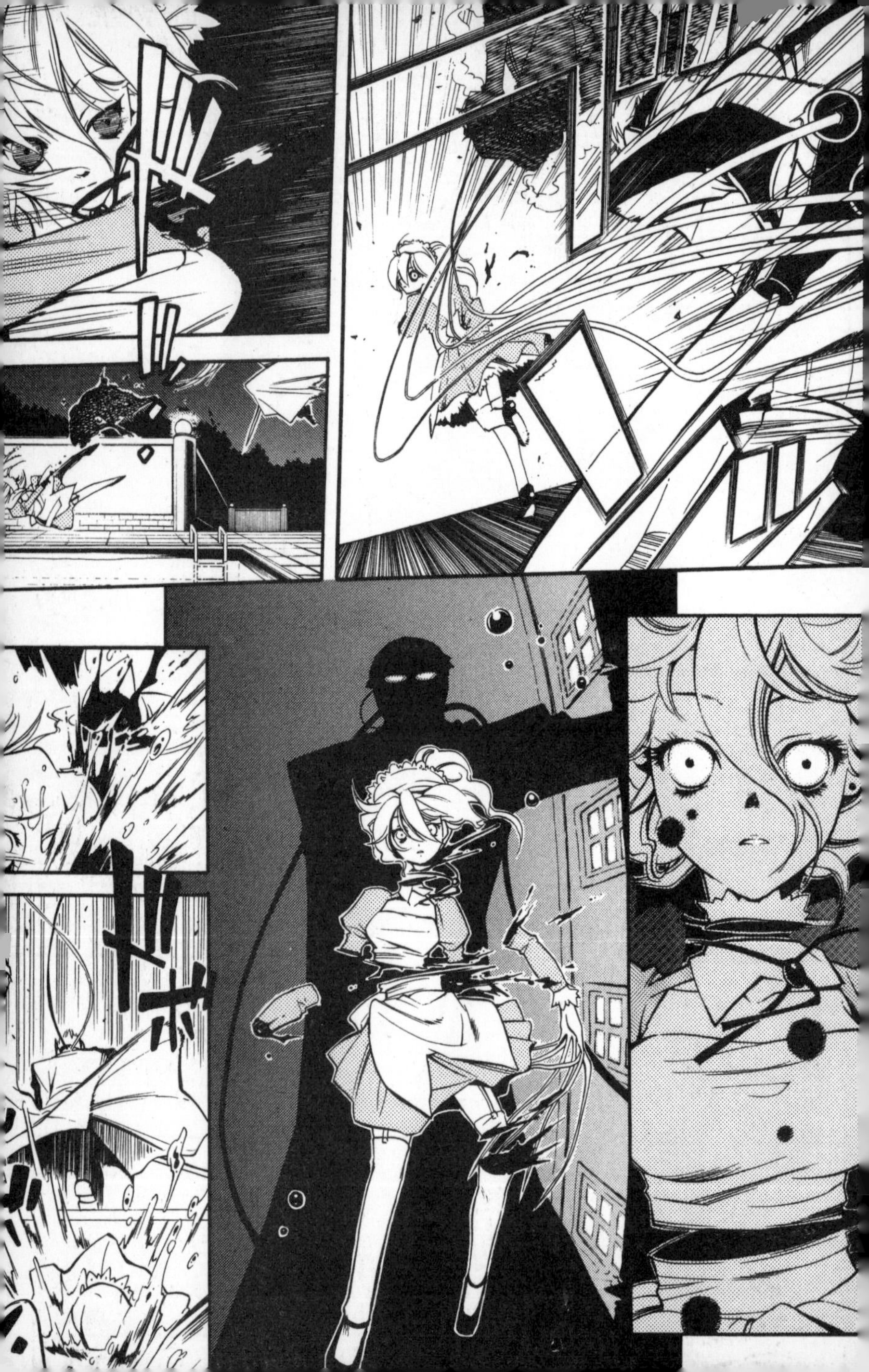

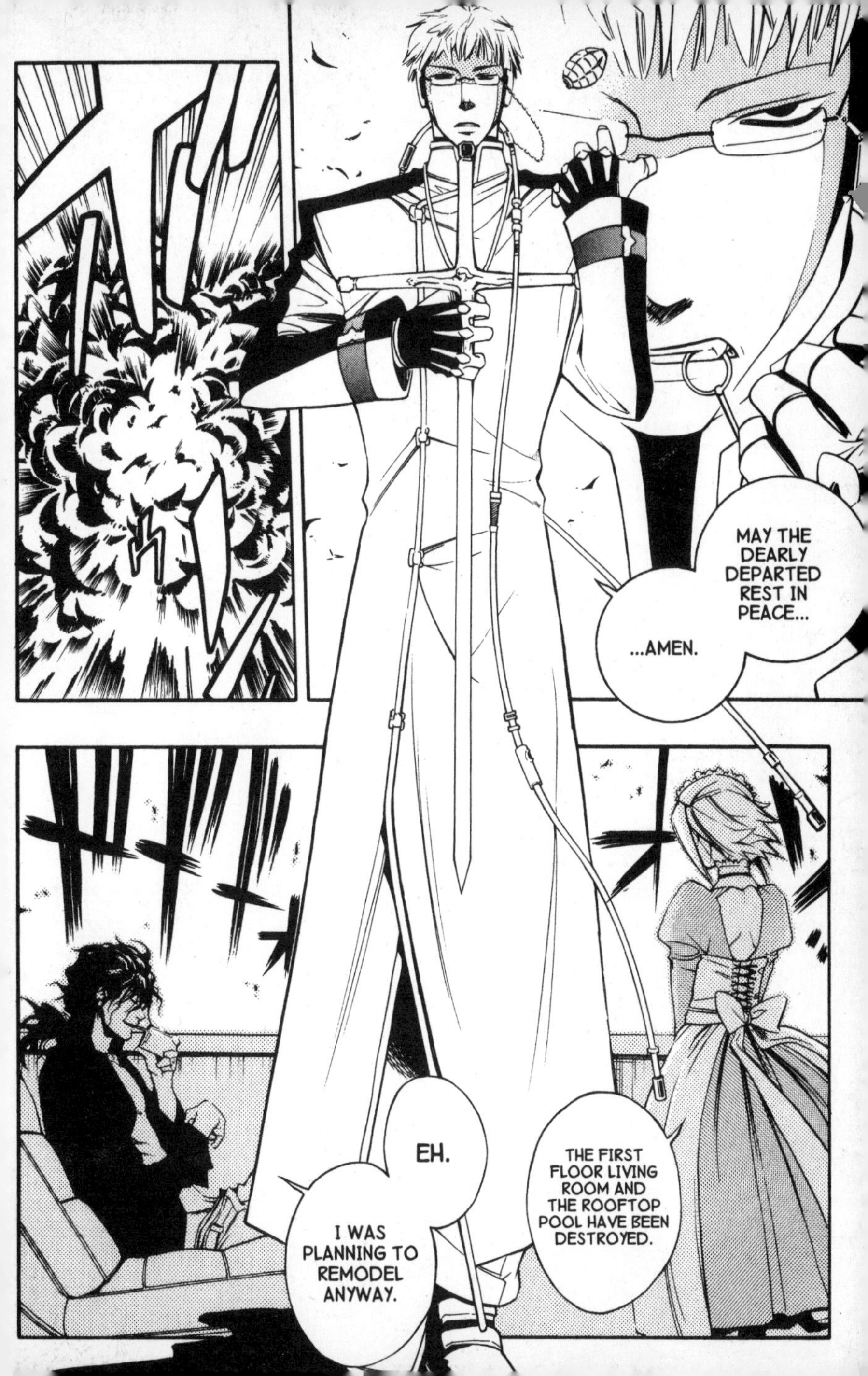
MAY THE DEARLY DEPARTED REST IN PEACE...
...AMEN.
THE FIRST FLOOR LIVING ROOM AND THE ROOFTOP POOL HAVE BEEN DESTROYED.
EH.
I WAS PLANNING TO REMODEL ANYWAY.

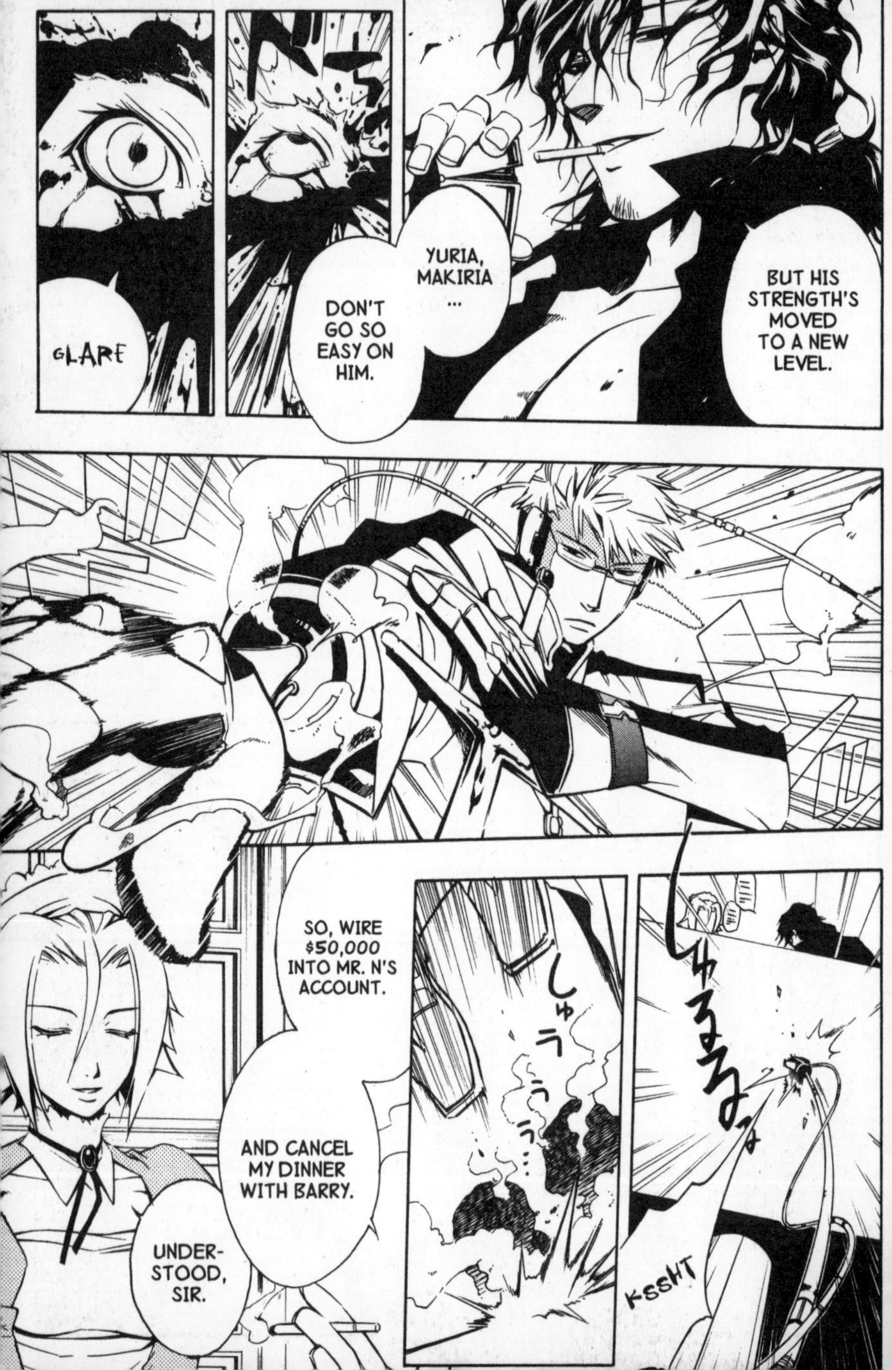
BUT HIS STRENGTH'S MOVED TO A NEW LEVEL.
YURIA, MAKIRIA ...
DON'T GO SO EASY ON HIM.
GLARE
KSSHT
SO, WIRE $50,000 INTO MR. N'S ACCOUNT.
AND CANCEL MY DINNER WITH BARRY.
UNDER-STOOD, SIR.

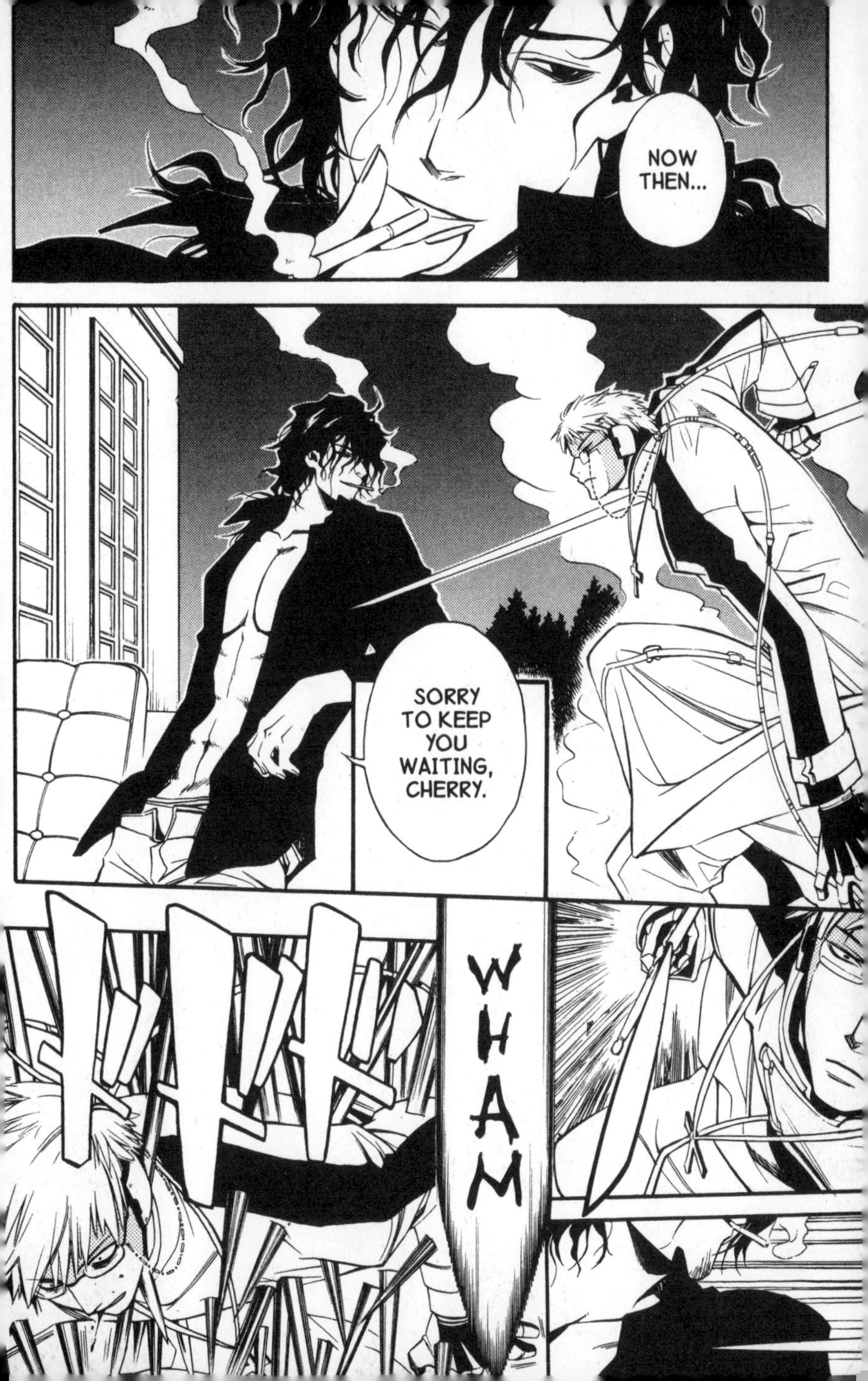
NOW THEN...
SORRY TO KEEP YOU WAITING, CHERRY.
WHAM

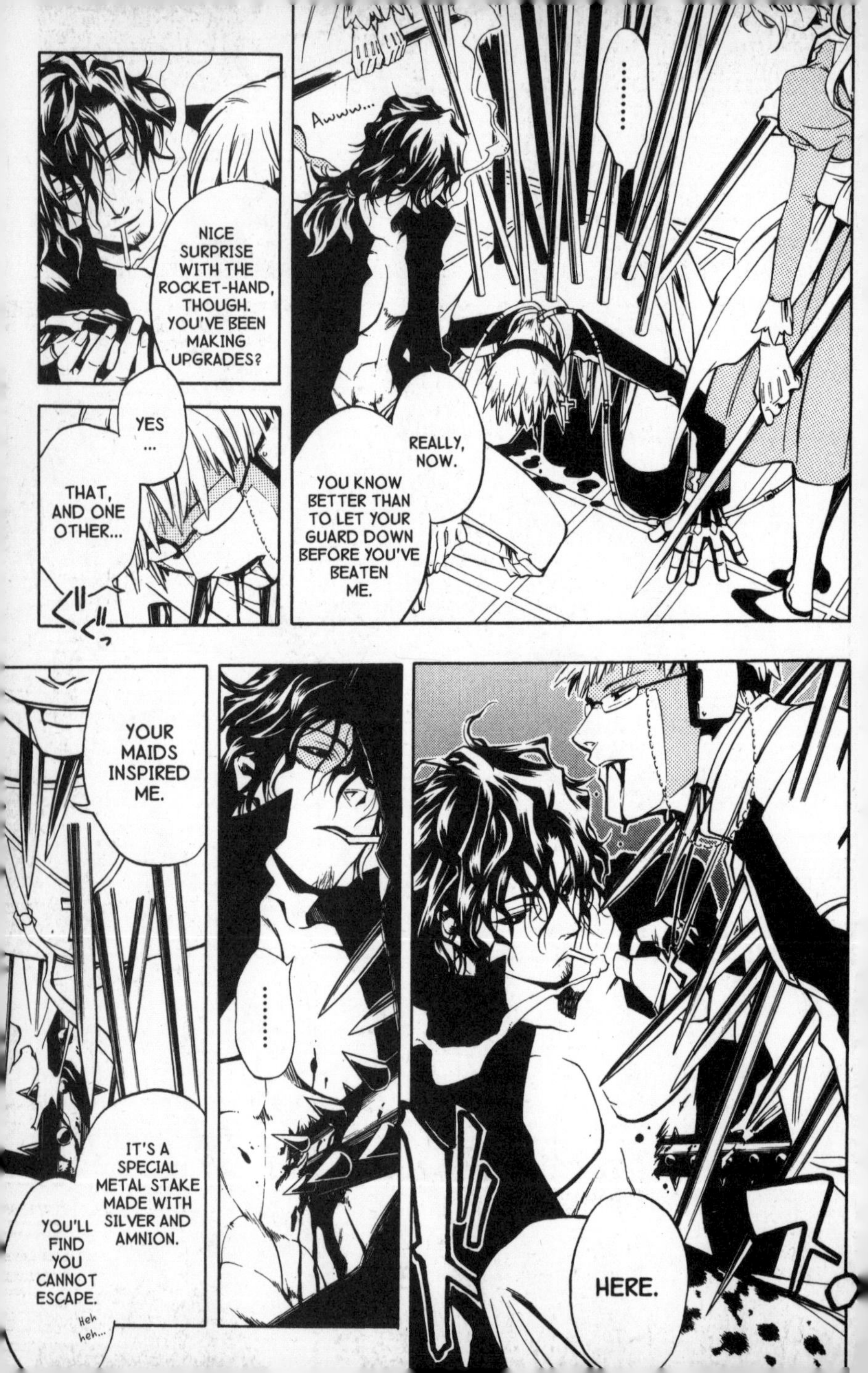
......
Awww...
REALLY, NOW.
YOU KNOW BETTER THAN TO LET YOUR GUARD DOWN BEFORE YOU'VE BEATEN ME.
NICE SURPRISE WITH THE ROCKET-HAND, THOUGH. YOU'VE BEEN MAKING UPGRADES?
YES ...
THAT, AND ONE OTHER...
HERE.
......
YOUR MAIDS INSPIRED ME.
IT'S A SPECIAL METAL STAKE MADE WITH SILVER AND AMNION.
YOU'LL FIND YOU CANNOT ESCAPE.
Heh heh...

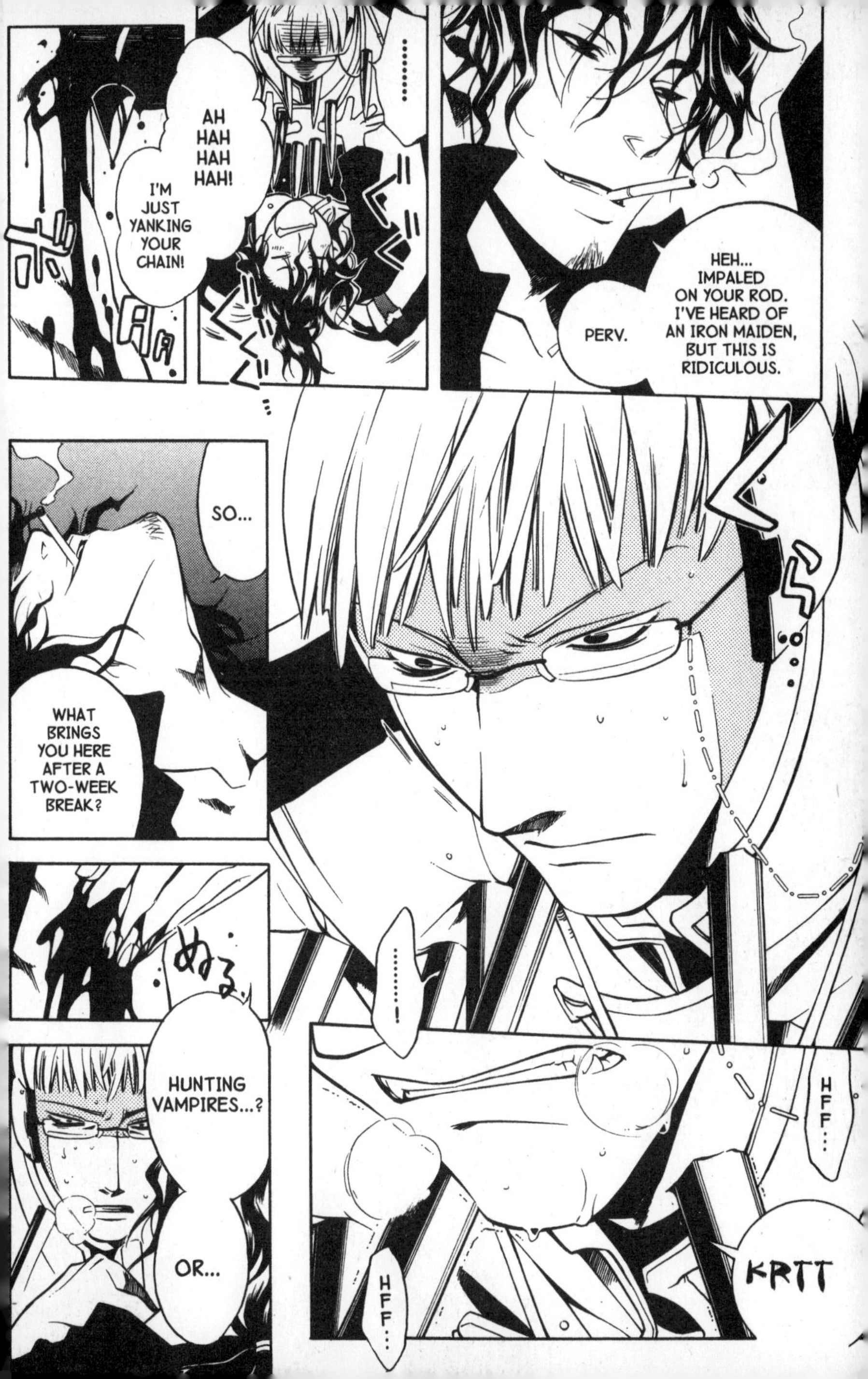
HEH... IMPALED ON YOUR ROD. I'VE HEARD OF AN IRON MAIDEN, BUT THIS IS RIDICULOUS.
PERV.
......
AH HAH HAH HAH!
I'M JUST YANKING YOUR CHAIN!
......!
SO...
WHAT BRINGS YOU HERE AFTER A TWO-WEEK BREAK?
ぬる
HFF...
KRTT
HFF...
HUNTING VAMPIRES...?
OR...

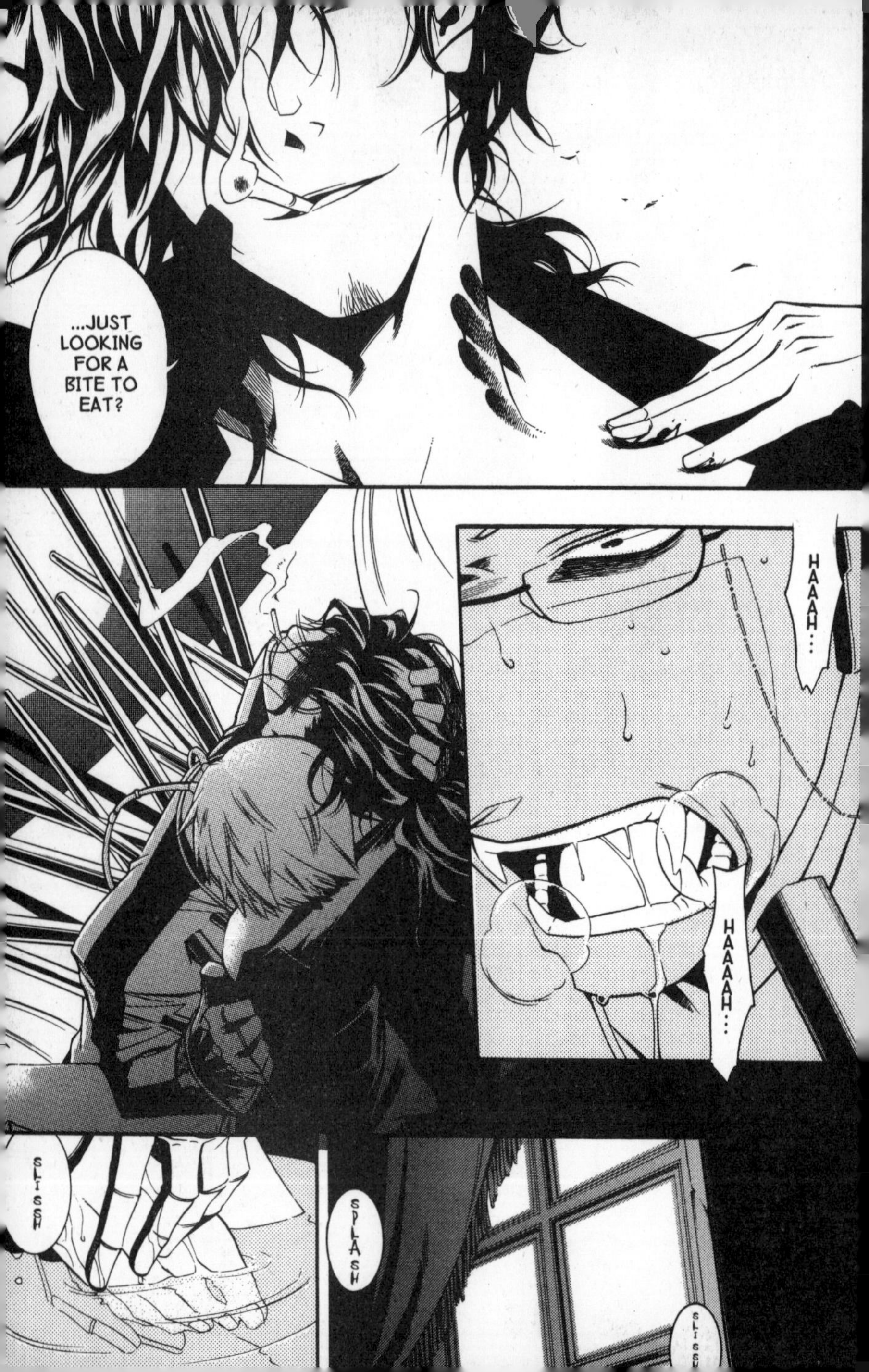
...JUST LOOKING FOR A BITE TO EAT?
HAAAH...
HAAAAH...
SPLASH
SLISS
SLISSH

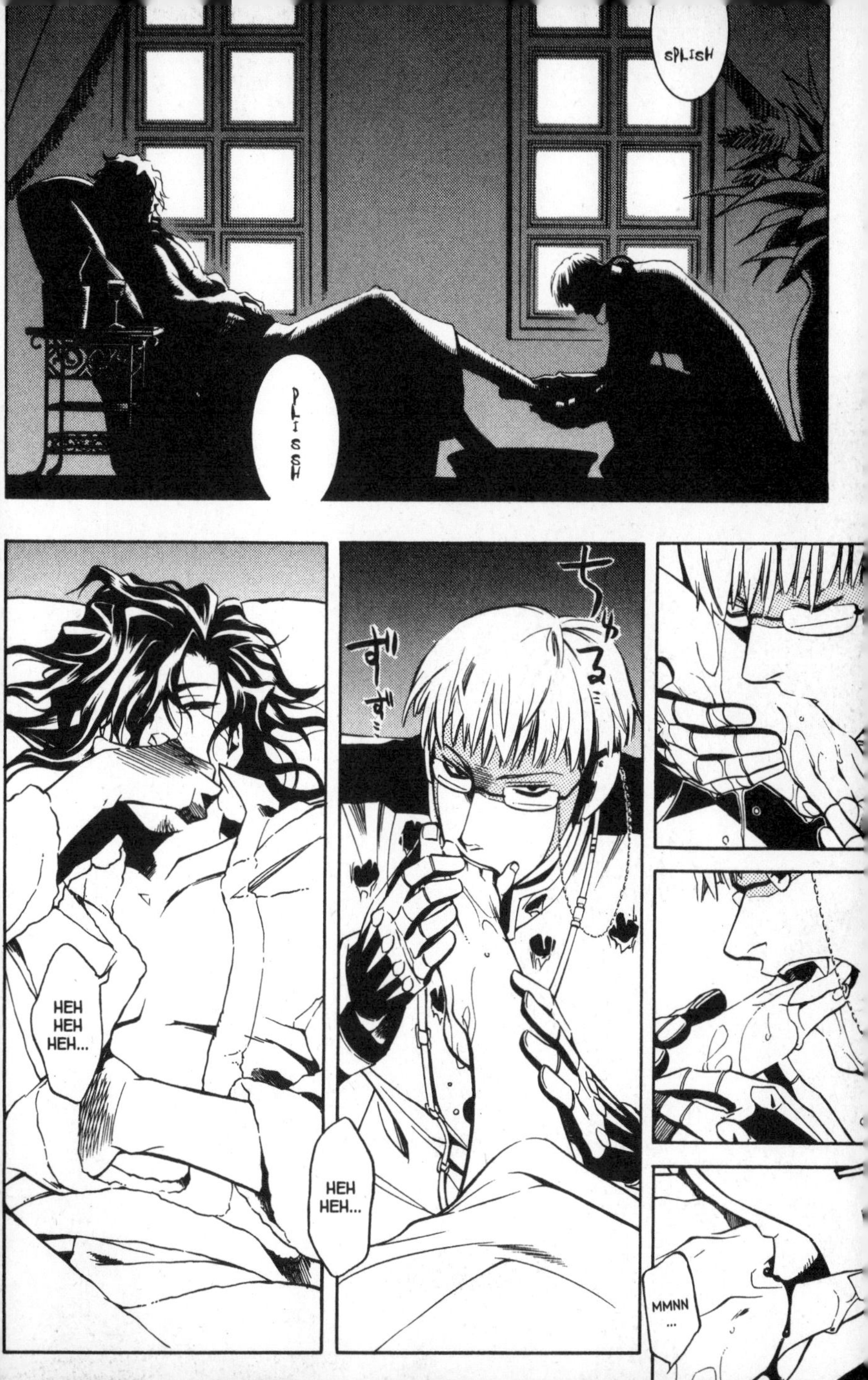
SPLISH
PLISSH
MMNN ...
ちゅる…
ずーず…
HEH HEH...
HEH HEH HEH...

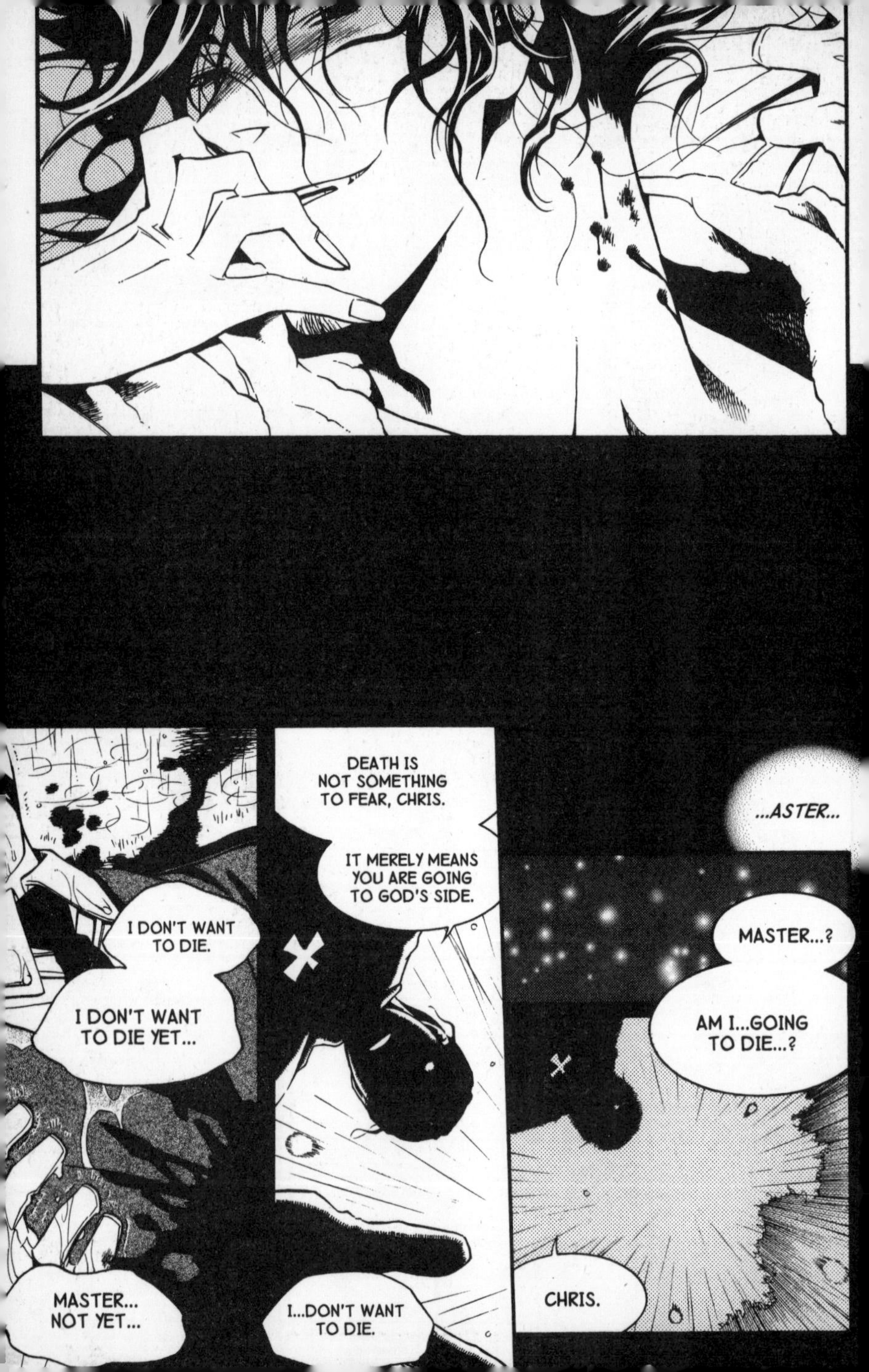
...ASTER...
MASTER...?
AM I...GOING TO DIE...?
CHRIS.
DEATH IS NOT SOMETHING TO FEAR, CHRIS.
IT MERELY MEANS YOU ARE GOING TO GOD'S SIDE.
I...DON'T WANT TO DIE.
I DON'T WANT TO DIE.
I DON'T WANT TO DIE YET...
MASTER... NOT YET...

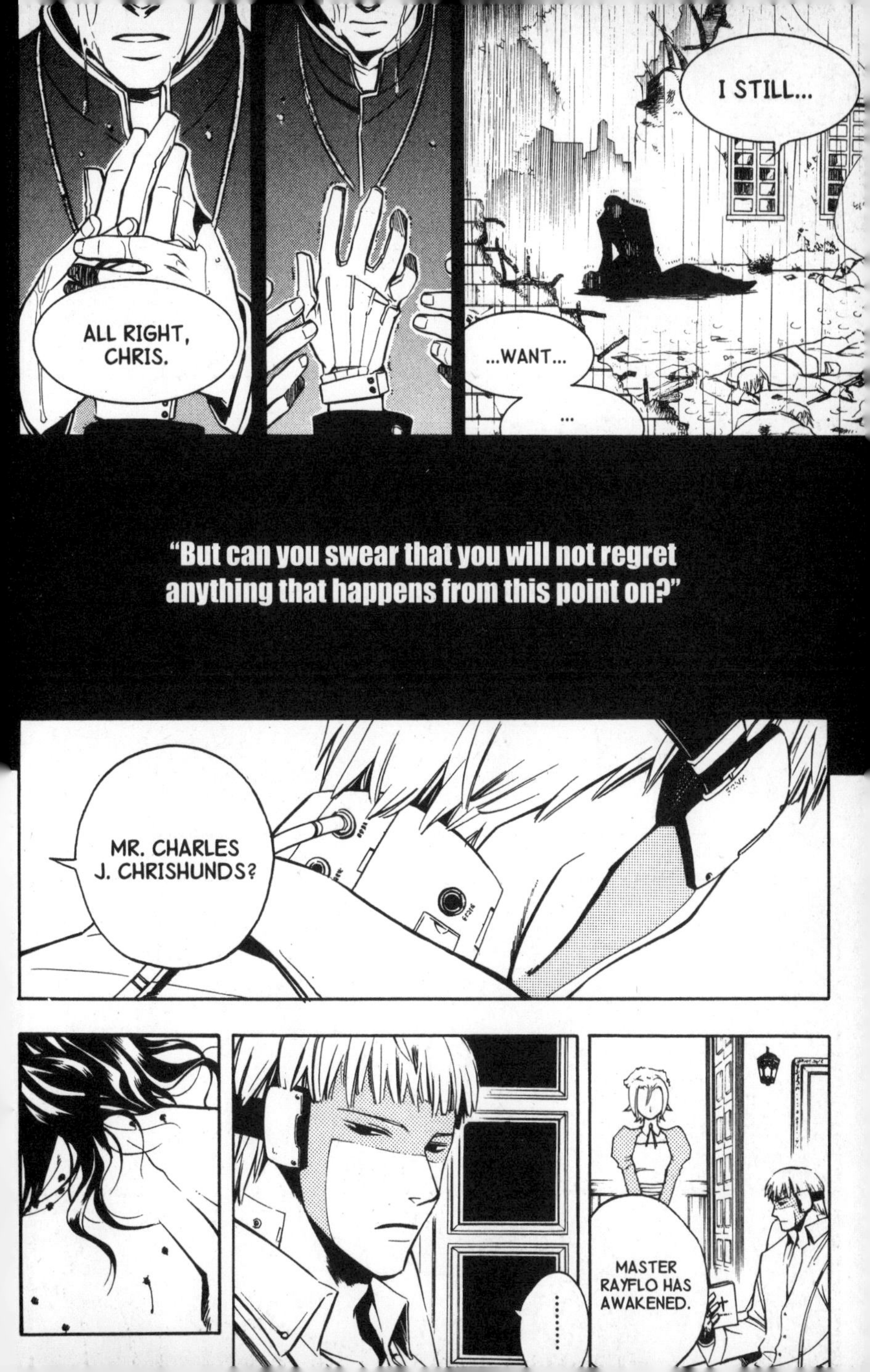
I STILL...
...WANT...
...
ALL RIGHT, CHRIS.
"But can you swear that you will not regret anything that happens from this point on?"
MR. CHARLES J. CHRISHUNDS?
MASTER RAYFLO HAS AWAKENED.
......

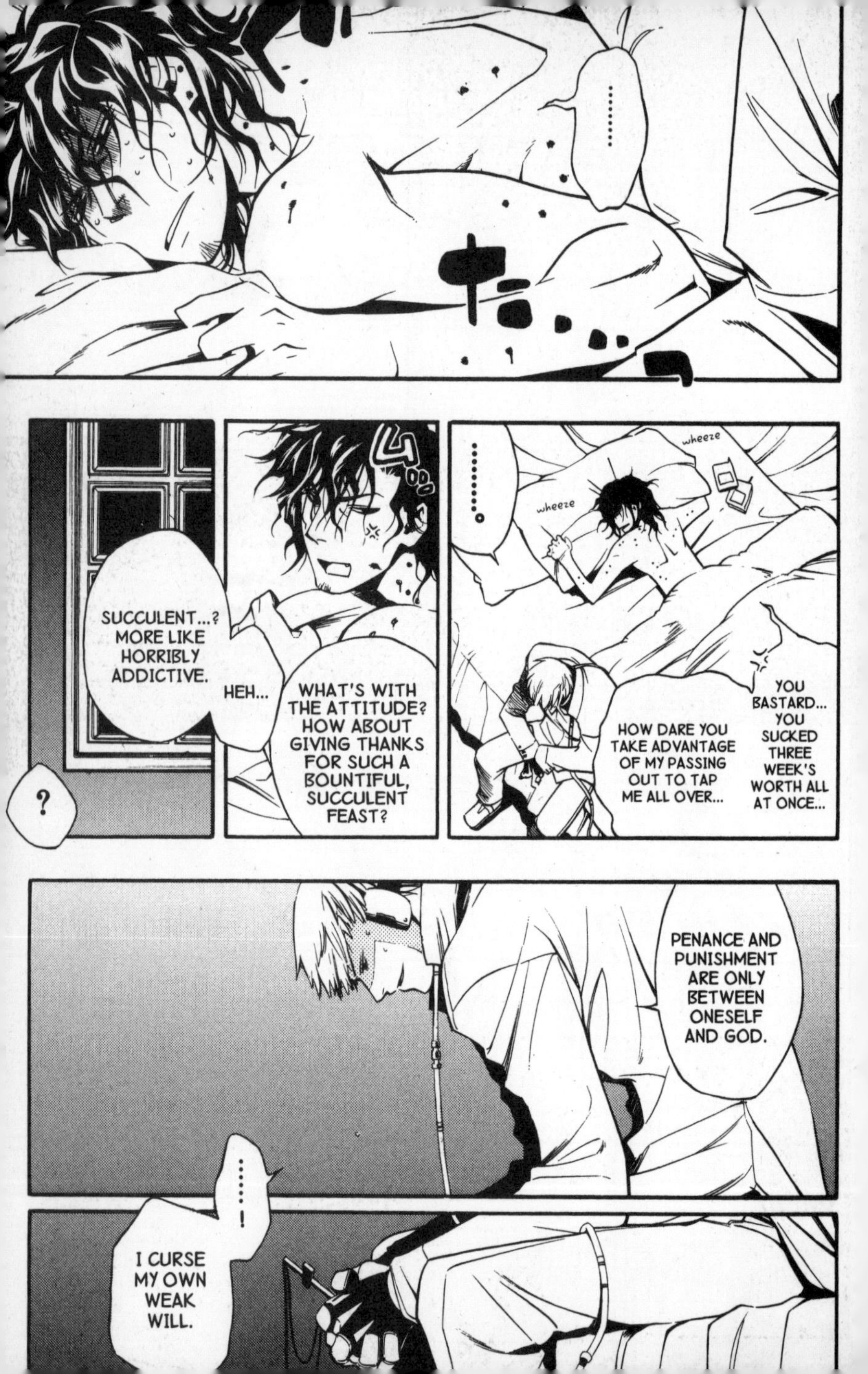
......
....
wheeze
wheeze
YOU BASTARD... YOU SUCKED THREE WEEK'S WORTH ALL AT ONCE...
HOW DARE YOU TAKE ADVANTAGE OF MY PASSING OUT TO TAP ME ALL OVER...
WHAT'S WITH THE ATTITUDE? HOW ABOUT GIVING THANKS FOR SUCH A BOUNTIFUL, SUCCULENT FEAST?
HEH...
SUCCULENT...? MORE LIKE HORRIBLY ADDICTIVE.
?
PENANCE AND PUNISHMENT ARE ONLY BETWEEN ONESELF AND GOD.
......
!
I CURSE MY OWN WEAK WILL.

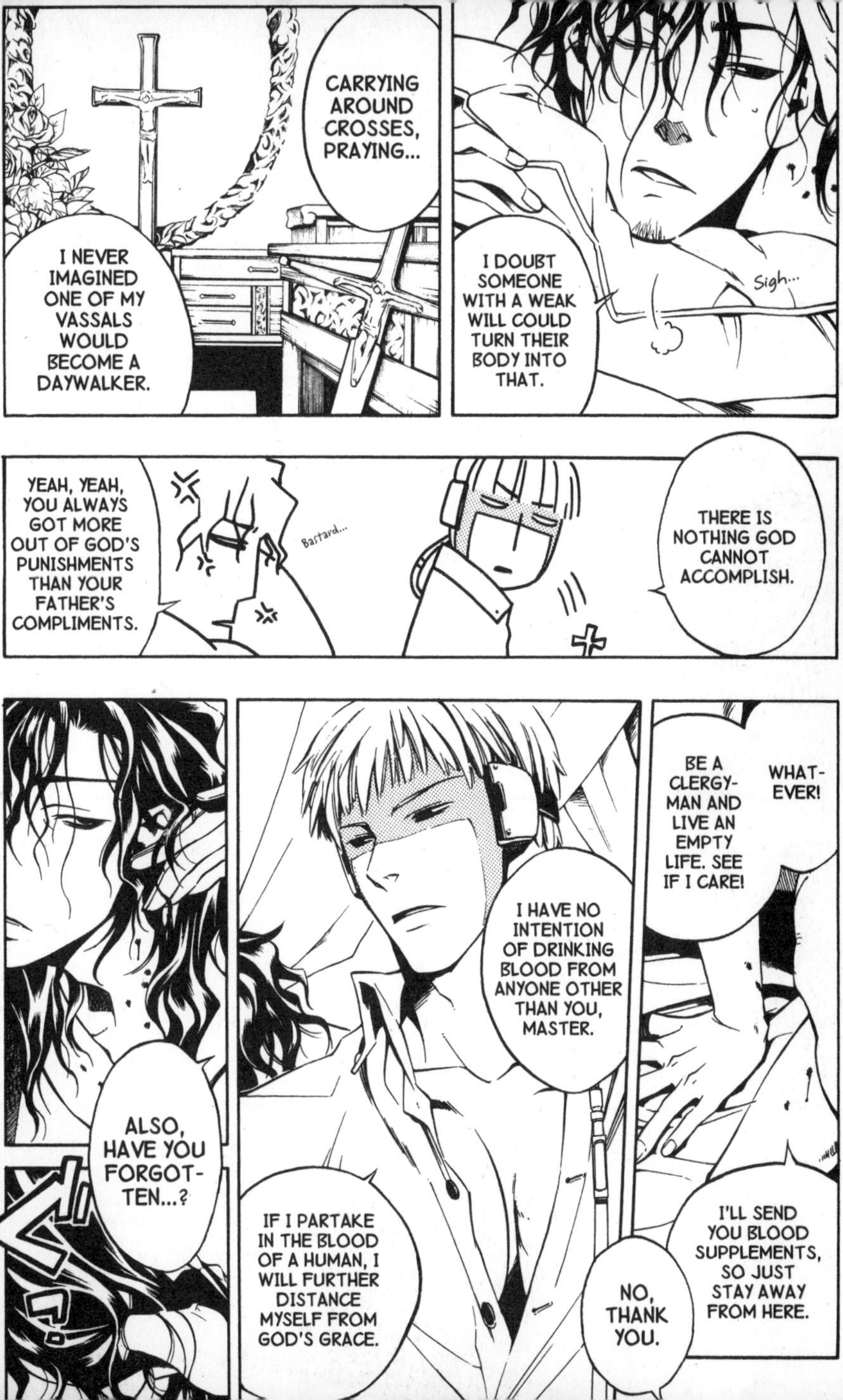
I DOUBT SOMEONE WITH A WEAK WILL COULD TURN THEIR BODY INTO THAT.
Sigh...
CARRYING AROUND CROSSES, PRAYING...
I NEVER IMAGINED ONE OF MY VASSALS WOULD BECOME A DAYWALKER.
THERE IS NOTHING GOD CANNOT ACCOMPLISH.
Bastard...
YEAH, YEAH, YOU ALWAYS GOT MORE OUT OF GOD'S PUNISHMENTS THAN YOUR FATHER'S COMPLIMENTS.
WHAT-EVER!
BE A CLERGY-MAN AND LIVE AN EMPTY LIFE. SEE IF I CARE!
I'LL SEND YOU BLOOD SUPPLEMENTS, SO JUST STAY AWAY FROM HERE.
NO, THANK YOU.
I HAVE NO INTENTION OF DRINKING BLOOD FROM ANYONE OTHER THAN YOU, MASTER.
IF I PARTAKE IN THE BLOOD OF A HUMAN, I WILL FURTHER DISTANCE MYSELF FROM GOD'S GRACE.
ALSO, HAVE YOU FORGOT-TEN...?

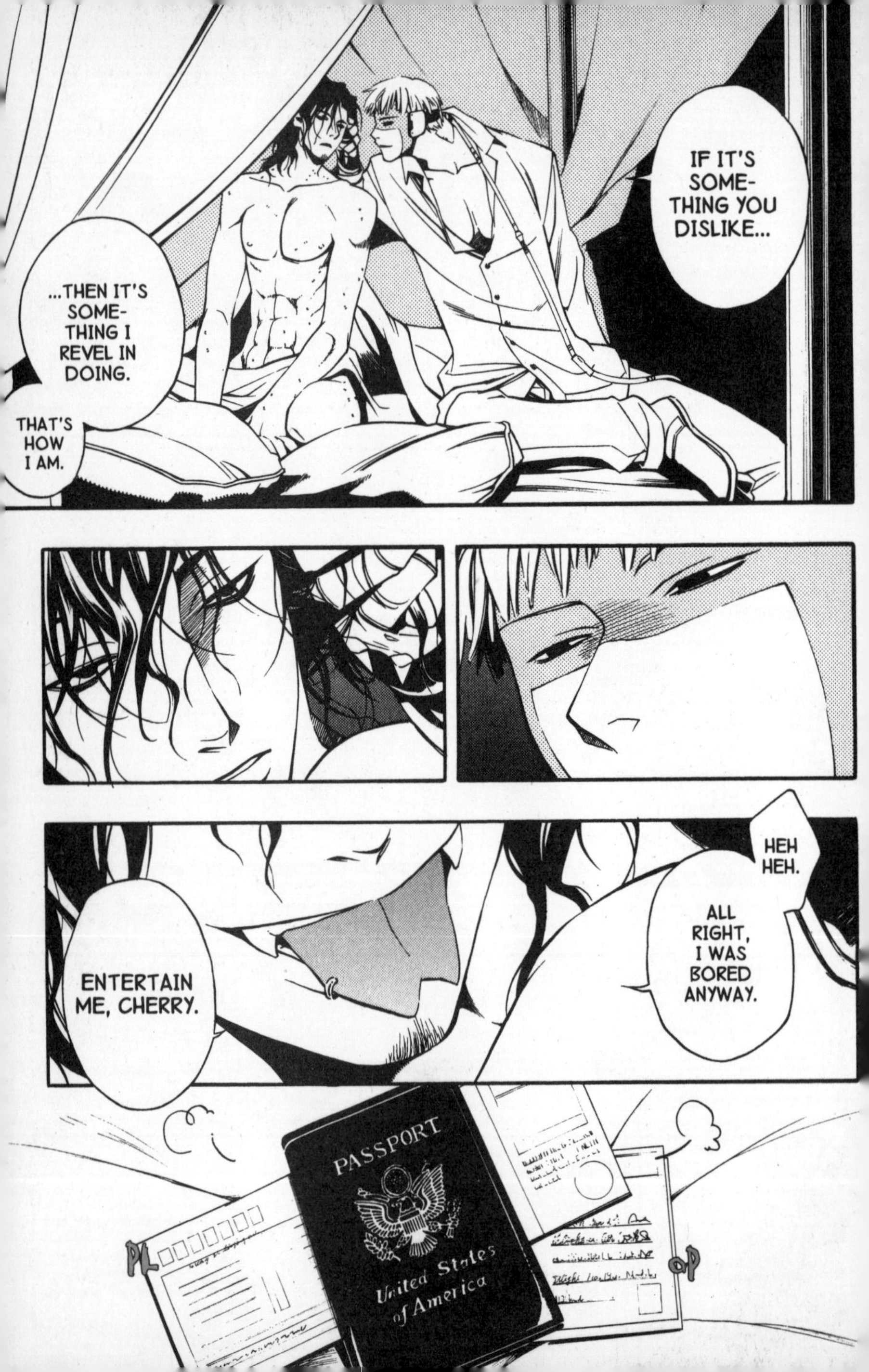
IF IT'S SOME- THING YOU DISLIKE...
...THEN IT'S SOME- THING I REVEL IN DOING.
THAT'S HOW I AM.
HEH HEH.
ALL RIGHT, I WAS BORED ANYWAY.
ENTERTAIN ME, CHERRY.
PASSPORT
United States of America
PL
oP

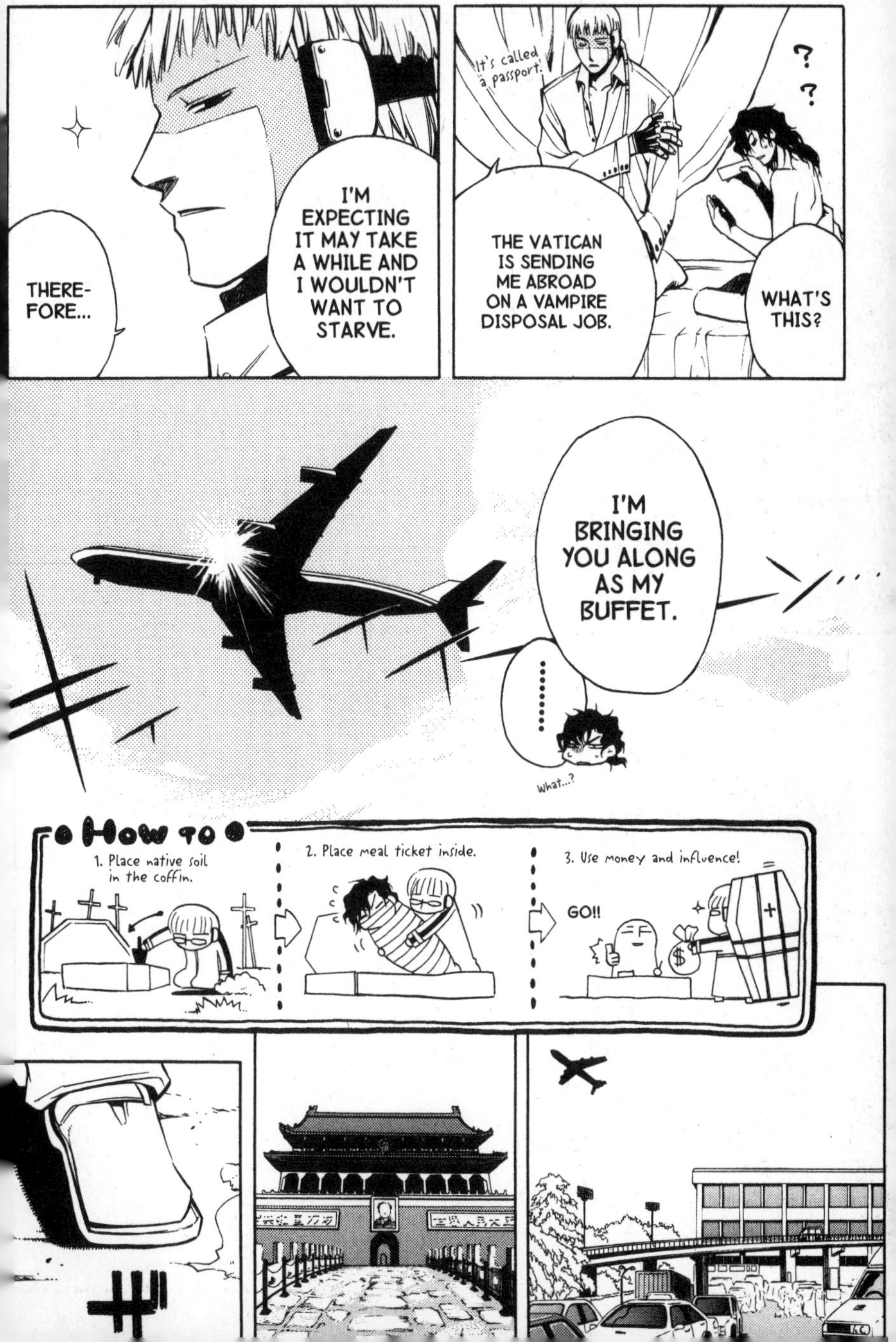
??
WHAT'S THIS?
THE VATICAN IS SENDING ME ABROAD ON A VAMPIRE DISPOSAL JOB.
It's called a passport.
I'M EXPECTING IT MAY TAKE A WHILE AND I WOULDN'T WANT TO STARVE.
THEREFORE...
I'M BRINGING YOU ALONG AS MY BUFFET.
......
What...?
How to
1. Place native soil in the coffin.
2. Place meal ticket inside.
3. Use money and influence!
GO!!

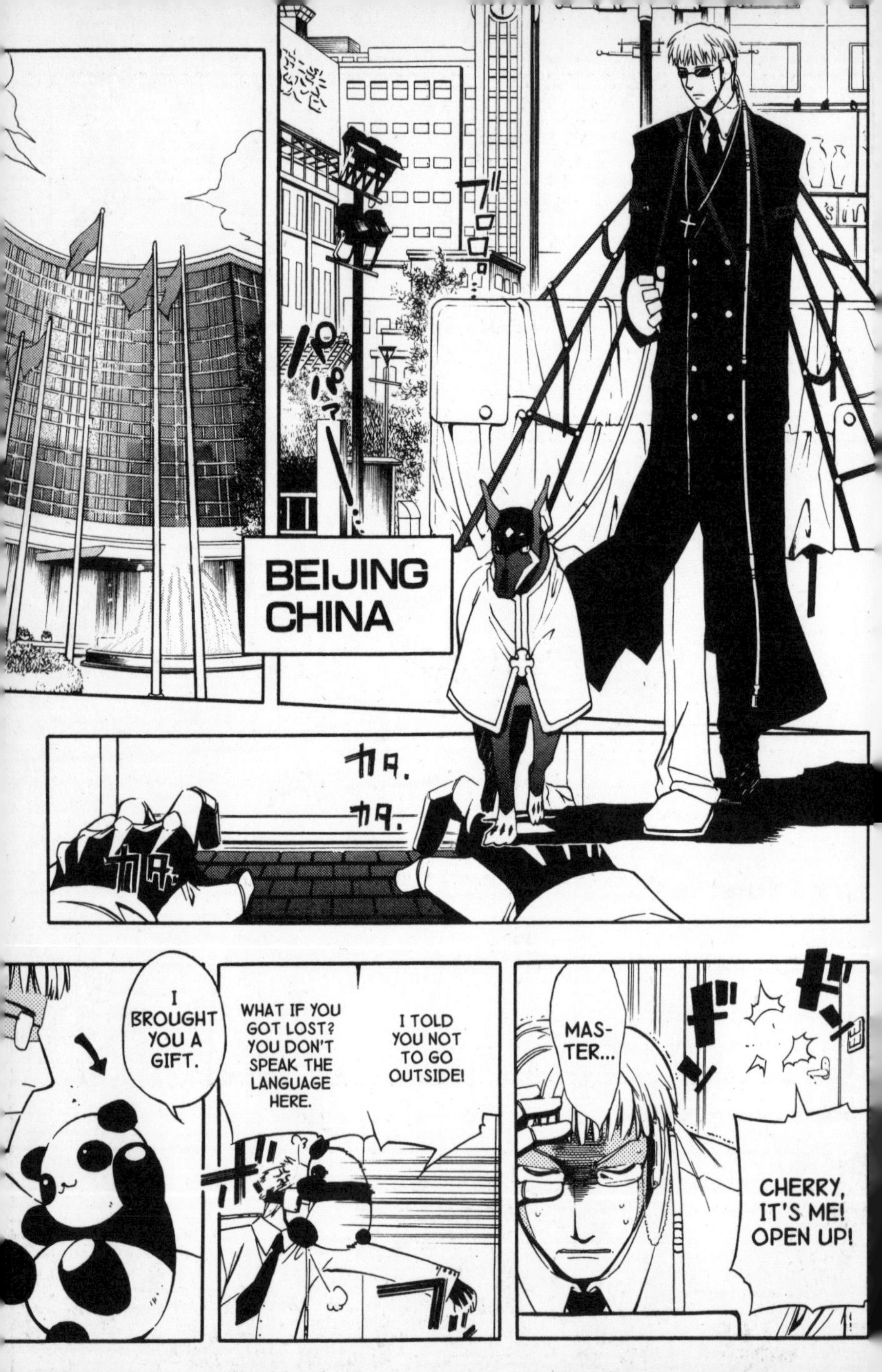

BEIJING CHINA
カタ.
カタ.
CHERRY, IT'S ME! OPEN UP!
MAS-TER...
I TOLD YOU NOT TO GO OUTSIDE!
WHAT IF YOU GOT LOST? YOU DON'T SPEAK THE LANGUAGE HERE.
I BROUGHT YOU A GIFT.

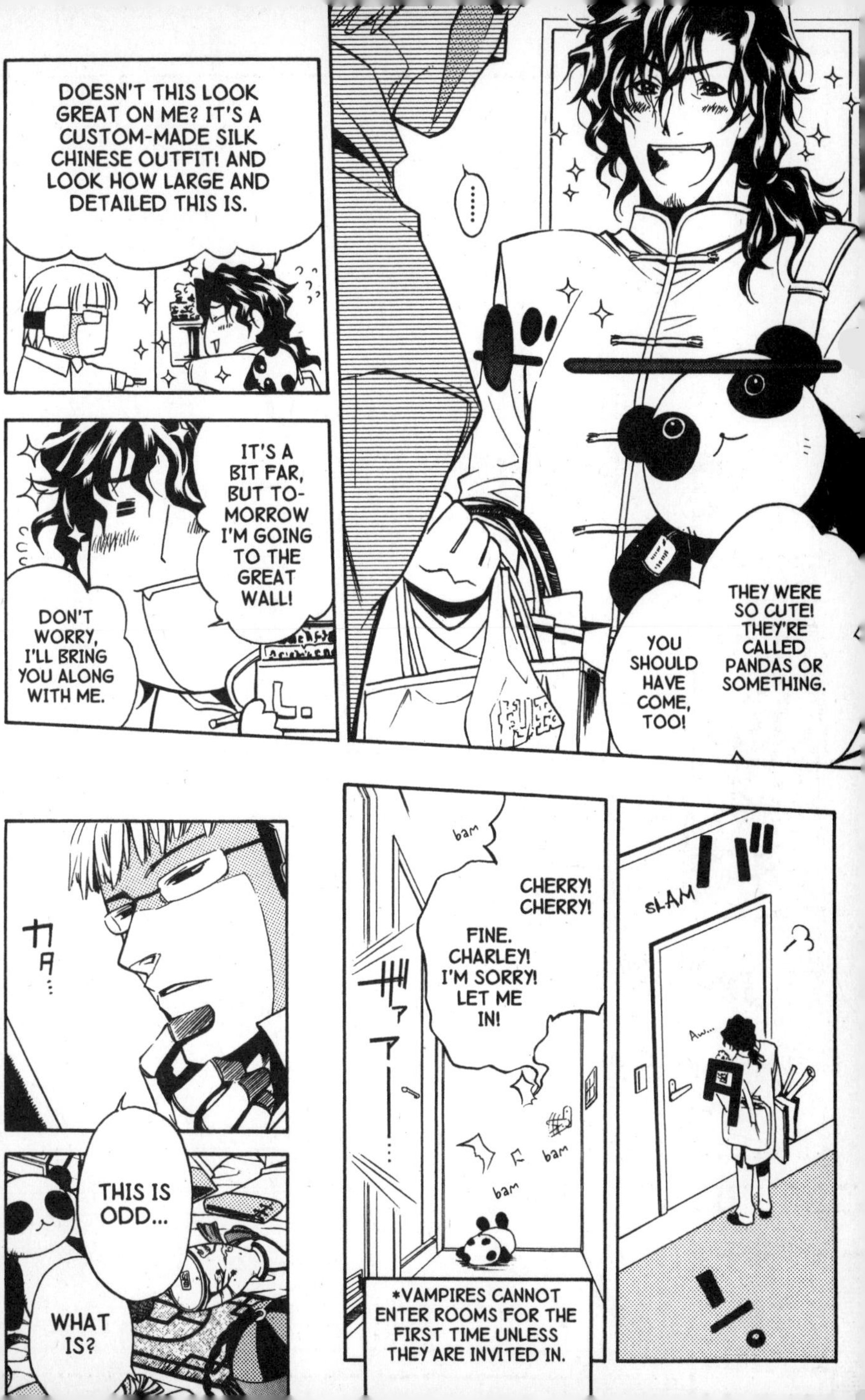
......
THEY WERE SO CUTE! THEY'RE CALLED PANDAS OR SOMETHING.
YOU SHOULD HAVE COME, TOO!
DOESN'T THIS LOOK GREAT ON ME? IT'S A CUSTOM-MADE SILK CHINESE OUTFIT! AND LOOK HOW LARGE AND DETAILED THIS IS.
IT'S A BIT FAR, BUT TO-MORROW I'M GOING TO THE GREAT WALL!
DON'T WORRY, I'LL BRING YOU ALONG WITH ME.
SLAM
Aw...
bam
CHERRY! CHERRY!
FINE. CHARLEY! I'M SORRY! LET ME IN!
bam
bam
*VAMPIRES CANNOT ENTER ROOMS FOR THE FIRST TIME UNLESS THEY ARE INVITED IN.
カタ…
THIS IS ODD...
WHAT IS?

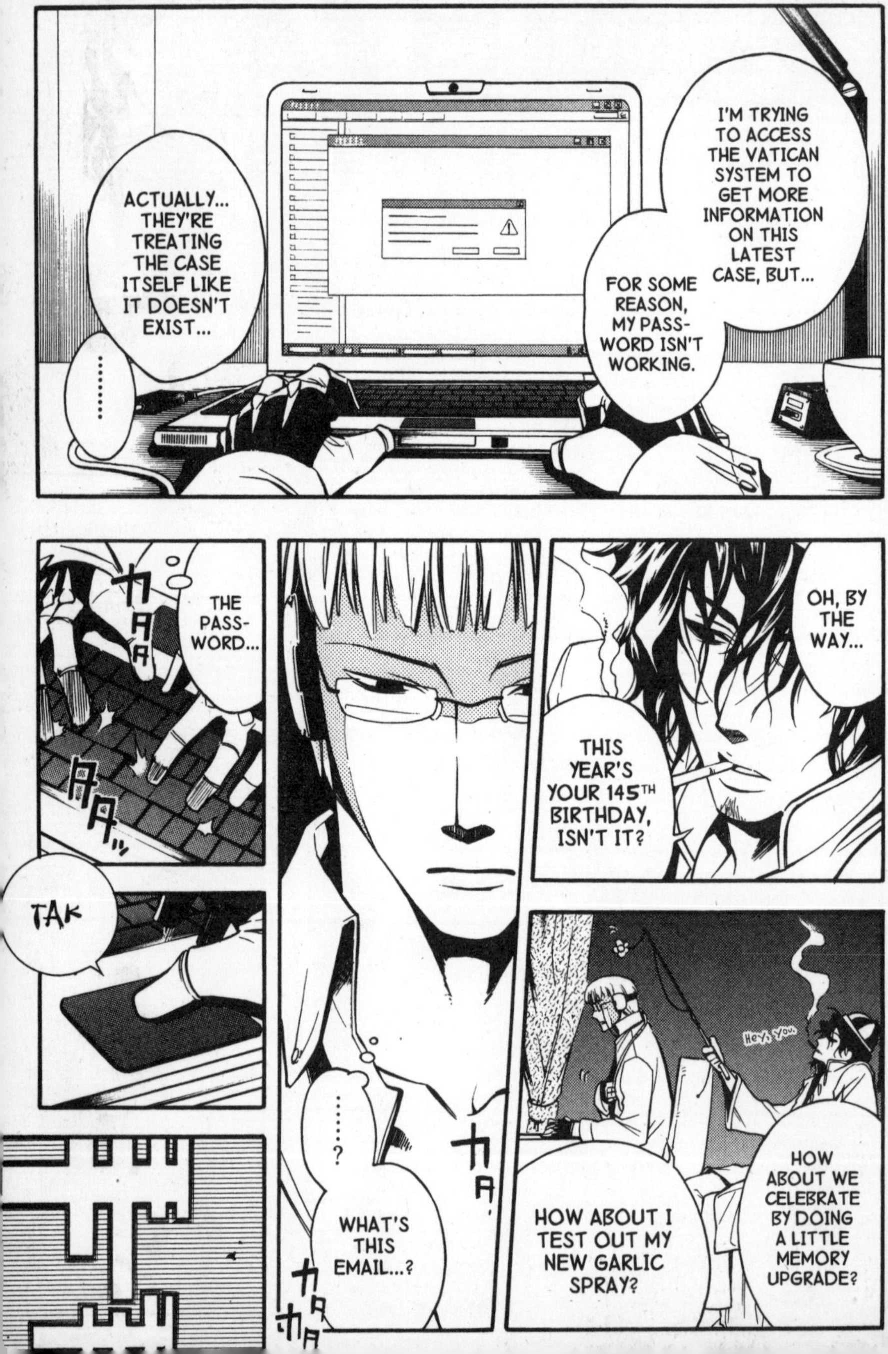
I'M TRYING TO ACCESS THE VATICAN SYSTEM TO GET MORE INFORMATION ON THIS LATEST CASE, BUT...
FOR SOME REASON, MY PASS-WORD ISN'T WORKING.
ACTUALLY... THEY'RE TREATING THE CASE ITSELF LIKE IT DOESN'T EXIST...
……
OH, BY THE WAY...
THIS YEAR'S YOUR 145th BIRTHDAY, ISN'T IT?
Hey, you.
HOW ABOUT WE CELEBRATE BY DOING A LITTLE MEMORY UPGRADE?
HOW ABOUT I TEST OUT MY NEW GARLIC SPRAY?
……?
WHAT'S THIS EMAIL...?
THE PASS-WORD...
TAK

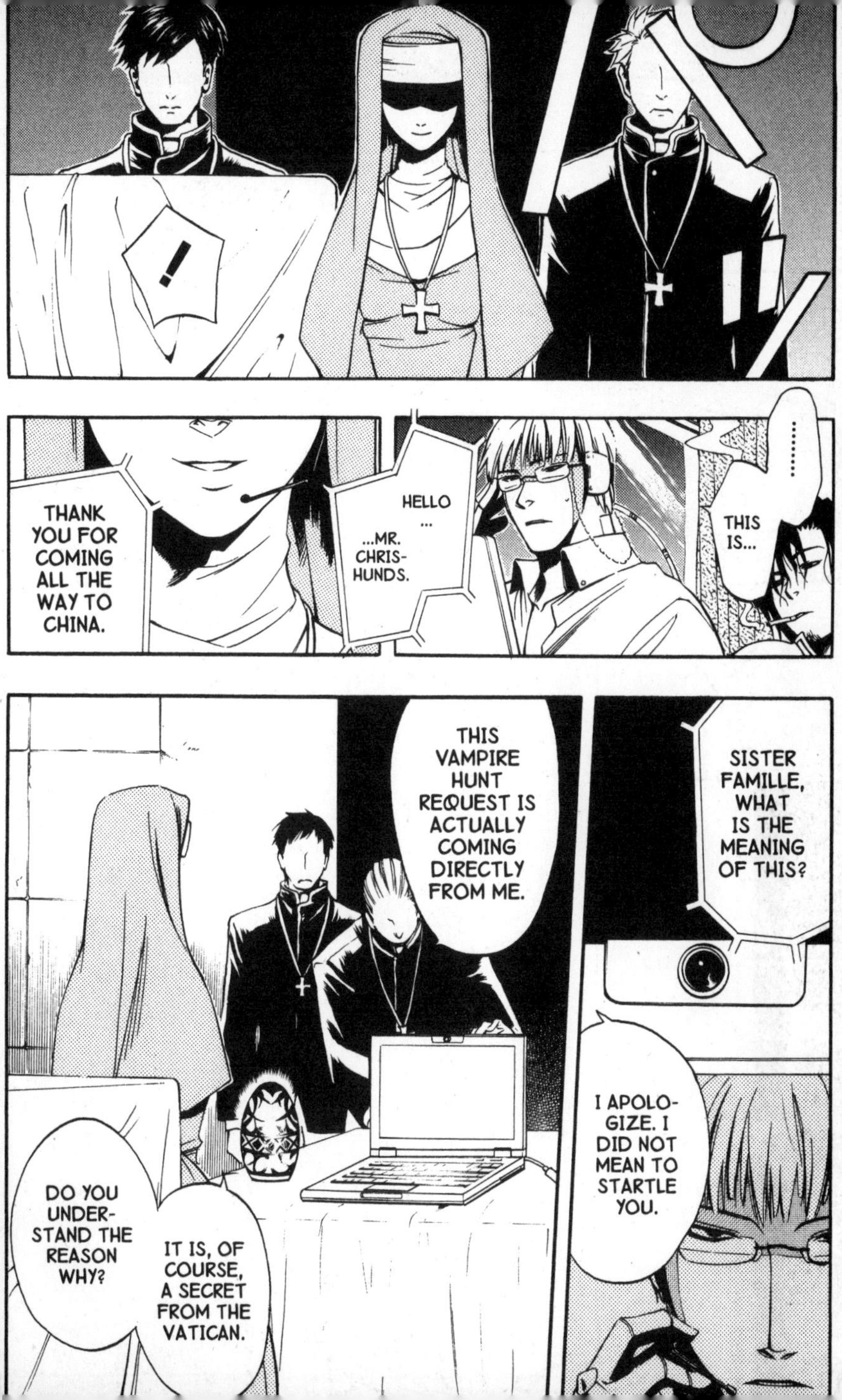
!
......
THIS IS...
HELLO ... ...MR. CHRIS-HUNDS.
THANK YOU FOR COMING ALL THE WAY TO CHINA.
SISTER FAMILLE, WHAT IS THE MEANING OF THIS?
I APOLO-GIZE. I DID NOT MEAN TO STARTLE YOU.
THIS VAMPIRE HUNT REQUEST IS ACTUALLY COMING DIRECTLY FROM ME.
IT IS, OF COURSE, A SECRET FROM THE VATICAN.
DO YOU UNDER-STAND THE REASON WHY?

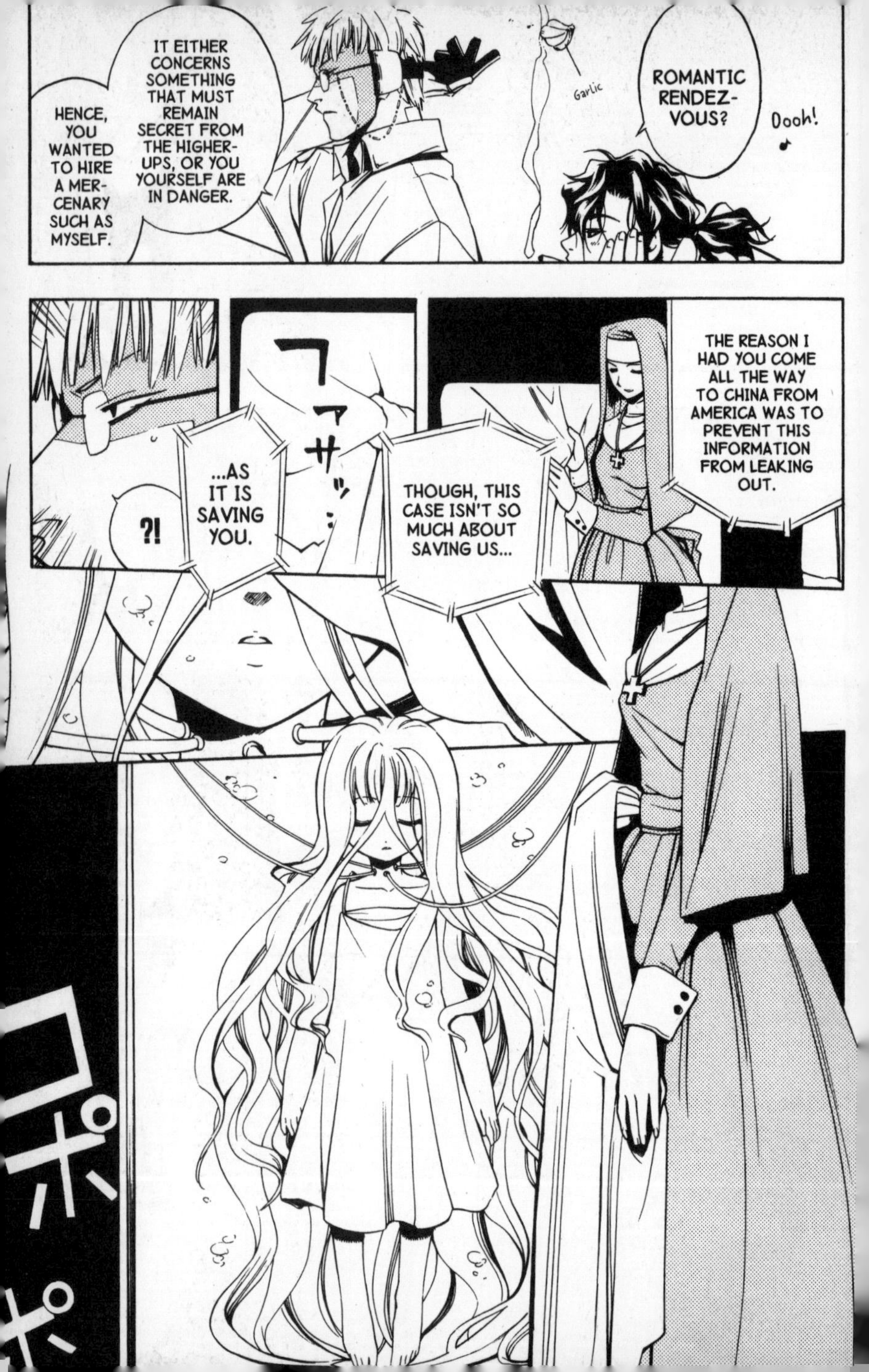
ROMANTIC RENDEZ-VOUS?
Oooh! ♪
Garlic
IT EITHER CONCERNS SOMETHING THAT MUST REMAIN SECRET FROM THE HIGHER-UPS, OR YOU YOURSELF ARE IN DANGER.
HENCE, YOU WANTED TO HIRE A MER-CENARY SUCH AS MYSELF.
THE REASON I HAD YOU COME ALL THE WAY TO CHINA FROM AMERICA WAS TO PREVENT THIS INFORMATION FROM LEAKING OUT.
THOUGH, THIS CASE ISN'T SO MUCH ABOUT SAVING US...
ファサッ
...AS IT IS SAVING YOU.
?!
コポ
ポ

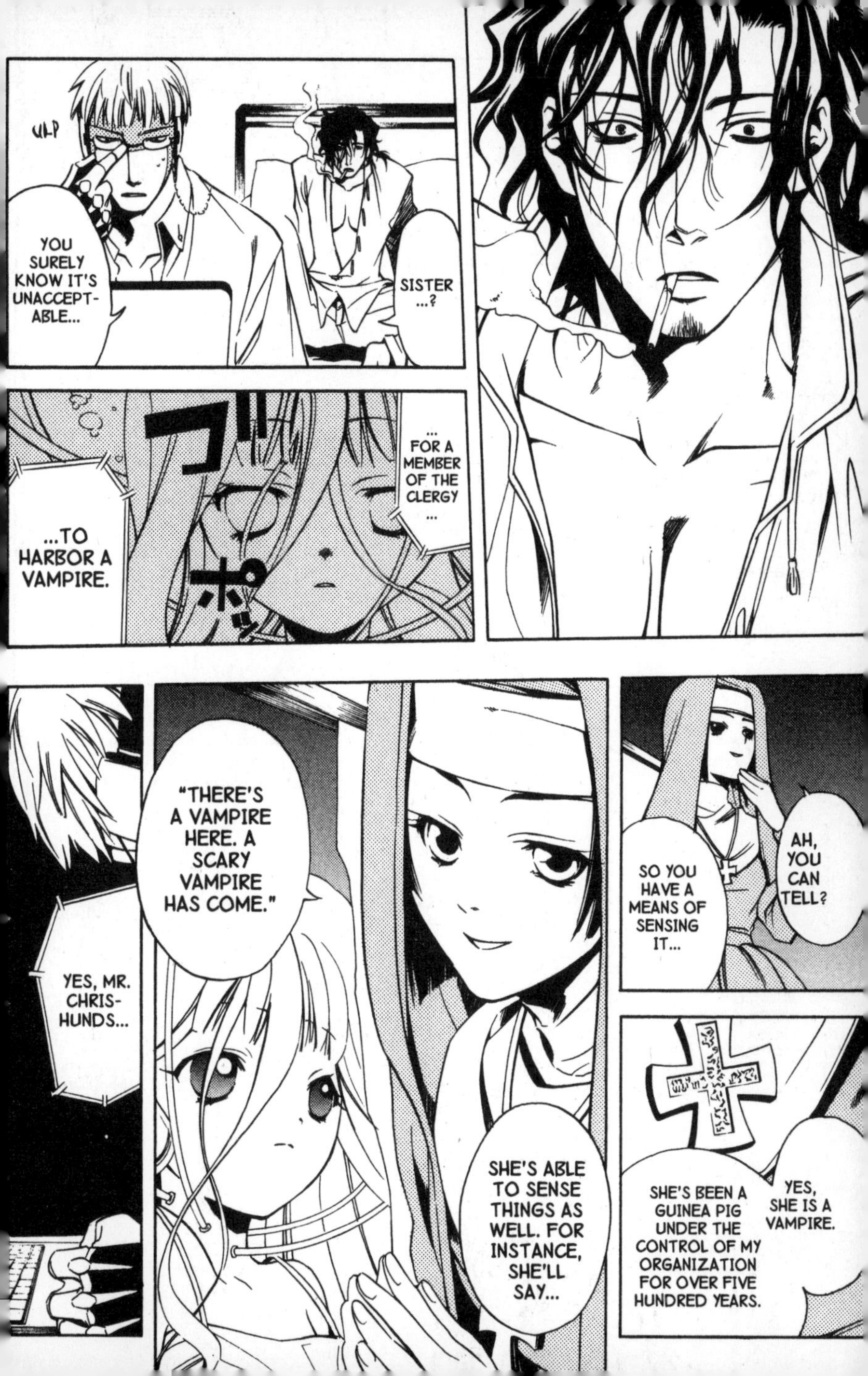
ULP
SISTER ...?
YOU SURELY KNOW IT'S UNACCEPT-ABLE...
... FOR A MEMBER OF THE CLERGY ...
...TO HARBOR A VAMPIRE.
AH, YOU CAN TELL?
SO YOU HAVE A MEANS OF SENSING IT...
YES, SHE IS A VAMPIRE.
SHE'S BEEN A GUINEA PIG UNDER THE CONTROL OF MY ORGANIZATION FOR OVER FIVE HUNDRED YEARS.
SHE'S ABLE TO SENSE THINGS AS WELL. FOR INSTANCE, SHE'LL SAY...
"THERE'S A VAMPIRE HERE. A SCARY VAMPIRE HAS COME."
YES, MR. CHRIS-HUNDS...

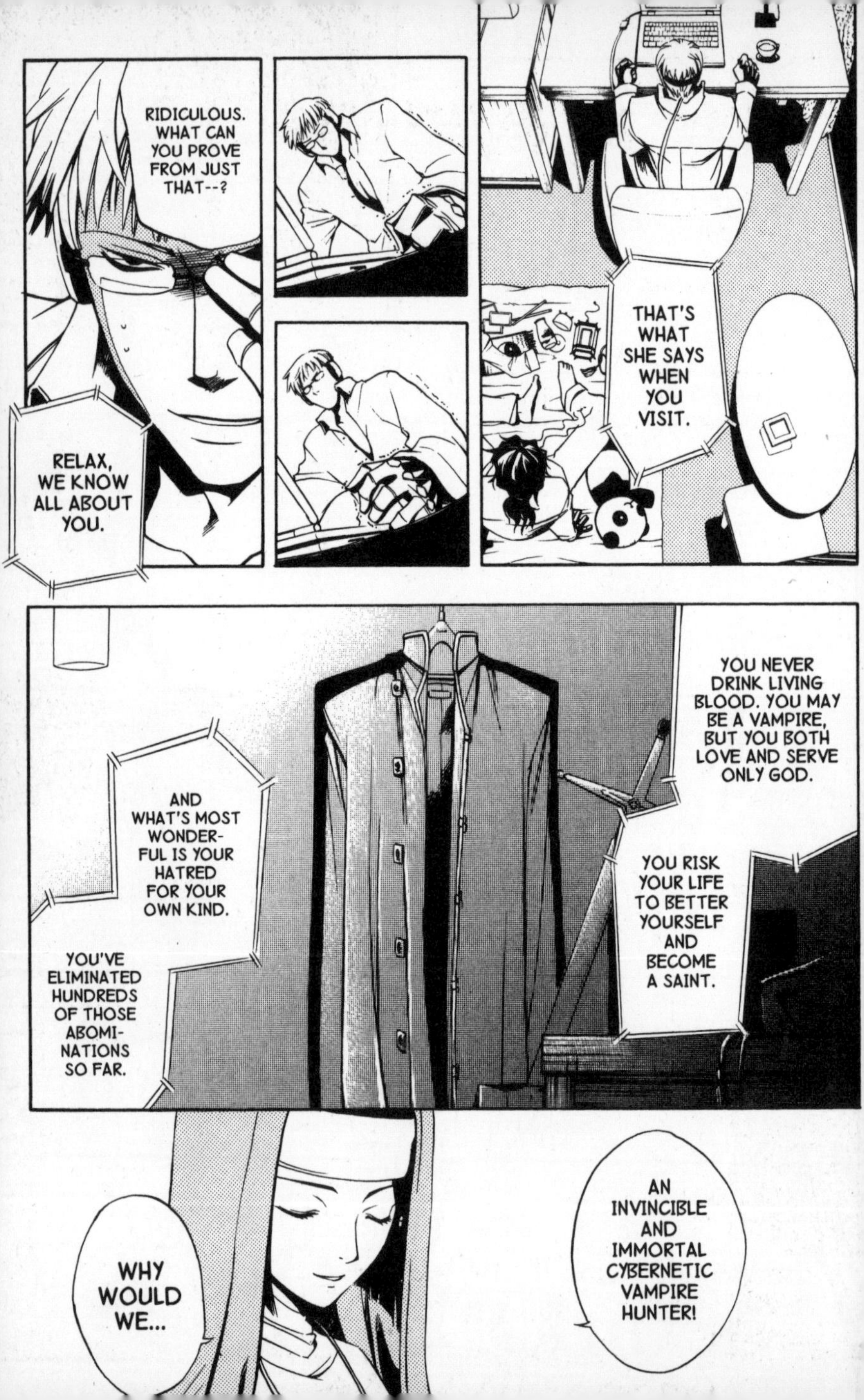
THAT'S WHAT SHE SAYS WHEN YOU VISIT.
RIDICULOUS. WHAT CAN YOU PROVE FROM JUST THAT--?
RELAX, WE KNOW ALL ABOUT YOU.
YOU NEVER DRINK LIVING BLOOD. YOU MAY BE A VAMPIRE, BUT YOU BOTH LOVE AND SERVE ONLY GOD.
YOU RISK YOUR LIFE TO BETTER YOURSELF AND BECOME A SAINT.
AND WHAT'S MOST WONDER-FUL IS YOUR HATRED FOR YOUR OWN KIND.
YOU'VE ELIMINATED HUNDREDS OF THOSE ABOMI-NATIONS SO FAR.
AN INVINCIBLE AND IMMORTAL CYBERNETIC VAMPIRE HUNTER!
WHY WOULD WE...

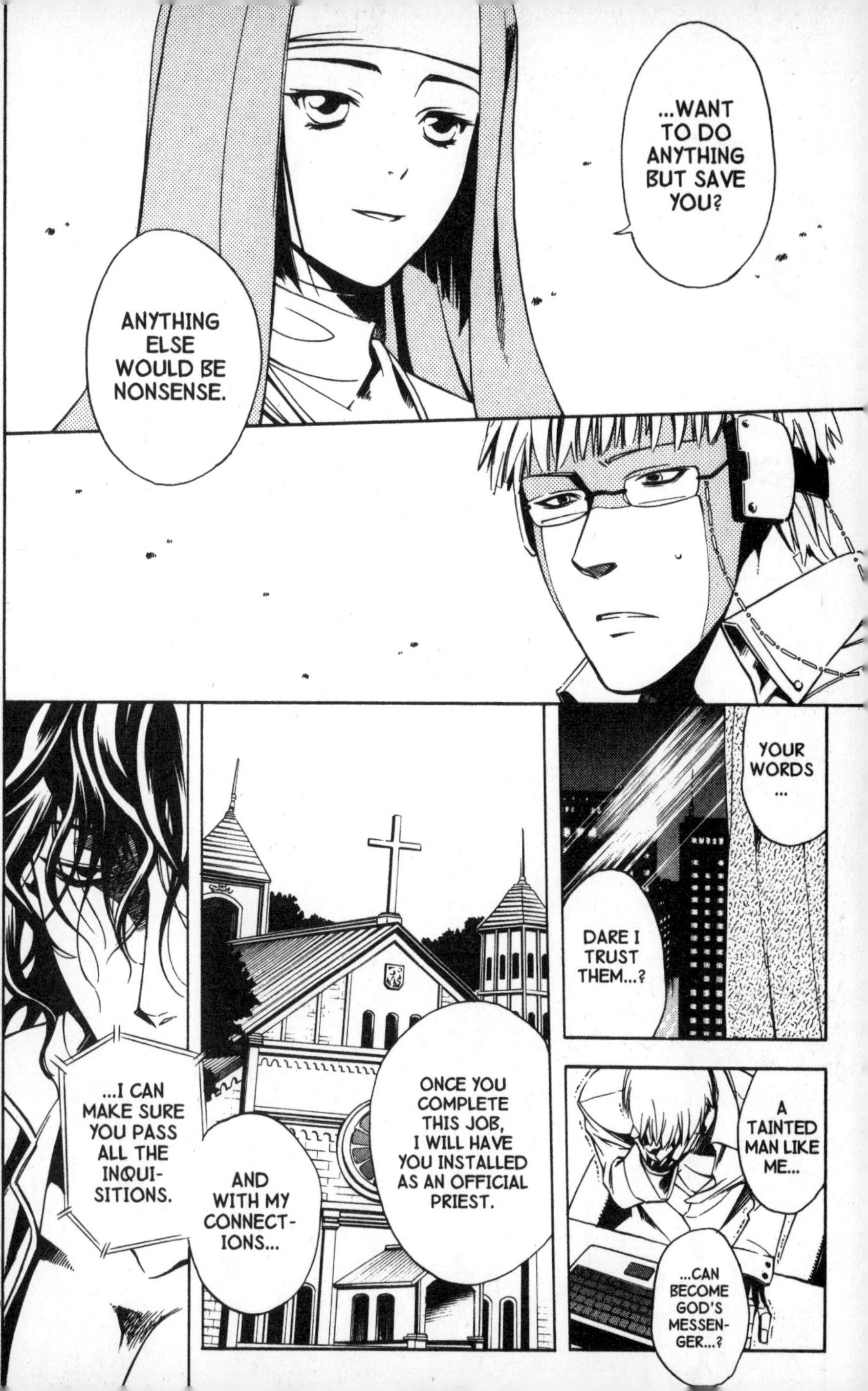
...WANT TO DO ANYTHING BUT SAVE YOU?
ANYTHING ELSE WOULD BE NONSENSE.
YOUR WORDS ...
DARE I TRUST THEM...?
A TAINTED MAN LIKE ME...
...CAN BECOME GOD'S MESSEN-GER...?
ONCE YOU COMPLETE THIS JOB, I WILL HAVE YOU INSTALLED AS AN OFFICIAL PRIEST.
AND WITH MY CONNECT-IONS...
...I CAN MAKE SURE YOU PASS ALL THE INQUI-SITIONS.

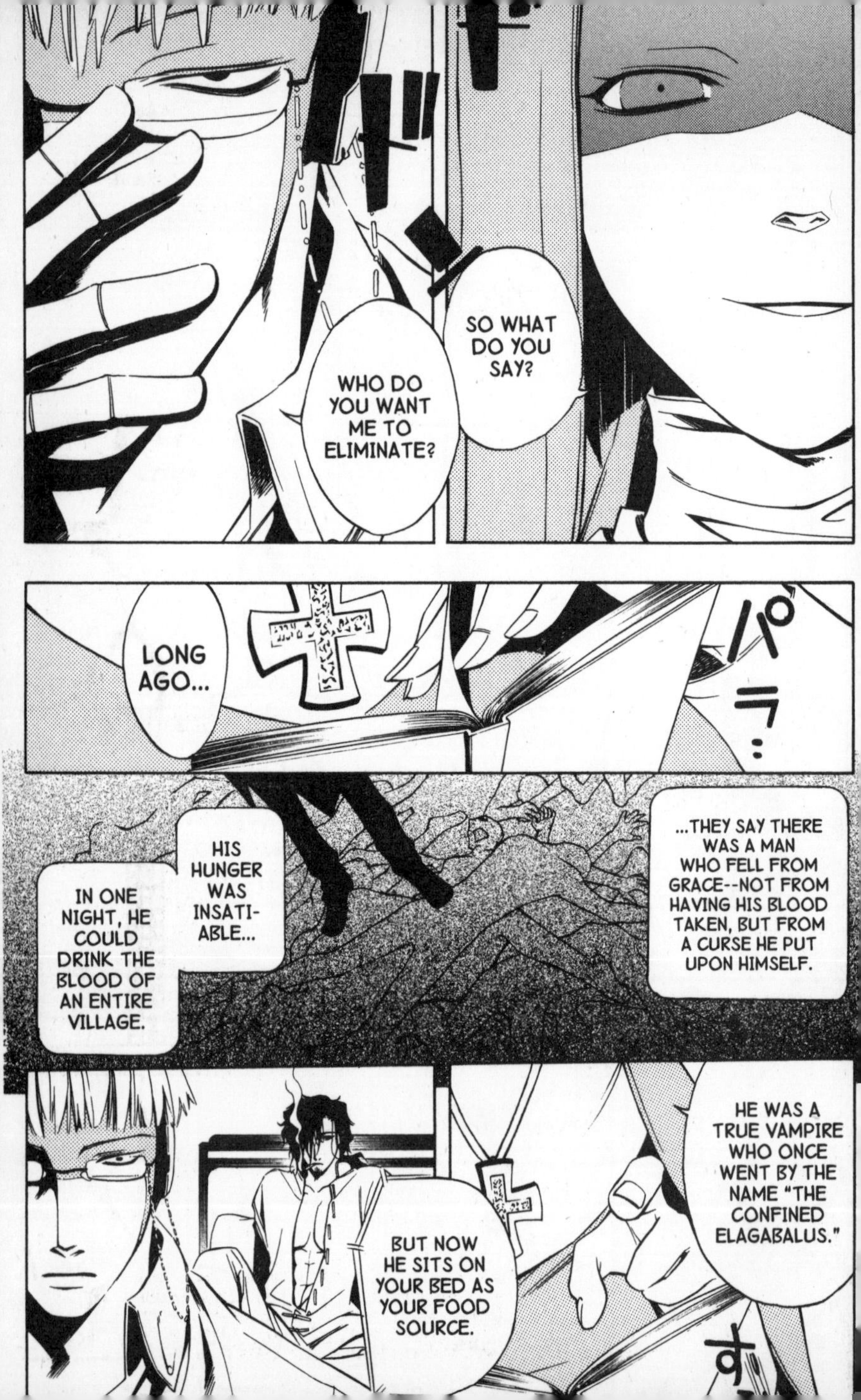
SO WHAT DO YOU SAY?
WHO DO YOU WANT ME TO ELIMINATE?
パラ
LONG AGO...
...THEY SAY THERE WAS A MAN WHO FELL FROM GRACE--NOT FROM HAVING HIS BLOOD TAKEN, BUT FROM A CURSE HE PUT UPON HIMSELF.
HIS HUNGER WAS INSATI-ABLE...
IN ONE NIGHT, HE COULD DRINK THE BLOOD OF AN ENTIRE VILLAGE.
HE WAS A TRUE VAMPIRE WHO ONCE WENT BY THE NAME "THE CONFINED ELAGABALUS."
BUT NOW HE SITS ON YOUR BED AS YOUR FOOD SOURCE.
す

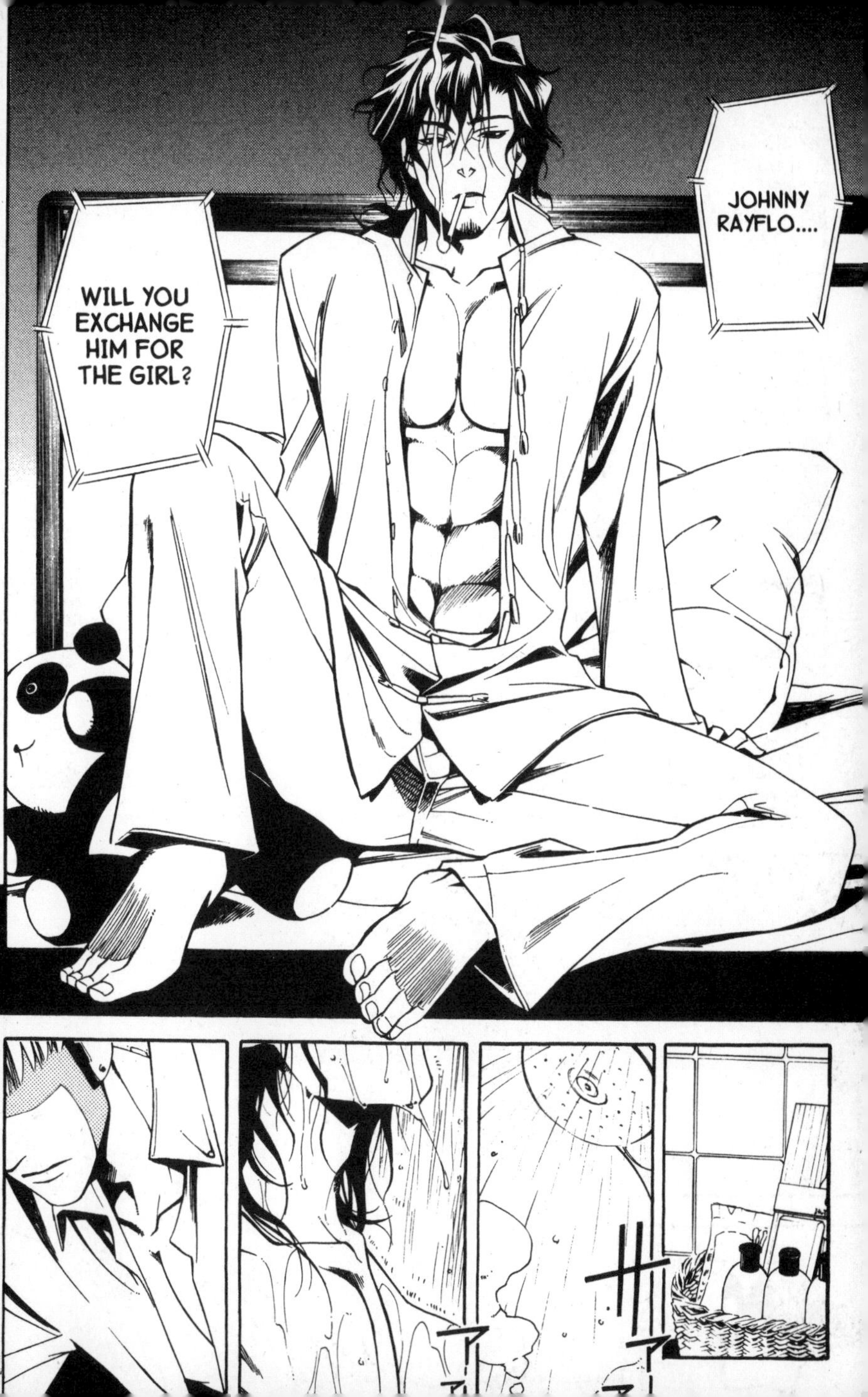
JOHNNY RAYFLO....
WILL YOU EXCHANGE HIM FOR THE GIRL?

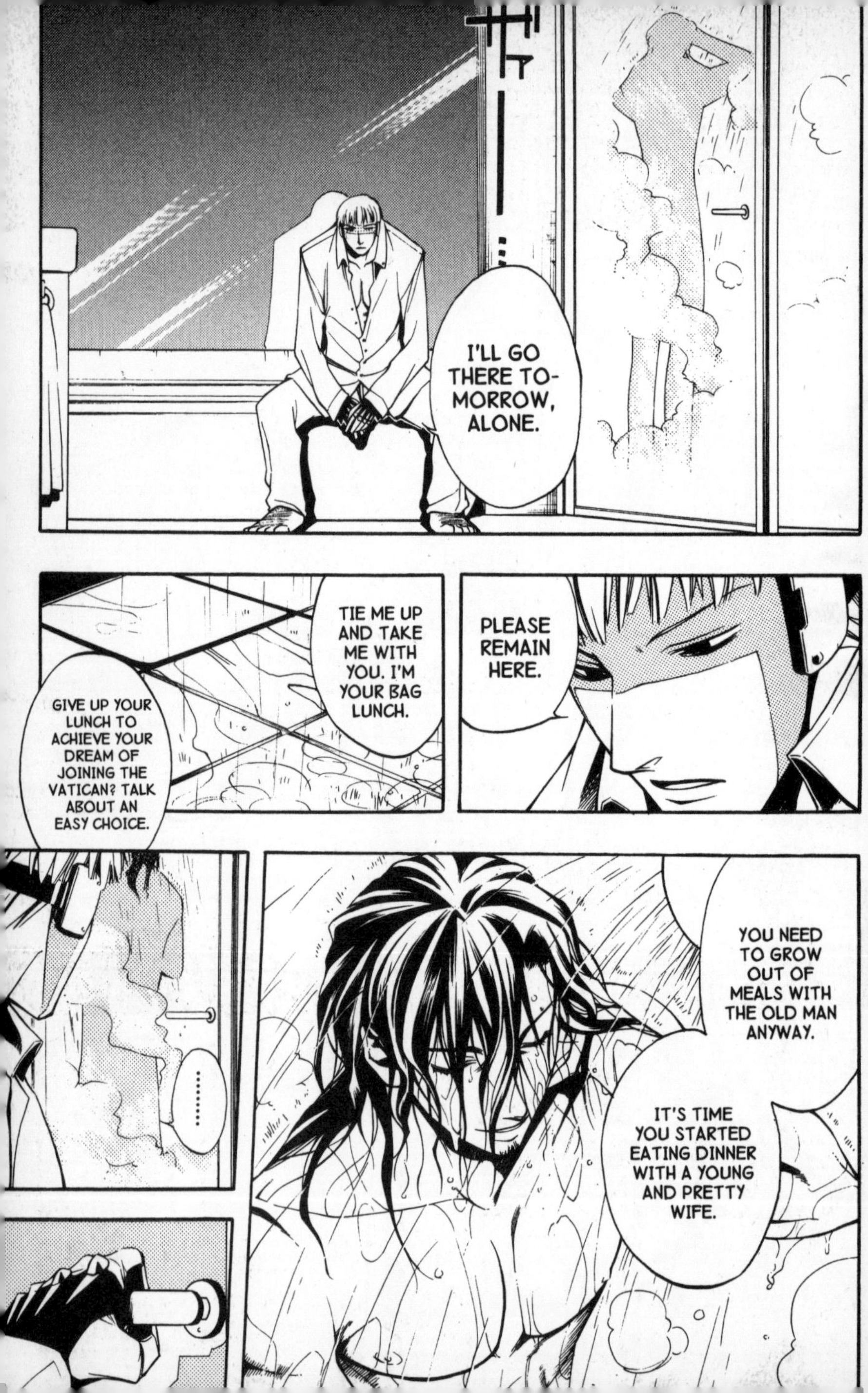
ザァー
I'LL GO THERE TO-MORROW, ALONE.
PLEASE REMAIN HERE.
TIE ME UP AND TAKE ME WITH YOU. I'M YOUR BAG LUNCH.
GIVE UP YOUR LUNCH TO ACHIEVE YOUR DREAM OF JOINING THE VATICAN? TALK ABOUT AN EASY CHOICE.
YOU NEED TO GROW OUT OF MEALS WITH THE OLD MAN ANYWAY.
IT'S TIME YOU STARTED EATING DINNER WITH A YOUNG AND PRETTY WIFE.
....

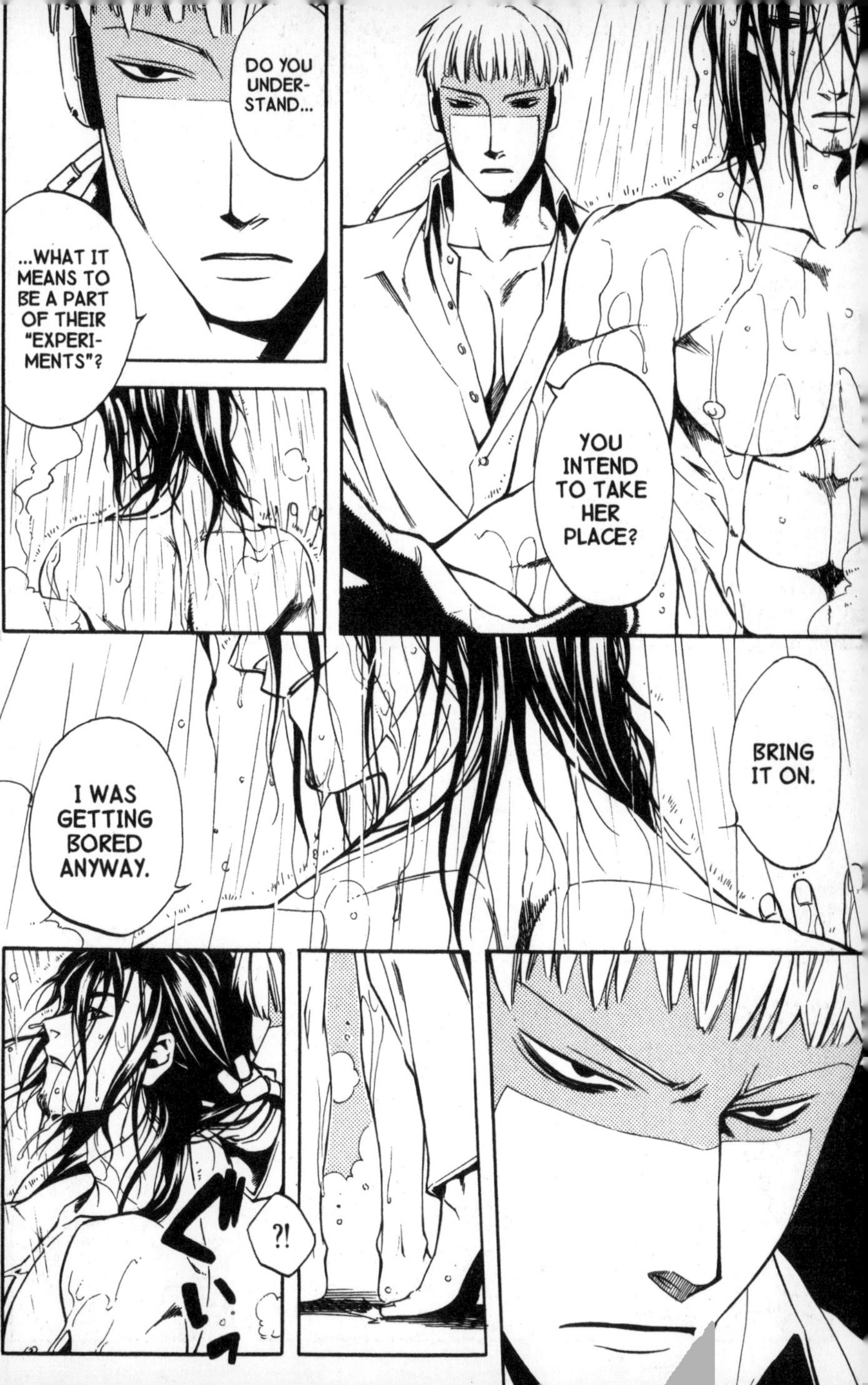
YOU INTEND TO TAKE HER PLACE?
DO YOU UNDERSTAND...
...WHAT IT MEANS TO BE A PART OF THEIR "EXPERIMENTS"?
BRING IT ON.
I WAS GETTING BORED ANYWAY.
?!

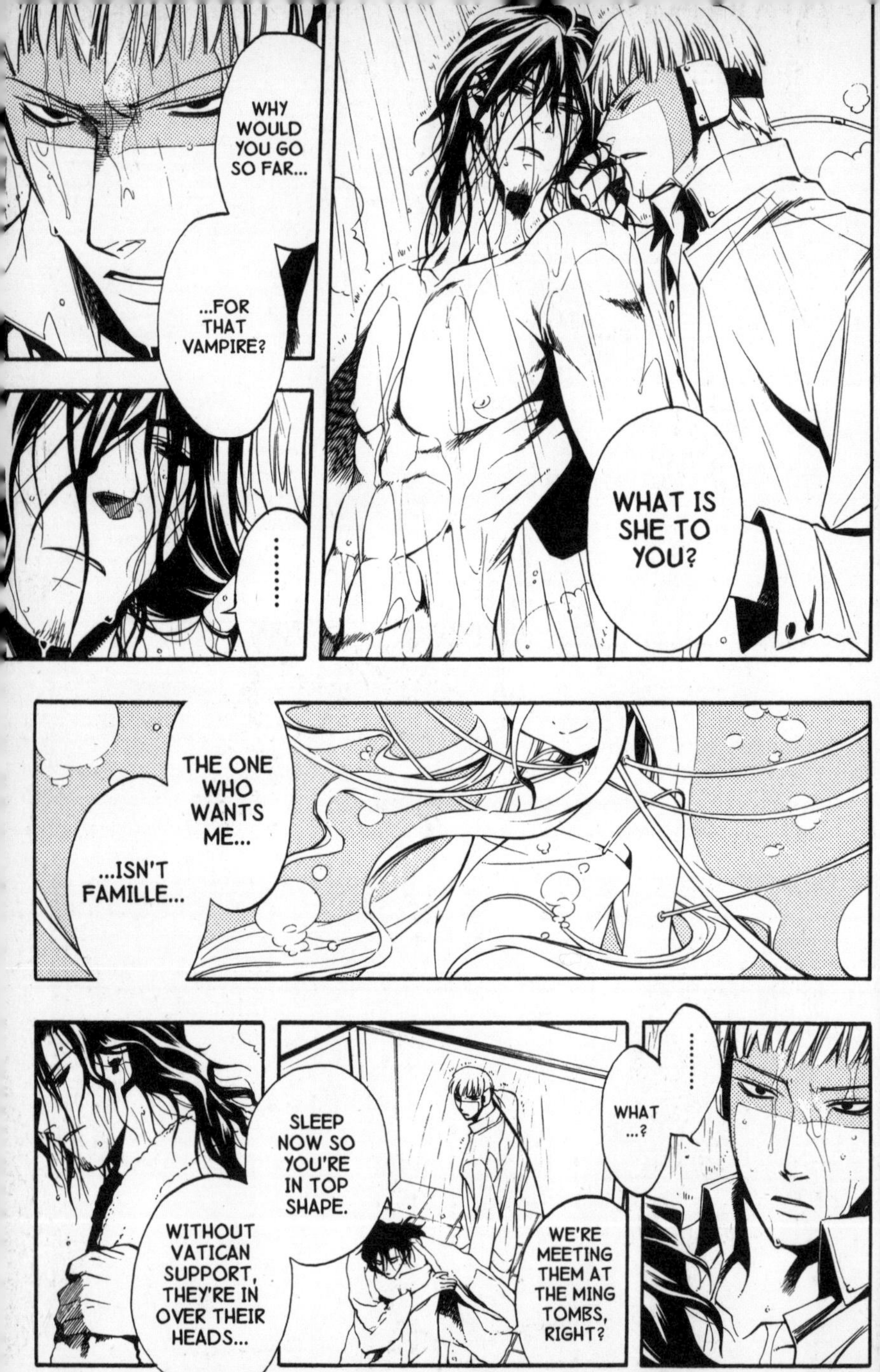
WHAT IS SHE TO YOU?
WHY WOULD YOU GO SO FAR...
...FOR THAT VAMPIRE?
......
THE ONE WHO WANTS ME...
...ISN'T FAMILLE...
......
WHAT ...?
WE'RE MEETING THEM AT THE MING TOMBS, RIGHT?
WITHOUT VATICAN SUPPORT, THEY'RE IN OVER THEIR HEADS...
SLEEP NOW SO YOU'RE IN TOP SHAPE.

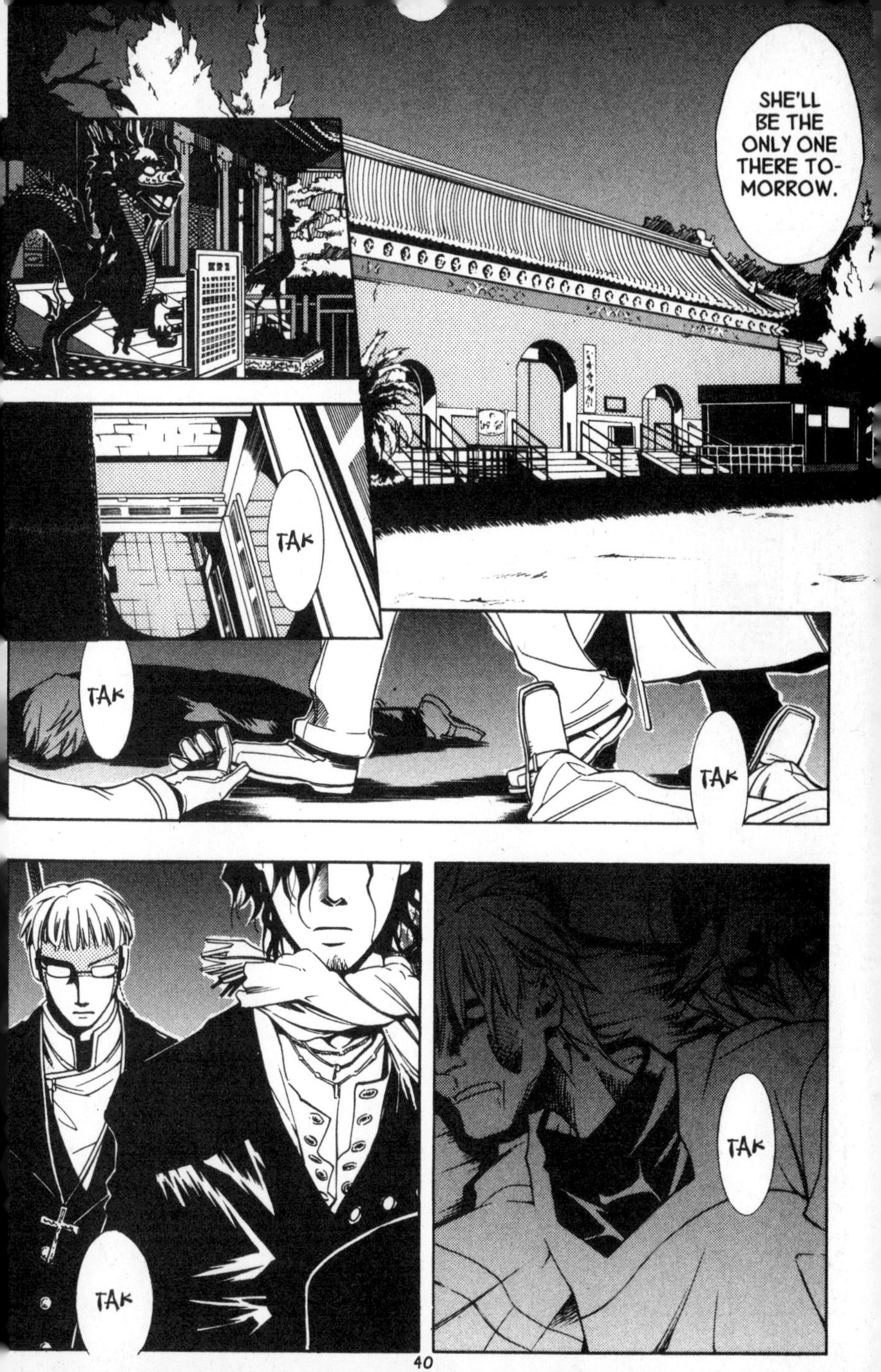
SHE'LL BE THE ONLY ONE THERE TO-MORROW.
TAK
TAK
TAK
TAK
TAK

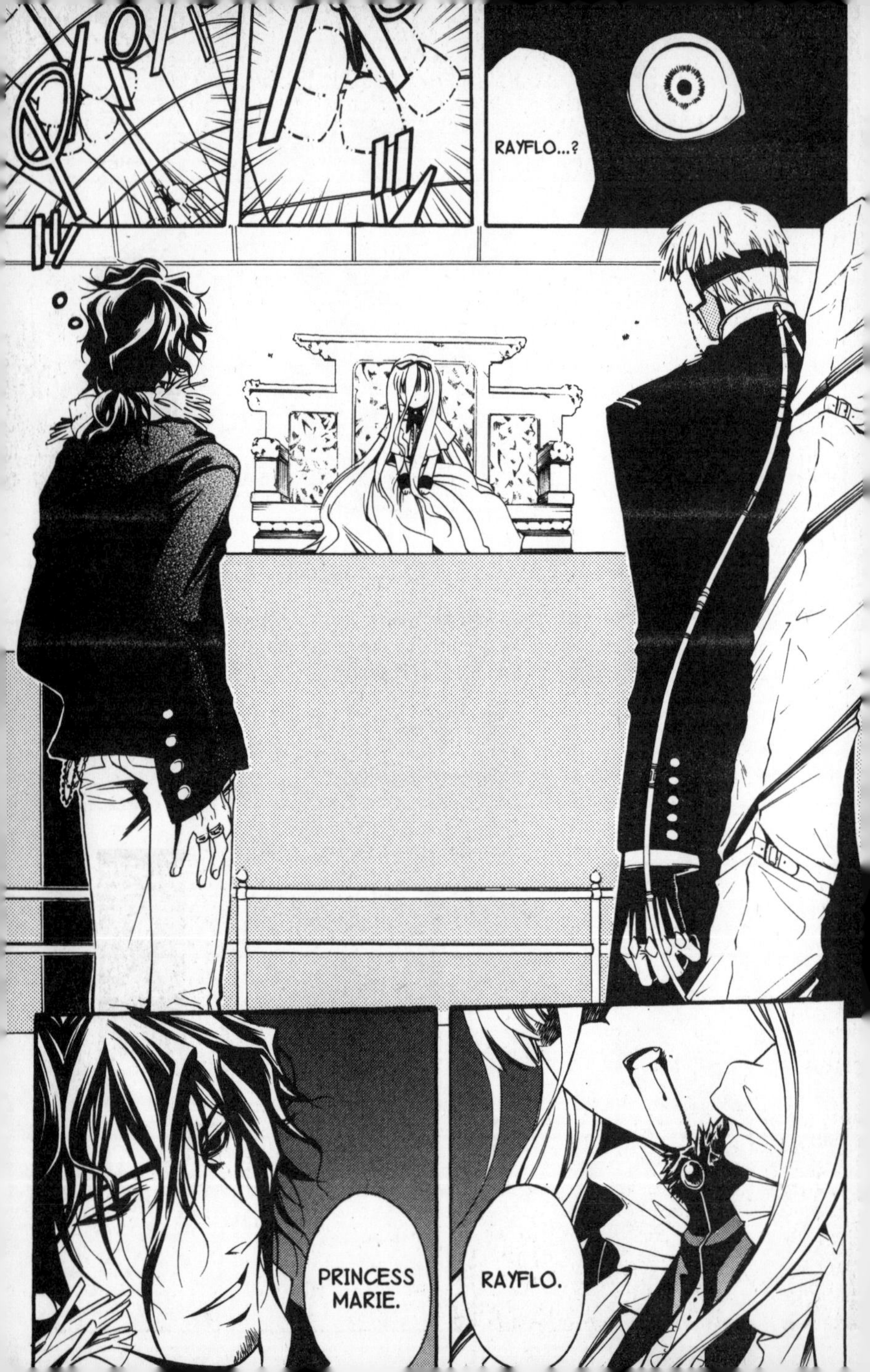
RAYFLO...?
RAYFLO.
PRINCESS MARIE.

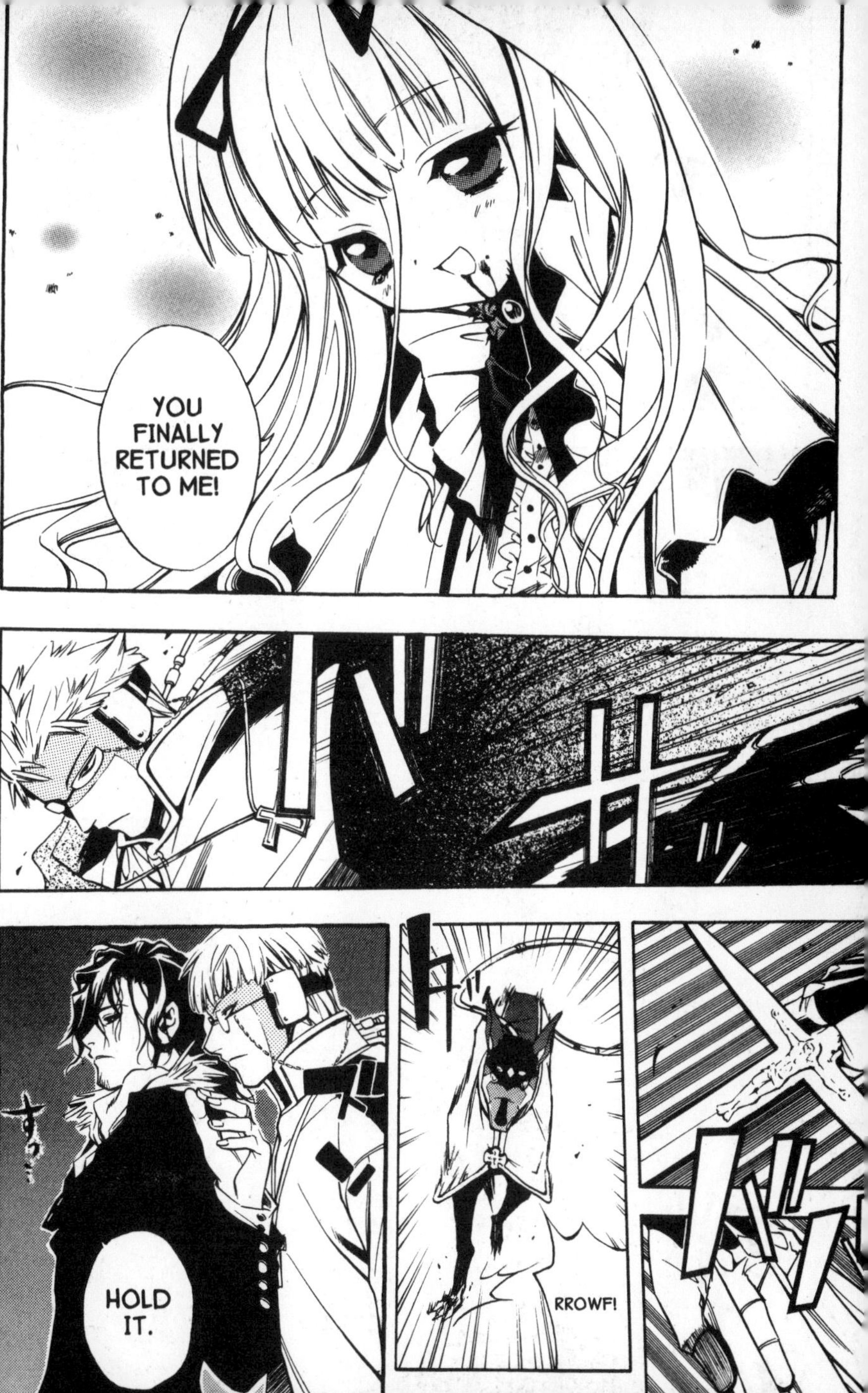
YOU FINALLY RETURNED TO ME!
RROWF!
HOLD IT.

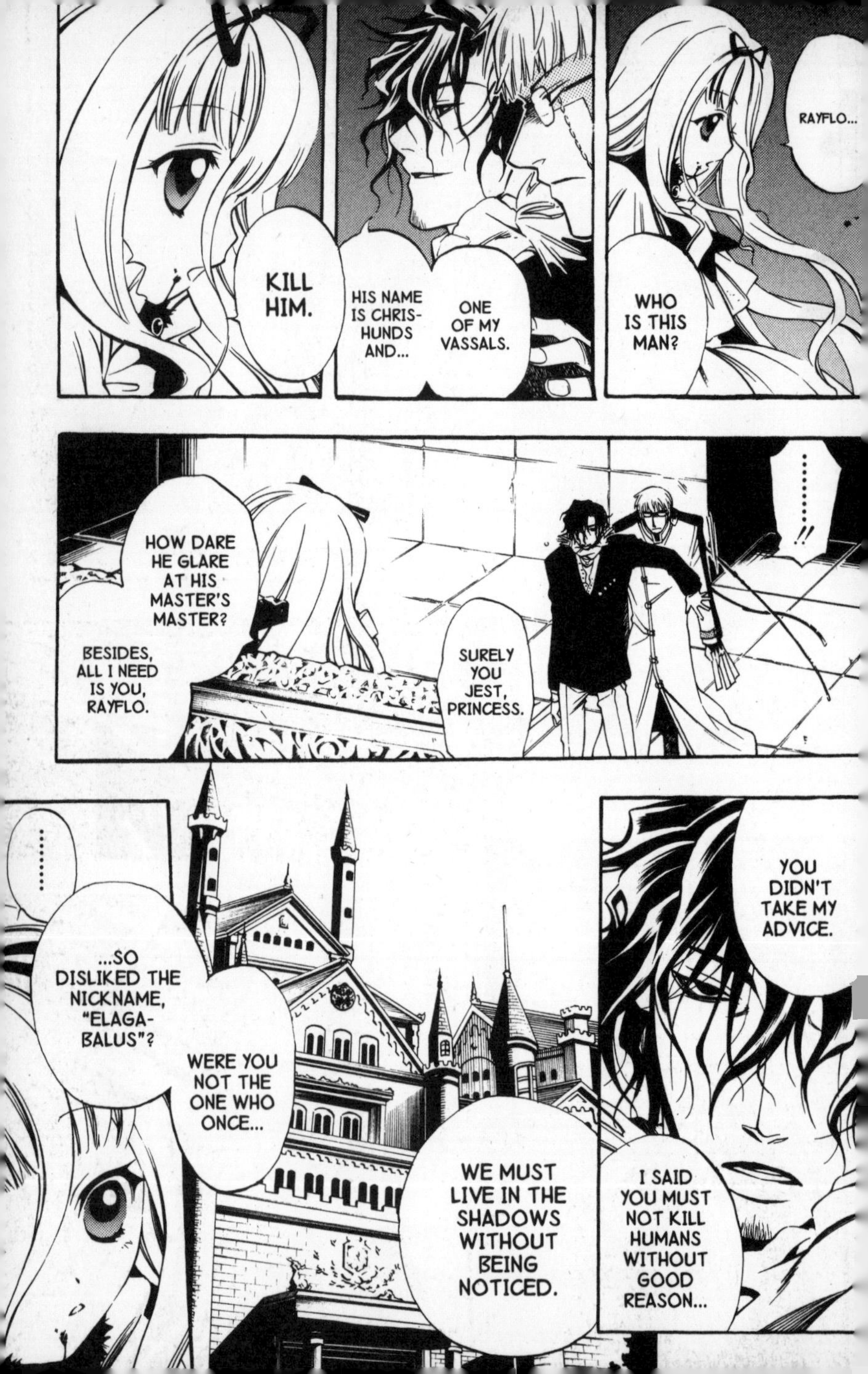
RAYFLO...
WHO IS THIS MAN?
ONE OF MY VASSALS.
HIS NAME IS CHRIS-HUNDS AND...
KILL HIM.
......!!
SURELY YOU JEST, PRINCESS.
HOW DARE HE GLARE AT HIS MASTER'S MASTER?
BESIDES, ALL I NEED IS YOU, RAYFLO.
YOU DIDN'T TAKE MY ADVICE.
I SAID YOU MUST NOT KILL HUMANS WITHOUT GOOD REASON...
WE MUST LIVE IN THE SHADOWS WITHOUT BEING NOTICED.
WERE YOU NOT THE ONE WHO ONCE...
...SO DISLIKED THE NICKNAME, "ELAGA-BALUS"?
......

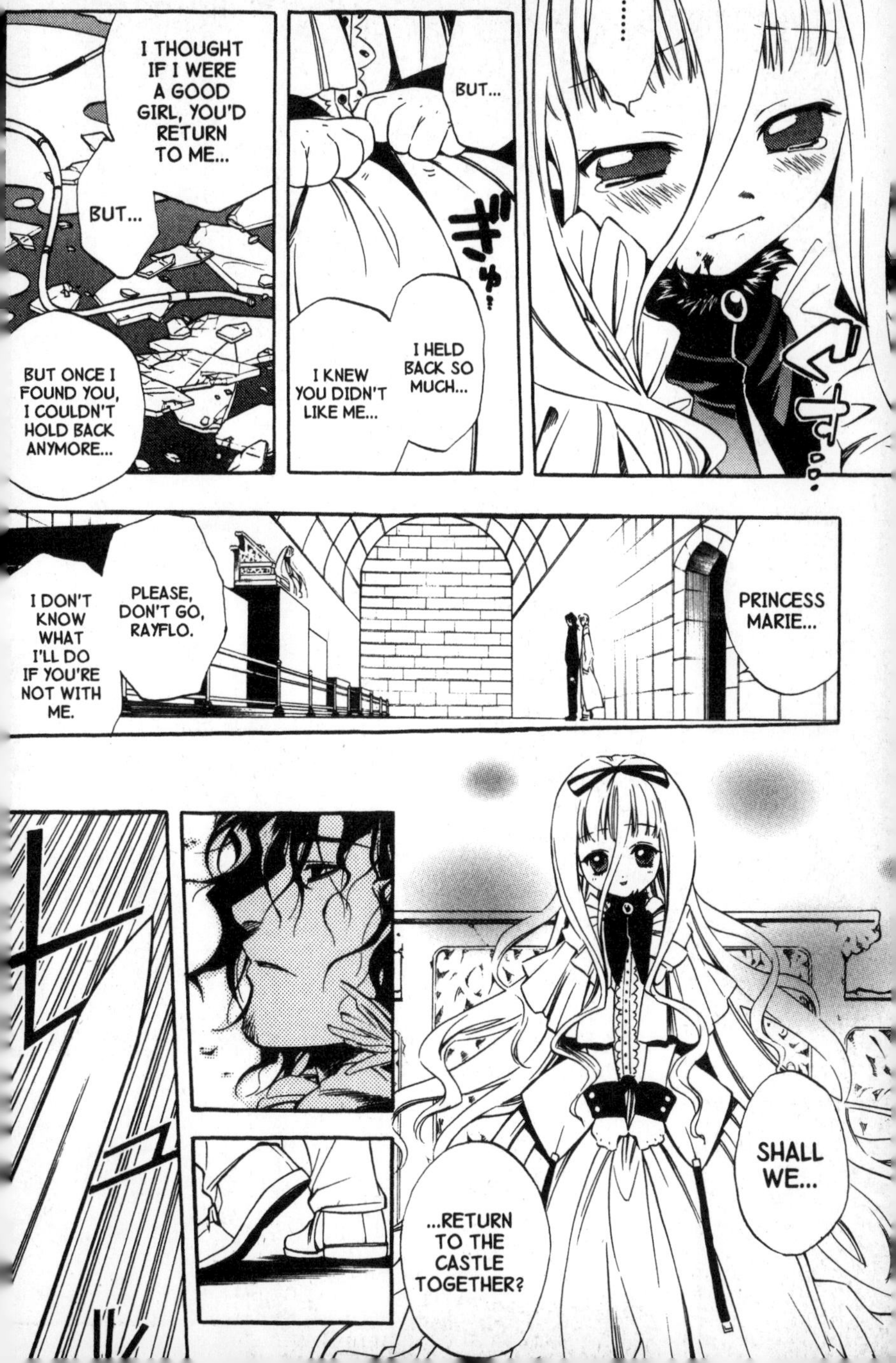
......
BUT...
ぎゅ
I HELD BACK SO MUCH...
I KNEW YOU DIDN'T LIKE ME...
I THOUGHT IF I WERE A GOOD GIRL, YOU'D RETURN TO ME...
BUT...
BUT ONCE I FOUND YOU, I COULDN'T HOLD BACK ANYMORE...
PRINCESS MARIE...
PLEASE, DON'T GO, RAYFLO.
I DON'T KNOW WHAT I'LL DO IF YOU'RE NOT WITH ME.
SHALL WE...
...RETURN TO THE CASTLE TOGETHER?

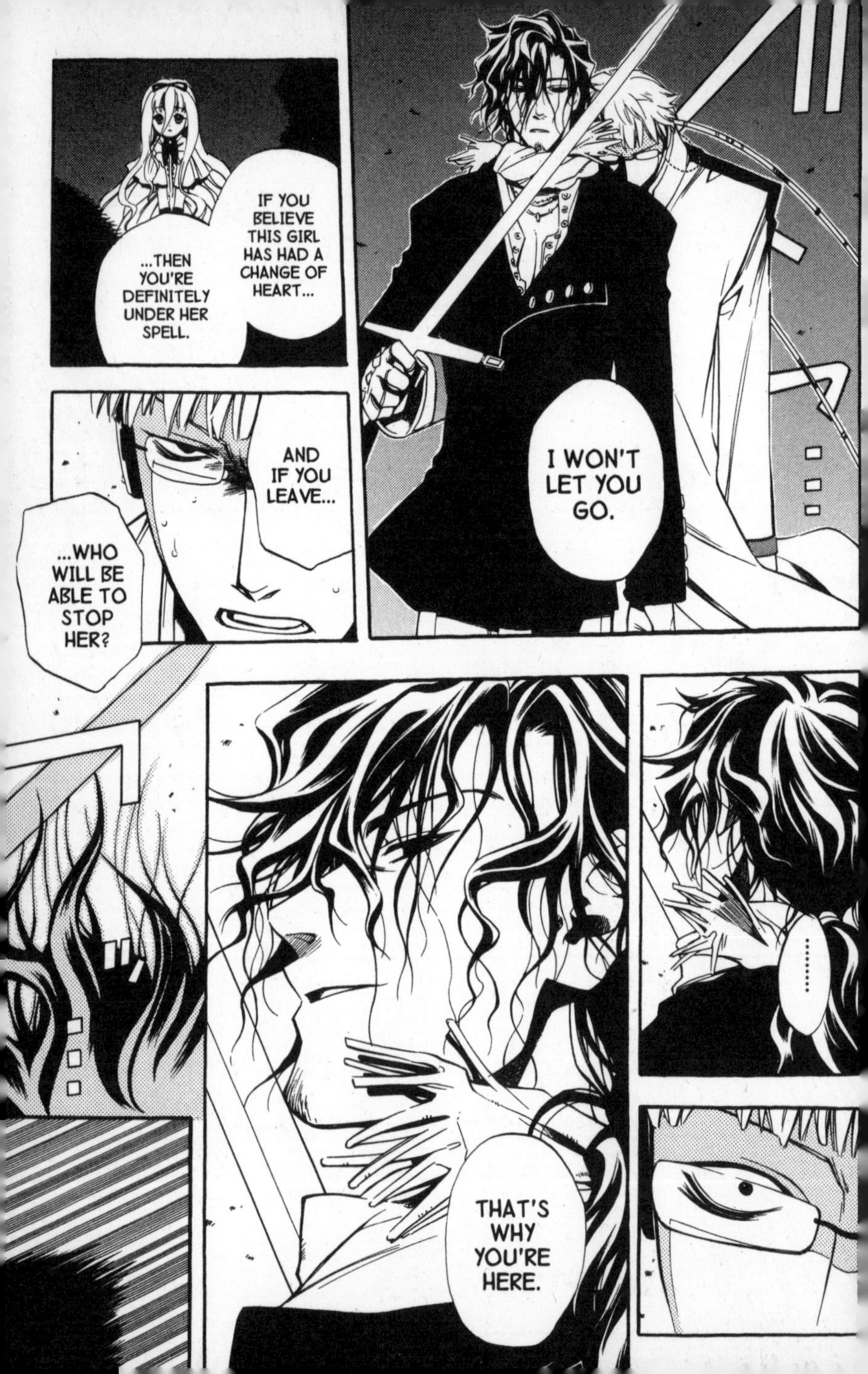
I WON'T LET YOU GO.
IF YOU BELIEVE THIS GIRL HAS HAD A CHANGE OF HEART...
...THEN YOU'RE DEFINITELY UNDER HER SPELL.
AND IF YOU LEAVE...
...WHO WILL BE ABLE TO STOP HER?
......
THAT'S WHY YOU'RE HERE.

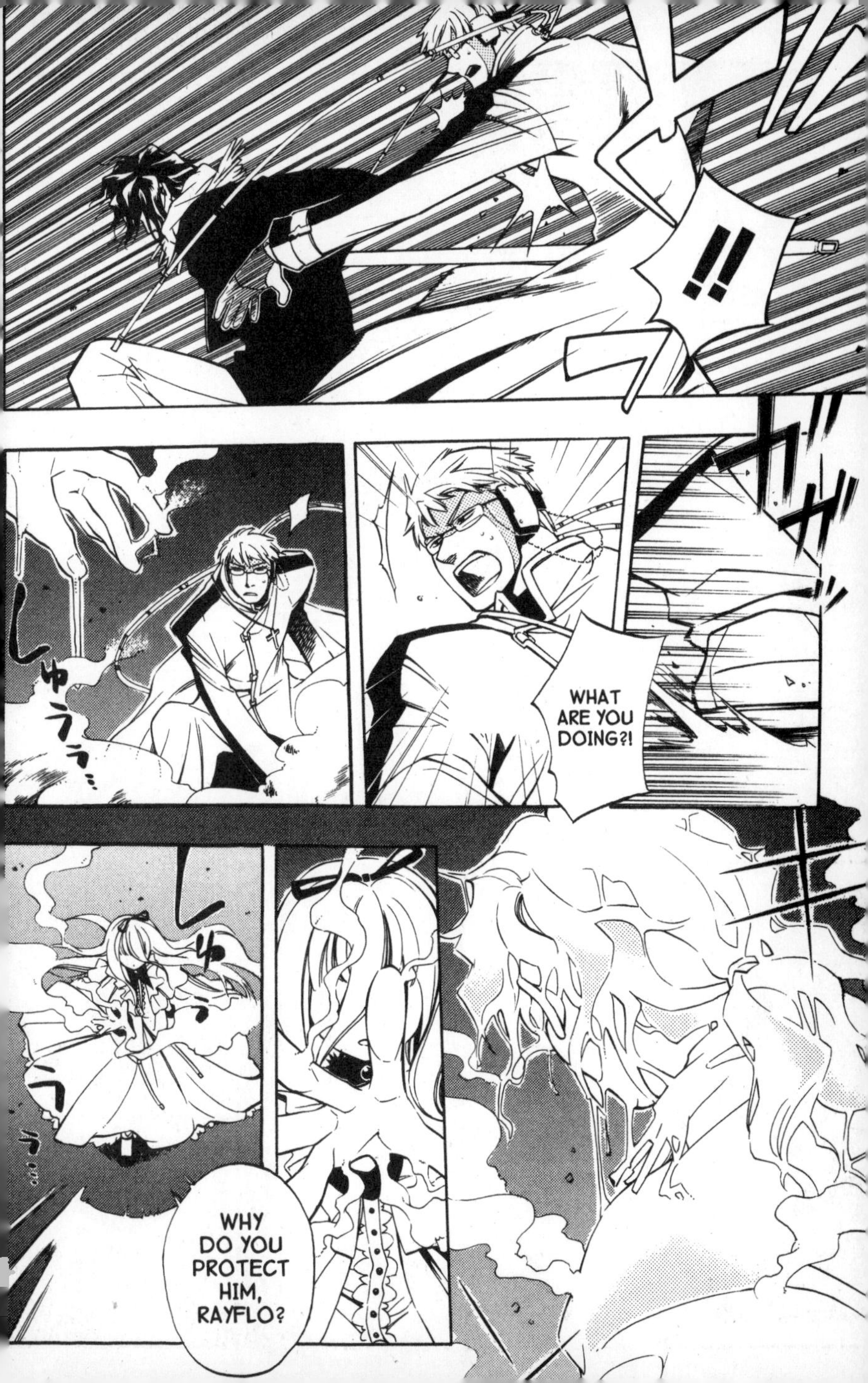
!!
WHAT ARE YOU DOING?!
WHY DO YOU PROTECT HIM, RAYFLO?

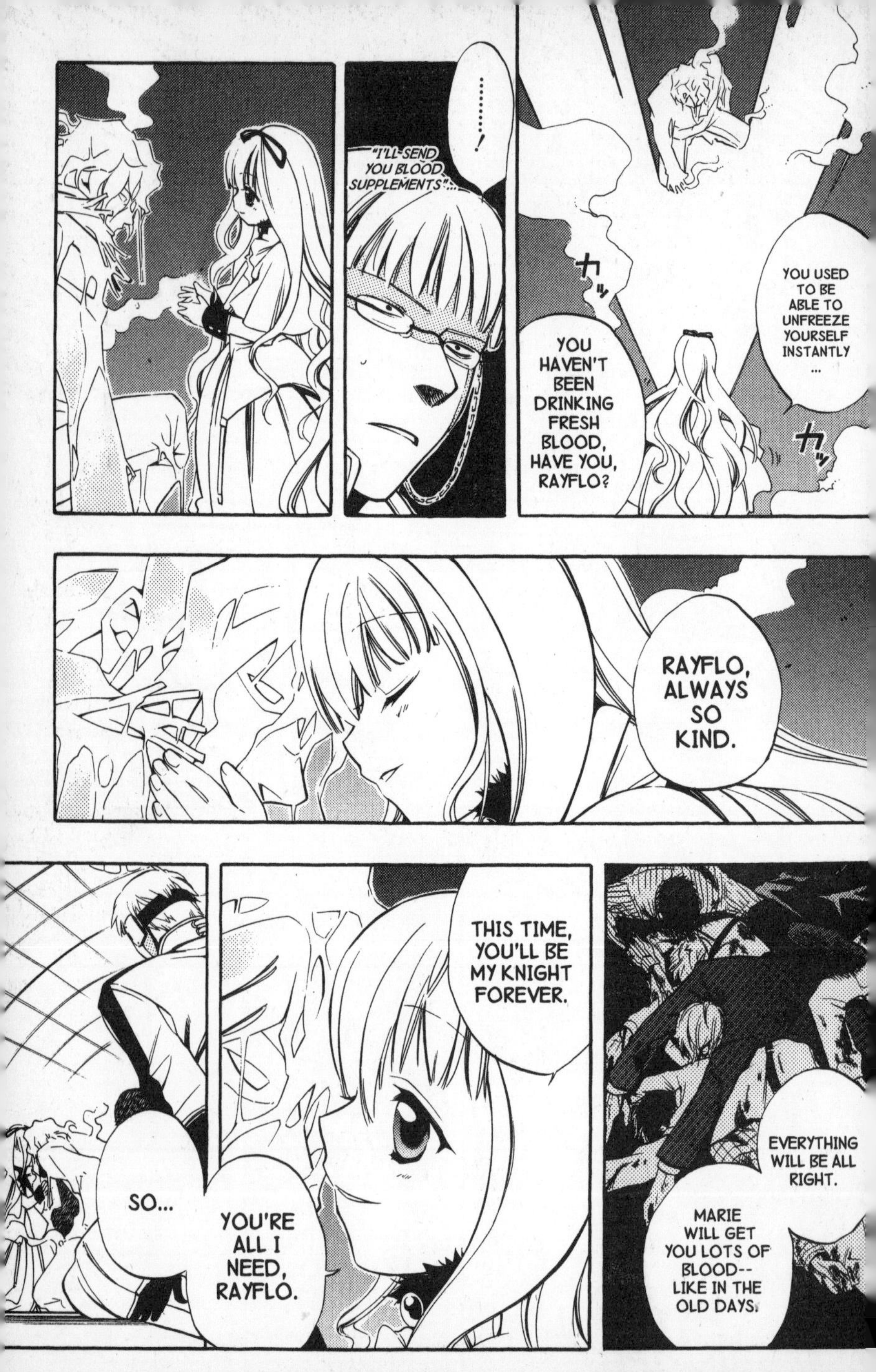

YOU USED TO BE ABLE TO UNFREEZE YOURSELF INSTANTLY ...
カッ
カッ
YOU HAVEN'T BEEN DRINKING FRESH BLOOD, HAVE YOU, RAYFLO?
......!
"I'LL SEND YOU BLOOD SUPPLEMENTS"...
RAYFLO, ALWAYS SO KIND.
EVERYTHING WILL BE ALL RIGHT.
MARIE WILL GET YOU LOTS OF BLOOD-- LIKE IN THE OLD DAYS.
THIS TIME, YOU'LL BE MY KNIGHT FOREVER.
SO...
YOU'RE ALL I NEED, RAYFLO.

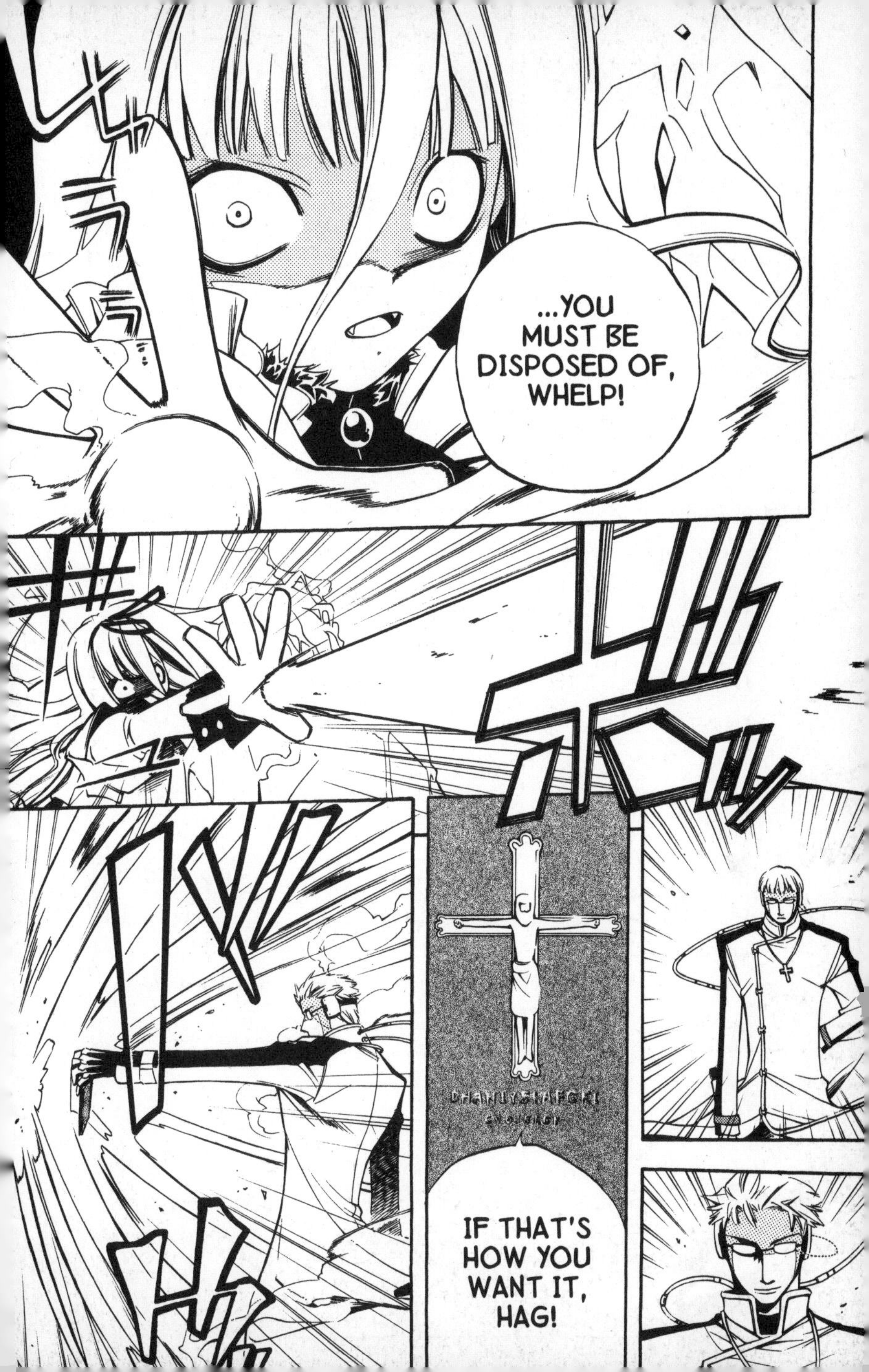
...YOU MUST BE DISPOSED OF, WHELP!
IF THAT'S HOW YOU WANT IT, HAG!

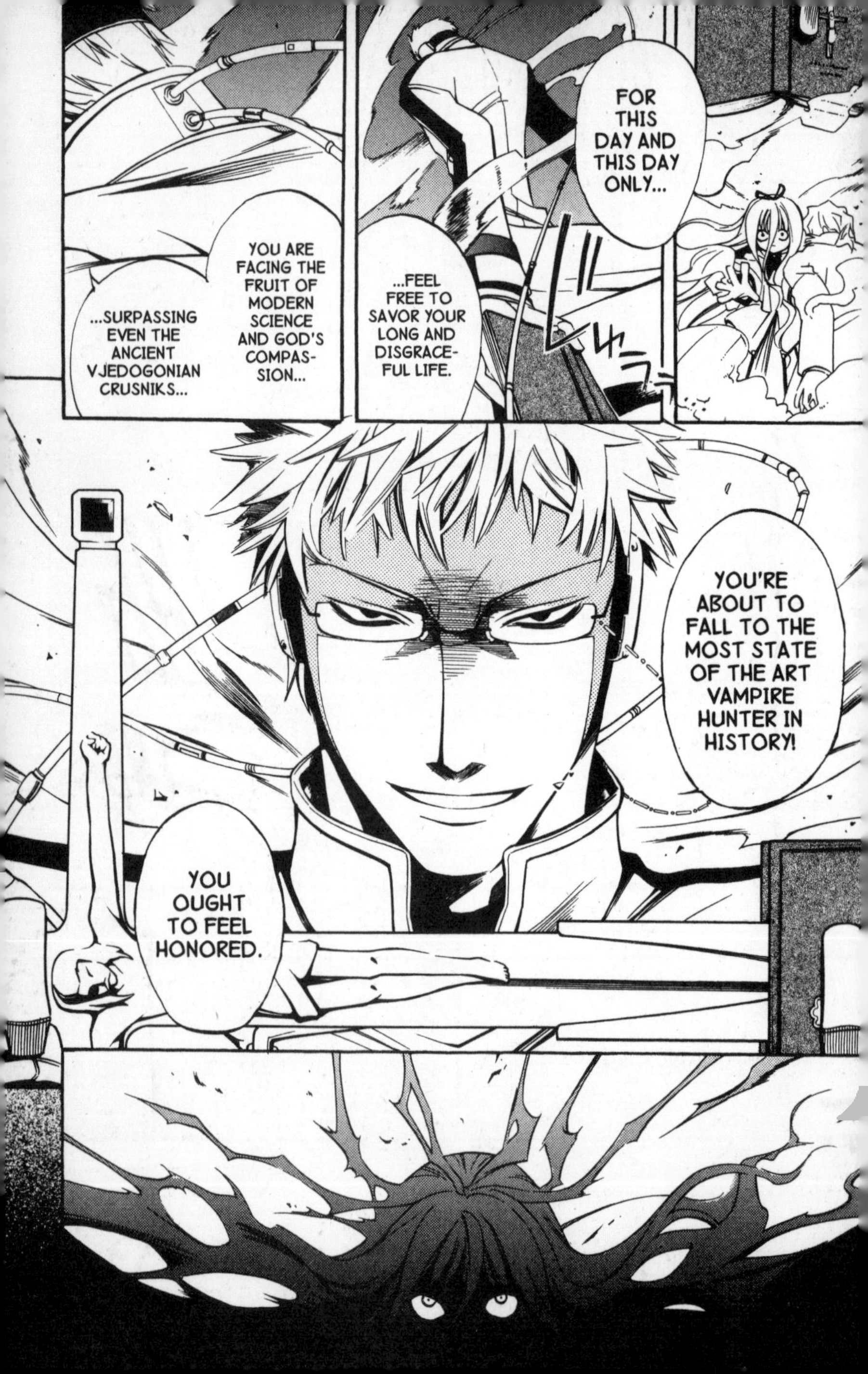
FOR THIS DAY AND THIS DAY ONLY...
...FEEL FREE TO SAVOR YOUR LONG AND DISGRACE-FUL LIFE.
YOU ARE FACING THE FRUIT OF MODERN SCIENCE AND GOD'S COMPAS-SION...
...SURPASSING EVEN THE ANCIENT VJEDOGONIAN CRUSNIKS...
YOU'RE ABOUT TO FALL TO THE MOST STATE OF THE ART VAMPIRE HUNTER IN HISTORY!
YOU OUGHT TO FEEL HONORED.

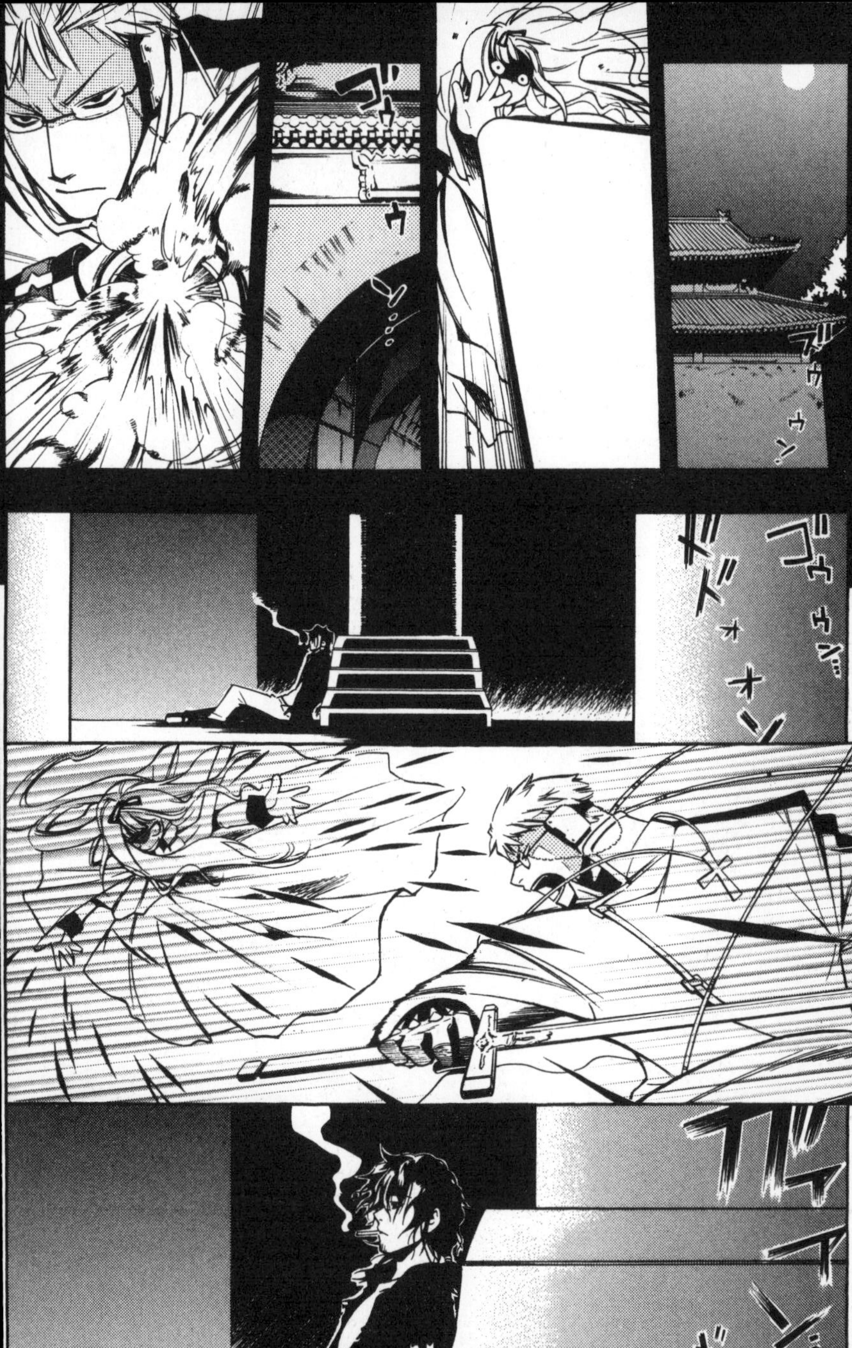
ズゥウン
ゴゥ
ウ
ゴゥェン…
ギドォオン
ガアン…ッ
ズッ

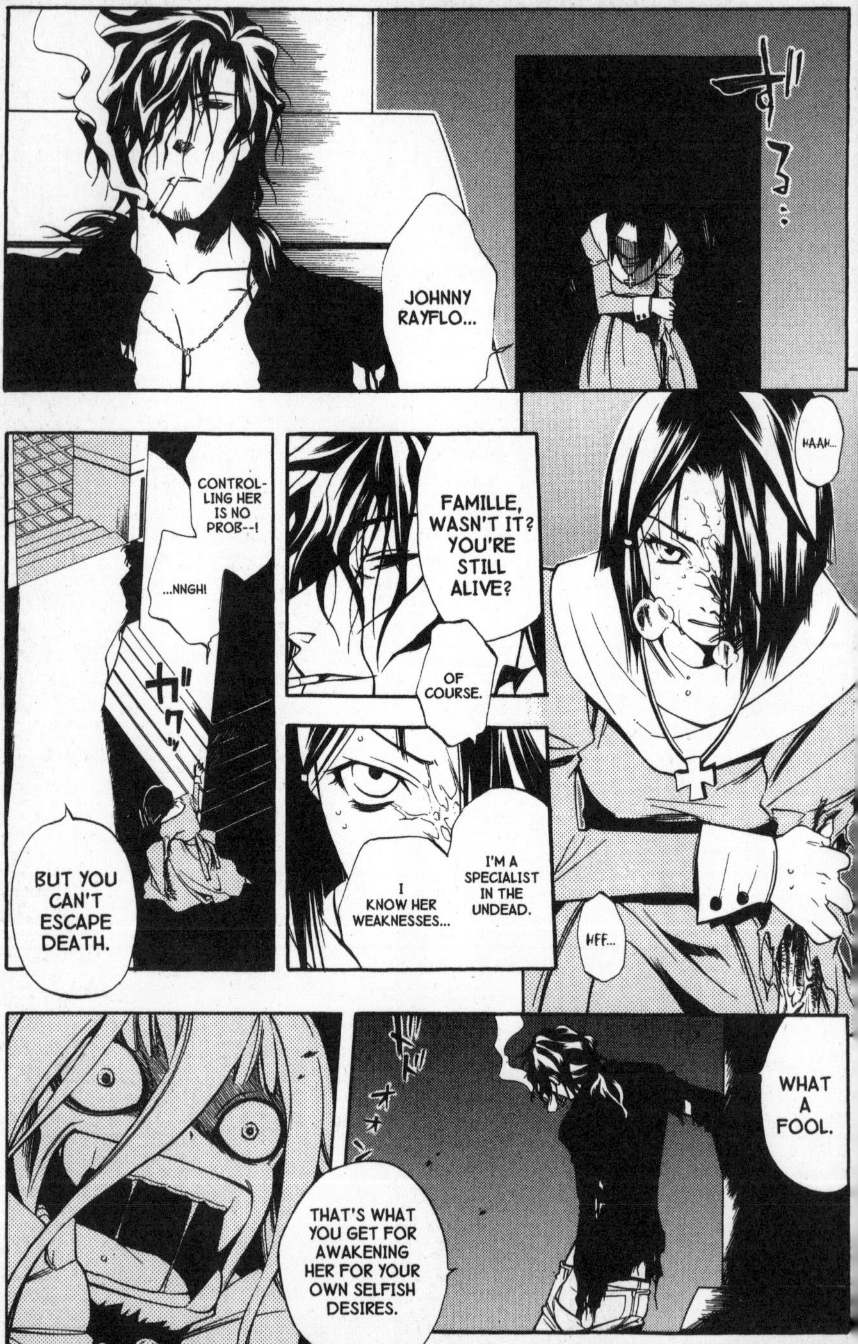
ずる..
JOHNNY RAYFLO...
HAAH...
HFF...
FAMILLE, WASN'T IT? YOU'RE STILL ALIVE?
OF COURSE.
I'M A SPECIALIST IN THE UNDEAD.
I KNOW HER WEAKNESSES...
CONTROL-LING HER IS NO PROB--!
...NNGH!
ガクッ
BUT YOU CAN'T ESCAPE DEATH.
WHAT A FOOL.
THAT'S WHAT YOU GET FOR AWAKENING HER FOR YOUR OWN SELFISH DESIRES.

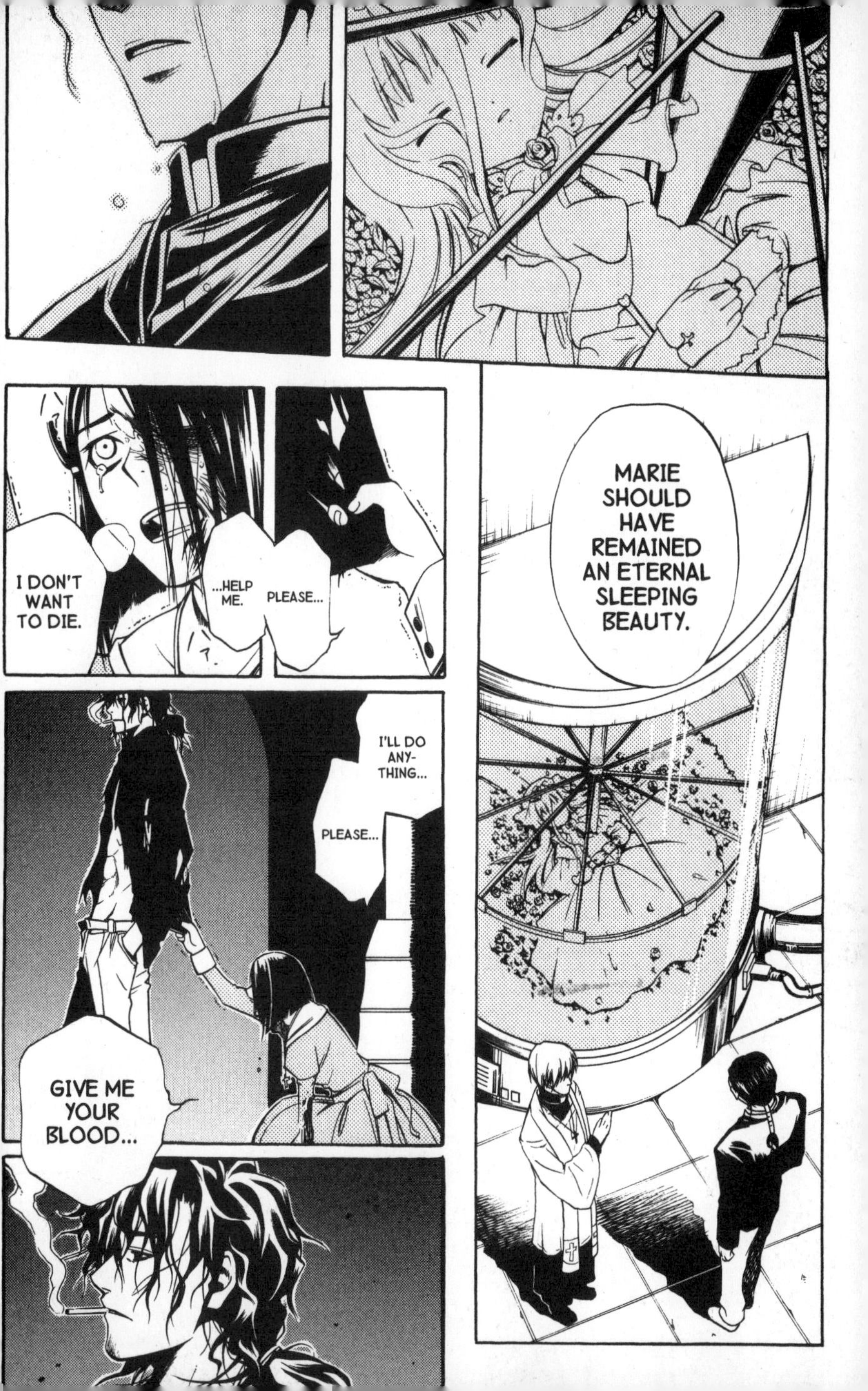
MARIE SHOULD HAVE REMAINED AN ETERNAL SLEEPING BEAUTY.
PLEASE...
...HELP ME.
I DON'T WANT TO DIE.
I'LL DO ANY-THING...
PLEASE...
GIVE ME YOUR BLOOD...

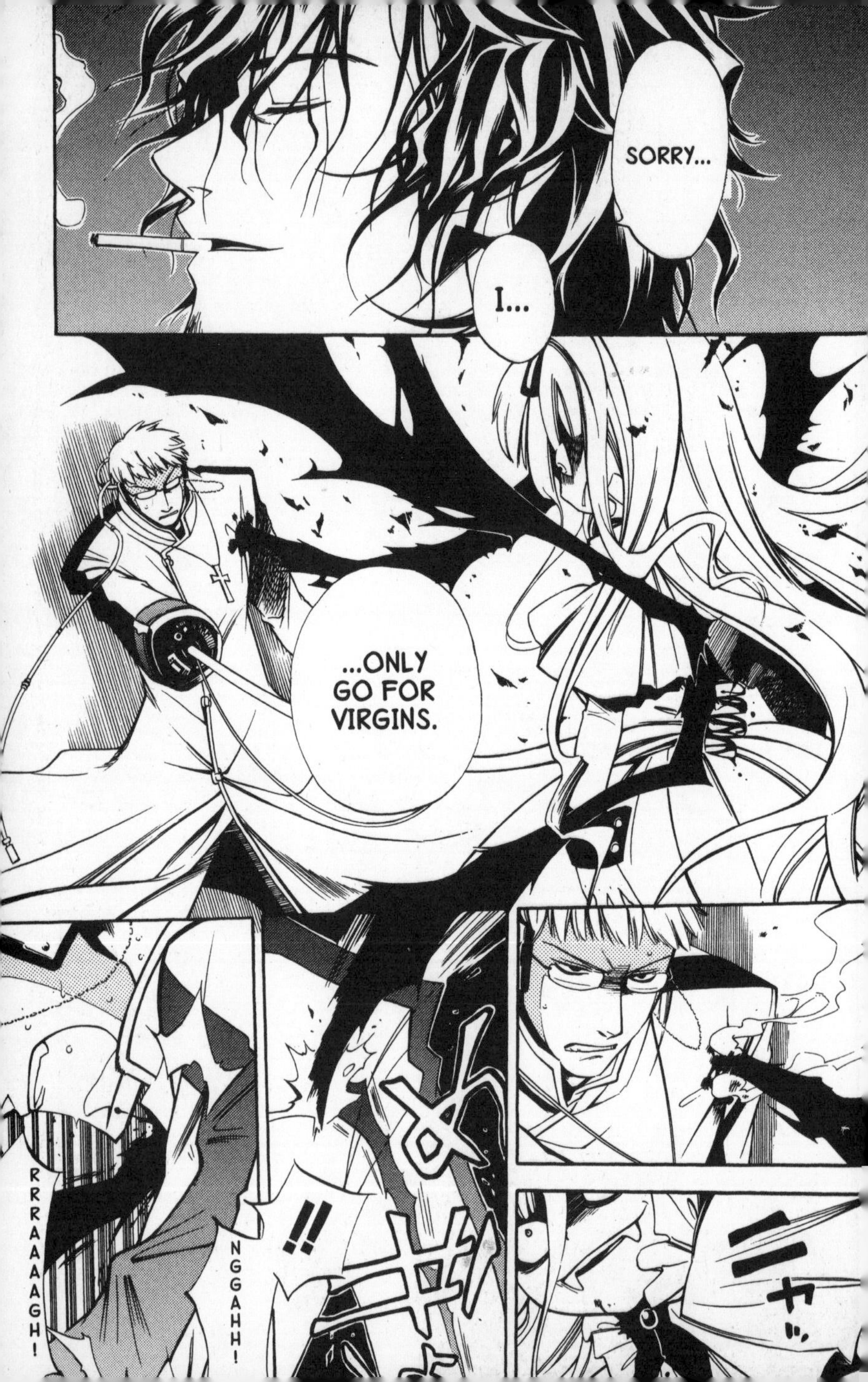
SORRY...
I...
...ONLY GO FOR VIRGINS.
ニヤッ
!!
NGGAHH!
RRRAAAAGH!

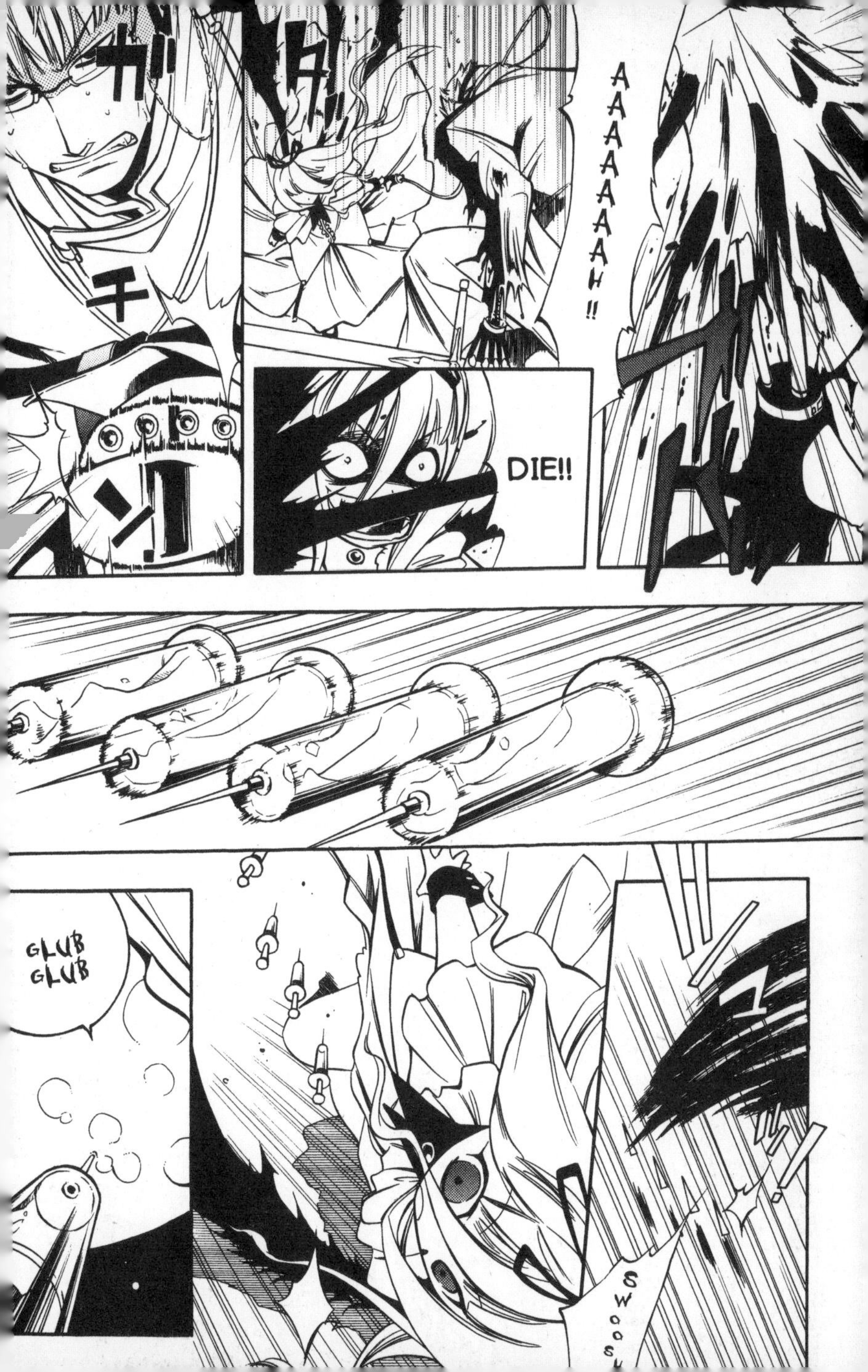
AAAAAAAAAH!!
DIE!!
SWOOSH
GLUB GLUB

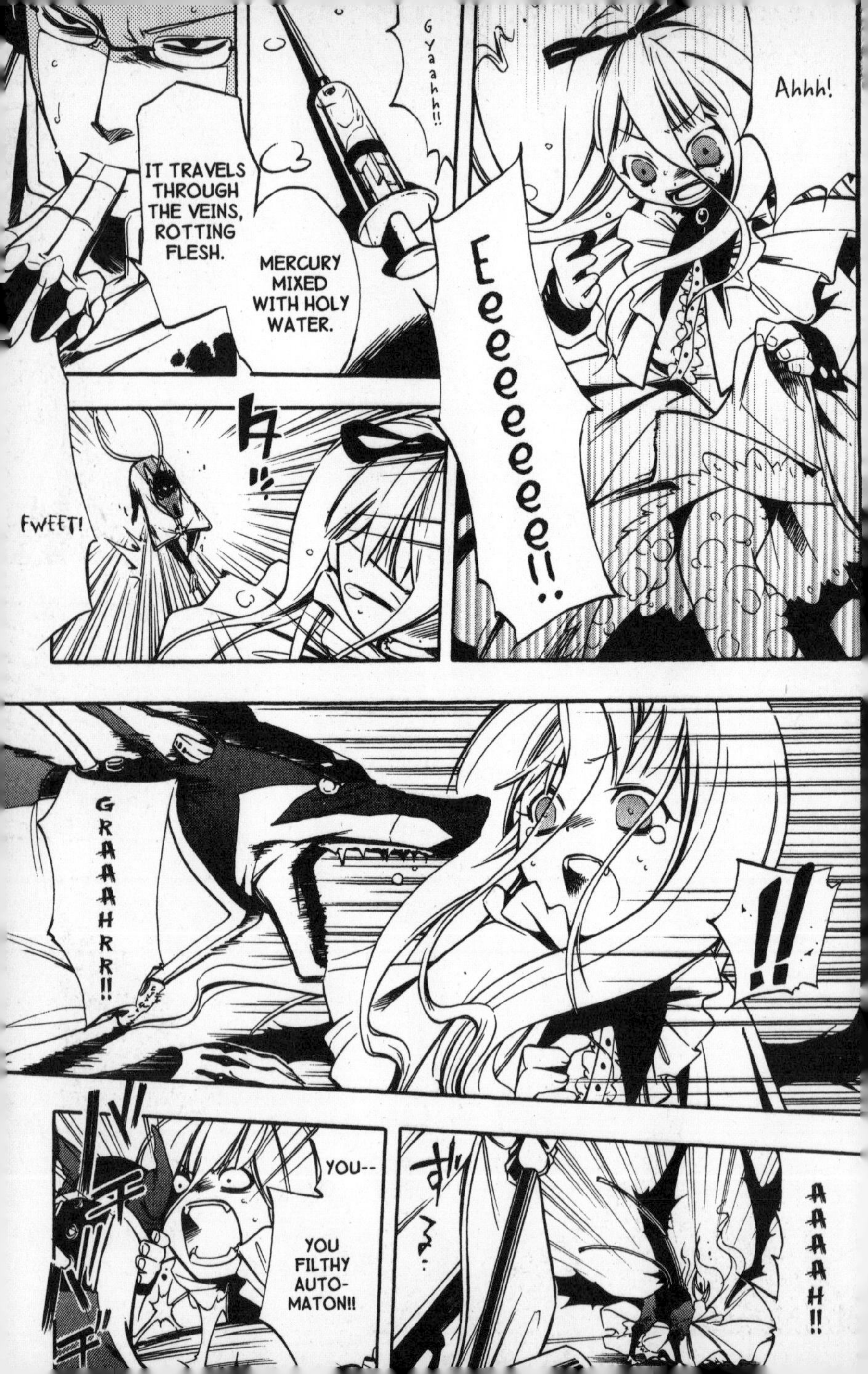
Ahhh!
Eeeeeeee!!
Gyaahh!!
MERCURY MIXED WITH HOLY WATER.
IT TRAVELS THROUGH THE VEINS, ROTTING FLESH.
FWEET!
!!
GRAAAAHRRR!!
AAAAAH!!
YOU--
YOU FILTHY AUTO-MATON!!

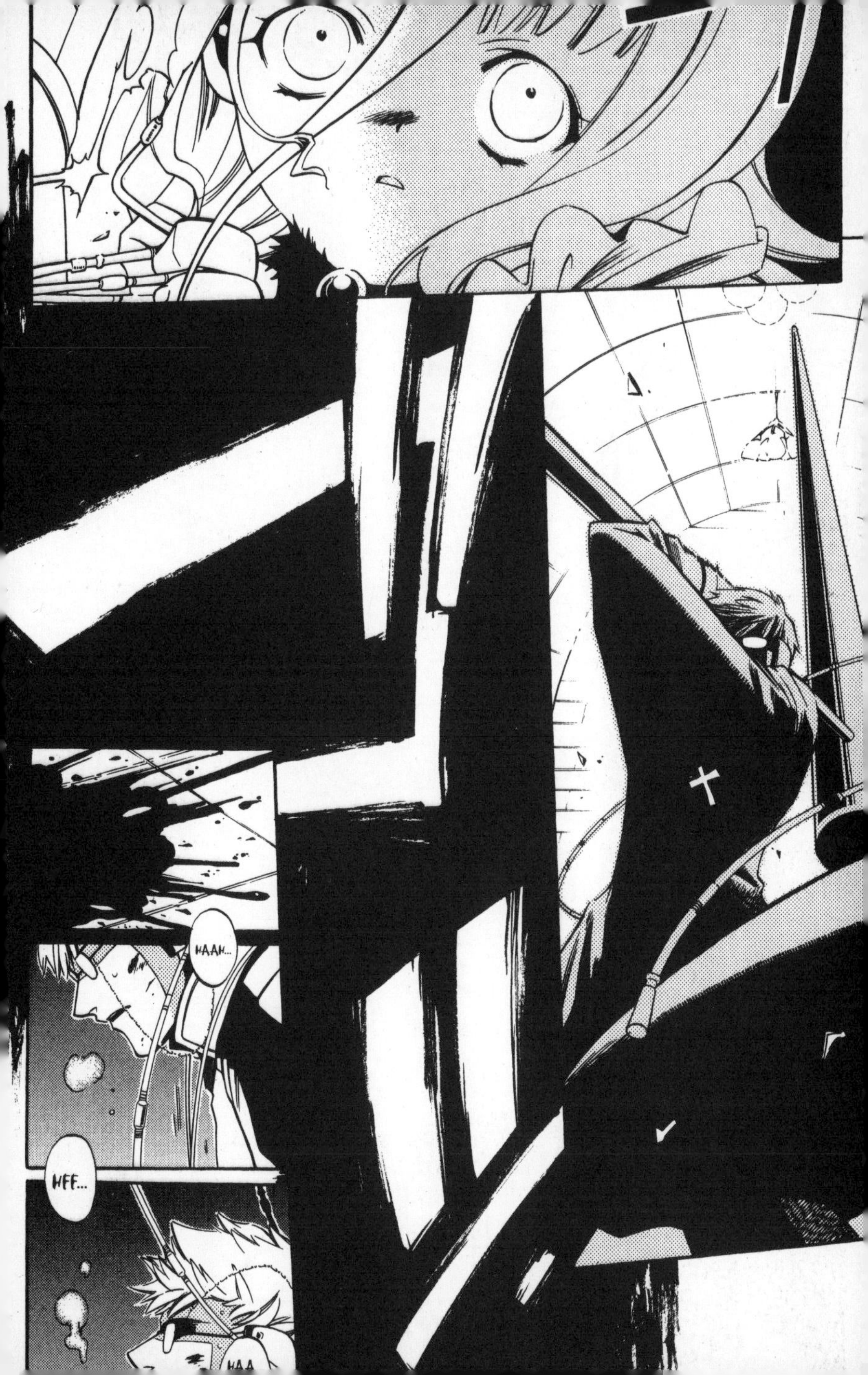
HAAH...
HFF...
HAA

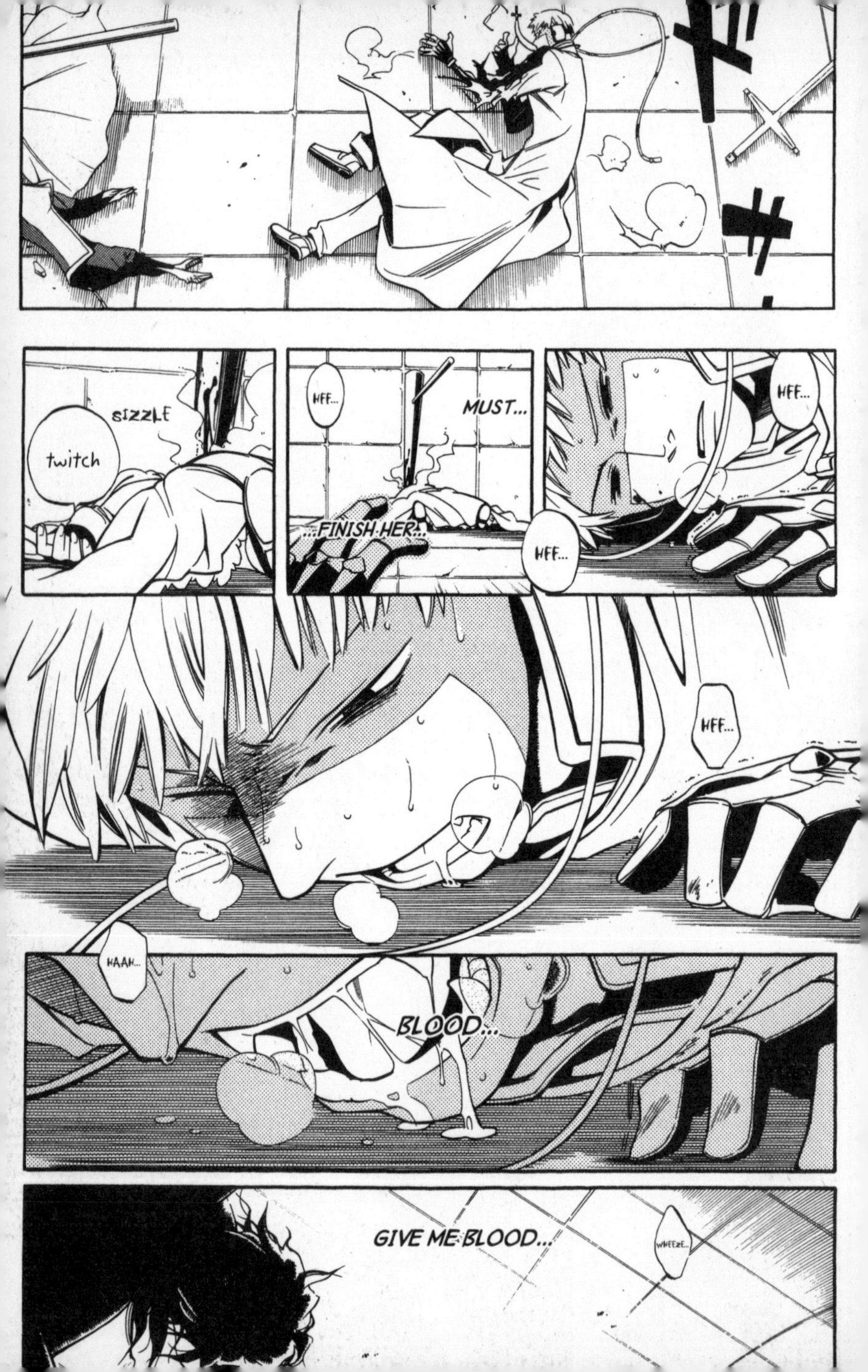
HFF...
HFF...
HFF...
MUST...
...FINISH HER...
SIZZLE
twitch
HFF...
BLOOD...
HAAH...
WHEEZE...
GIVE ME BLOOD...

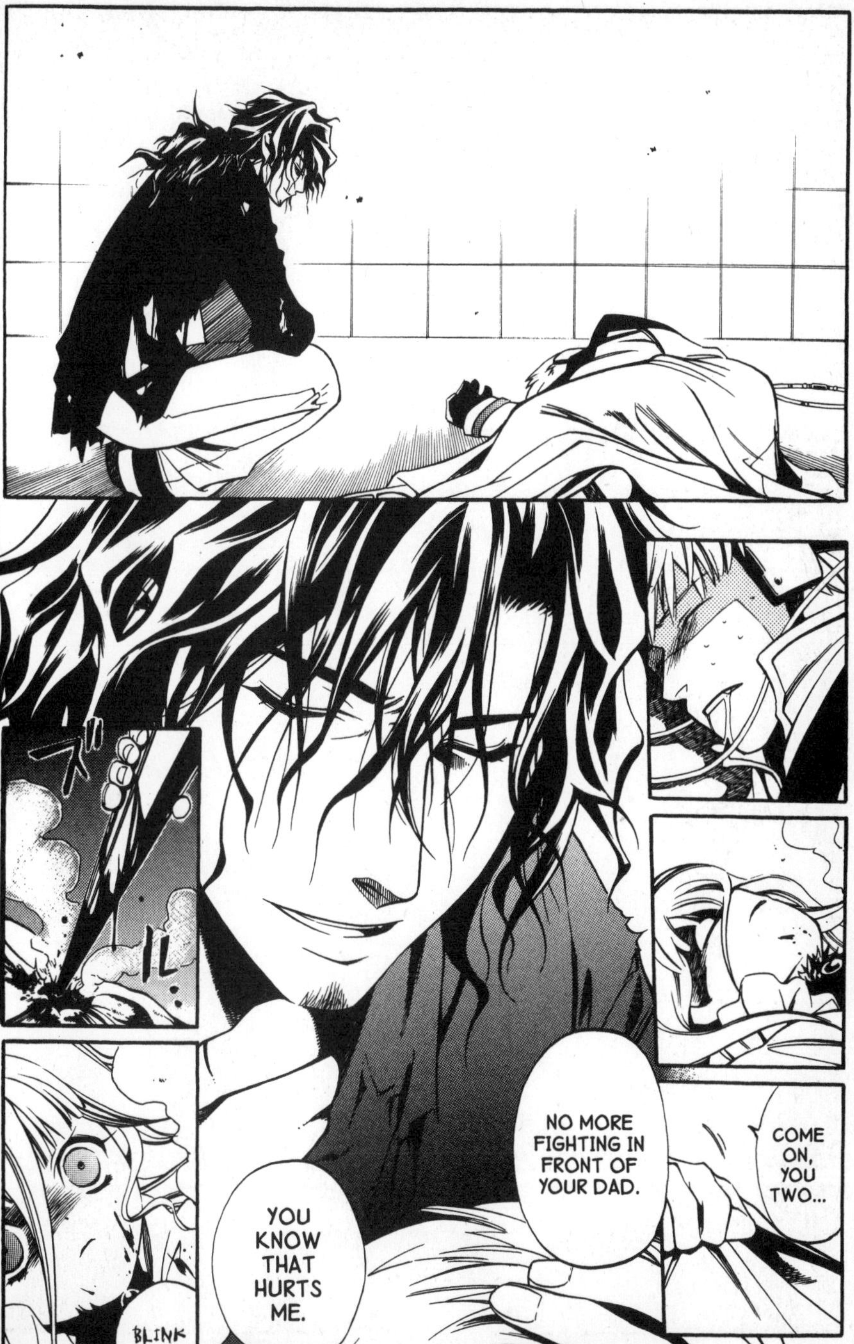
ズル
COME ON, YOU TWO...
NO MORE FIGHTING IN FRONT OF YOUR DAD.
YOU KNOW THAT HURTS ME.
BLINK

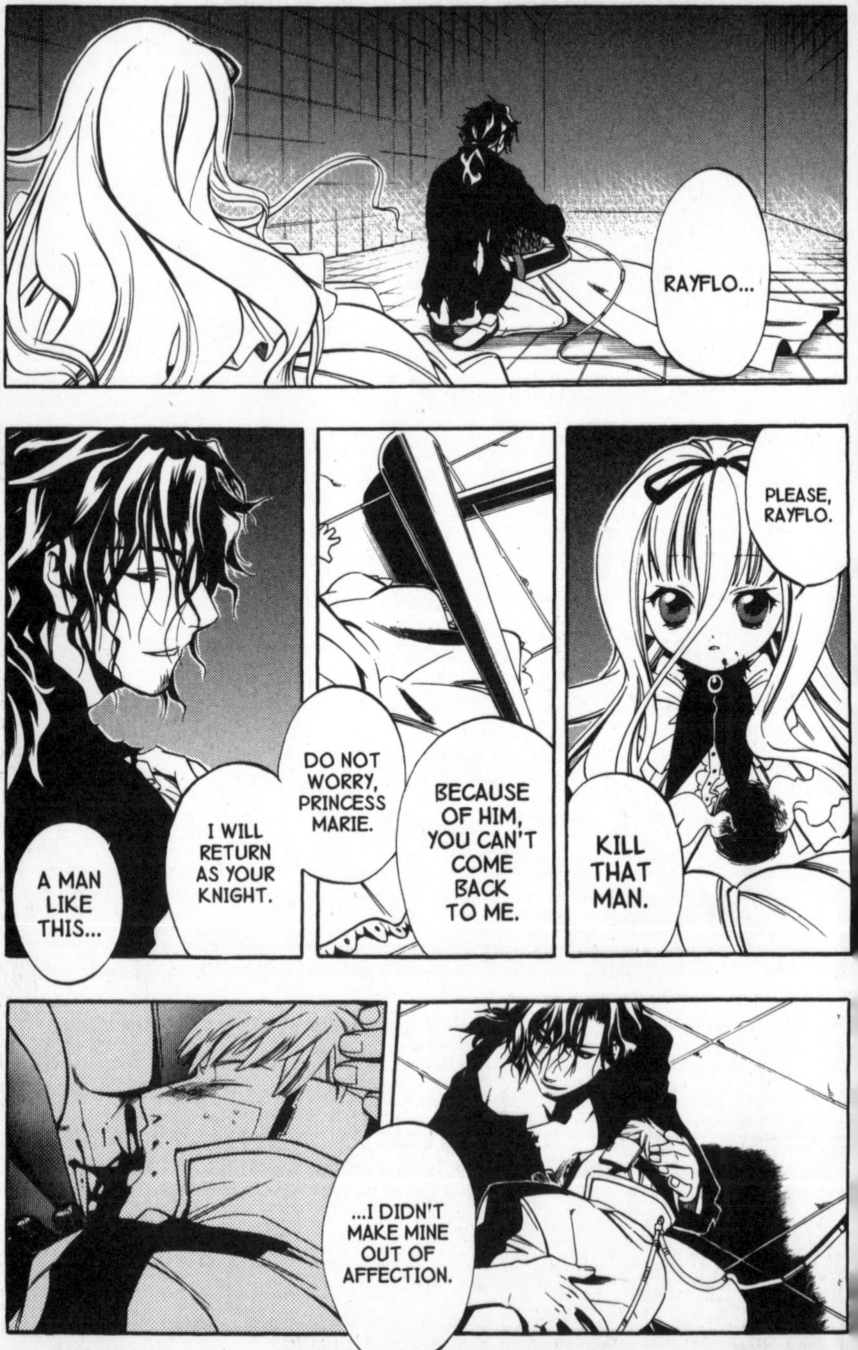
RAYFLO...
PLEASE, RAYFLO.
KILL THAT MAN.
BECAUSE OF HIM, YOU CAN'T COME BACK TO ME.
DO NOT WORRY, PRINCESS MARIE.
I WILL RETURN AS YOUR KNIGHT.
A MAN LIKE THIS...
...I DIDN'T MAKE MINE OUT OF AFFECTION.

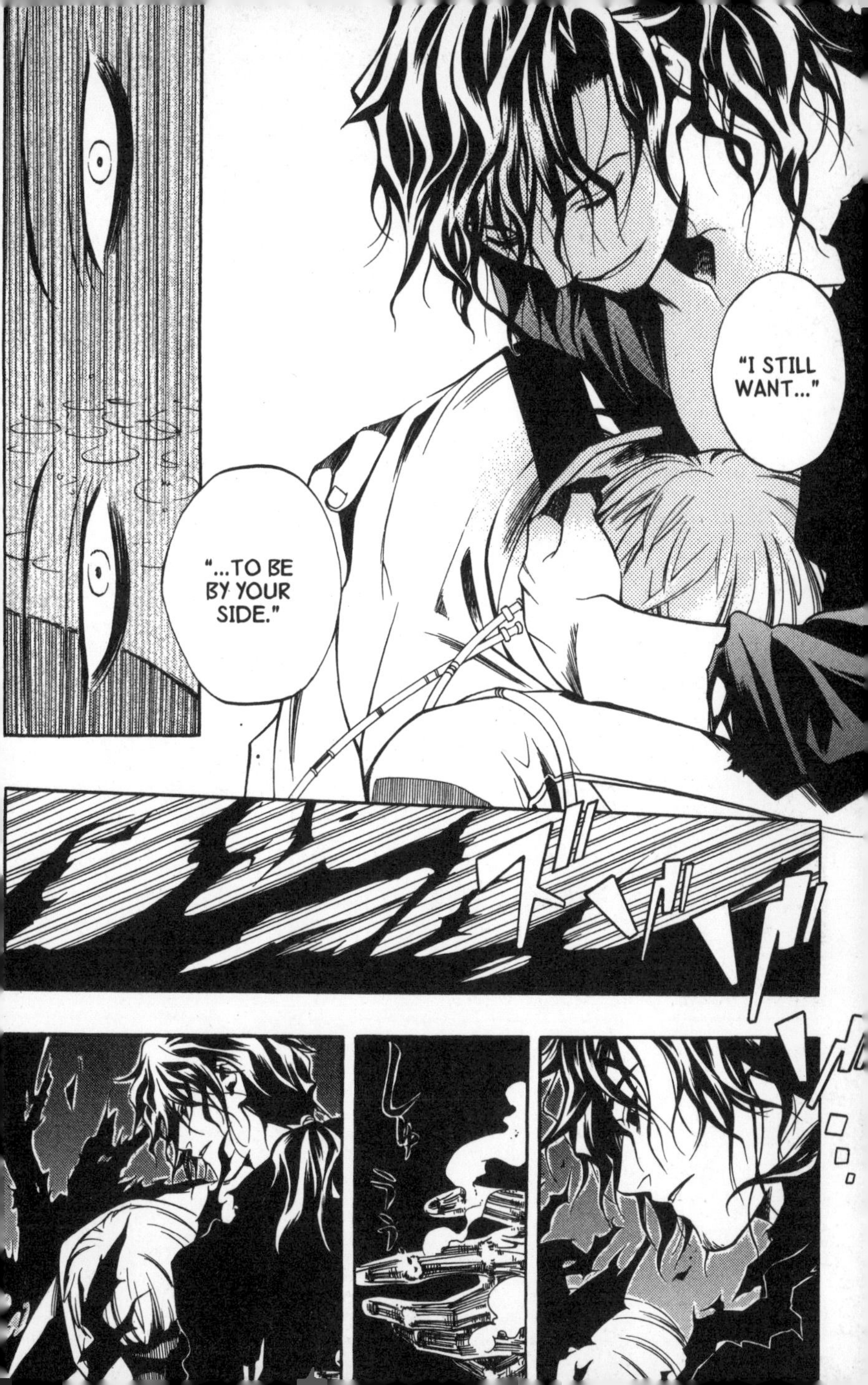
"I STILL WANT..."
"...TO BE BY YOUR SIDE."

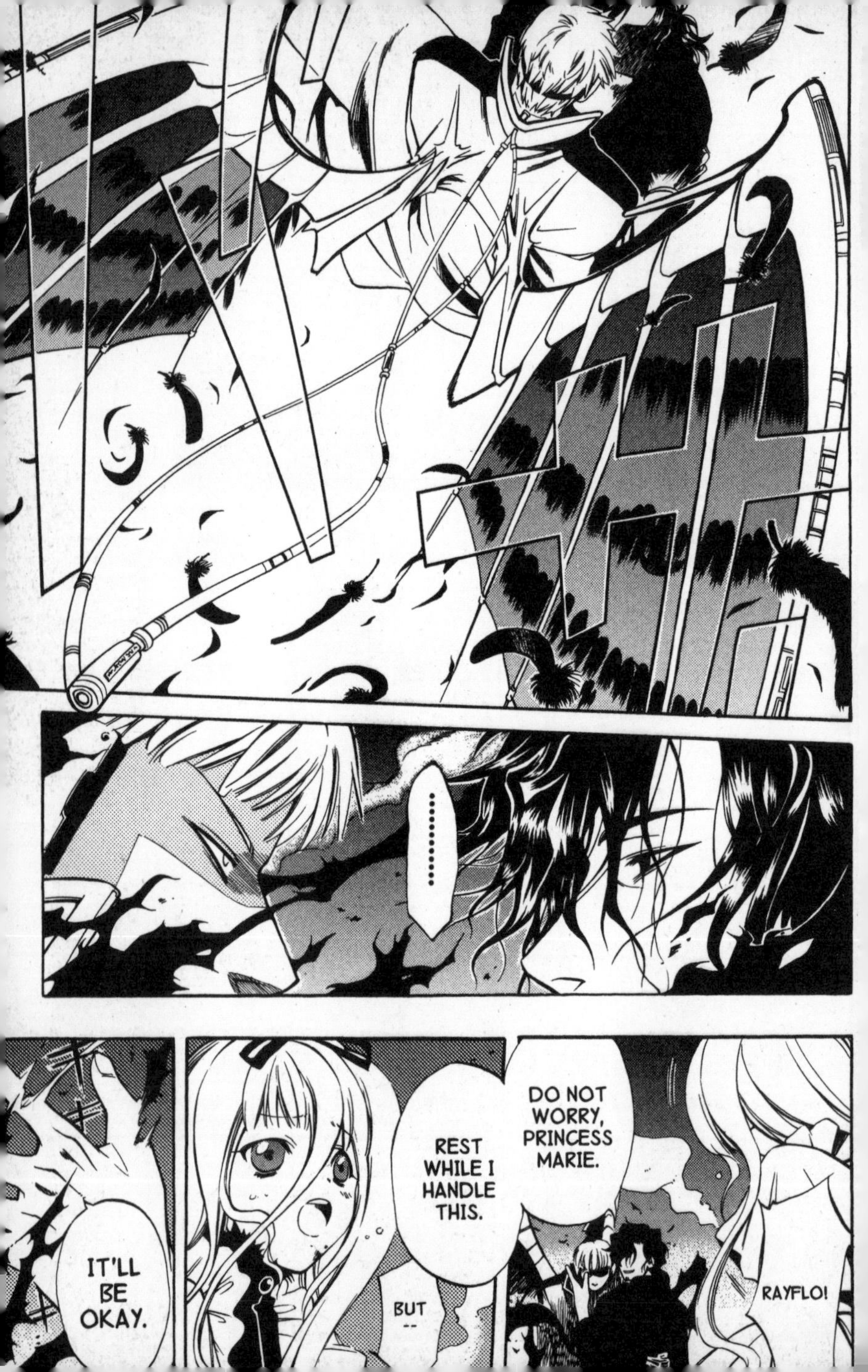
....
RAYFLO!
DO NOT WORRY, PRINCESS MARIE.
REST WHILE I HANDLE THIS.
BUT --
IT'LL BE OKAY.

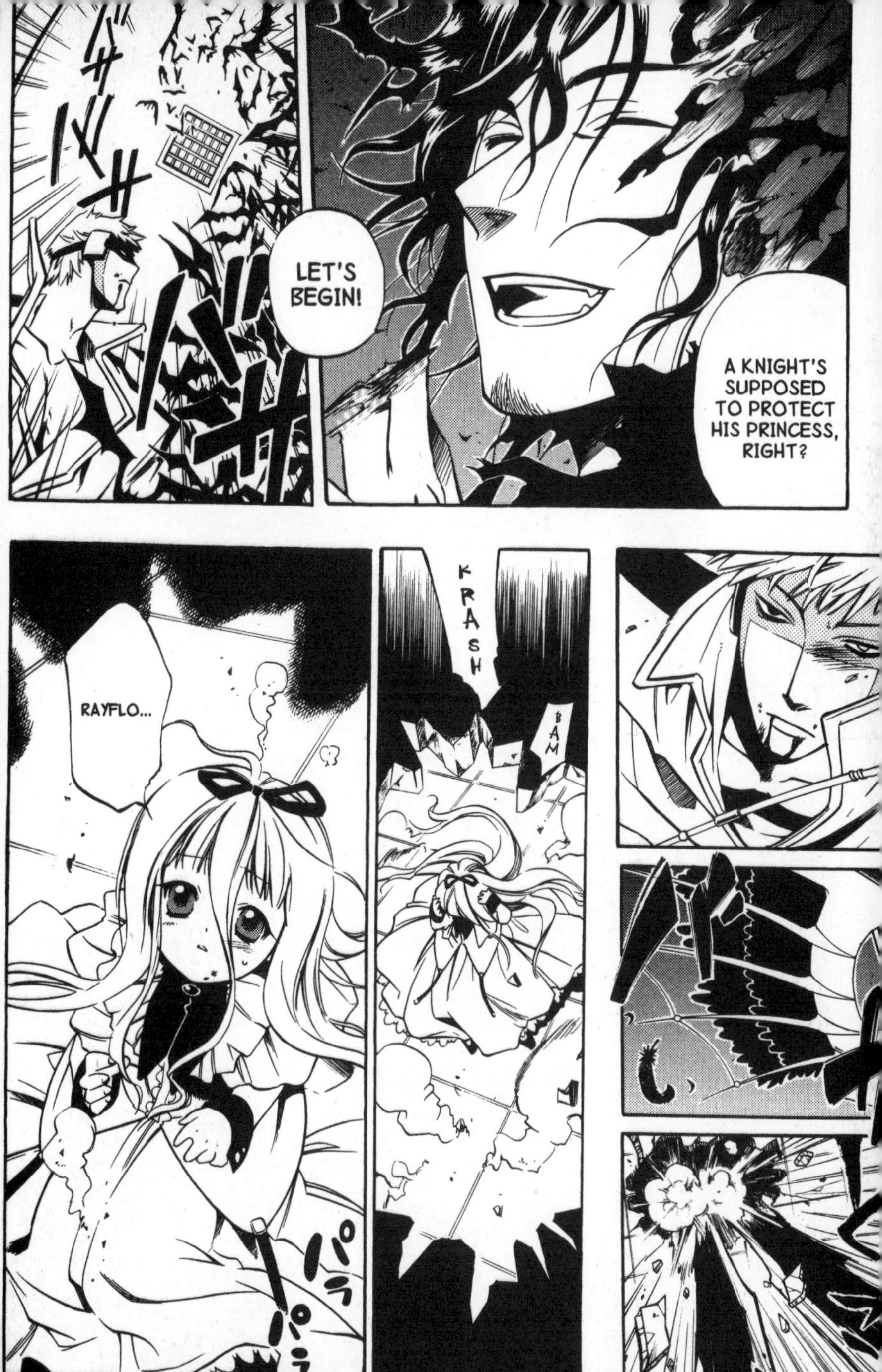
A KNIGHT'S SUPPOSED TO PROTECT HIS PRINCESS, RIGHT?
LET'S BEGIN!
KRASH
BAM
RAYFLO...
パラパラ…

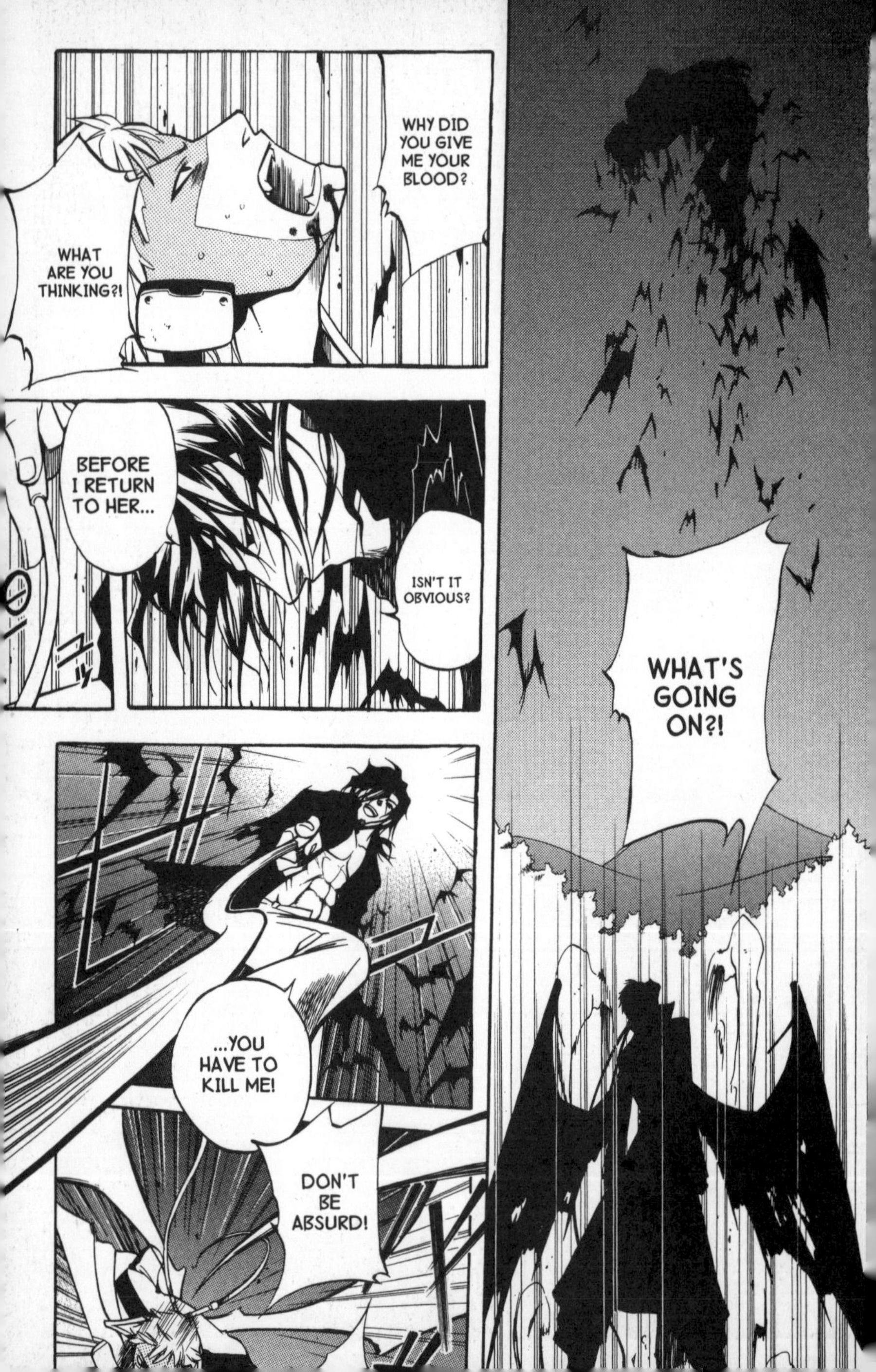
WHAT'S GOING ON?!
WHY DID YOU GIVE ME YOUR BLOOD?
WHAT ARE YOU THINKING?!
ISN'T IT OBVIOUS?
BEFORE I RETURN TO HER...
...YOU HAVE TO KILL ME!
DON'T BE ABSURD!

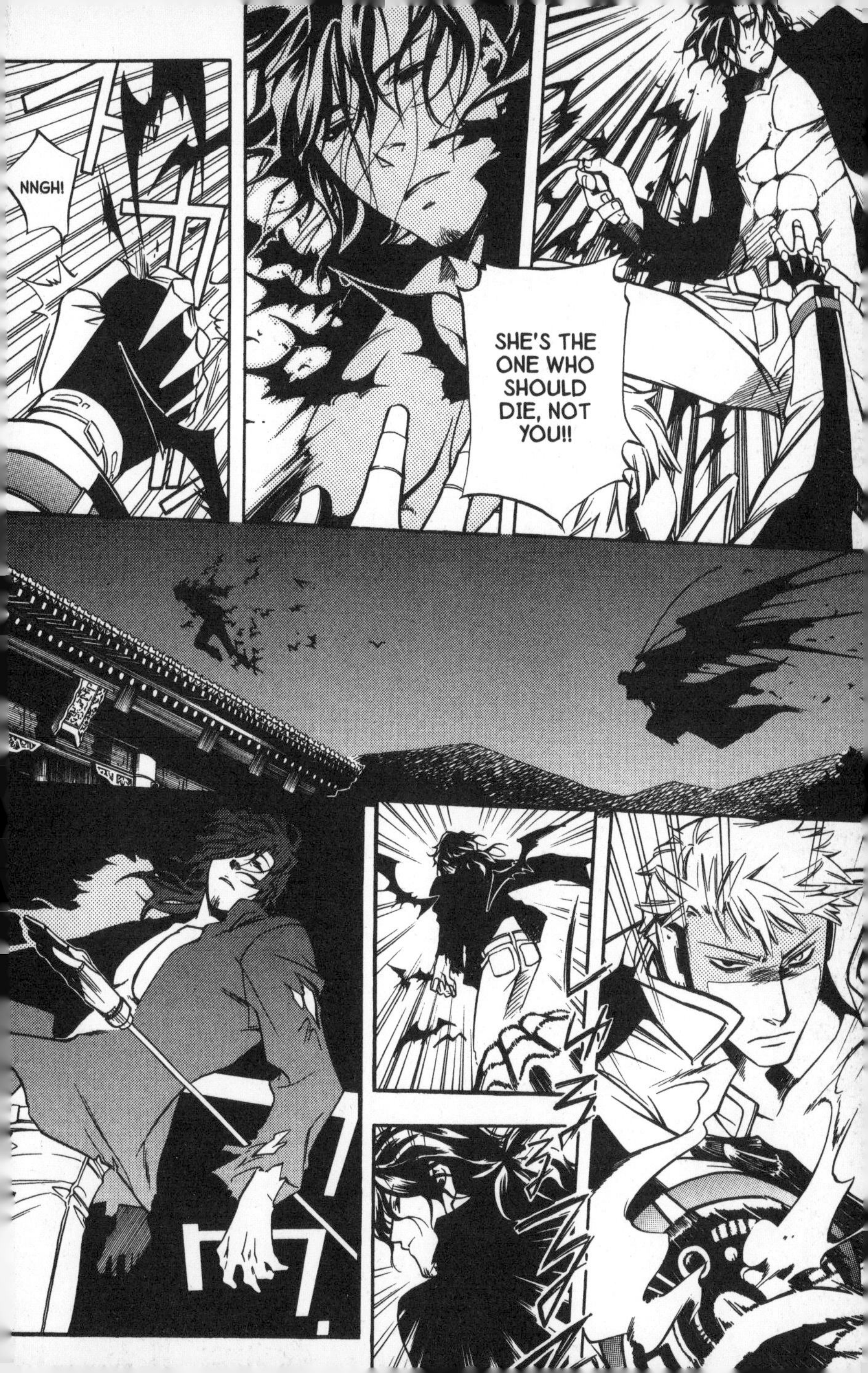
SHE'S THE ONE WHO SHOULD DIE, NOT YOU!!
NNGH!

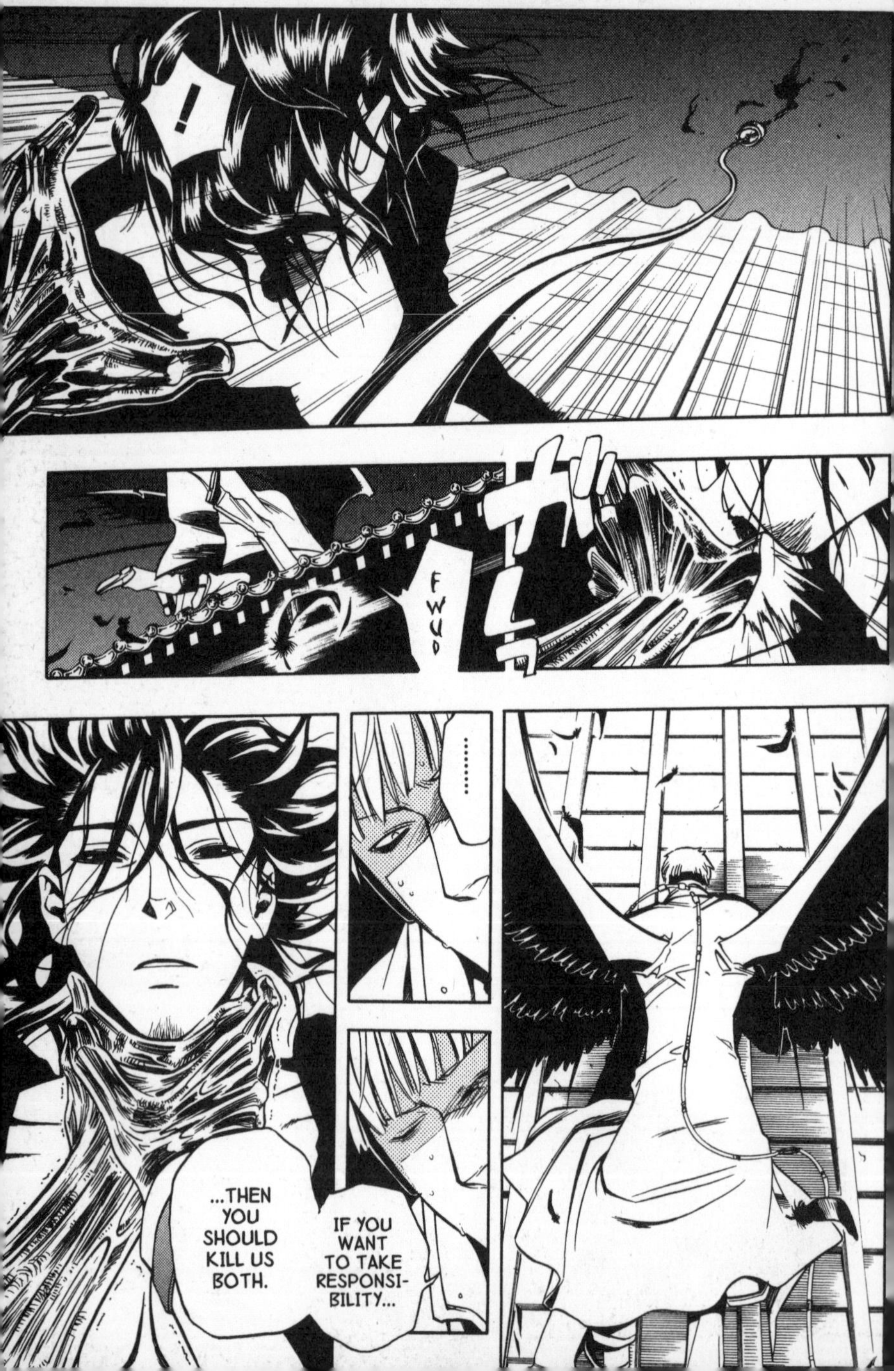
!
FWUD
......
IF YOU WANT TO TAKE RESPONSI-BILITY...
...THEN YOU SHOULD KILL US BOTH.

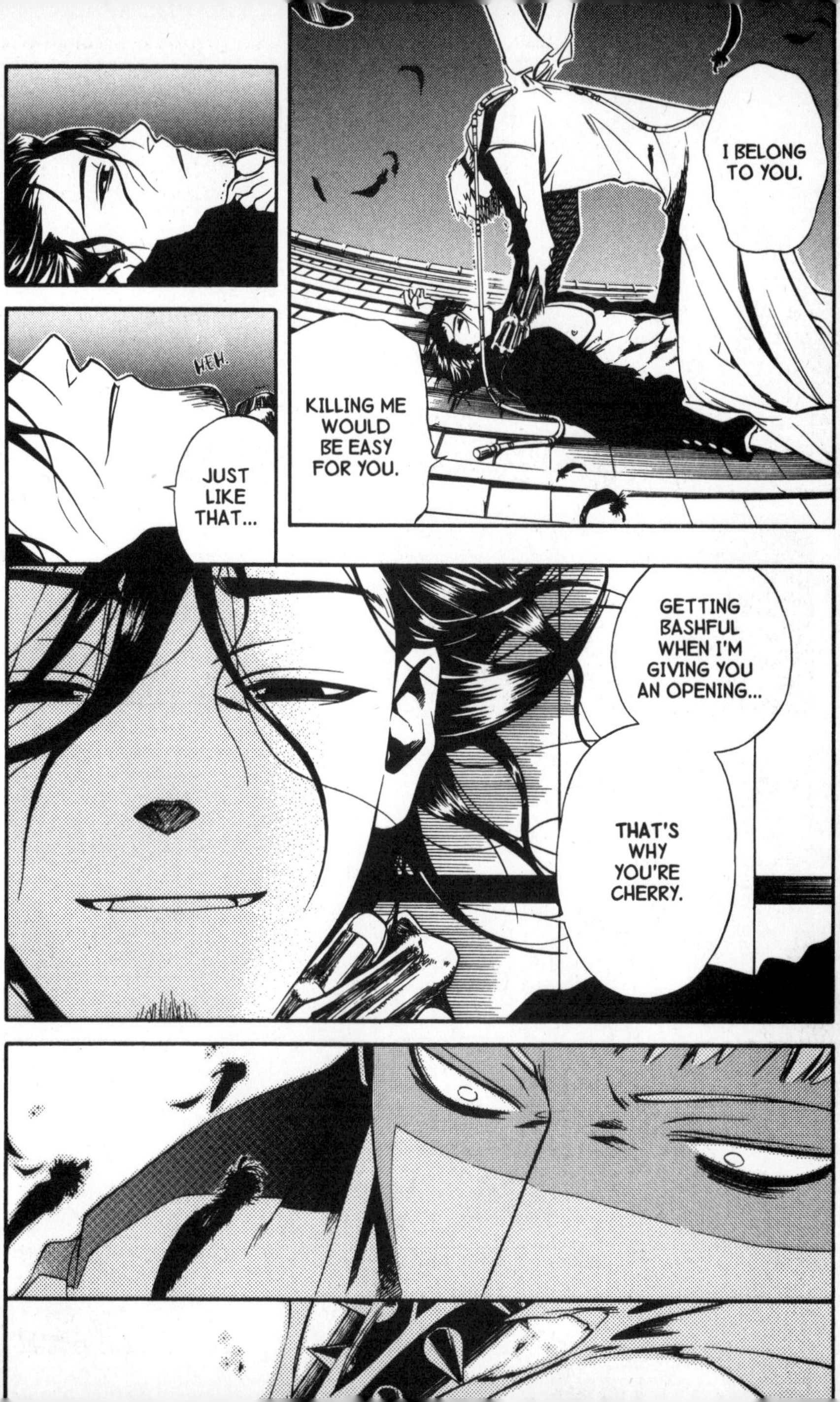
I BELONG TO YOU.
KILLING ME WOULD BE EASY FOR YOU.
HEH.
JUST LIKE THAT...
GETTING BASHFUL WHEN I'M GIVING YOU AN OPENING...
THAT'S WHY YOU'RE CHERRY.

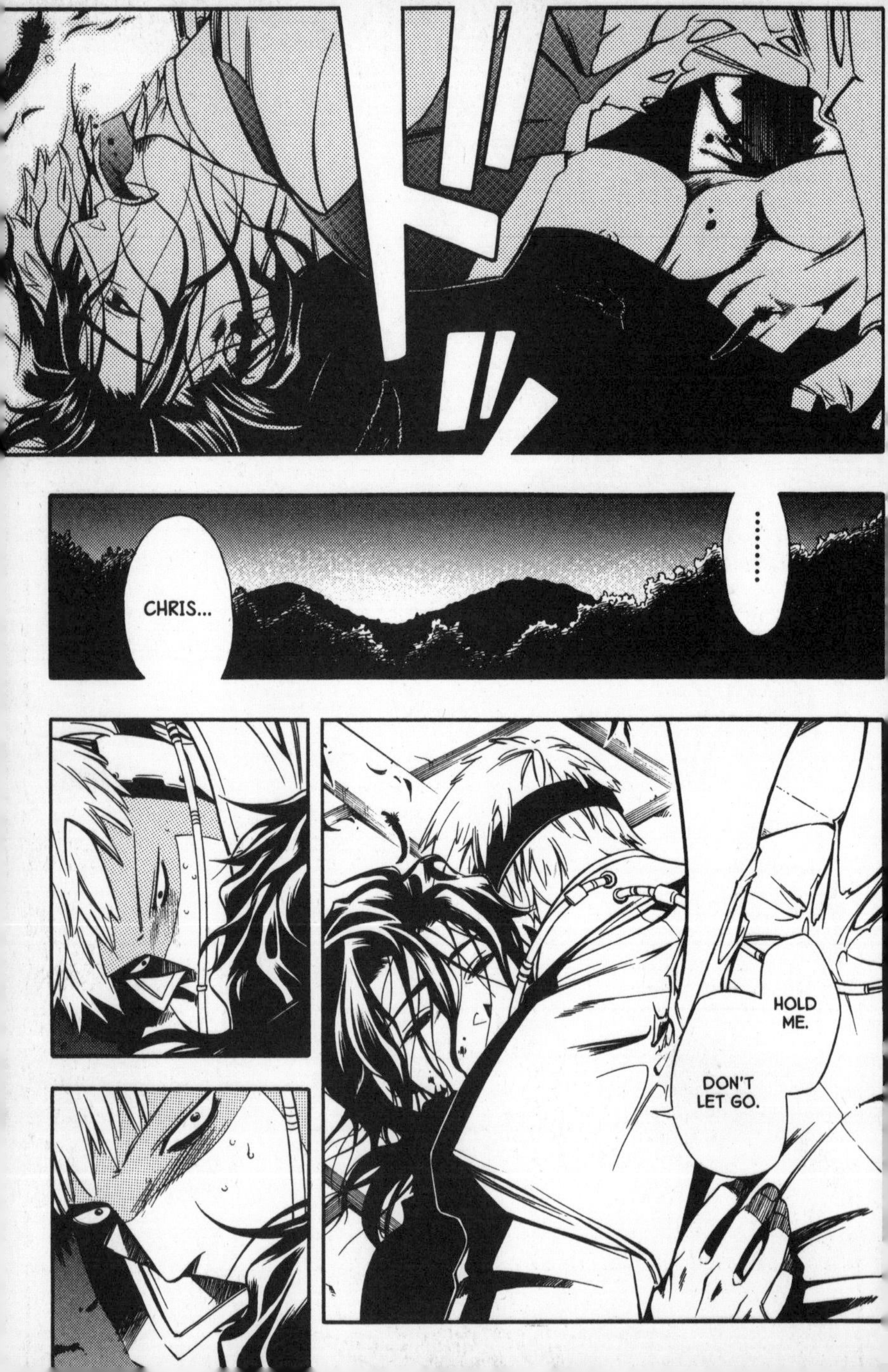
....
CHRIS...
HOLD ME.
DON'T LET GO.

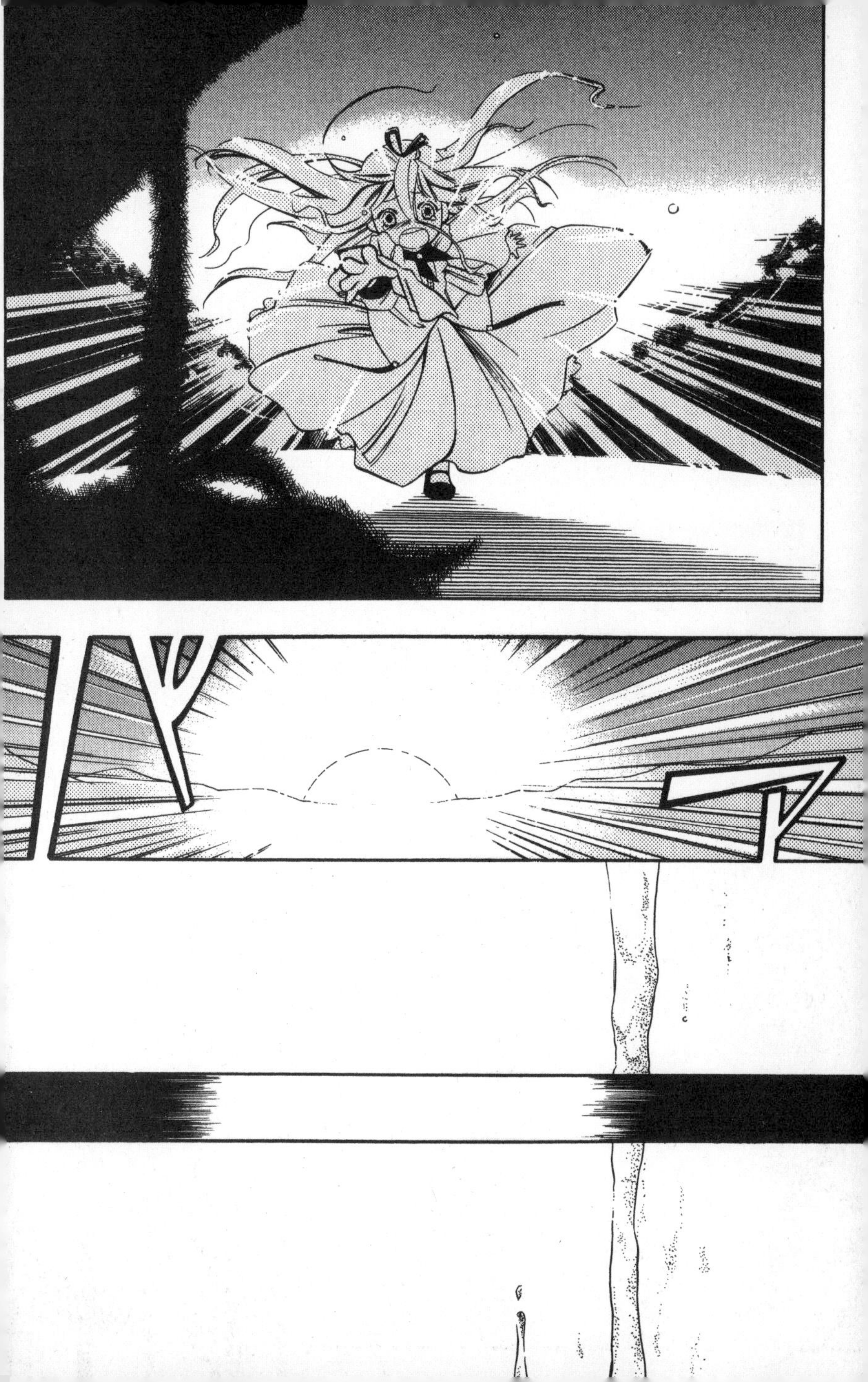

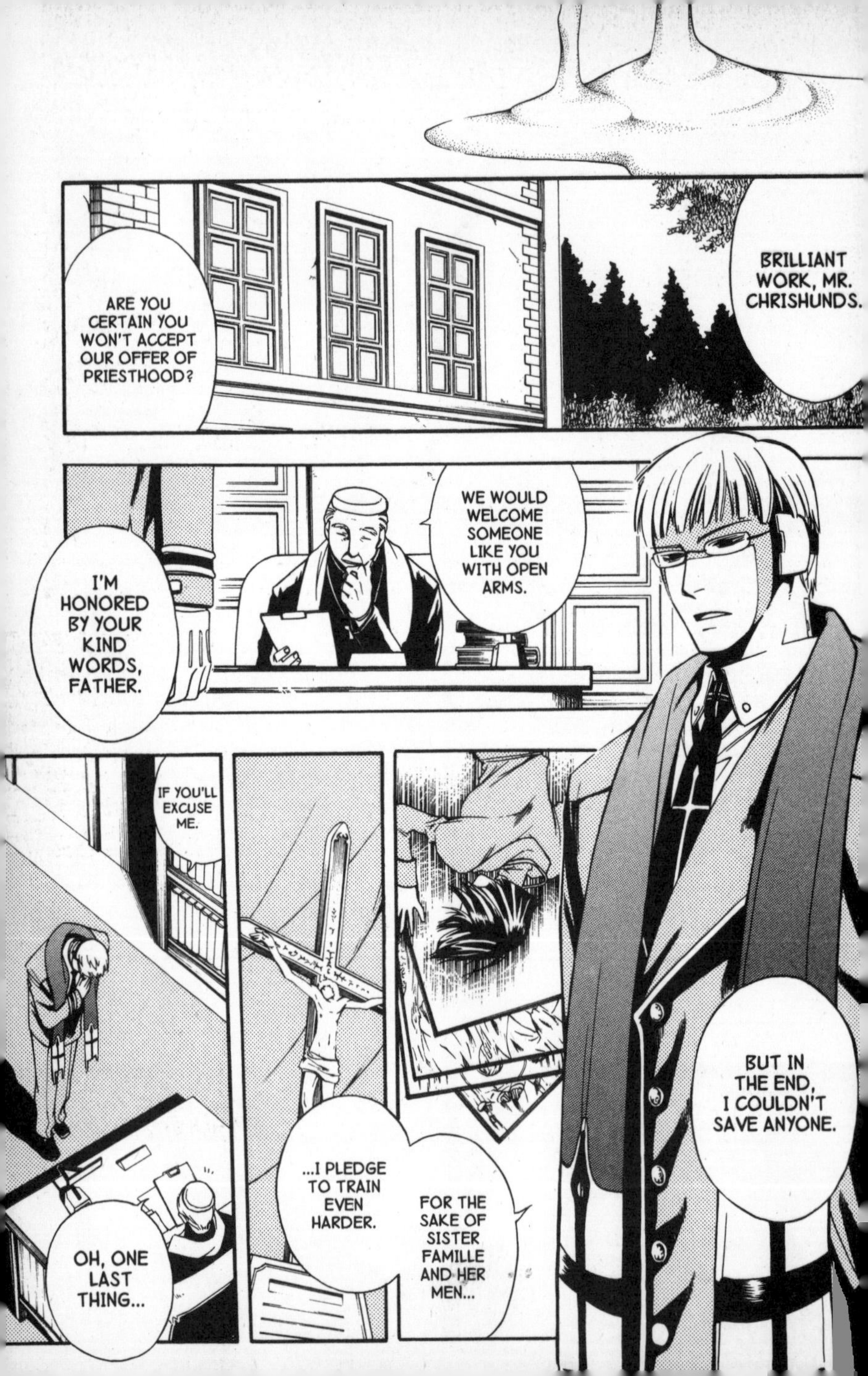
BRILLIANT WORK, MR. CHRISHUNDS.
ARE YOU CERTAIN YOU WON'T ACCEPT OUR OFFER OF PRIESTHOOD?
WE WOULD WELCOME SOMEONE LIKE YOU WITH OPEN ARMS.
I'M HONORED BY YOUR KIND WORDS, FATHER.
BUT IN THE END, I COULDN'T SAVE ANYONE.
FOR THE SAKE OF SISTER FAMILLE AND HER MEN...
...I PLEDGE TO TRAIN EVEN HARDER.
IF YOU'LL EXCUSE ME.
OH, ONE LAST THING...

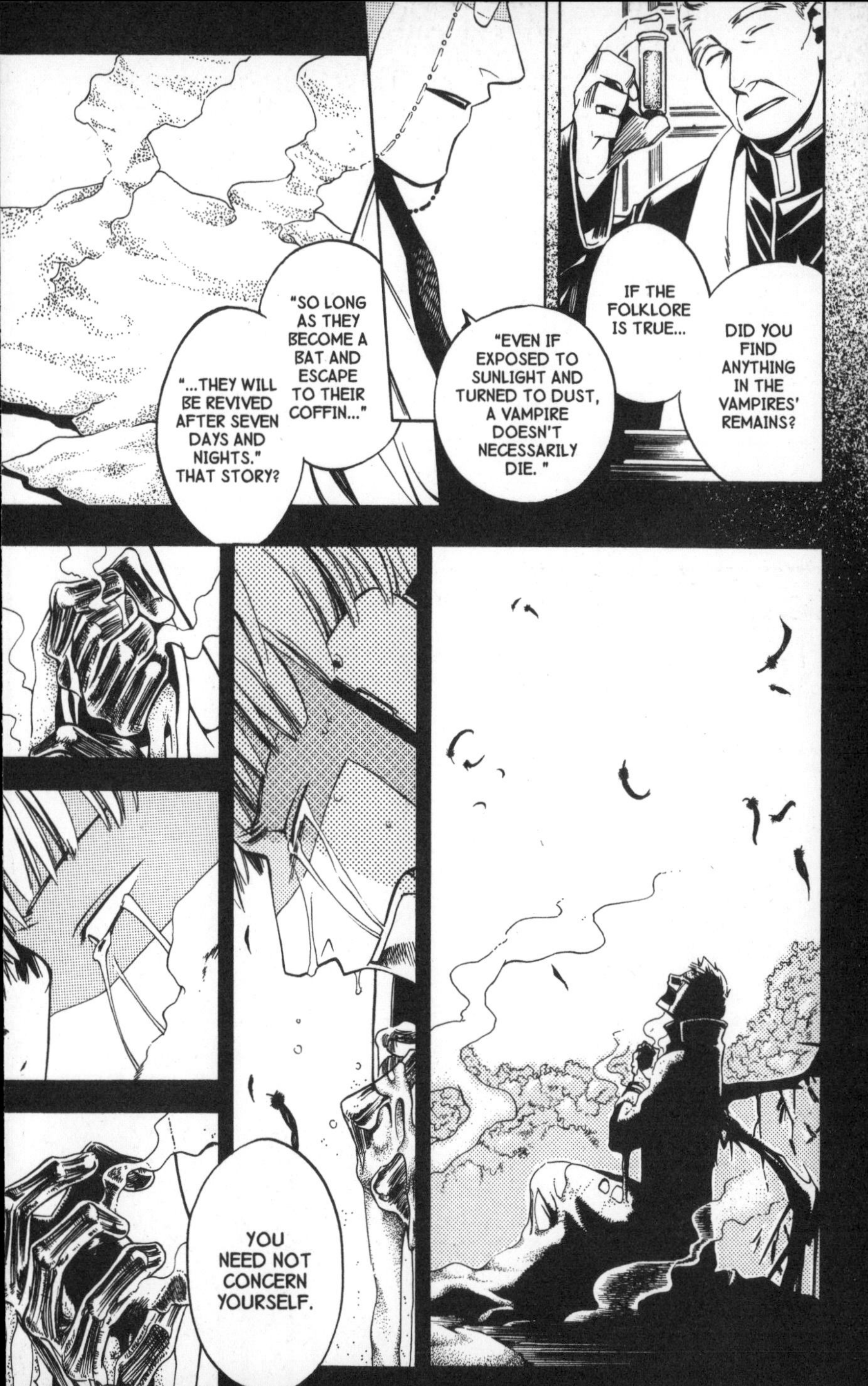
DID YOU FIND ANYTHING IN THE VAMPIRES' REMAINS?
IF THE FOLKLORE IS TRUE...
"EVEN IF EXPOSED TO SUNLIGHT AND TURNED TO DUST, A VAMPIRE DOESN'T NECESSARILY DIE."
"SO LONG AS THEY BECOME A BAT AND ESCAPE TO THEIR COFFIN..."
"...THEY WILL BE REVIVED AFTER SEVEN DAYS AND NIGHTS." THAT STORY?
YOU NEED NOT CONCERN YOURSELF.

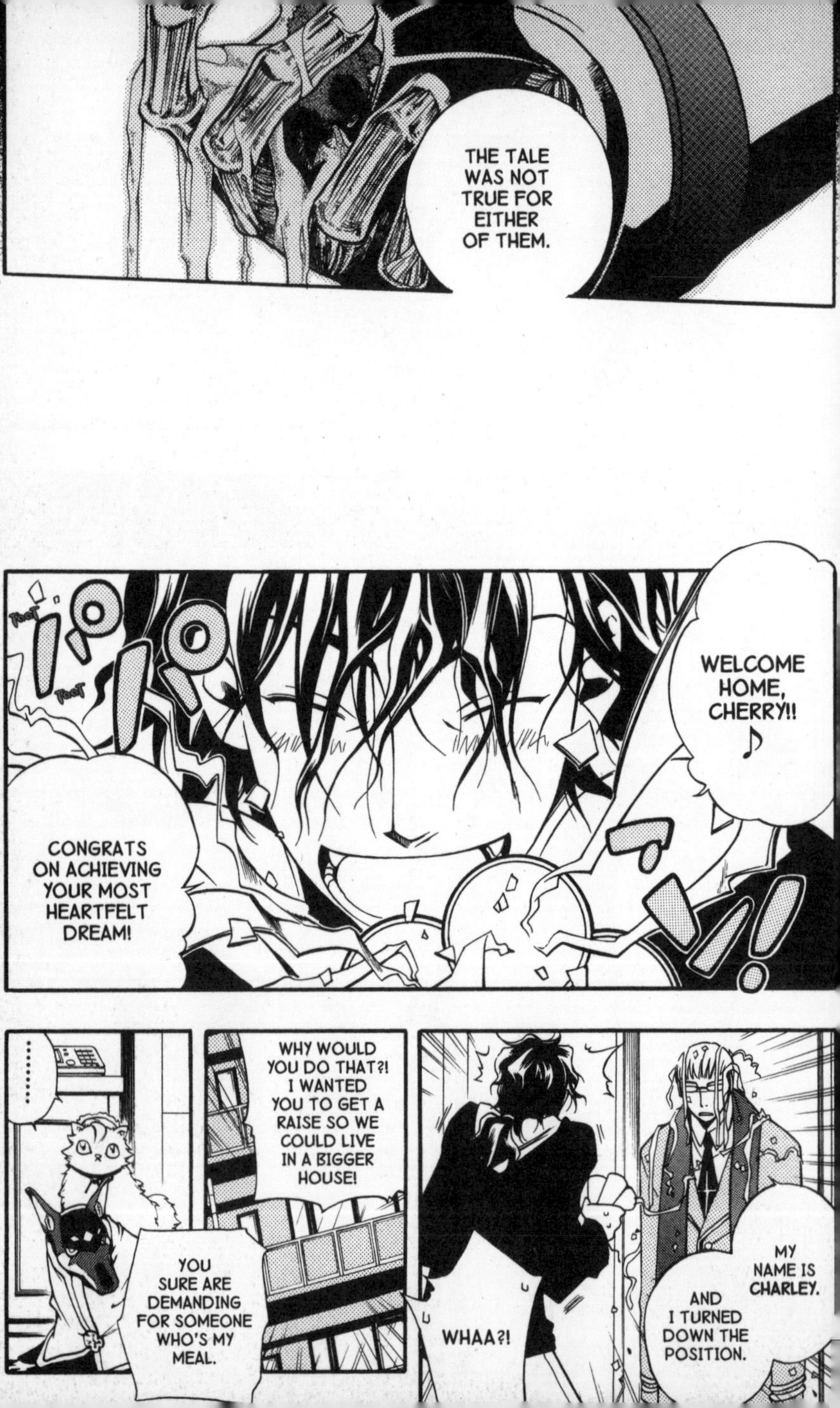
THE TALE WAS NOT TRUE FOR EITHER OF THEM.
WELCOME HOME, CHERRY!! ♪
TOOT
TOOT
CONGRATS ON ACHIEVING YOUR MOST HEARTFELT DREAM!
MY NAME IS CHARLEY.
AND I TURNED DOWN THE POSITION.
WHAA?!
WHY WOULD YOU DO THAT?! I WANTED YOU TO GET A RAISE SO WE COULD LIVE IN A BIGGER HOUSE!
......
YOU SURE ARE DEMANDING FOR SOMEONE WHO'S MY MEAL.

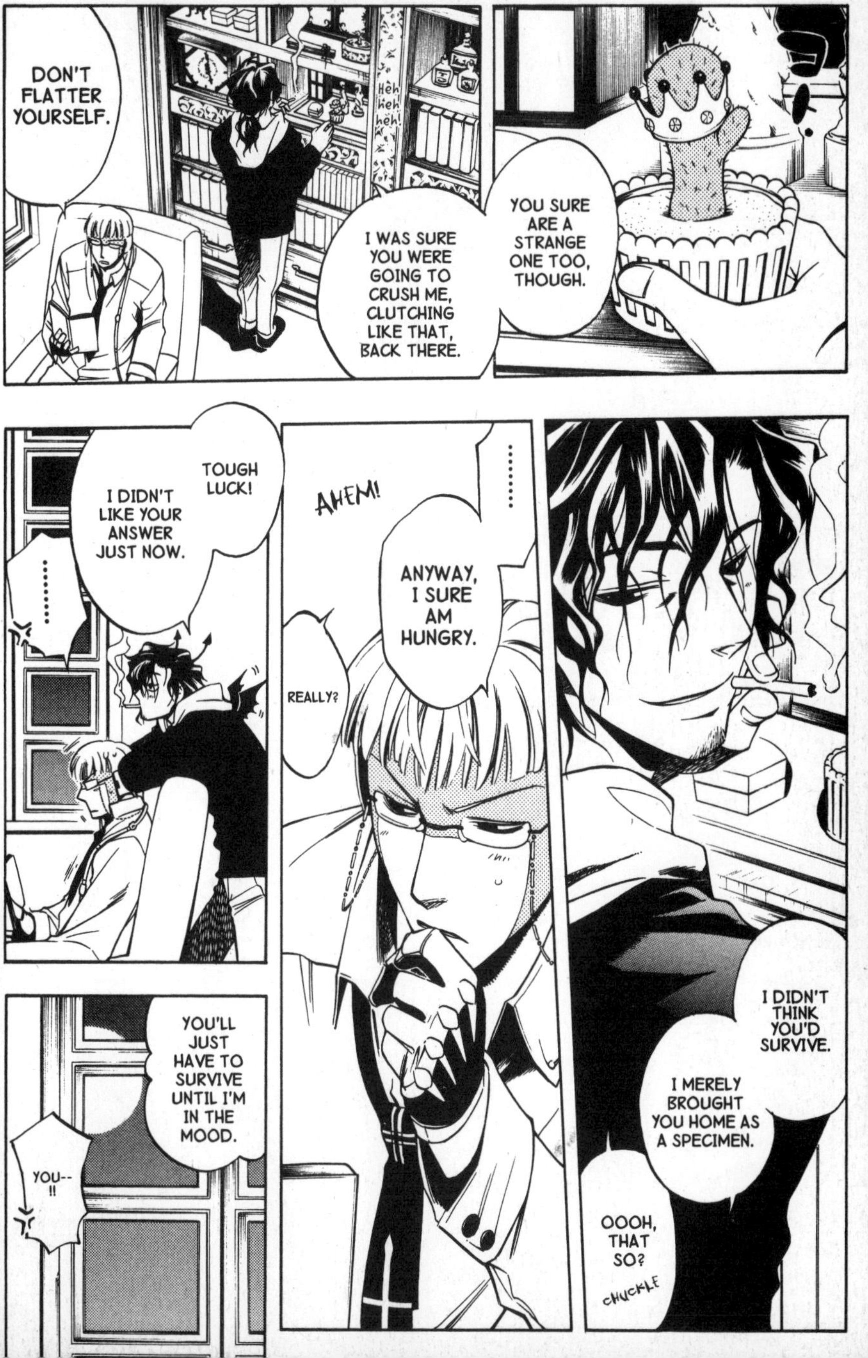
YOU SURE ARE A STRANGE ONE TOO, THOUGH.
I WAS SURE YOU WERE GOING TO CRUSH ME, CLUTCHING LIKE THAT, BACK THERE.
Heh heh heh!
DON'T FLATTER YOURSELF.
I DIDN'T THINK YOU'D SURVIVE.
I MERELY BROUGHT YOU HOME AS A SPECIMEN.
OOOH, THAT SO?
CHUCKLE
......
AHEM!
ANYWAY, I SURE AM HUNGRY.
REALLY?
TOUGH LUCK!
I DIDN'T LIKE YOUR ANSWER JUST NOW.
......
YOU'LL JUST HAVE TO SURVIVE UNTIL I'M IN THE MOOD.
YOU-- !!

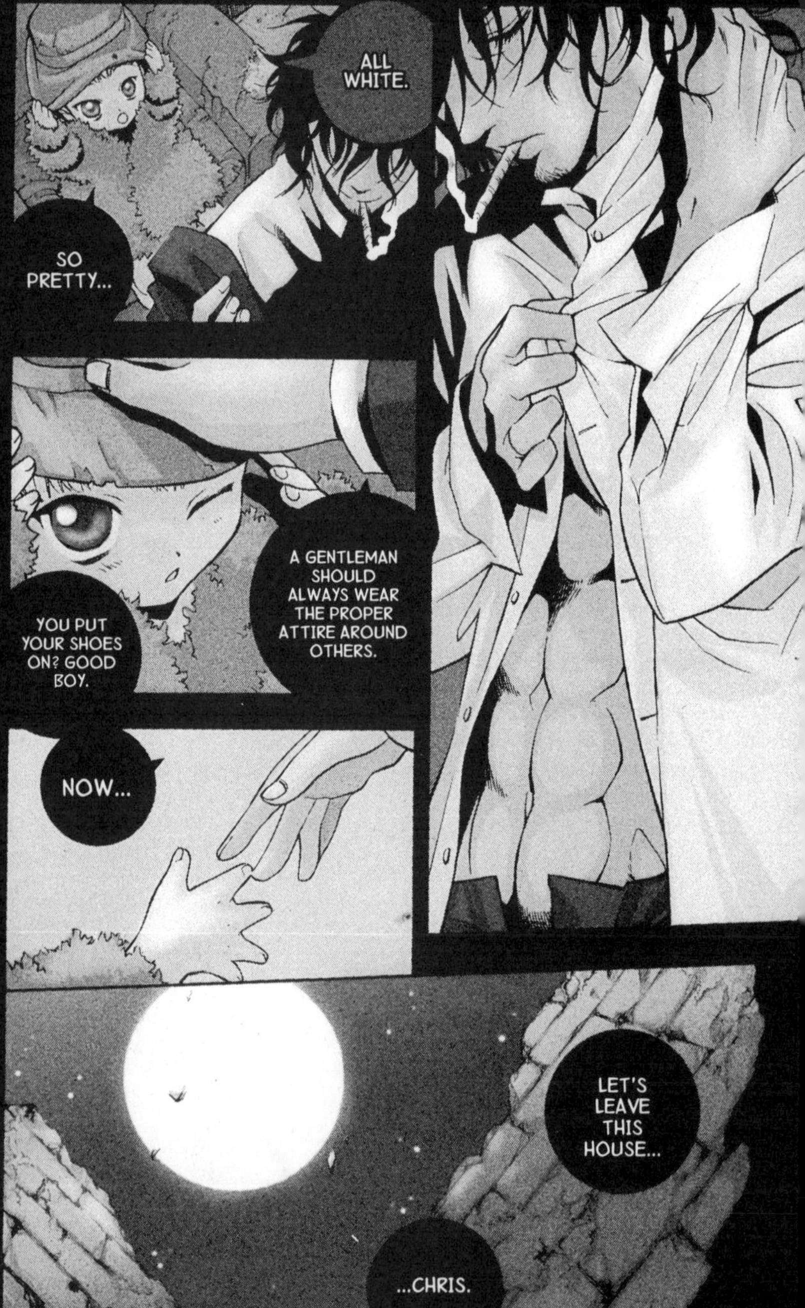
ALL WHITE.
SO PRETTY...
A GENTLEMAN SHOULD ALWAYS WEAR THE PROPER ATTIRE AROUND OTHERS.
YOU PUT YOUR SHOES ON? GOOD BOY.
NOW...
LET'S LEAVE THIS HOUSE...
...CHRIS.

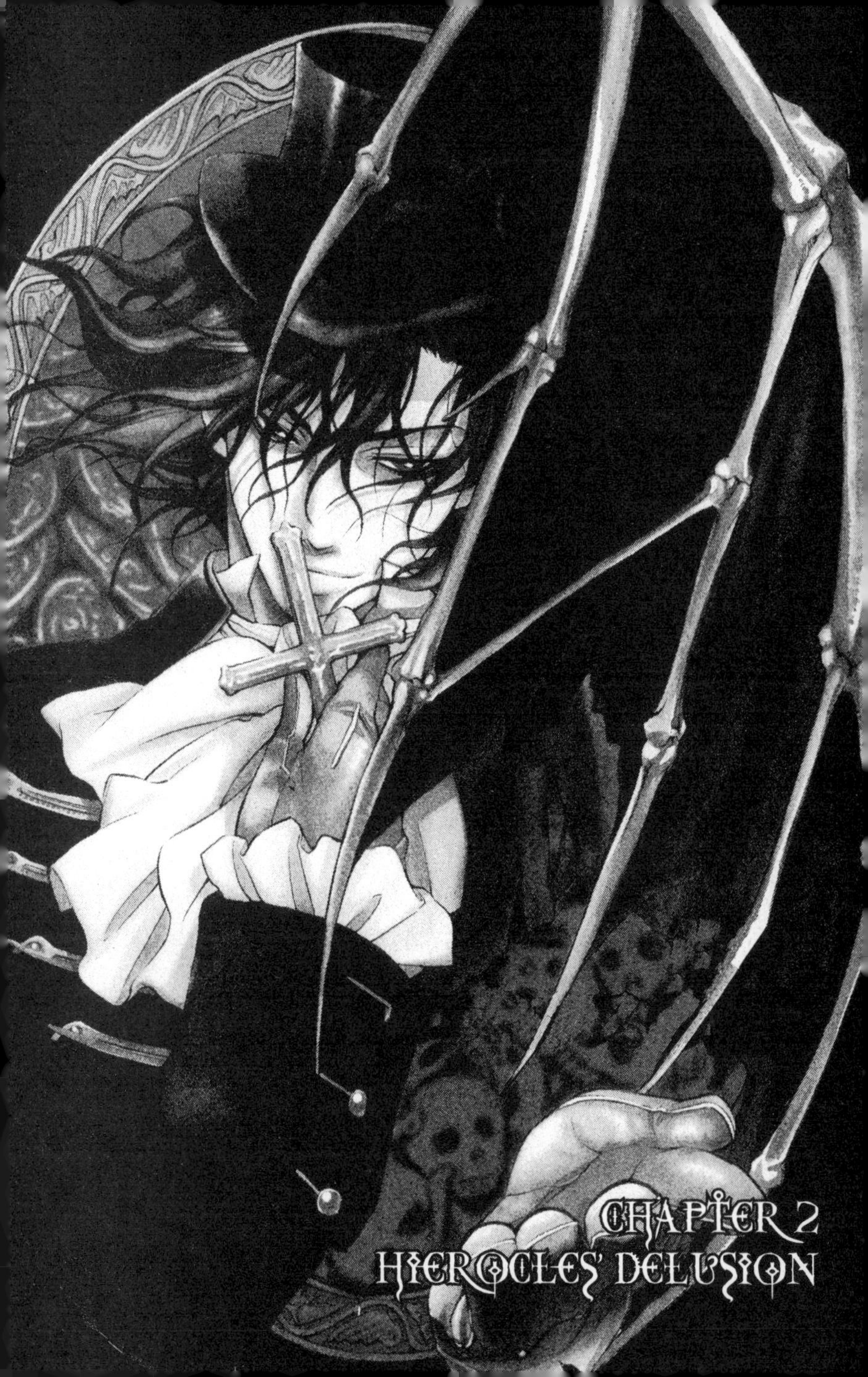
CHAPTER 2
HIEROCLES' DELUSION

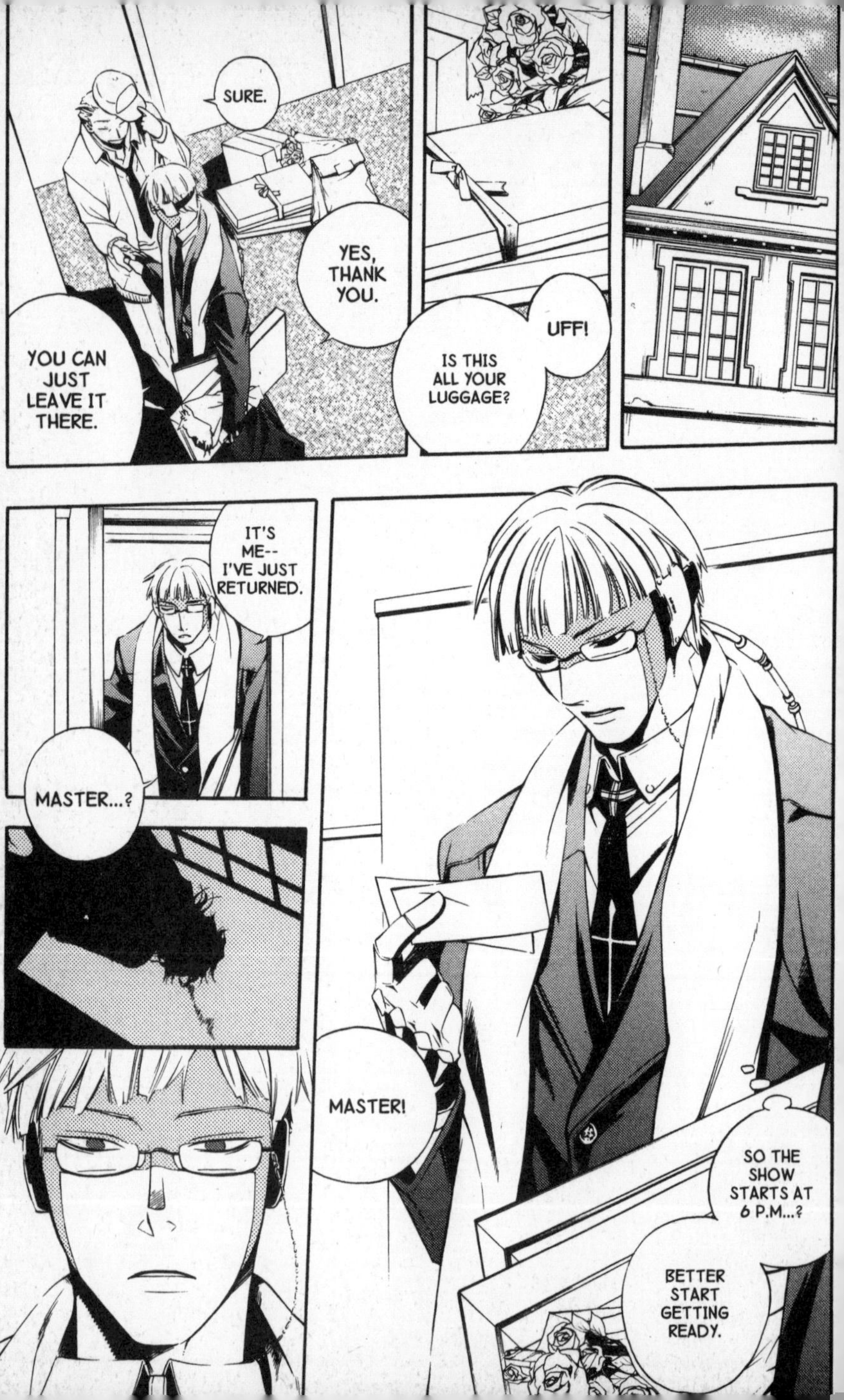
UFF!
IS THIS ALL YOUR LUGGAGE?
SURE.
YES, THANK YOU.
YOU CAN JUST LEAVE IT THERE.
MASTER!
SO THE SHOW STARTS AT 6 P.M...?
BETTER START GETTING READY.
IT'S ME-- I'VE JUST RETURNED.
MASTER...?

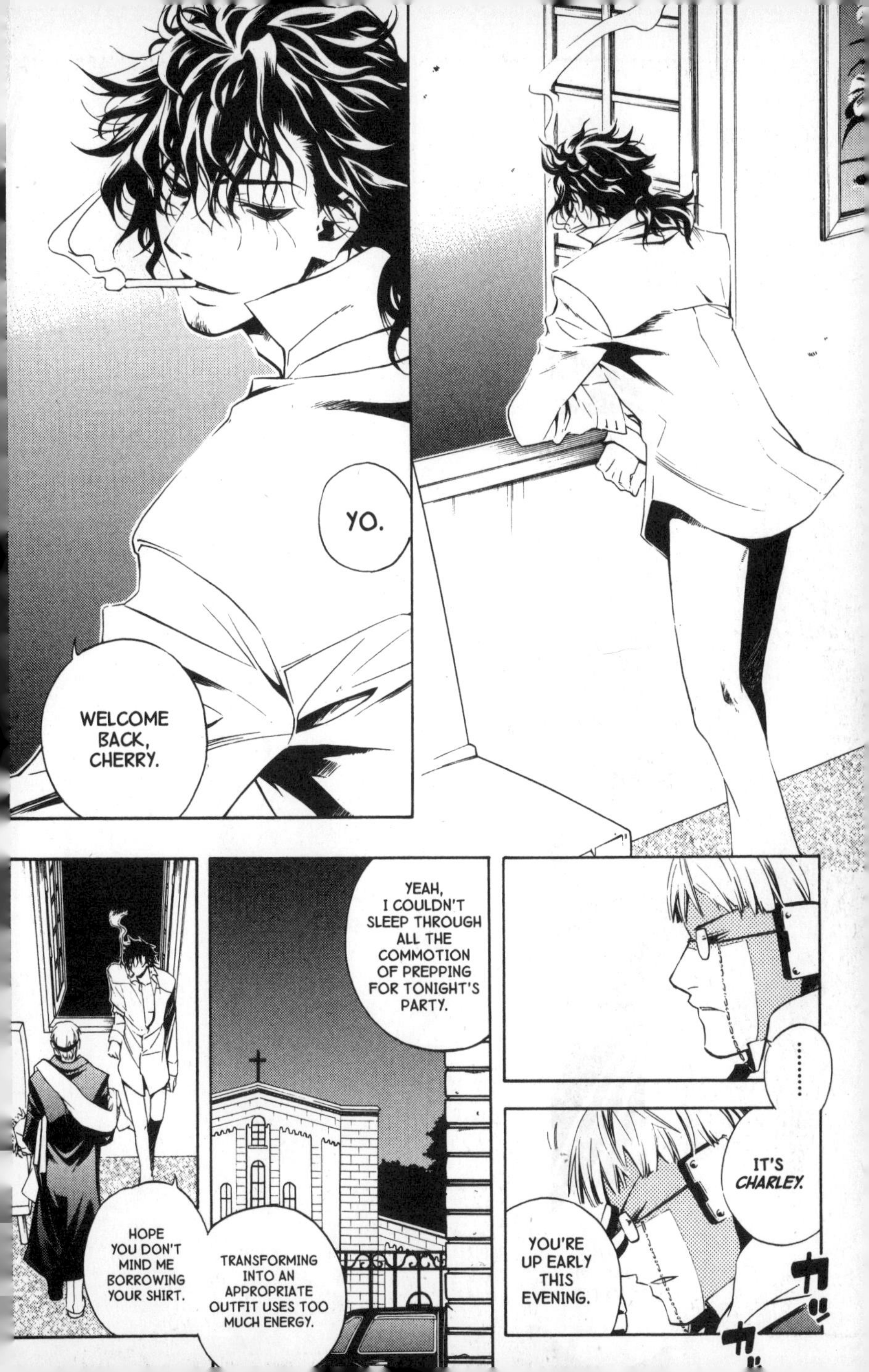
YO.
WELCOME BACK, CHERRY.
....
IT'S CHARLEY.
YOU'RE UP EARLY THIS EVENING.
YEAH, I COULDN'T SLEEP THROUGH ALL THE COMMOTION OF PREPPING FOR TONIGHT'S PARTY.
HOPE YOU DON'T MIND ME BORROWING YOUR SHIRT.
TRANSFORMING INTO AN APPROPRIATE OUTFIT USES TOO MUCH ENERGY.

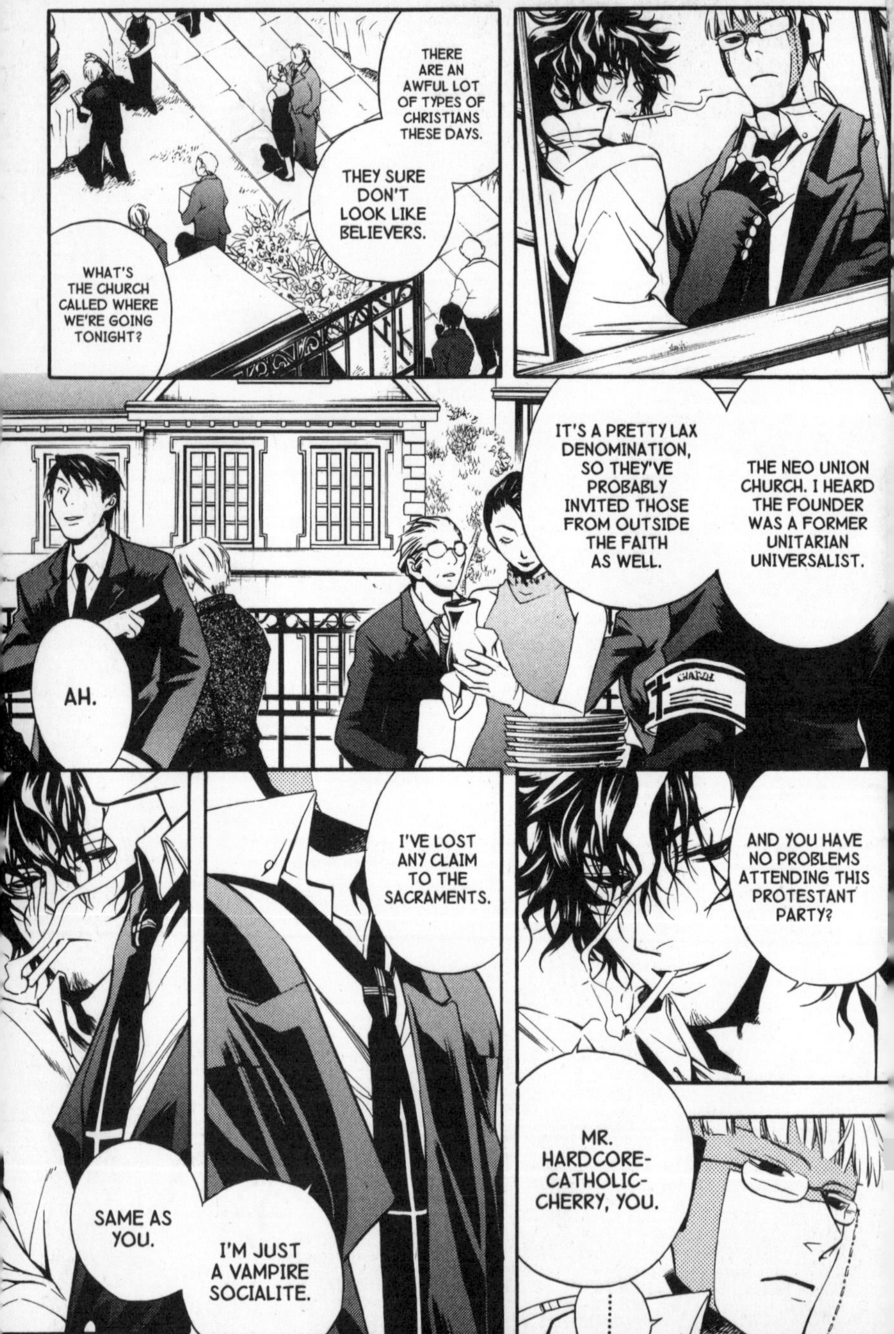
THERE ARE AN AWFUL LOT OF TYPES OF CHRISTIANS THESE DAYS.
THEY SURE DON'T LOOK LIKE BELIEVERS.
WHAT'S THE CHURCH CALLED WHERE WE'RE GOING TONIGHT?
THE NEO UNION CHURCH. I HEARD THE FOUNDER WAS A FORMER UNITARIAN UNIVERSALIST.
IT'S A PRETTY LAX DENOMINATION, SO THEY'VE PROBABLY INVITED THOSE FROM OUTSIDE THE FAITH AS WELL.
AH.
AND YOU HAVE NO PROBLEMS ATTENDING THIS PROTESTANT PARTY?
MR. HARDCORE-CATHOLIC-CHERRY, YOU.
......
I'VE LOST ANY CLAIM TO THE SACRAMENTS.
SAME AS YOU.
I'M JUST A VAMPIRE SOCIALITE.

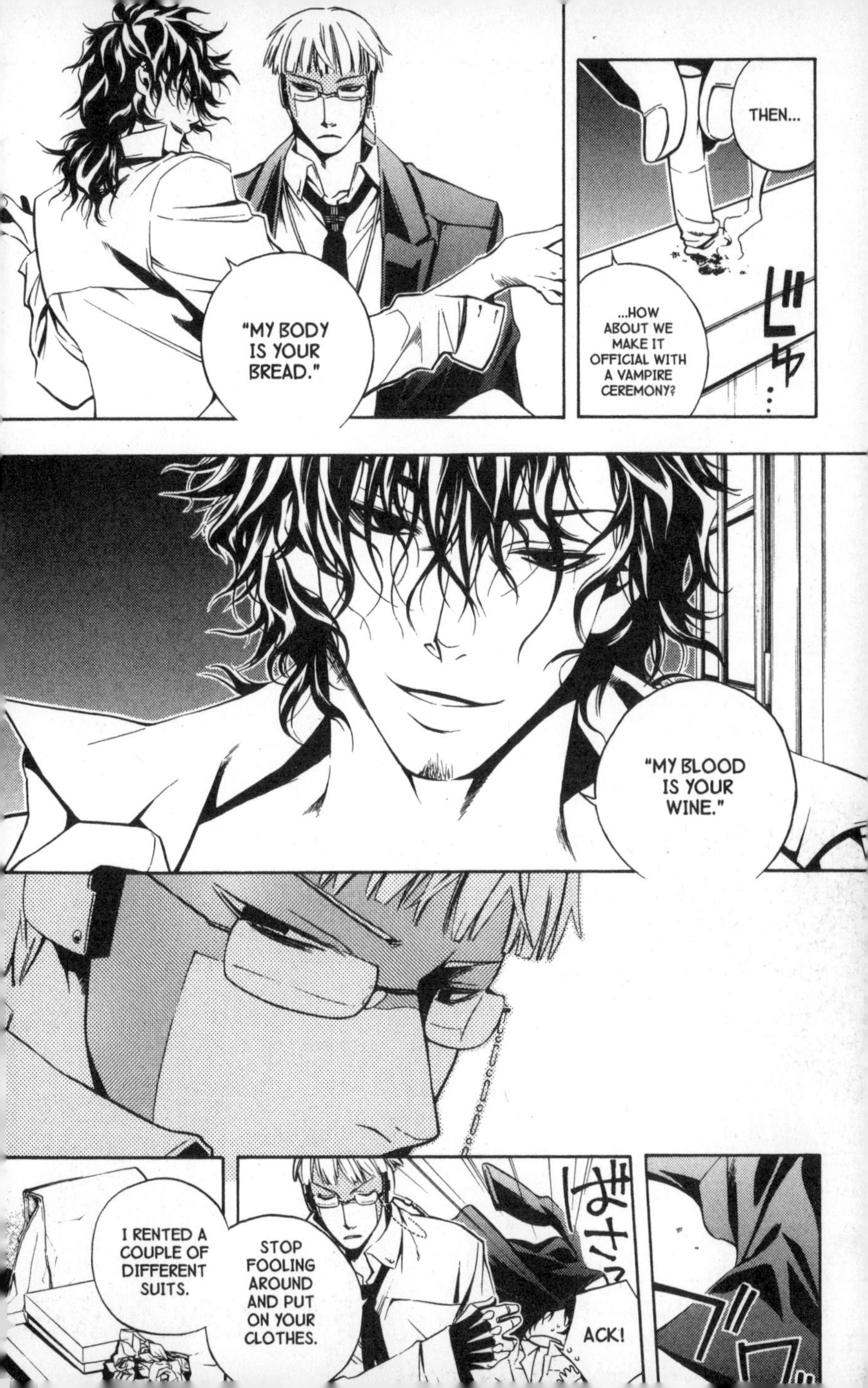
THEN...
...HOW ABOUT WE MAKE IT OFFICIAL WITH A VAMPIRE CEREMONY?
"MY BODY IS YOUR BREAD."
"MY BLOOD IS YOUR WINE."
ACK!
STOP FOOLING AROUND AND PUT ON YOUR CLOTHES.
I RENTED A COUPLE OF DIFFERENT SUITS.

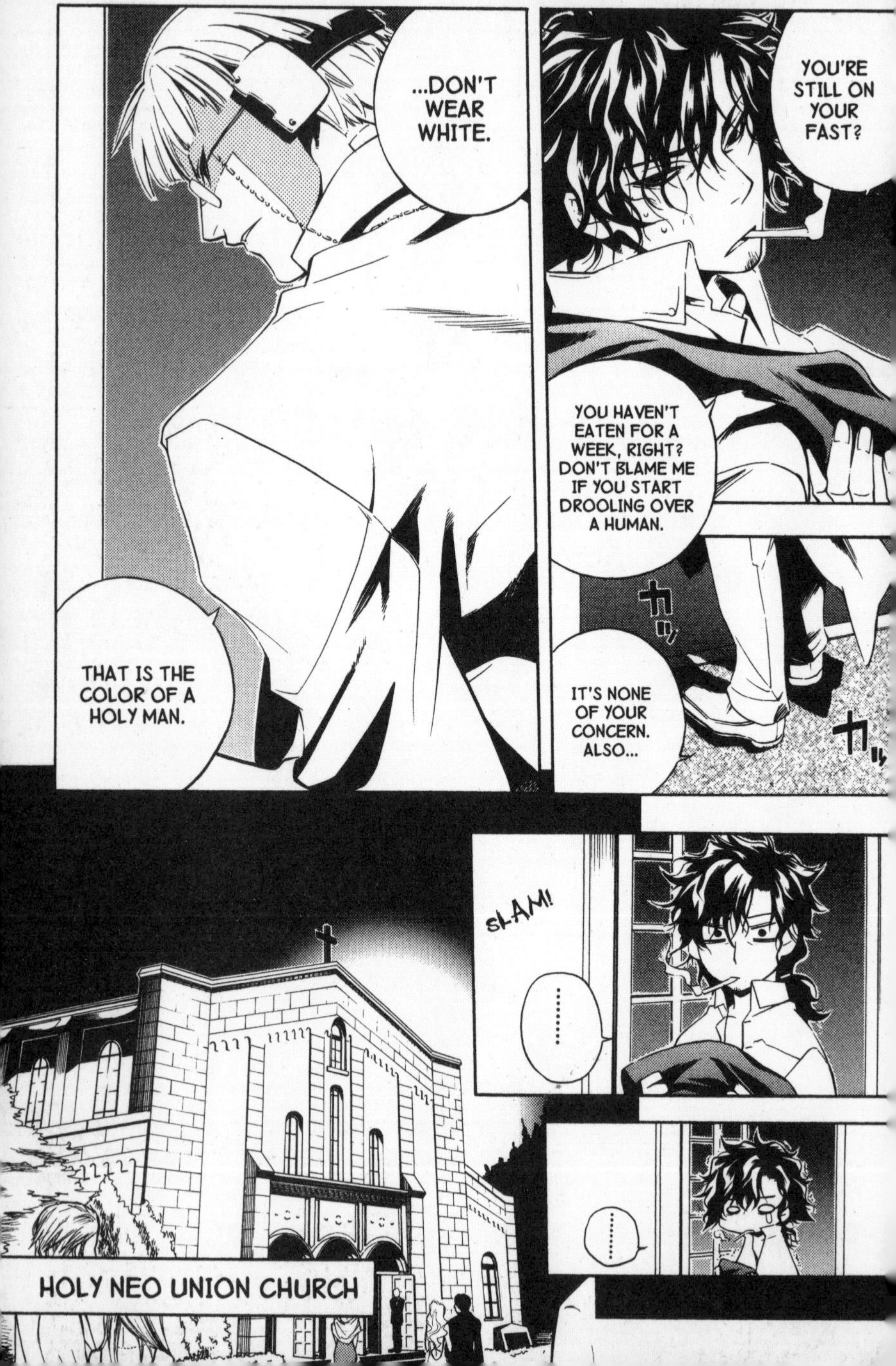
YOU'RE STILL ON YOUR FAST?
YOU HAVEN'T EATEN FOR A WEEK, RIGHT? DON'T BLAME ME IF YOU START DROOLING OVER A HUMAN.
カッ
カッ
IT'S NONE OF YOUR CONCERN. ALSO...
...DON'T WEAR WHITE.
THAT IS THE COLOR OF A HOLY MAN.
SLAM!
......
......
HOLY NEO UNION CHURCH

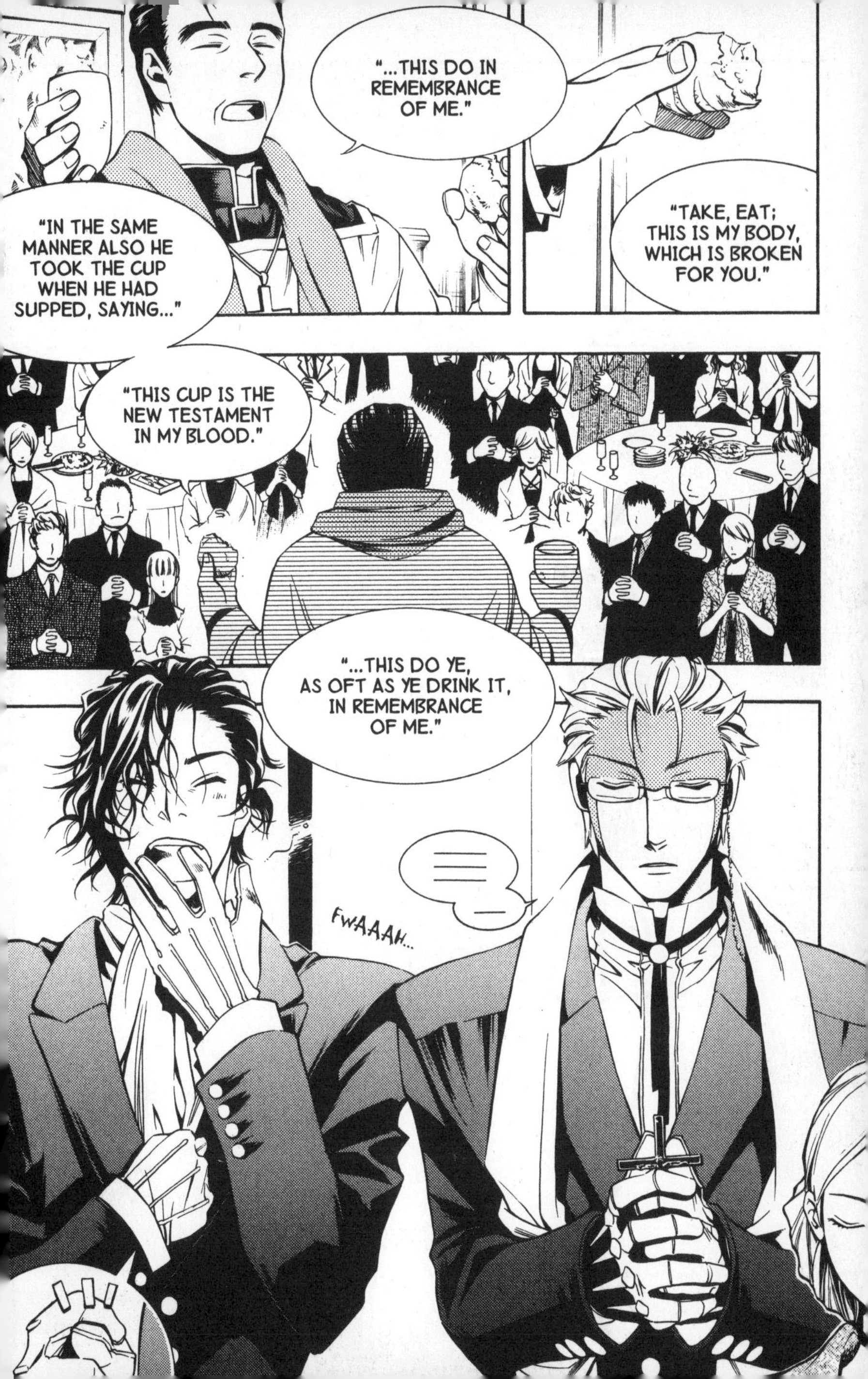
"TAKE, EAT; THIS IS MY BODY, WHICH IS BROKEN FOR YOU."
"...THIS DO IN REMEMBRANCE OF ME."
"IN THE SAME MANNER ALSO HE TOOK THE CUP WHEN HE HAD SUPPED, SAYING..."
"THIS CUP IS THE NEW TESTAMENT IN MY BLOOD."
"...THIS DO YE, AS OFT AS YE DRINK IT, IN REMEMBRANCE OF ME."
FWAAAH...

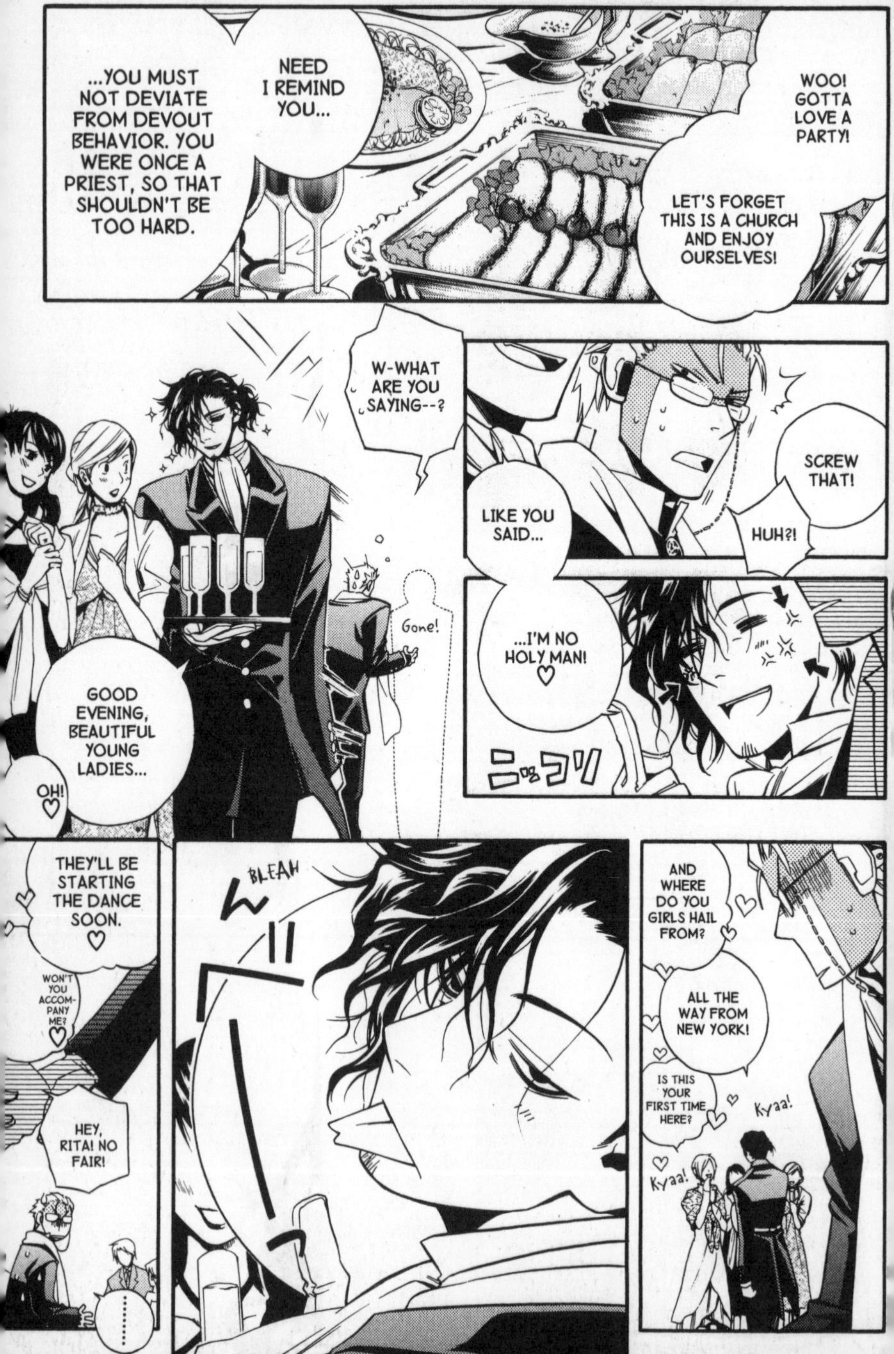
WOO! GOTTA LOVE A PARTY!
LET'S FORGET THIS IS A CHURCH AND ENJOY OURSELVES!
NEED I REMIND YOU...
...YOU MUST NOT DEVIATE FROM DEVOUT BEHAVIOR. YOU WERE ONCE A PRIEST, SO THAT SHOULDN'T BE TOO HARD.
SCREW THAT!
HUH?!
LIKE YOU SAID...
...I'M NO HOLY MAN! ♡
ニッコリ
W-WHAT ARE YOU SAYING--?
Gone!
GOOD EVENING, BEAUTIFUL YOUNG LADIES...
OH! ♡
AND WHERE DO YOU GIRLS HAIL FROM?
ALL THE WAY FROM NEW YORK!
Kyaa!
IS THIS YOUR FIRST TIME HERE?
Kyaa!
BLEAH
THEY'LL BE STARTING THE DANCE SOON. ♡
WON'T YOU ACCOMPANY ME? ♡
HEY, RITA! NO FAIR!
......

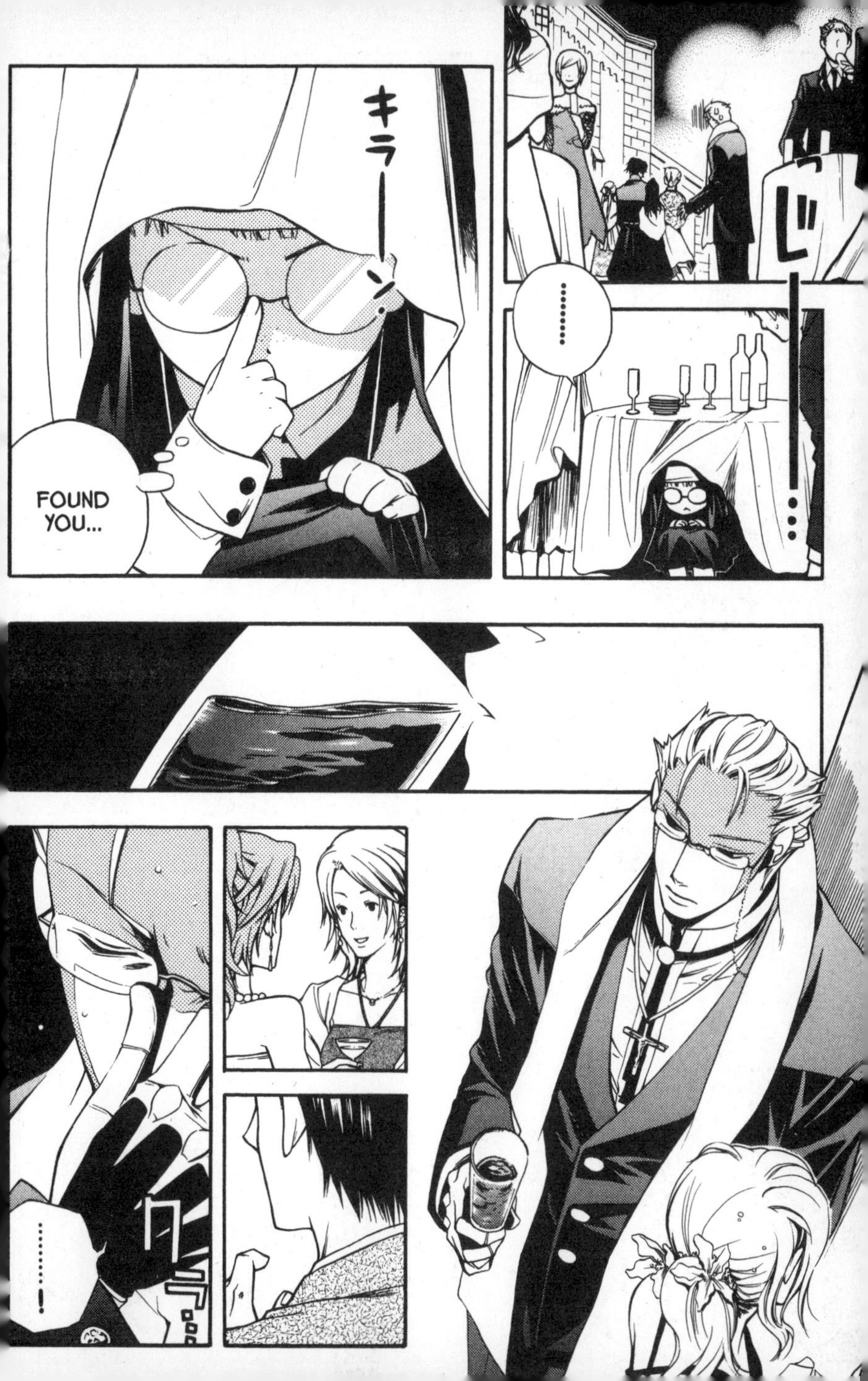

....
キラーン
FOUND YOU...
.........!

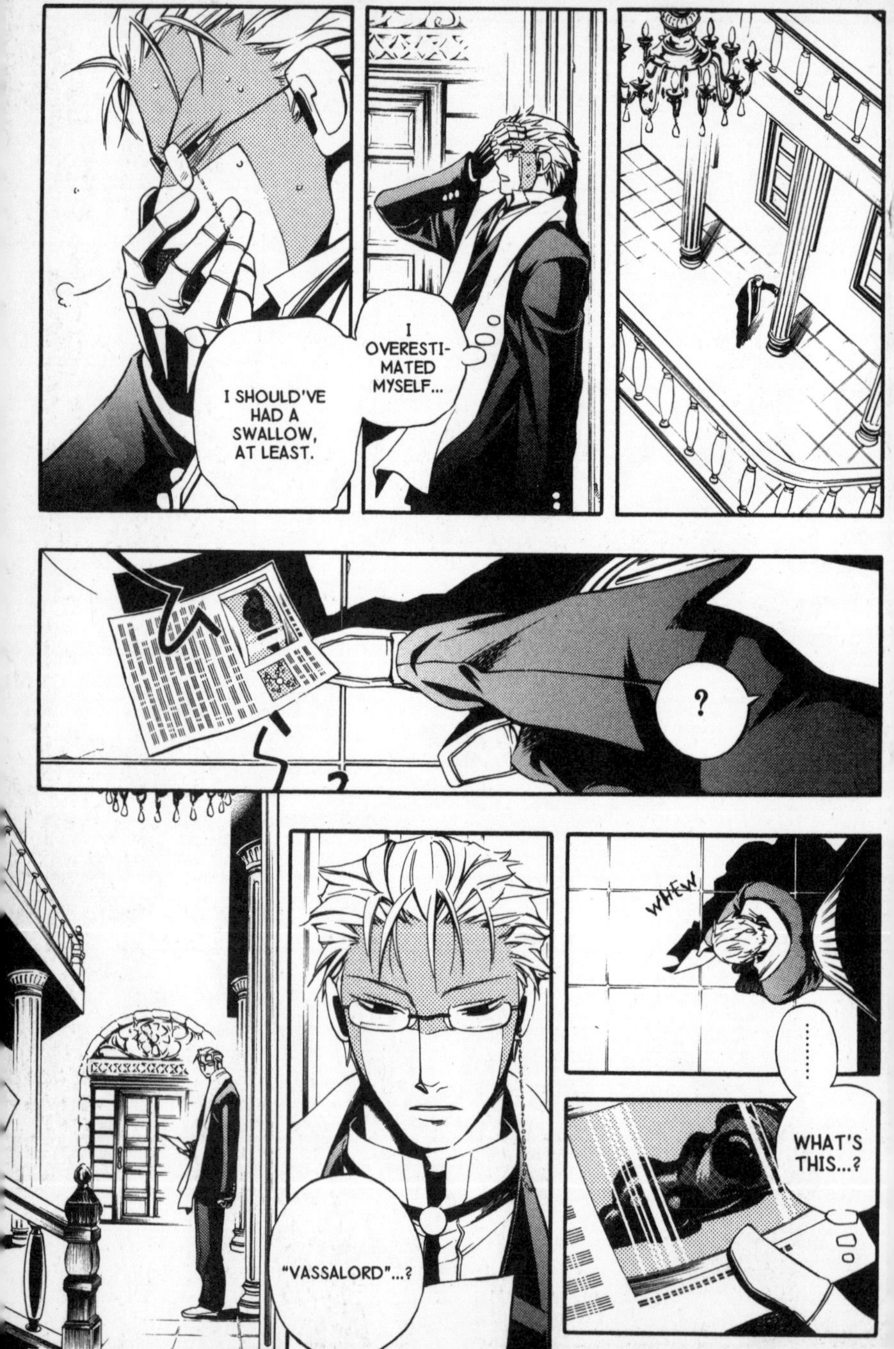
I OVERESTI-MATED MYSELF...
I SHOULD'VE HAD A SWALLOW, AT LEAST.
?
WHEW
......
WHAT'S THIS...?
"VASSALORD"...?

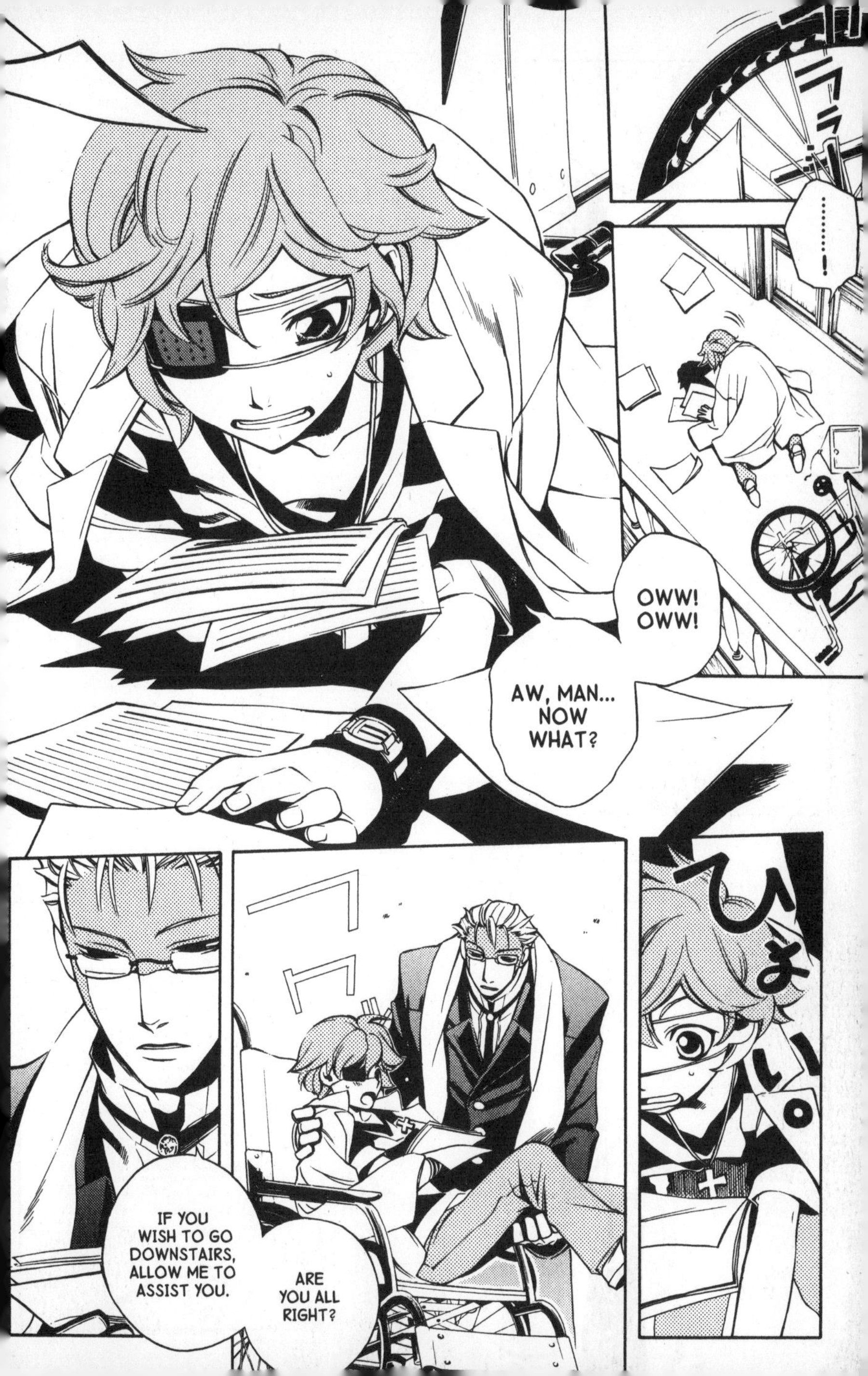

......!
OWW! OWW!
AW, MAN... NOW WHAT?
ひょい。
ARE YOU ALL RIGHT?
IF YOU WISH TO GO DOWNSTAIRS, ALLOW ME TO ASSIST YOU.

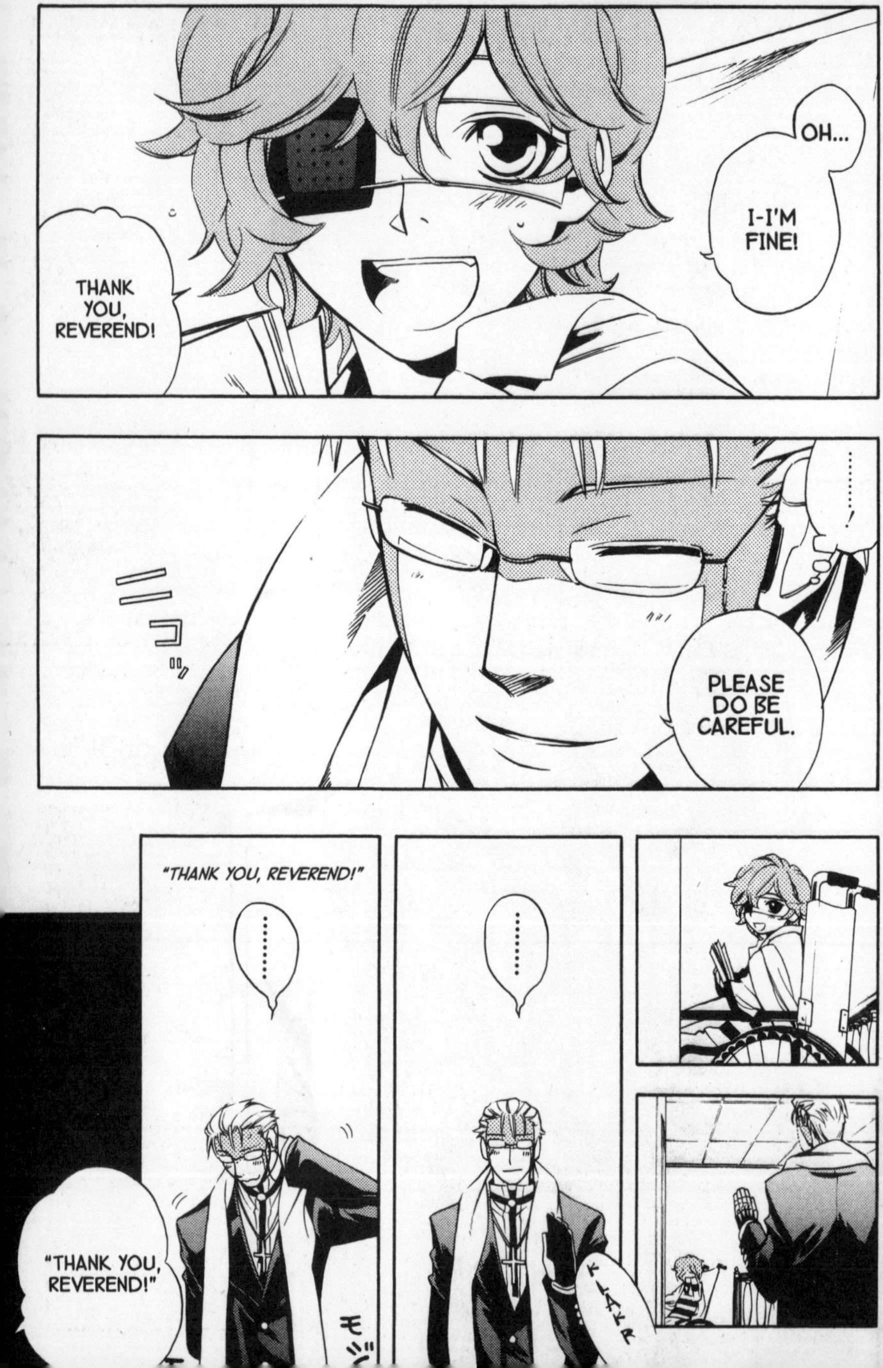
OH...
I-I'M FINE!
THANK YOU, REVEREND!
......!
PLEASE DO BE CAREFUL.
ニコッ
......
KLAKR
"THANK YOU, REVEREND!"
......
"THANK YOU, REVEREND!"
モジ

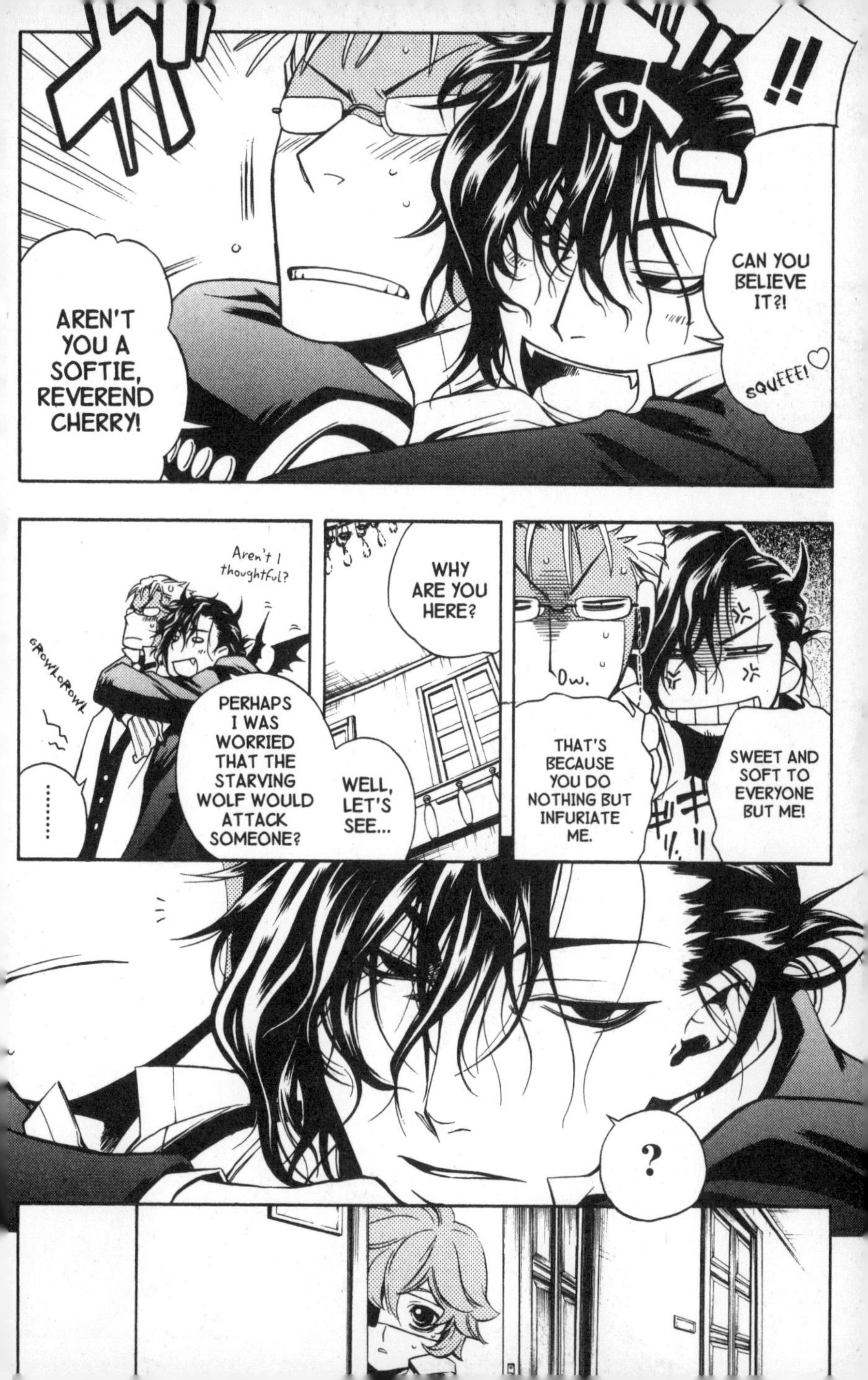
CAN YOU BELIEVE IT?!
SQUEEE!♡
AREN'T YOU A SOFTIE, REVEREND CHERRY!
SWEET AND SOFT TO EVERYONE BUT ME!
Ow.
THAT'S BECAUSE YOU DO NOTHING BUT INFURIATE ME.
WHY ARE YOU HERE?
WELL, LET'S SEE...
Aren't I thoughtful?
PERHAPS I WAS WORRIED THAT THE STARVING WOLF WOULD ATTACK SOMEONE?
GROWLOROWL
....
?

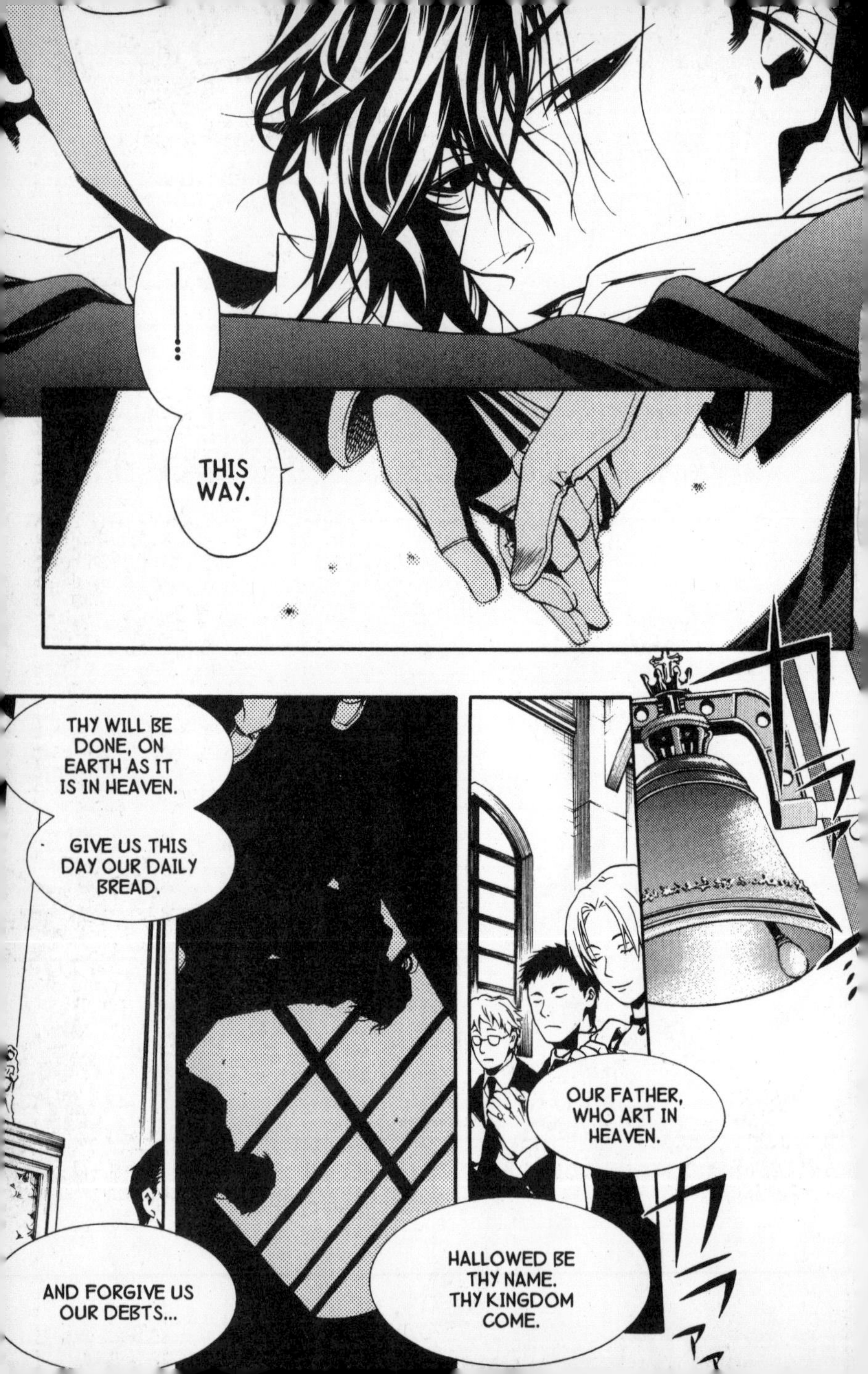
THIS WAY.
OUR FATHER, WHO ART IN HEAVEN.
HALLOWED BE THY NAME. THY KINGDOM COME.
THY WILL BE DONE, ON EARTH AS IT IS IN HEAVEN.
GIVE US THIS DAY OUR DAILY BREAD.
AND FORGIVE US OUR DEBTS...

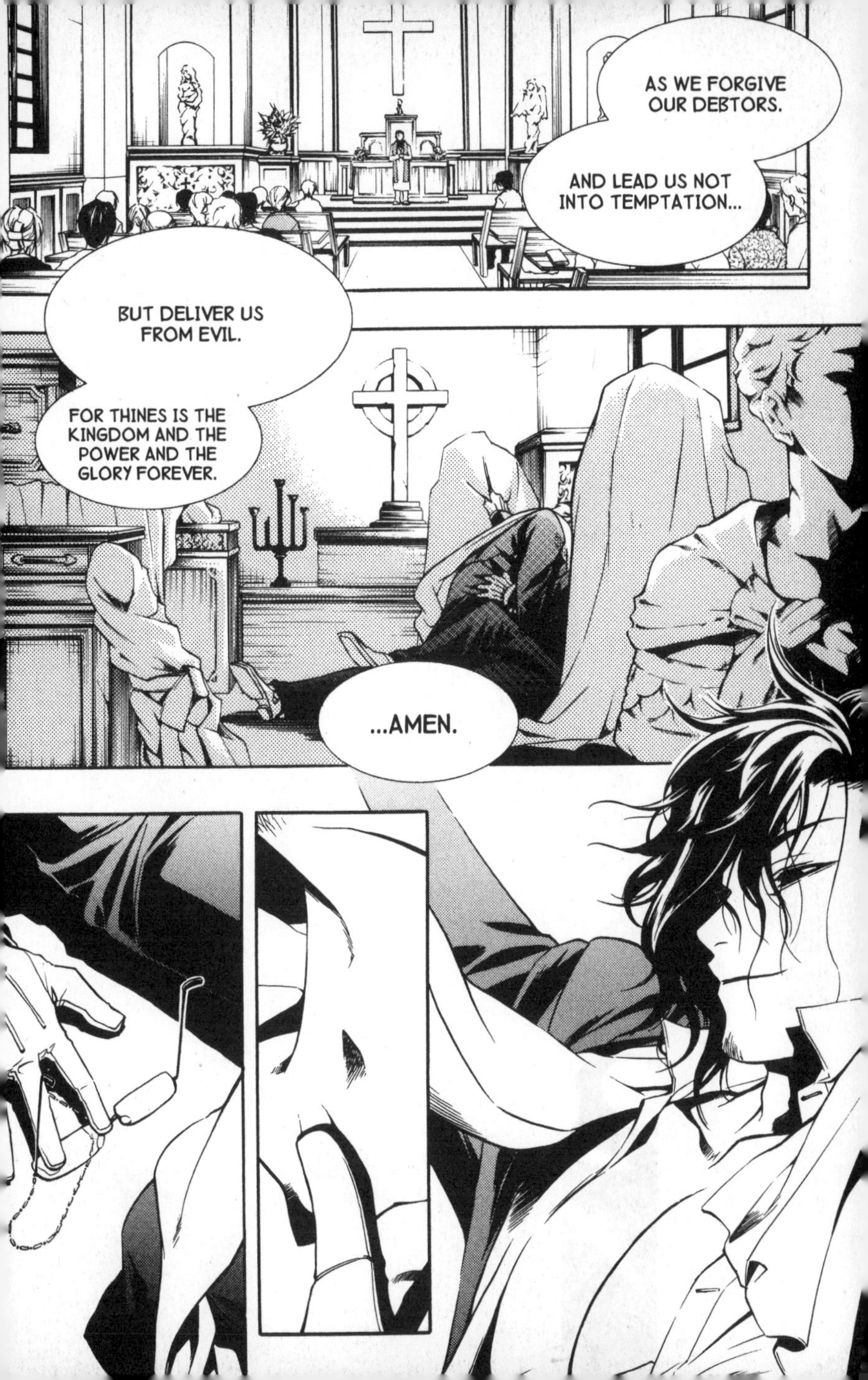
AS WE FORGIVE OUR DEBTORS.
AND LEAD US NOT INTO TEMPTATION...
BUT DELIVER US FROM EVIL.
FOR THINES IS THE KINGDOM AND THE POWER AND THE GLORY FOREVER.
...AMEN.

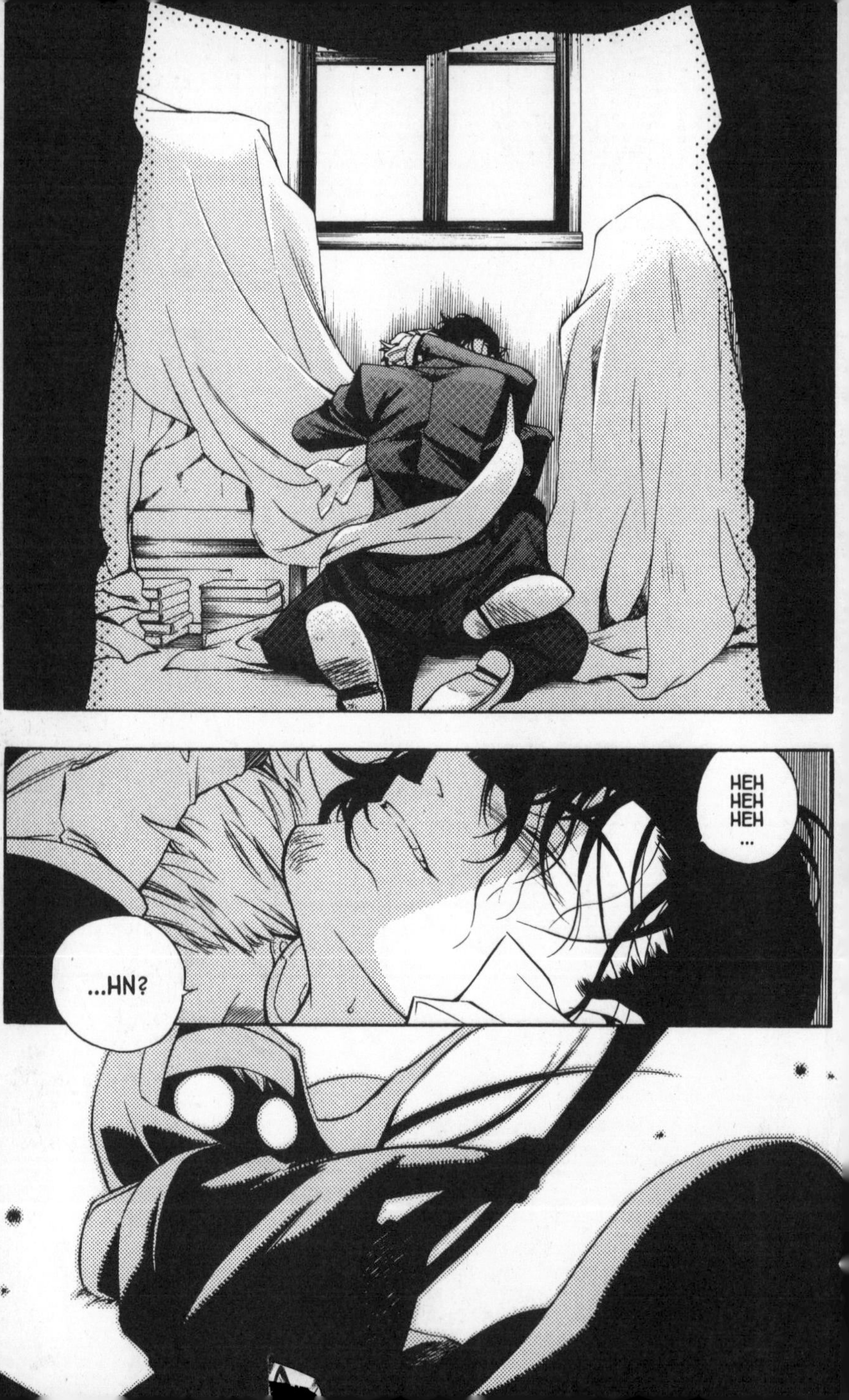
HEH HEH HEH ...
...HN?

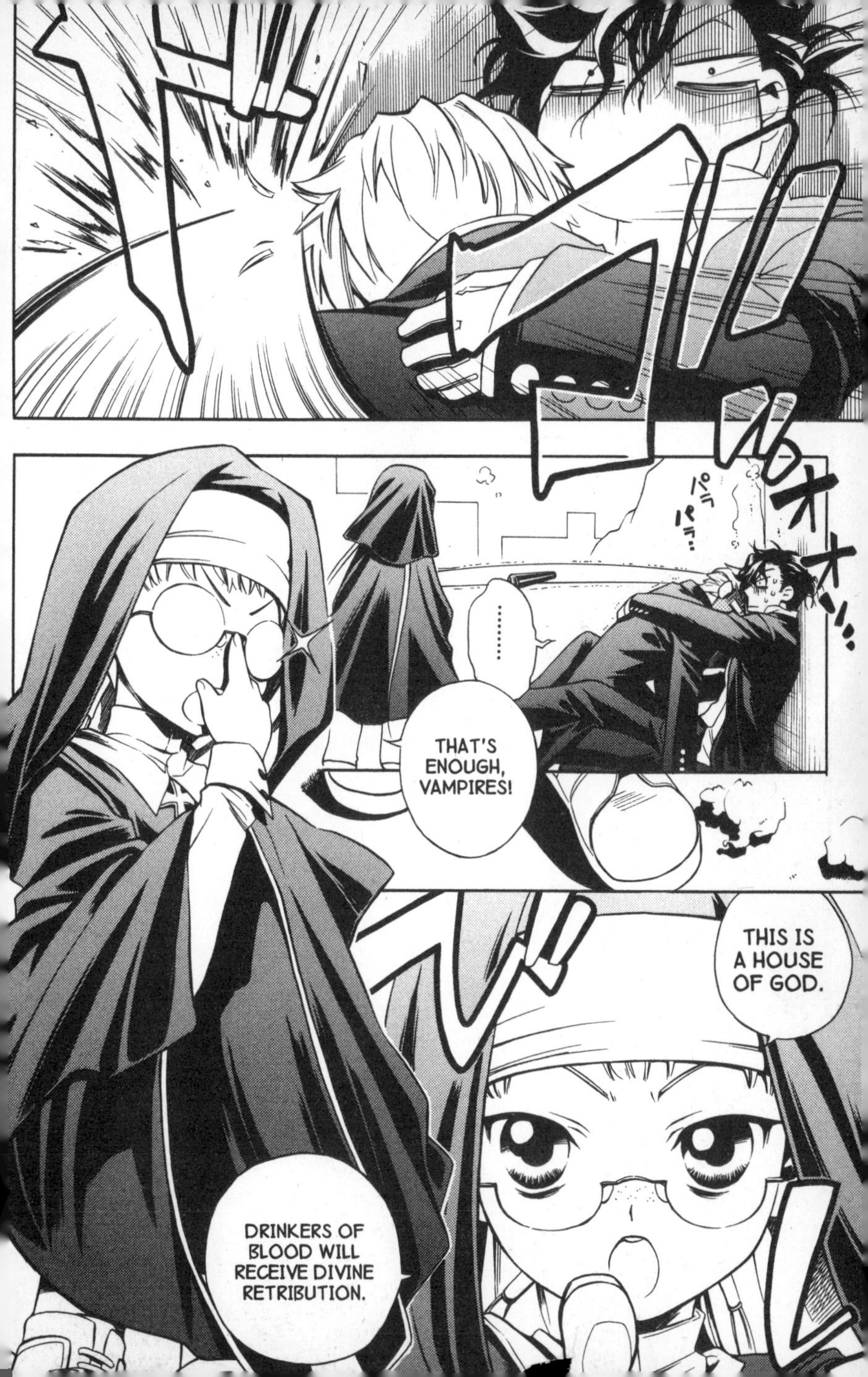
パラ
パラ…
………
THAT'S ENOUGH, VAMPIRES!
THIS IS A HOUSE OF GOD.
DRINKERS OF BLOOD WILL RECEIVE DIVINE RETRIBUTION.

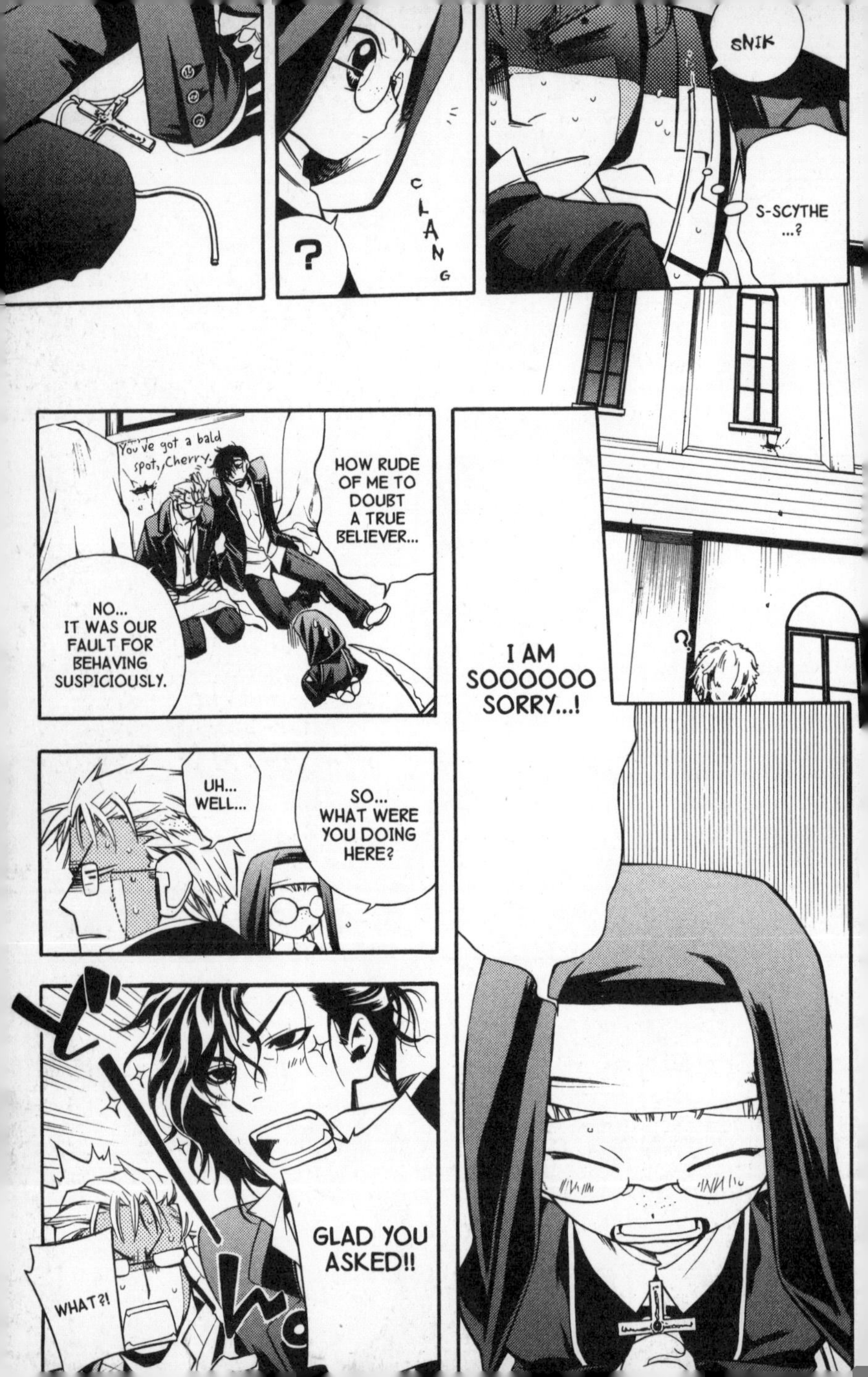
SNIK
S-SCYTHE ...?
?
CLANG
I AM SOOOOOO SORRY...!
HOW RUDE OF ME TO DOUBT A TRUE BELIEVER...
You've got a bald spot, Cherry.
NO... IT WAS OUR FAULT FOR BEHAVING SUSPICIOUSLY.
SO... WHAT WERE YOU DOING HERE?
UH... WELL...
GLAD YOU ASKED!!
WHAT?!

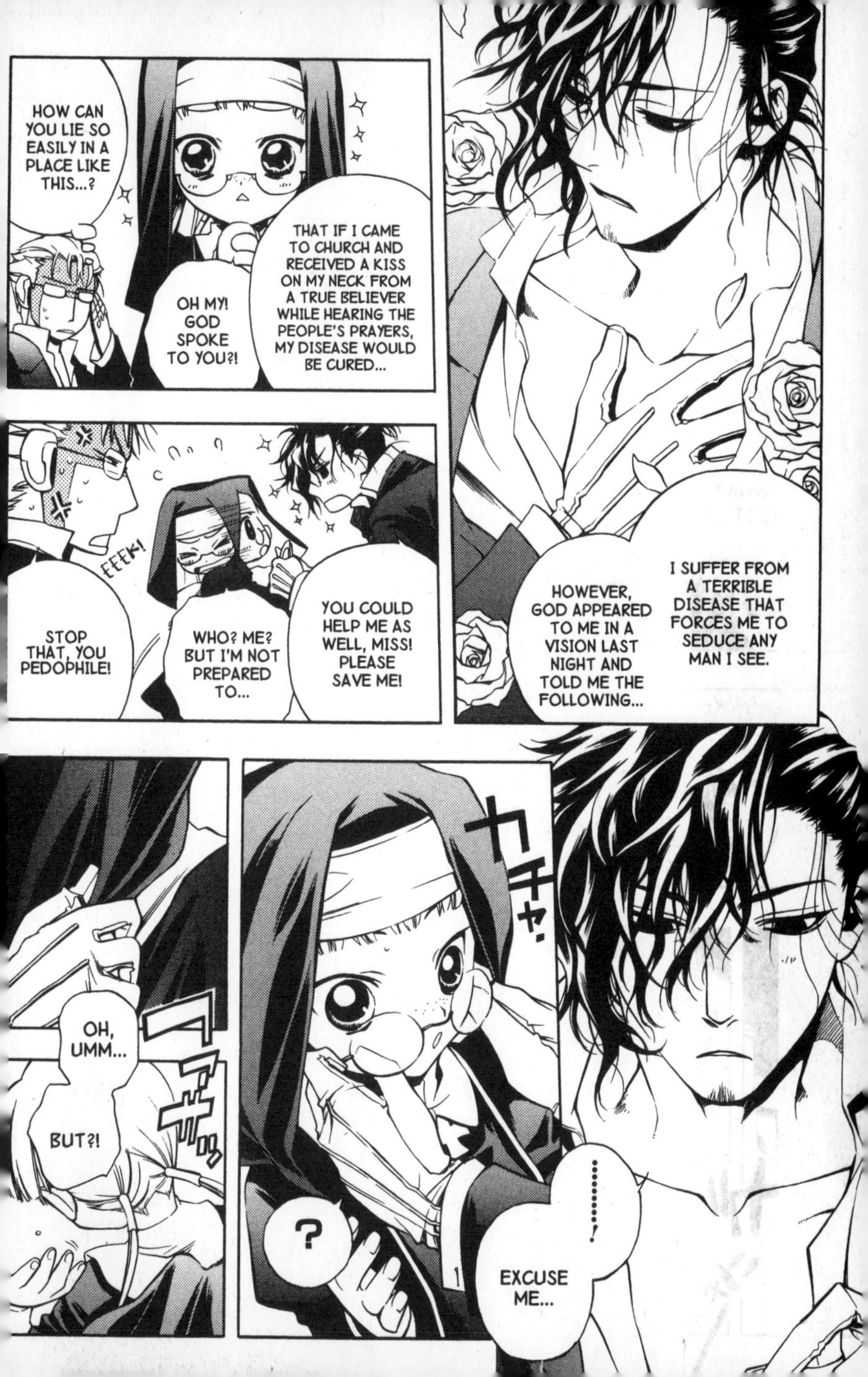
I SUFFER FROM A TERRIBLE DISEASE THAT FORCES ME TO SEDUCE ANY MAN I SEE.
HOWEVER, GOD APPEARED TO ME IN A VISION LAST NIGHT AND TOLD ME THE FOLLOWING...
THAT IF I CAME TO CHURCH AND RECEIVED A KISS ON MY NECK FROM A TRUE BELIEVER WHILE HEARING THE PEOPLE'S PRAYERS, MY DISEASE WOULD BE CURED...
OH MY! GOD SPOKE TO YOU?!
HOW CAN YOU LIE SO EASILY IN A PLACE LIKE THIS...?
YOU COULD HELP ME AS WELL, MISS! PLEASE SAVE ME!
WHO? ME? BUT I'M NOT PREPARED TO...
EEEK!
STOP THAT, YOU PEDOPHILE!
........!
EXCUSE ME...
カチャ
?
OH, UMM...
BUT?!

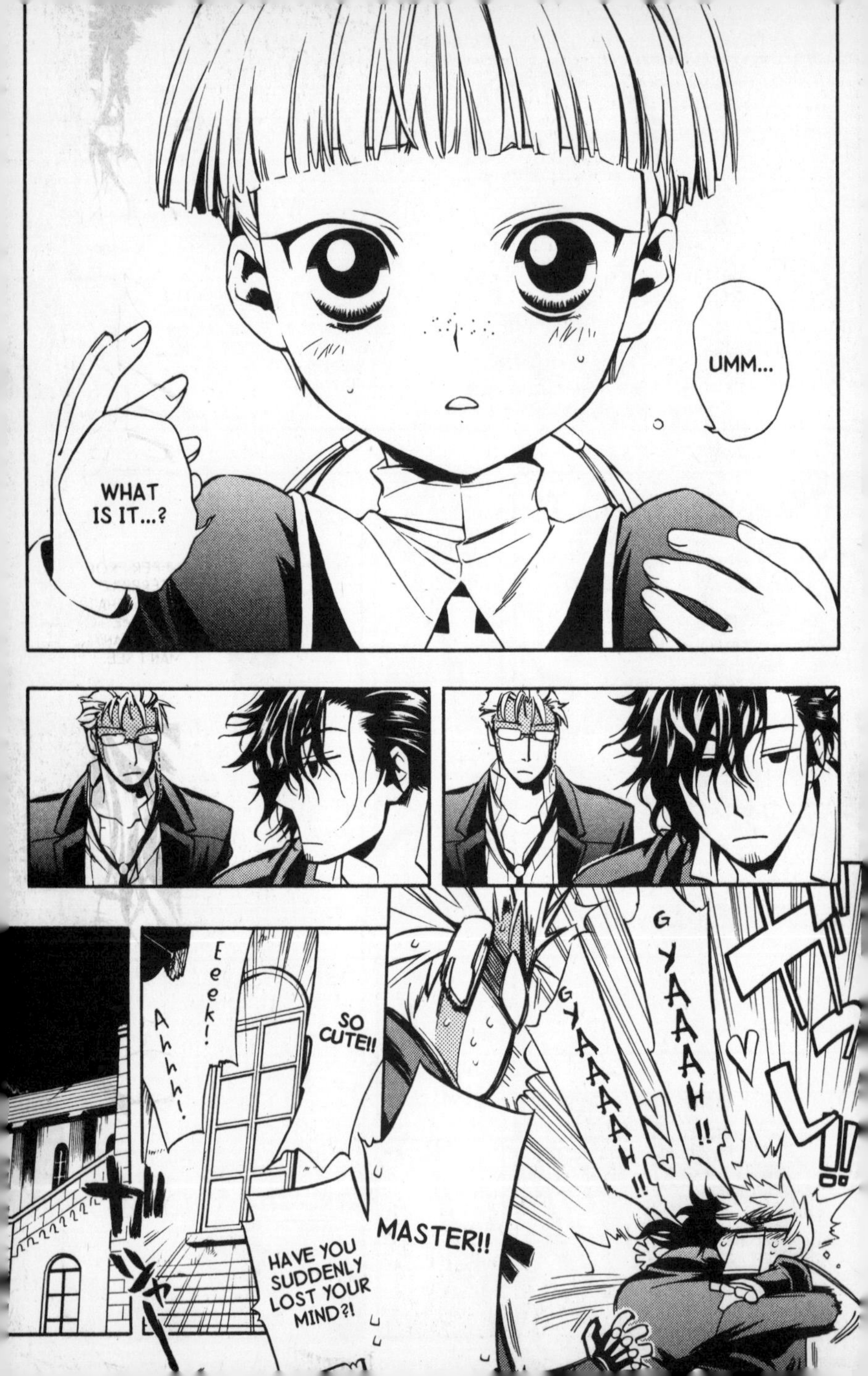
UMM...
WHAT IS IT...?
GYAAAH!!
GYAAAAH!!
MASTER!!
HAVE YOU SUDDENLY LOST YOUR MIND?!
SO CUTE!!
Eeek!
Ahhh!

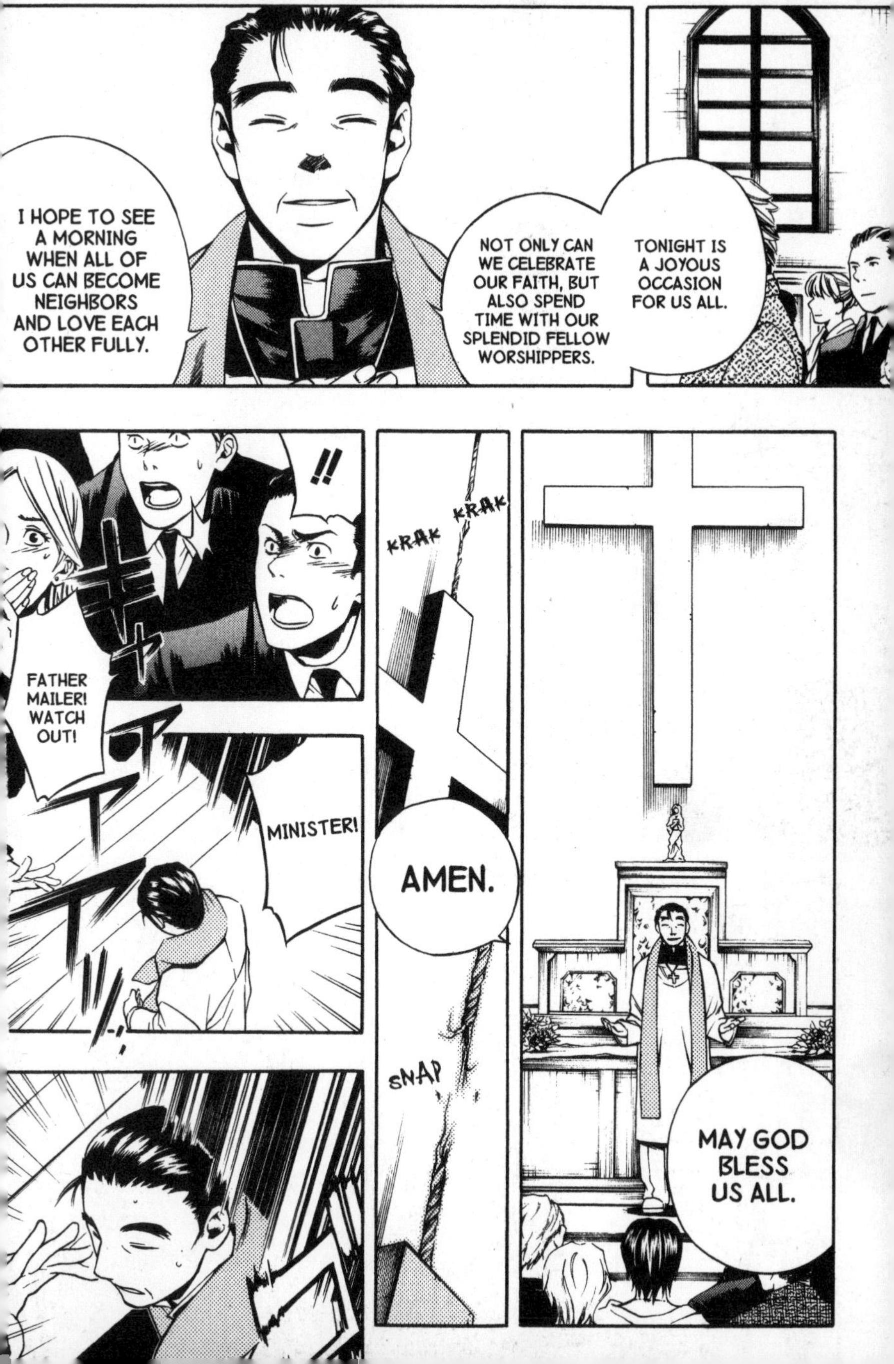
TONIGHT IS A JOYOUS OCCASION FOR US ALL.
NOT ONLY CAN WE CELEBRATE OUR FAITH, BUT ALSO SPEND TIME WITH OUR SPLENDID FELLOW WORSHIPPERS.
I HOPE TO SEE A MORNING WHEN ALL OF US CAN BECOME NEIGHBORS AND LOVE EACH OTHER FULLY.
MAY GOD BLESS US ALL.
KRAK
KRAK
AMEN.
SNAP
!!
FATHER MAILER! WATCH OUT!
MINISTER!

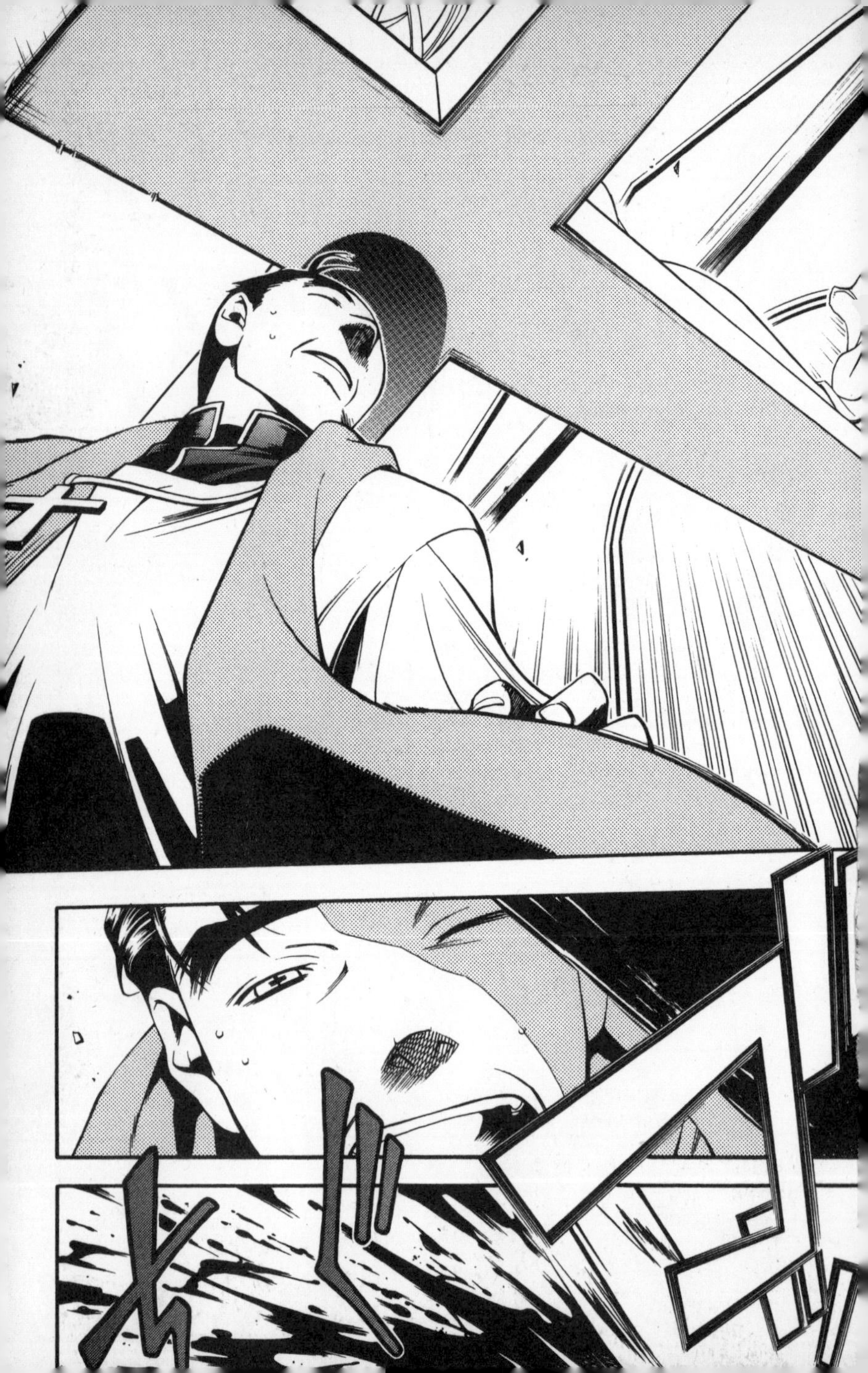

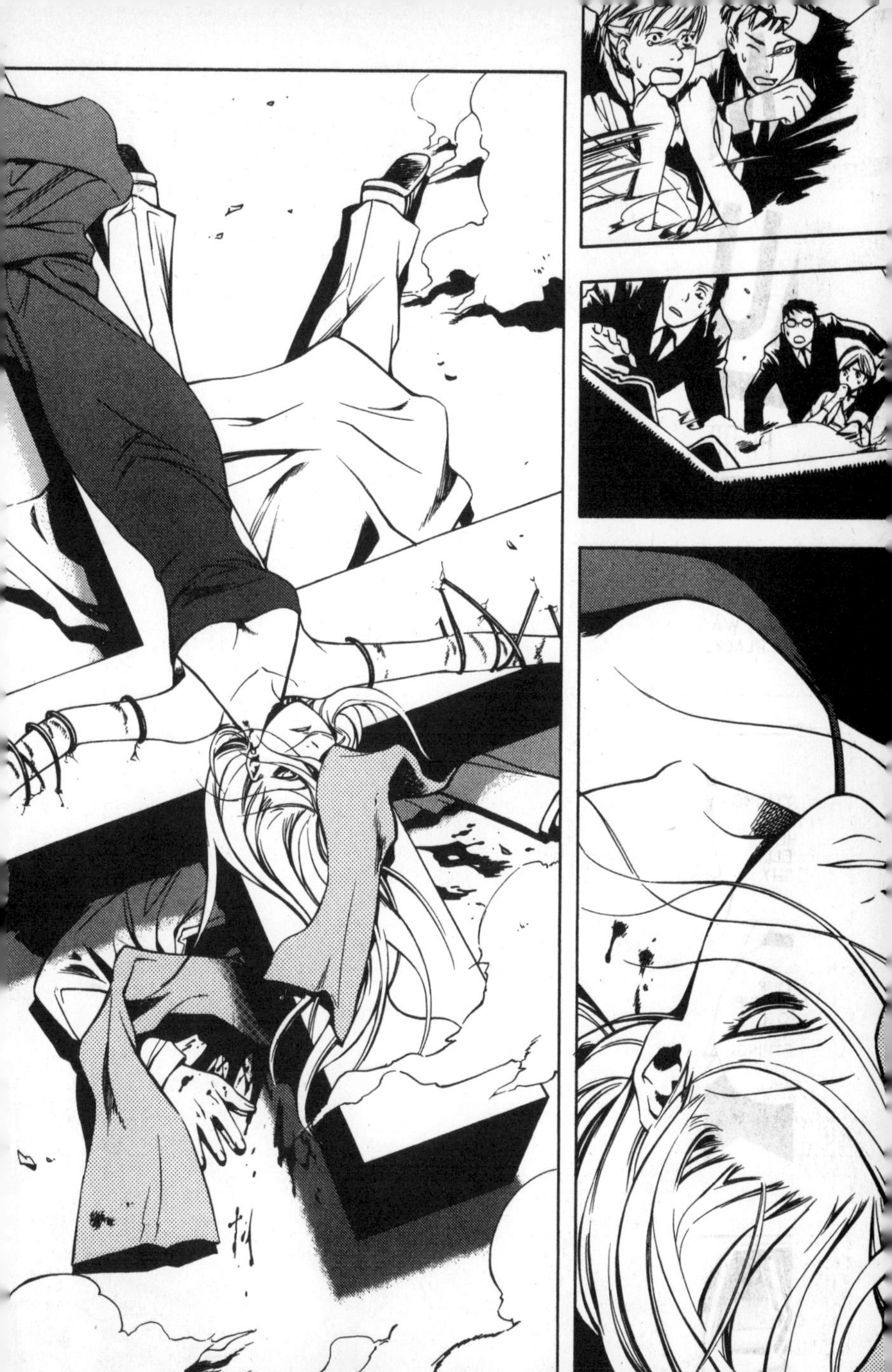

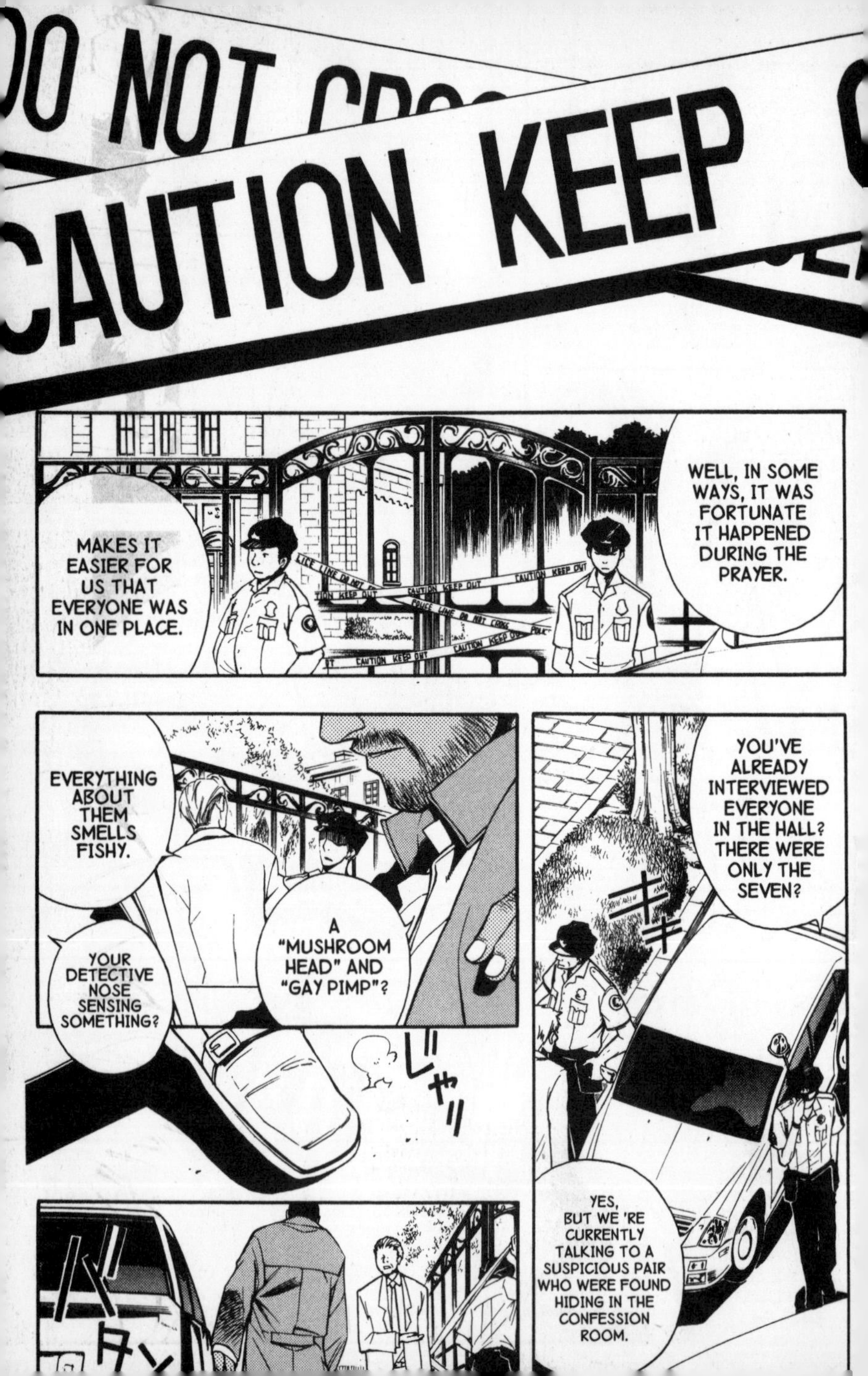
DO NOT
CAUTION KEEP
WELL, IN SOME WAYS, IT WAS FORTUNATE IT HAPPENED DURING THE PRAYER.
MAKES IT EASIER FOR US THAT EVERYONE WAS IN ONE PLACE.
YOU'VE ALREADY INTERVIEWED EVERYONE IN THE HALL? THERE WERE ONLY THE SEVEN?
YES, BUT WE 'RE CURRENTLY TALKING TO A SUSPICIOUS PAIR WHO WERE FOUND HIDING IN THE CONFESSION ROOM.
A "MUSHROOM HEAD" AND "GAY PIMP"?
EVERYTHING ABOUT THEM SMELLS FISHY.
YOUR DETECTIVE NOSE SENSING SOMETHING?
ジャリ

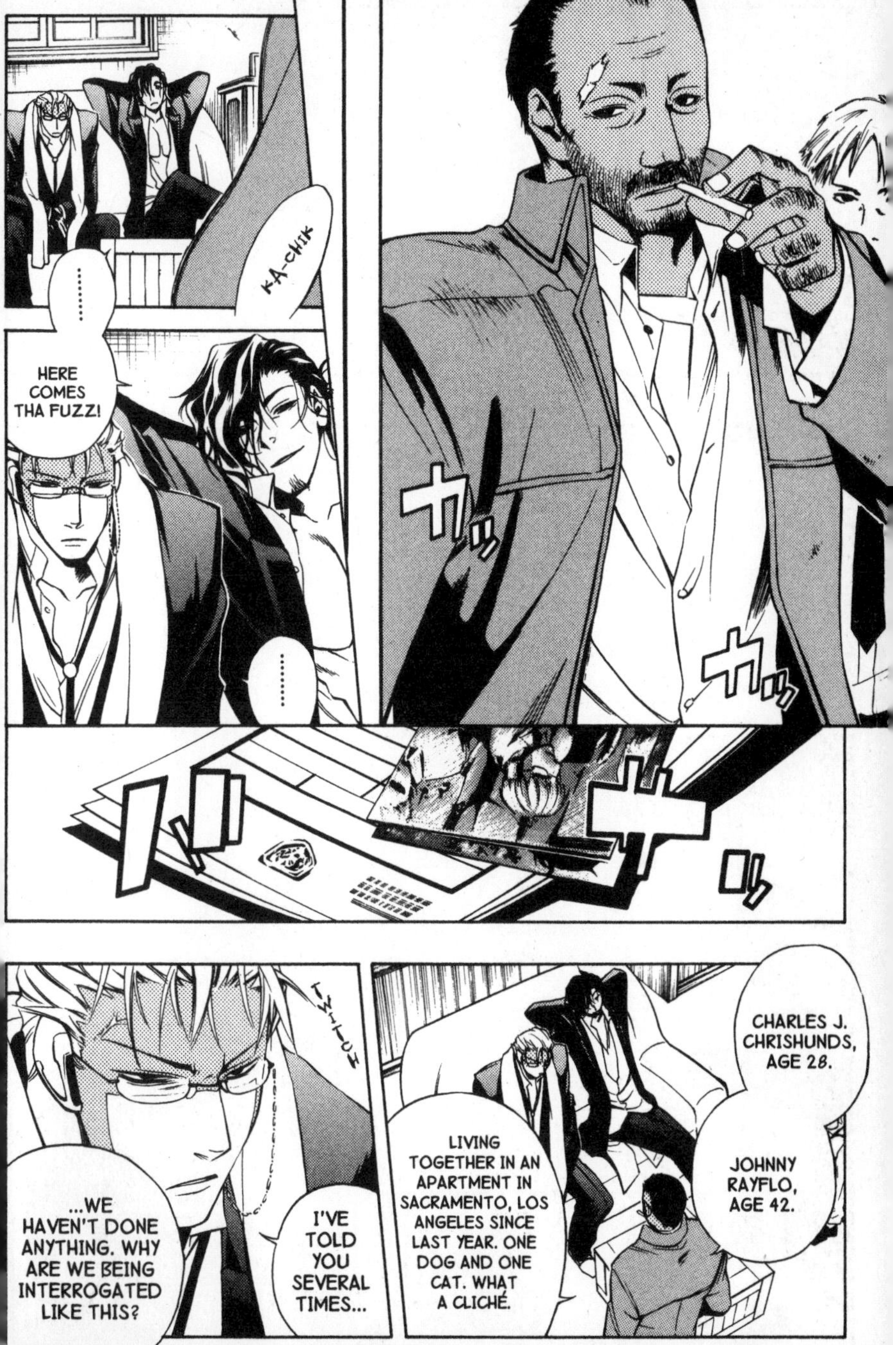
カッ
カッ
KA-CHIK
......
HERE COMES THA FUZZ!
......
CHARLES J. CHRISHUNDS, AGE 28.
JOHNNY RAYFLO, AGE 42.
LIVING TOGETHER IN AN APARTMENT IN SACRAMENTO, LOS ANGELES SINCE LAST YEAR. ONE DOG AND ONE CAT. WHAT A CLICHÉ.
TWITCH
I'VE TOLD YOU SEVERAL TIMES...
...WE HAVEN'T DONE ANYTHING. WHY ARE WE BEING INTERROGATED LIKE THIS?

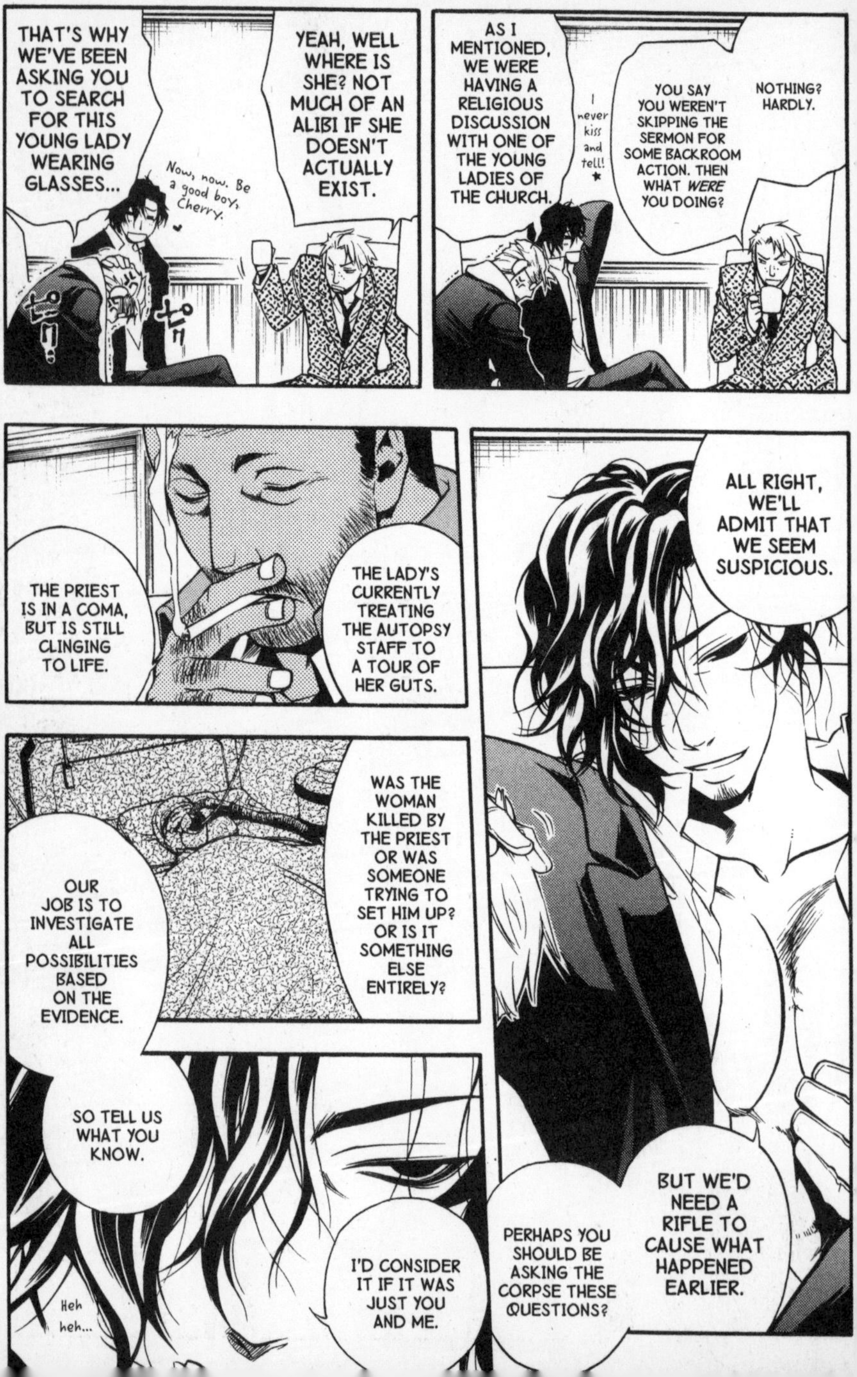
NOTHING? HARDLY.
YOU SAY YOU WEREN'T SKIPPING THE SERMON FOR SOME BACKROOM ACTION. THEN WHAT *WERE* YOU DOING?
I never kiss and tell! ★
AS I MENTIONED, WE WERE HAVING A RELIGIOUS DISCUSSION WITH ONE OF THE YOUNG LADIES OF THE CHURCH.
YEAH, WELL WHERE IS SHE? NOT MUCH OF AN ALIBI IF SHE DOESN'T ACTUALLY EXIST.
THAT'S WHY WE'VE BEEN ASKING YOU TO SEARCH FOR THIS YOUNG LADY WEARING GLASSES...
Now, now. Be a good boy, Cherry.
ALL RIGHT, WE'LL ADMIT THAT WE SEEM SUSPICIOUS.
BUT WE'D NEED A RIFLE TO CAUSE WHAT HAPPENED EARLIER.
PERHAPS YOU SHOULD BE ASKING THE CORPSE THESE QUESTIONS?
THE LADY'S CURRENTLY TREATING THE AUTOPSY STAFF TO A TOUR OF HER GUTS.
THE PRIEST IS IN A COMA, BUT IS STILL CLINGING TO LIFE.
WAS THE WOMAN KILLED BY THE PRIEST OR WAS SOMEONE TRYING TO SET HIM UP? OR IS IT SOMETHING ELSE ENTIRELY?
OUR JOB IS TO INVESTIGATE ALL POSSIBILITIES BASED ON THE EVIDENCE.
SO TELL US WHAT YOU KNOW.
I'D CONSIDER IT IF IT WAS JUST YOU AND ME.
Heh heh...

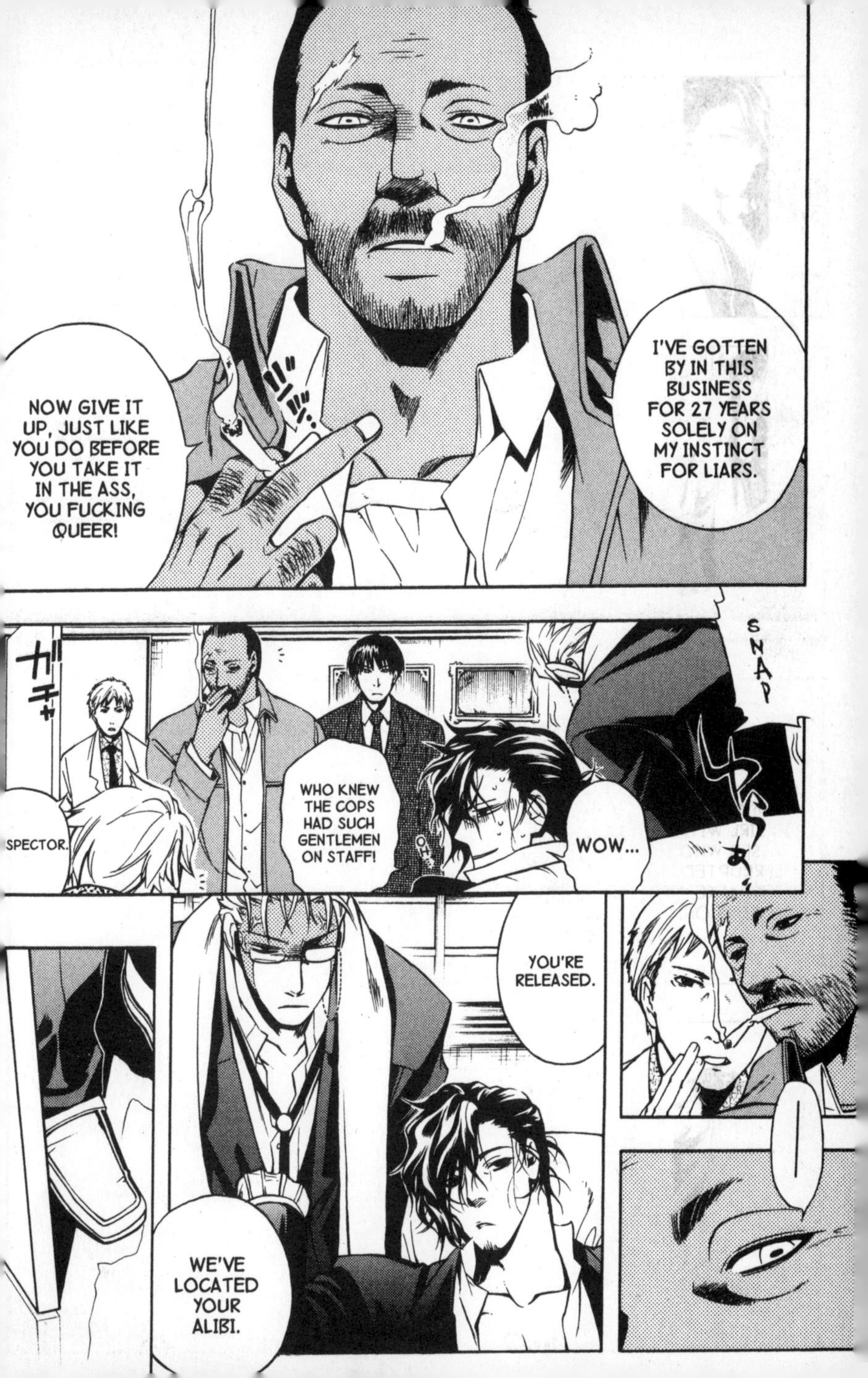
I'VE GOTTEN BY IN THIS BUSINESS FOR 27 YEARS SOLELY ON MY INSTINCT FOR LIARS.
NOW GIVE IT UP, JUST LIKE YOU DO BEFORE YOU TAKE IT IN THE ASS, YOU FUCKING QUEER!
SNAP
WOW...
OH...
WHO KNEW THE COPS HAD SUCH GENTLEMEN ON STAFF!
SPECTOR.
ガチャ
!
YOU'RE RELEASED.
WE'VE LOCATED YOUR ALIBI.

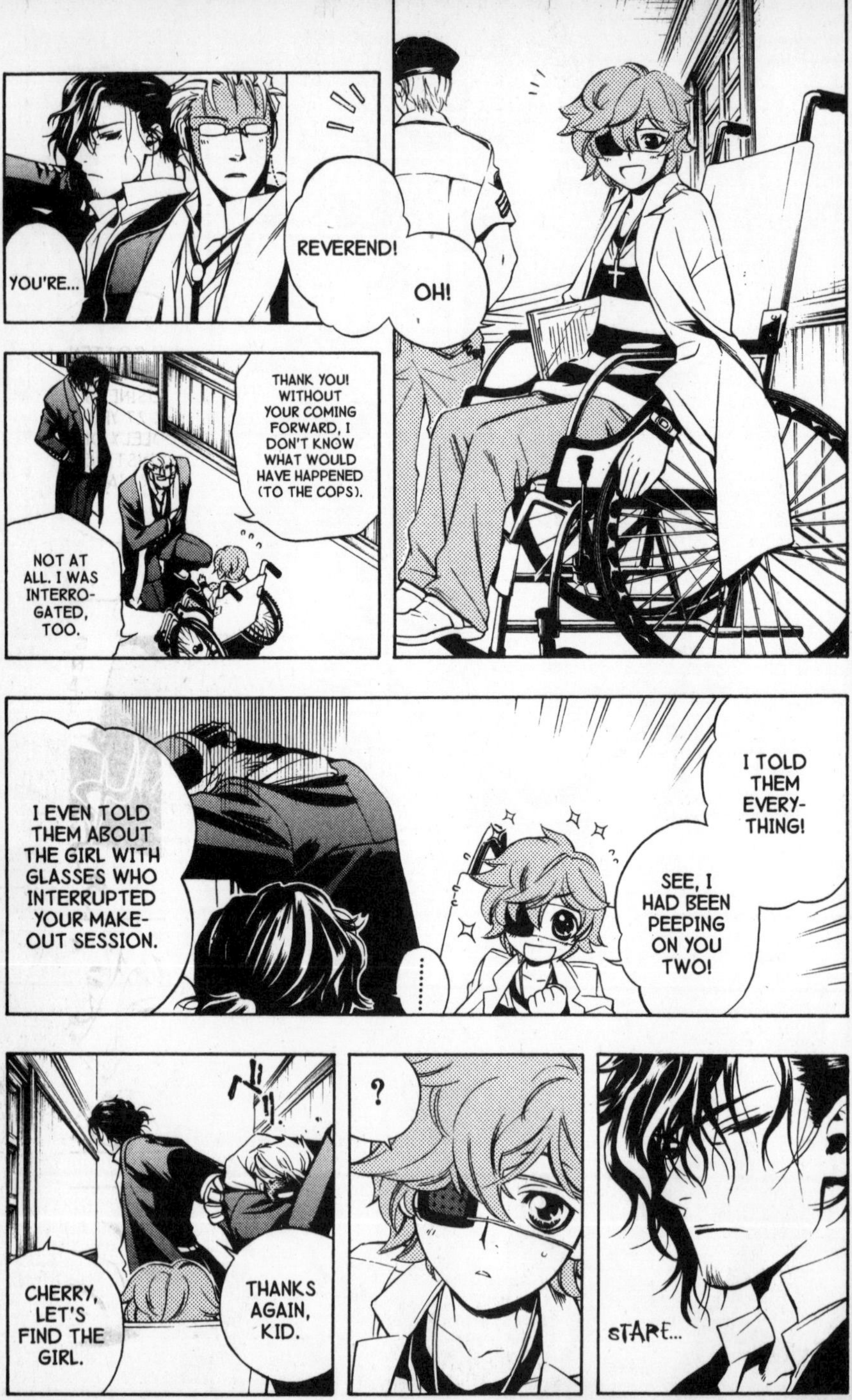
OH!
REVEREND!
YOU'RE...
THANK YOU! WITHOUT YOUR COMING FORWARD, I DON'T KNOW WHAT WOULD HAVE HAPPENED (TO THE COPS).
NOT AT ALL. I WAS INTERRO-GATED, TOO.
I TOLD THEM EVERY-THING!
SEE, I HAD BEEN PEEPING ON YOU TWO!
....
I EVEN TOLD THEM ABOUT THE GIRL WITH GLASSES WHO INTERRUPTED YOUR MAKE-OUT SESSION.
STARE...
?
THANKS AGAIN, KID.
CHERRY, LET'S FIND THE GIRL.

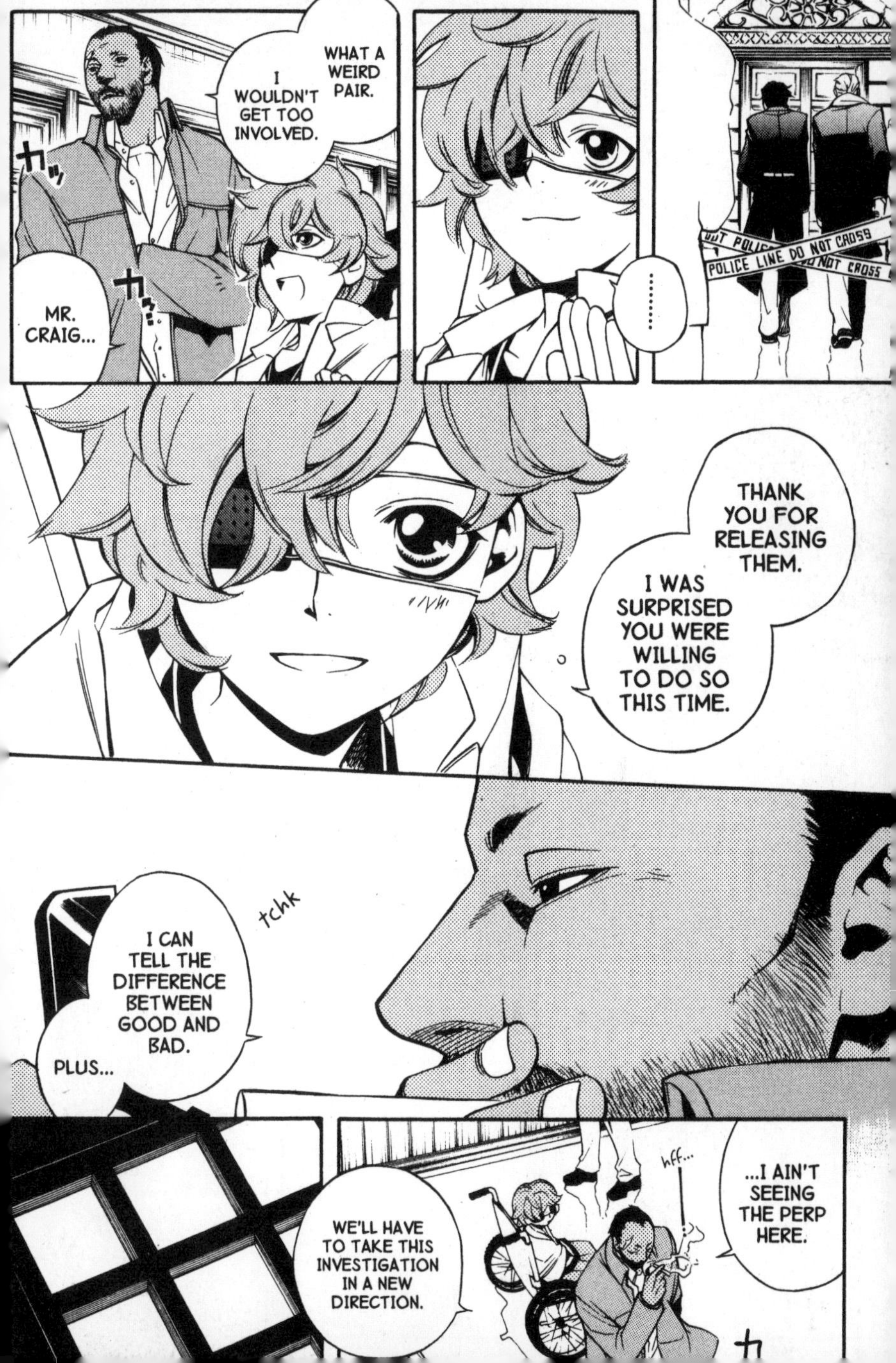
POLICE LINE DO NOT CROSS
......
WHAT A WEIRD PAIR.
I WOULDN'T GET TOO INVOLVED.
MR. CRAIG...
THANK YOU FOR RELEASING THEM.
I WAS SURPRISED YOU WERE WILLING TO DO SO THIS TIME.
tchk
I CAN TELL THE DIFFERENCE BETWEEN GOOD AND BAD.
PLUS...
...I AIN'T SEEING THE PERP HERE.
hff...
WE'LL HAVE TO TAKE THIS INVESTIGATION IN A NEW DIRECTION.

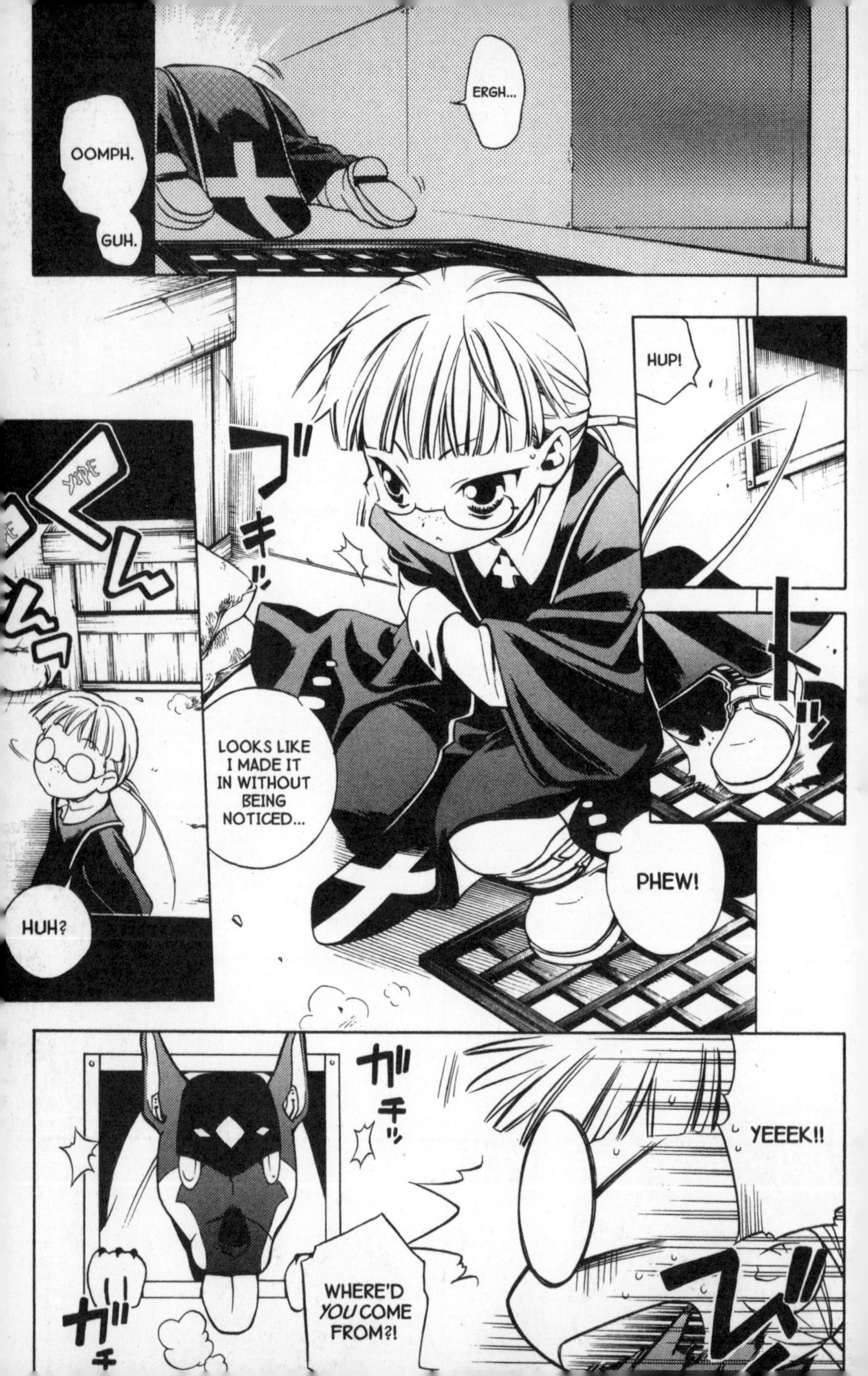
ERGH...
OOMPH.
GUH.
HUP!
LOOKS LIKE I MADE IT IN WITHOUT BEING NOTICED...
PHEW!
YIPE
HUH?
YEEEK!!
WHERE'D *YOU* COME FROM?!

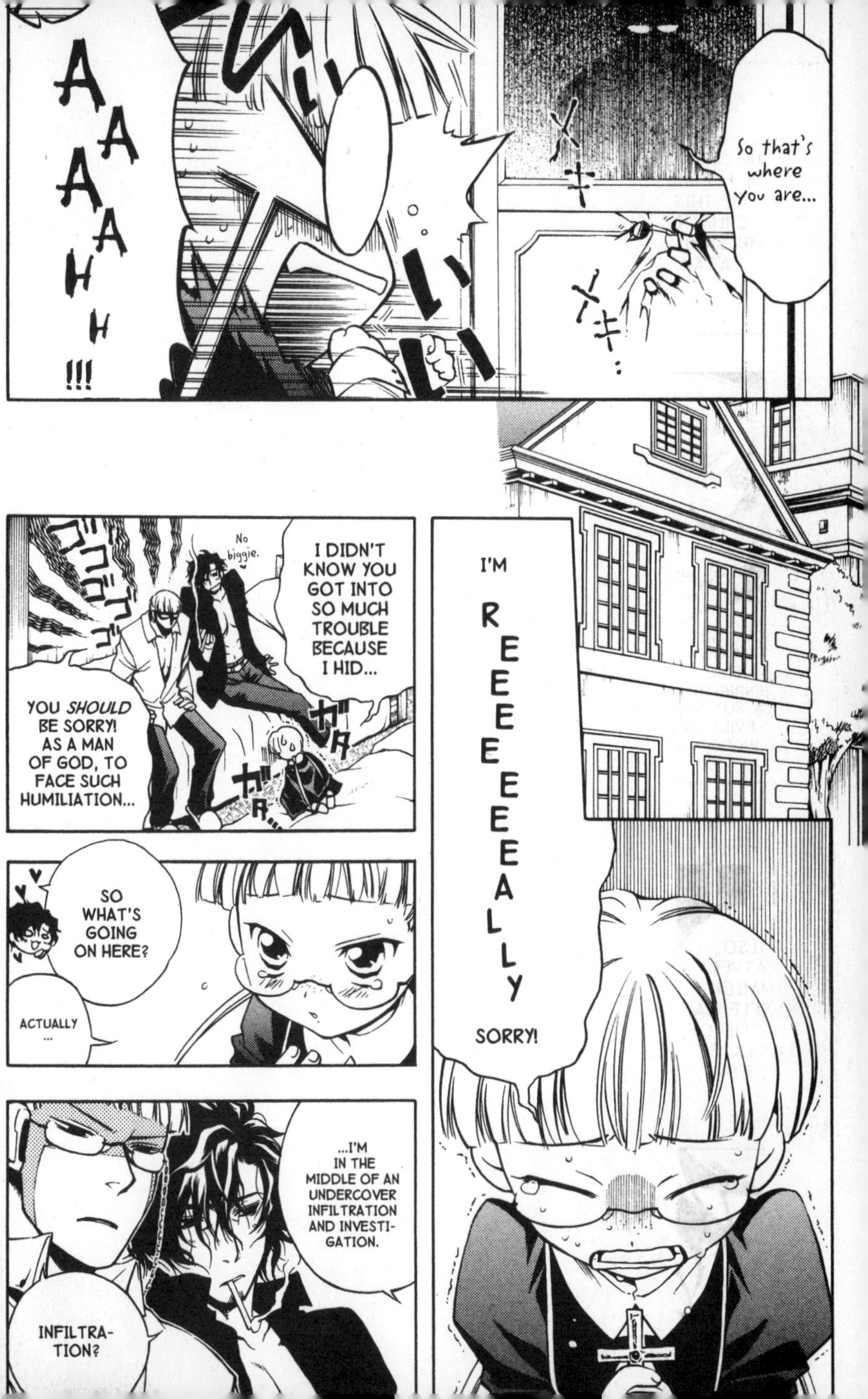
So that's where you are...
AAAAHH!!!
I'M REEEEEEEALLY SORRY!
I DIDN'T KNOW YOU GOT INTO SO MUCH TROUBLE BECAUSE I HID...
No biggie.
YOU *SHOULD* BE SORRY! AS A MAN OF GOD, TO FACE SUCH HUMILIATION...
SO WHAT'S GOING ON HERE?
ACTUALLY ...
...I'M IN THE MIDDLE OF AN UNDERCOVER INFILTRATION AND INVESTIGATION.
INFILTRATION?

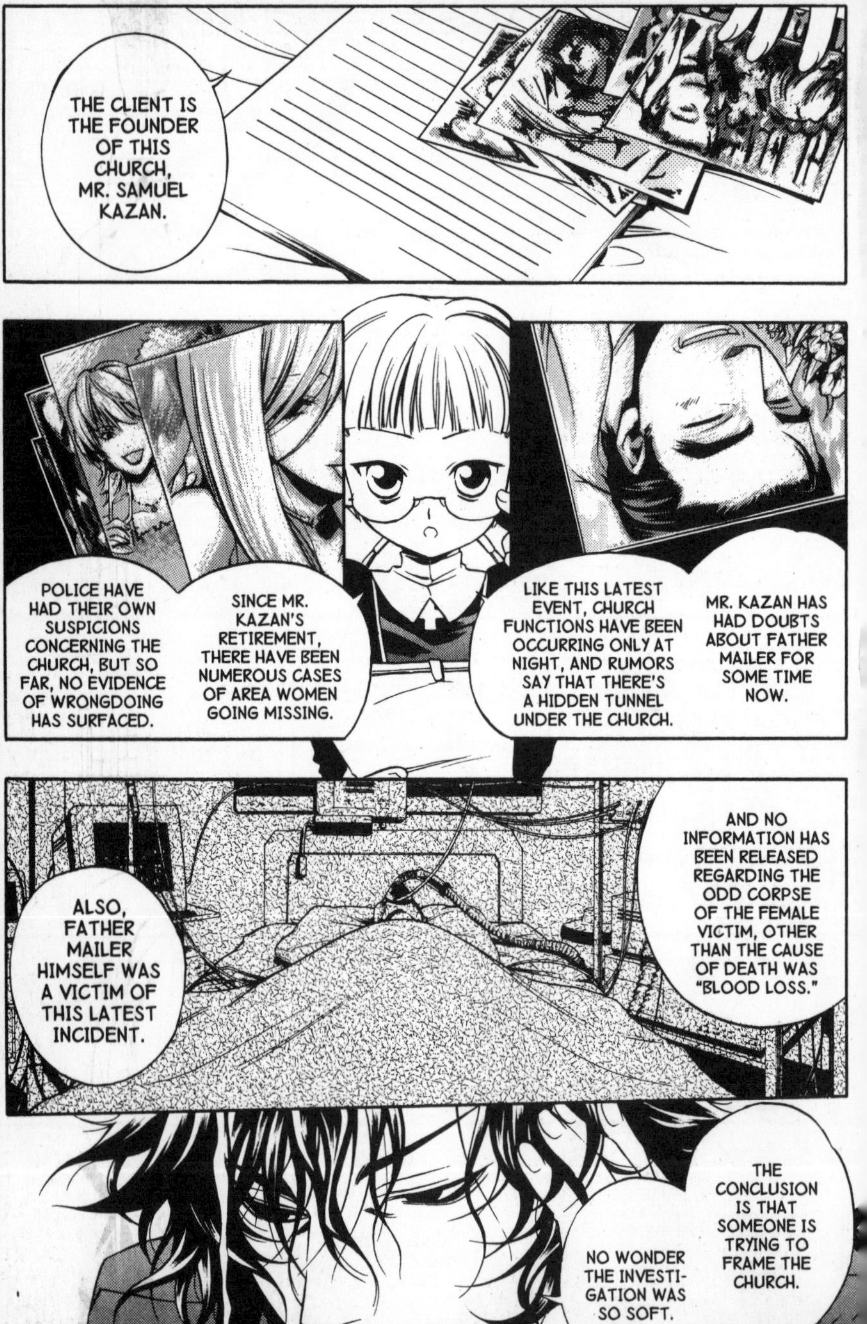
THE CLIENT IS THE FOUNDER OF THIS CHURCH, MR. SAMUEL KAZAN.
MR. KAZAN HAS HAD DOUBTS ABOUT FATHER MAILER FOR SOME TIME NOW.
LIKE THIS LATEST EVENT, CHURCH FUNCTIONS HAVE BEEN OCCURRING ONLY AT NIGHT, AND RUMORS SAY THAT THERE'S A HIDDEN TUNNEL UNDER THE CHURCH.
SINCE MR. KAZAN'S RETIREMENT, THERE HAVE BEEN NUMEROUS CASES OF AREA WOMEN GOING MISSING.
POLICE HAVE HAD THEIR OWN SUSPICIONS CONCERNING THE CHURCH, BUT SO FAR, NO EVIDENCE OF WRONGDOING HAS SURFACED.
AND NO INFORMATION HAS BEEN RELEASED REGARDING THE ODD CORPSE OF THE FEMALE VICTIM, OTHER THAN THE CAUSE OF DEATH WAS "BLOOD LOSS."
ALSO, FATHER MAILER HIMSELF WAS A VICTIM OF THIS LATEST INCIDENT.
THE CONCLUSION IS THAT SOMEONE IS TRYING TO FRAME THE CHURCH.
NO WONDER THE INVESTI-GATION WAS SO SOFT.

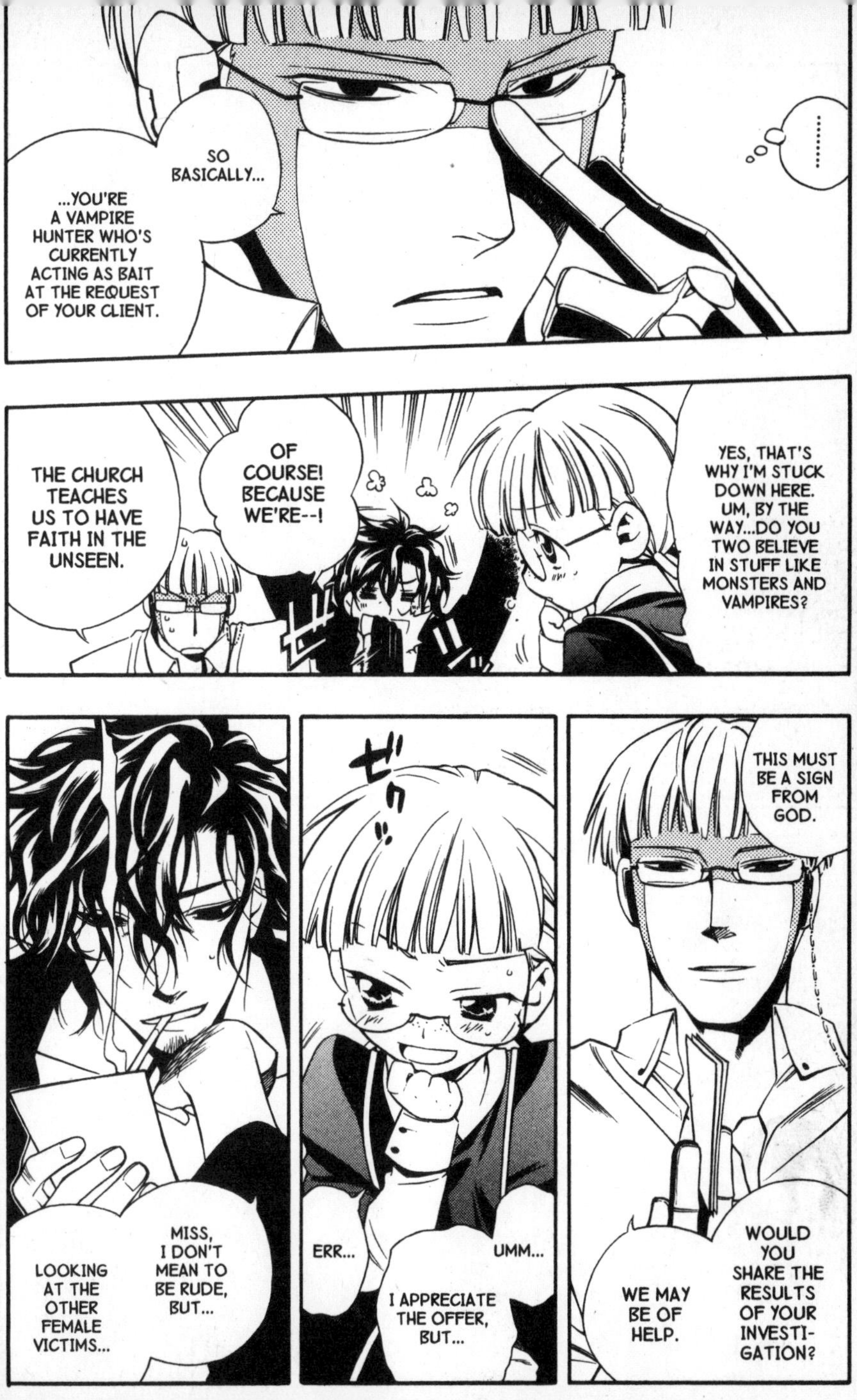

......
SO BASICALLY...
...YOU'RE A VAMPIRE HUNTER WHO'S CURRENTLY ACTING AS BAIT AT THE REQUEST OF YOUR CLIENT.
YES, THAT'S WHY I'M STUCK DOWN HERE. UM, BY THE WAY...DO YOU TWO BELIEVE IN STUFF LIKE MONSTERS AND VAMPIRES?
OF COURSE! BECAUSE WE'RE--!
THE CHURCH TEACHES US TO HAVE FAITH IN THE UNSEEN.
THIS MUST BE A SIGN FROM GOD.
WOULD YOU SHARE THE RESULTS OF YOUR INVESTI-GATION?
WE MAY BE OF HELP.
UMM...
ERR...
I APPRECIATE THE OFFER, BUT...
MISS, I DON'T MEAN TO BE RUDE, BUT...
LOOKING AT THE OTHER FEMALE VICTIMS...

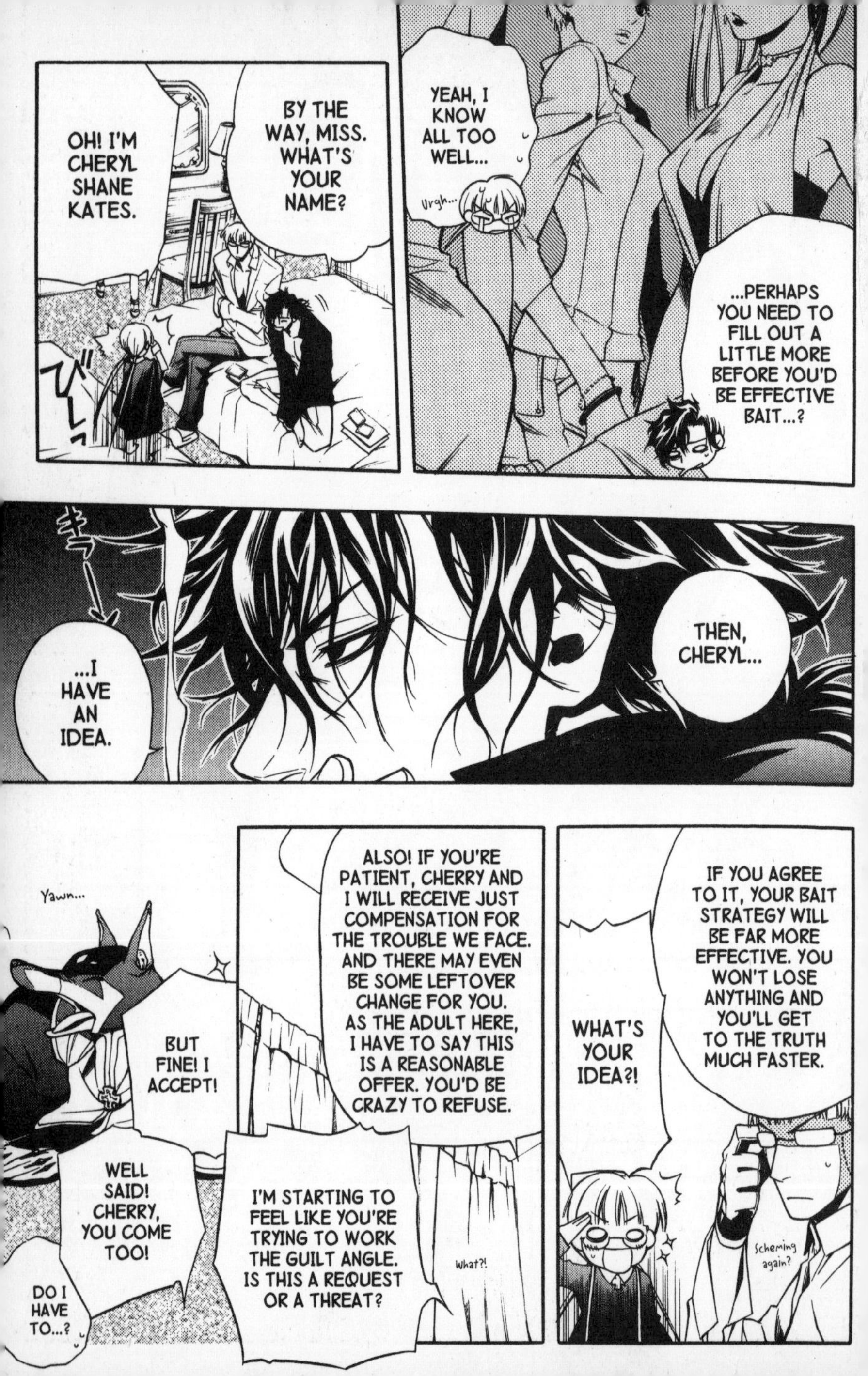
YEAH, I KNOW ALL TOO WELL...
Urgh...
...PERHAPS YOU NEED TO FILL OUT A LITTLE MORE BEFORE YOU'D BE EFFECTIVE BAIT...?
BY THE WAY, MISS. WHAT'S YOUR NAME?
OH! I'M CHERYL SHANE KATES.
THEN, CHERYL...
...I HAVE AN IDEA.
IF YOU AGREE TO IT, YOUR BAIT STRATEGY WILL BE FAR MORE EFFECTIVE. YOU WON'T LOSE ANYTHING AND YOU'LL GET TO THE TRUTH MUCH FASTER.
WHAT'S YOUR IDEA?!
Scheming again?
ALSO! IF YOU'RE PATIENT, CHERRY AND I WILL RECEIVE JUST COMPENSATION FOR THE TROUBLE WE FACE. AND THERE MAY EVEN BE SOME LEFTOVER CHANGE FOR YOU. AS THE ADULT HERE, I HAVE TO SAY THIS IS A REASONABLE OFFER. YOU'D BE CRAZY TO REFUSE.
I'M STARTING TO FEEL LIKE YOU'RE TRYING TO WORK THE GUILT ANGLE. IS THIS A REQUEST OR A THREAT?
What?!
BUT FINE! I ACCEPT!
Yawn...
WELL SAID! CHERRY, YOU COME TOO!
DO I HAVE TO...?

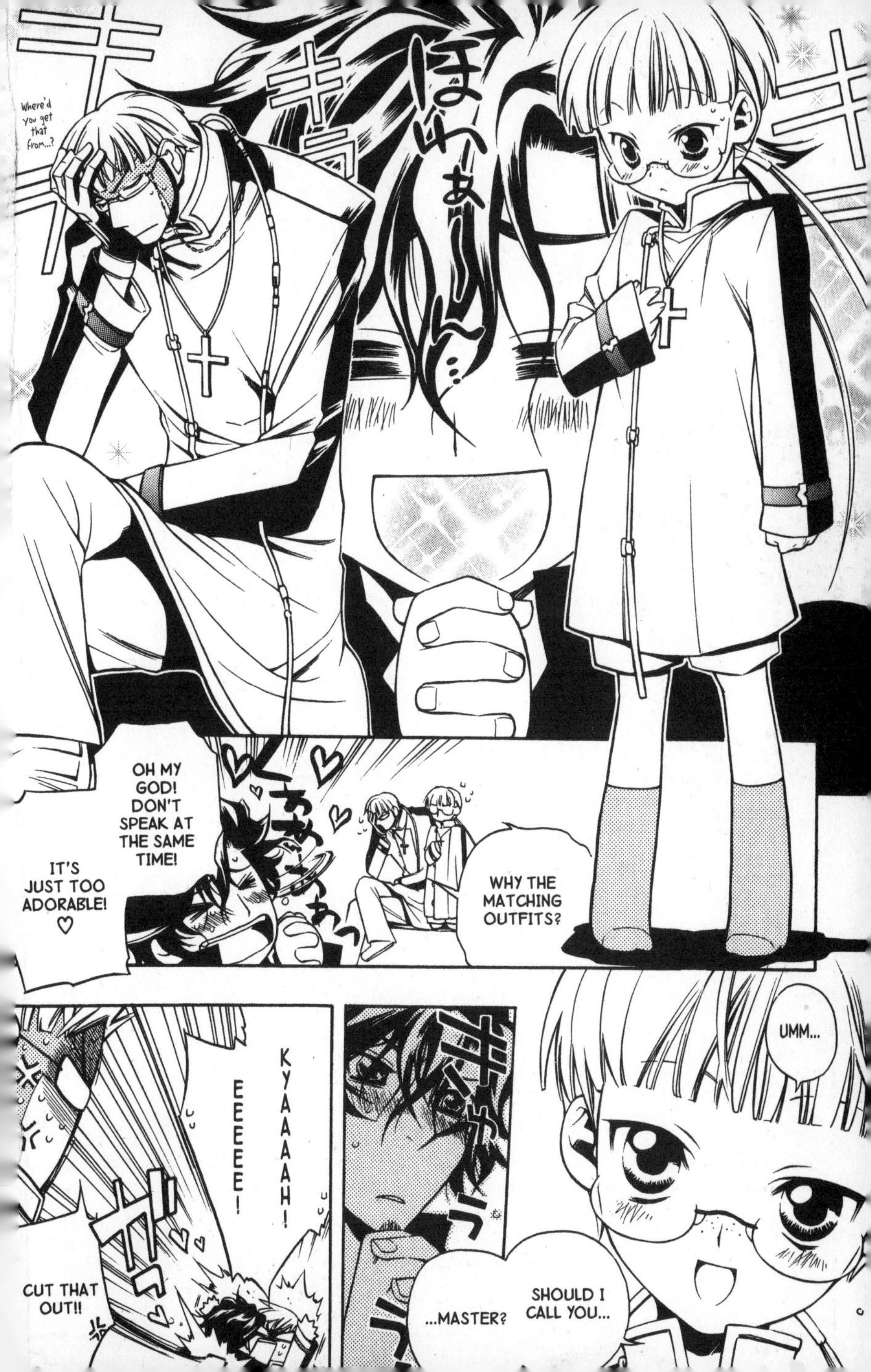
Where'd you get that from...?
WHY THE MATCHING OUTFITS?
OH MY GOD! DON'T SPEAK AT THE SAME TIME!
IT'S JUST TOO ADORABLE! ♡
UMM...
SHOULD I CALL YOU...
...MASTER?
KYAAAAAH!
EEEEEE!
CUT THAT OUT!!

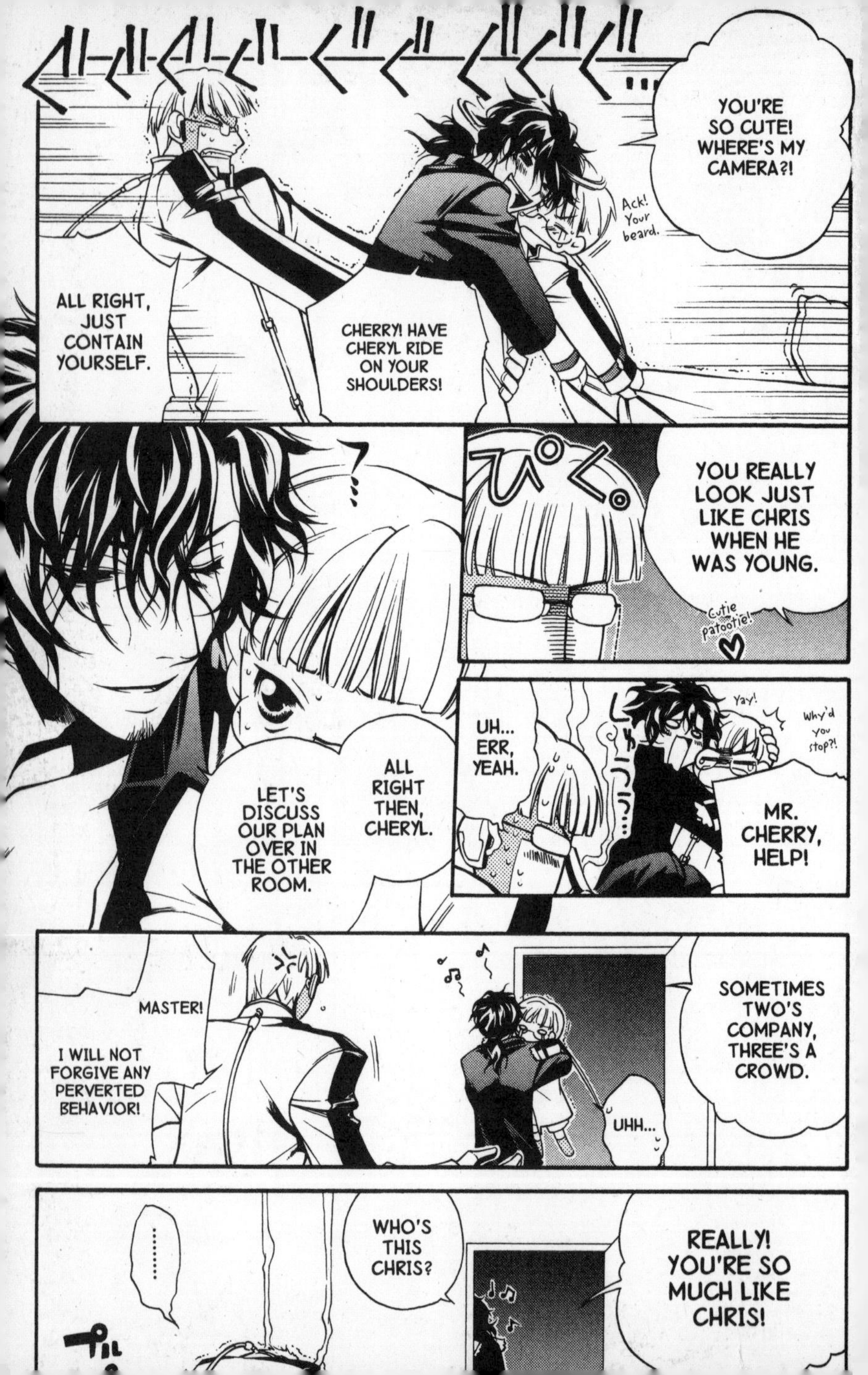
YOU'RE SO CUTE! WHERE'S MY CAMERA?!
Ack! Your beard.
CHERRY! HAVE CHERYL RIDE ON YOUR SHOULDERS!
ALL RIGHT, JUST CONTAIN YOURSELF.
YOU REALLY LOOK JUST LIKE CHRIS WHEN HE WAS YOUNG.
Cutie patootie!
Yay!
Why'd you stop?!
MR. CHERRY, HELP!
UH... ERR, YEAH.
ALL RIGHT THEN, CHERYL.
LET'S DISCUSS OUR PLAN OVER IN THE OTHER ROOM.
SOMETIMES TWO'S COMPANY, THREE'S A CROWD.
UHH...
MASTER!
I WILL NOT FORGIVE ANY PERVERTED BEHAVIOR!
REALLY! YOU'RE SO MUCH LIKE CHRIS!
WHO'S THIS CHRIS?
....

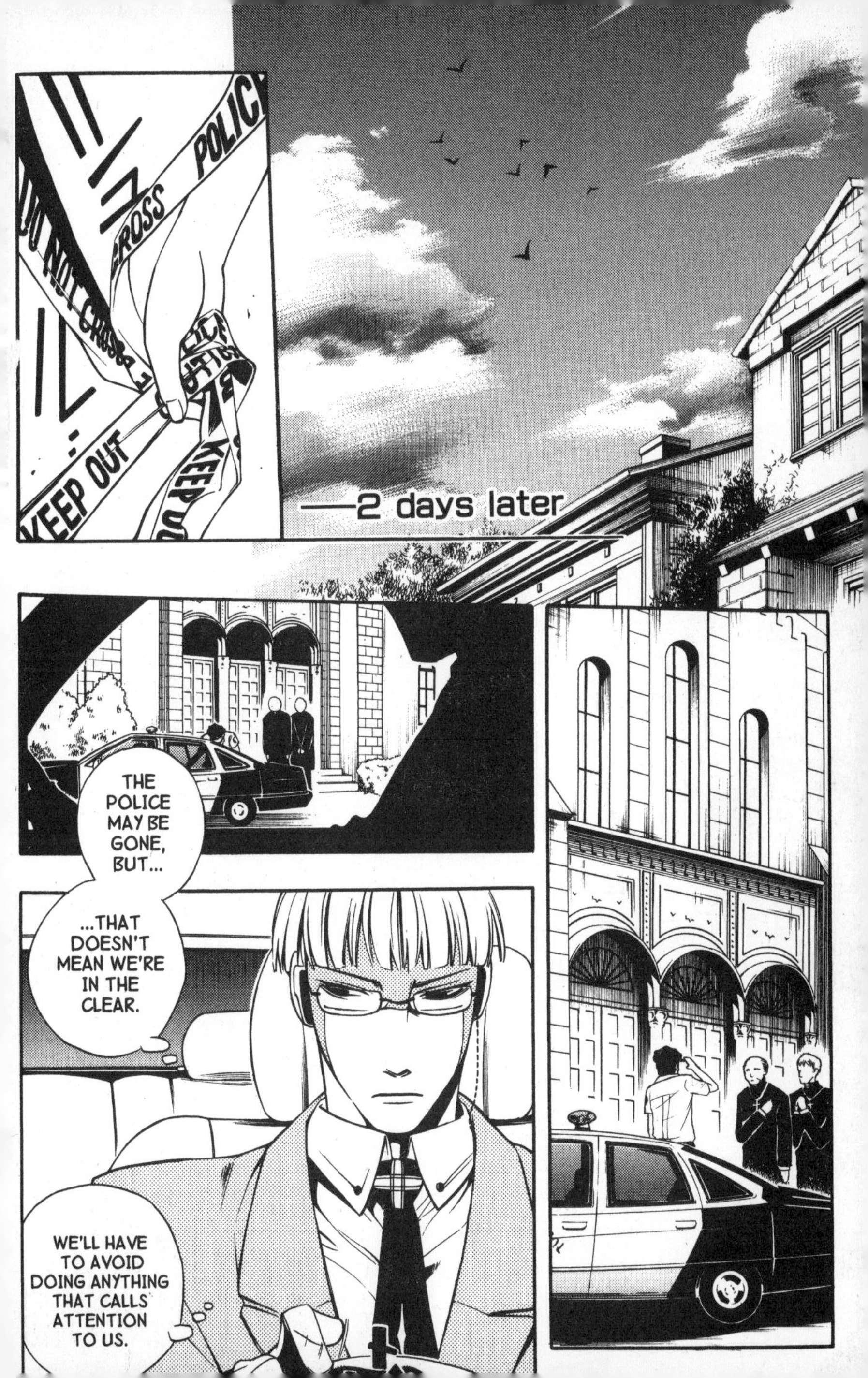
—2 days later
POLICE
DO NOT CROSS
KEEP OUT
THE POLICE MAY BE GONE, BUT...
...THAT DOESN'T MEAN WE'RE IN THE CLEAR.
WE'LL HAVE TO AVOID DOING ANYTHING THAT CALLS ATTENTION TO US.

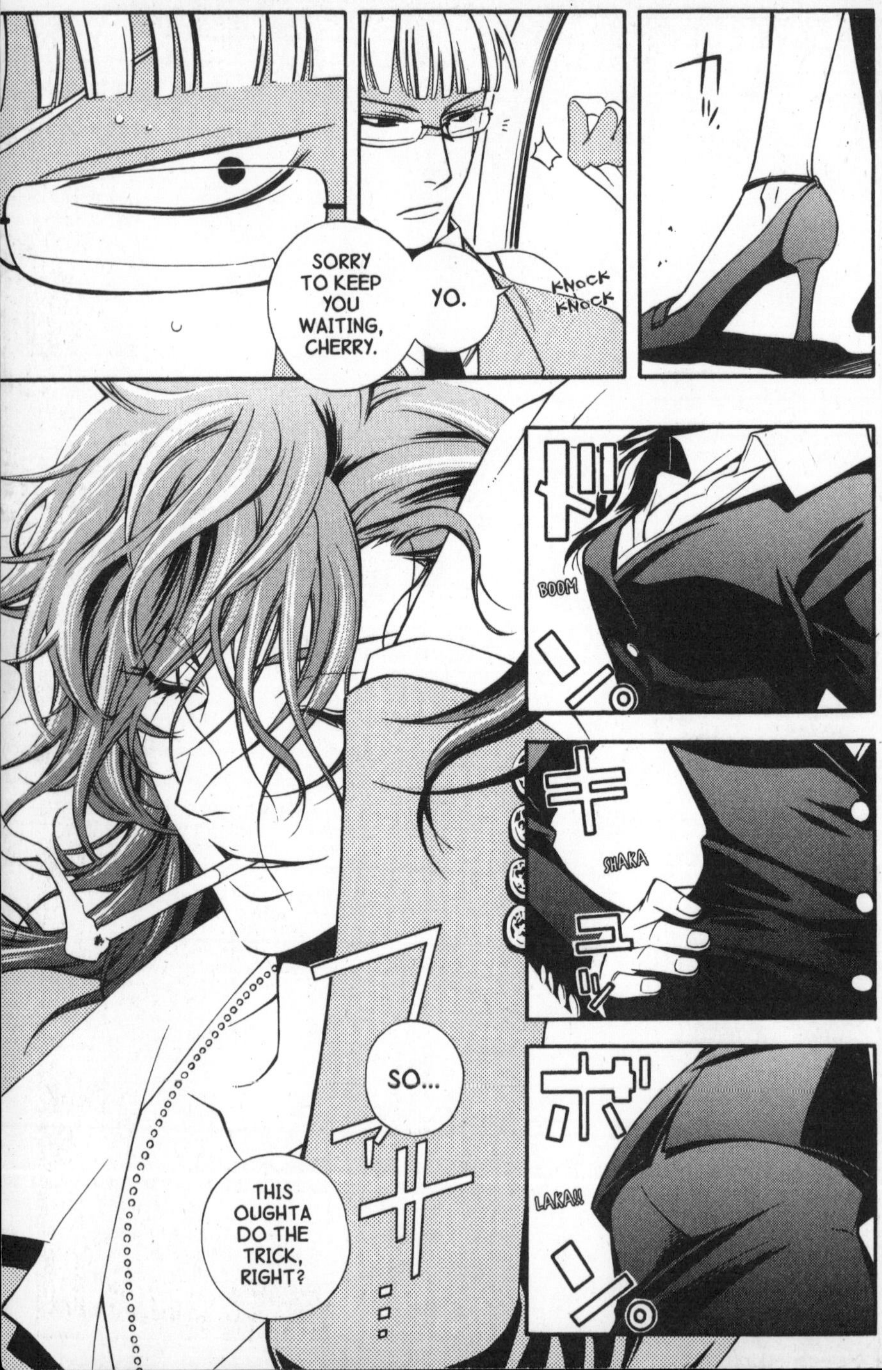
KNOCK KNOCK
YO.
SORRY TO KEEP YOU WAITING, CHERRY.
BOOM
SHAKA
LAKA!!
SO...
THIS OUGHTA DO THE TRICK, RIGHT?

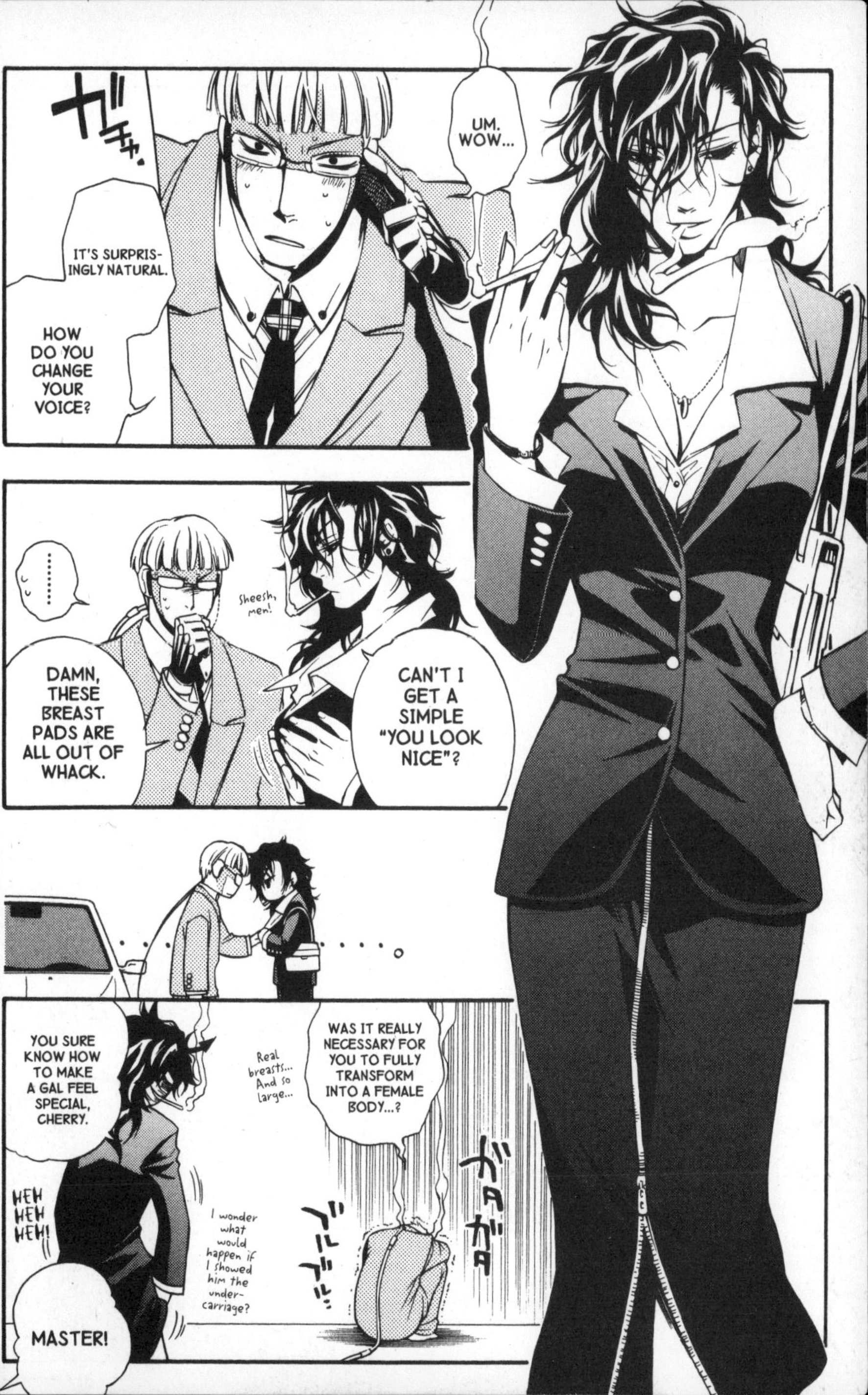
UM. WOW...
ガチャ
IT'S SURPRIS-INGLY NATURAL.
HOW DO YOU CHANGE YOUR VOICE?
CAN'T I GET A SIMPLE "YOU LOOK NICE"?
Sheesh, men!
....
DAMN, THESE BREAST PADS ARE ALL OUT OF WHACK.
....
ガタガタ
WAS IT REALLY NECESSARY FOR YOU TO FULLY TRANSFORM INTO A FEMALE BODY...?
Real breasts... And so large...
ブルブル
I wonder what would happen if I showed him the under-carriage?
YOU SURE KNOW HOW TO MAKE A GAL FEEL SPECIAL, CHERRY.
HEH HEH HEH!
MASTER!

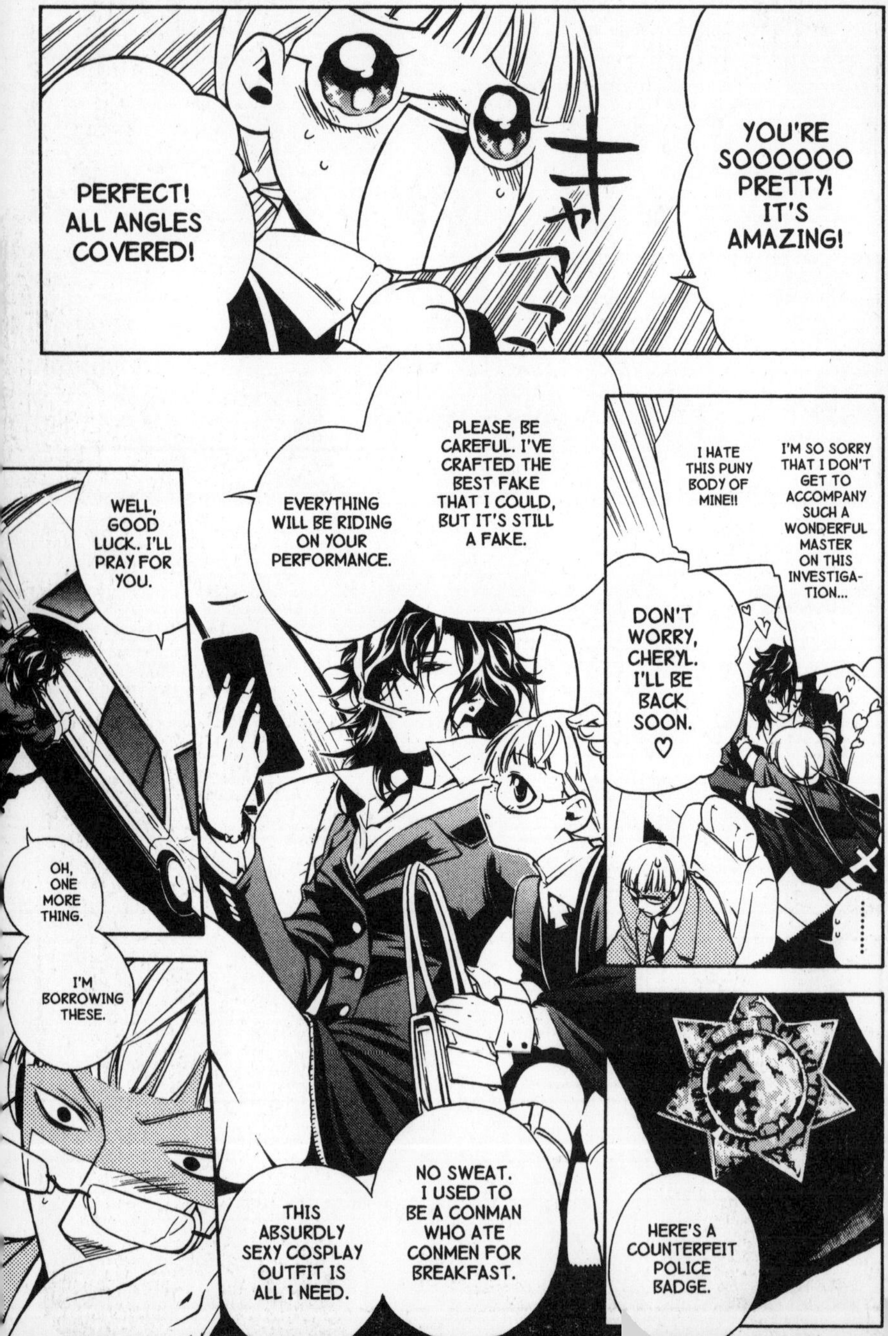
YOU'RE SOOOOOO PRETTY! IT'S AMAZING!
PERFECT! ALL ANGLES COVERED!
I'M SO SORRY THAT I DON'T GET TO ACCOMPANY SUCH A WONDERFUL MASTER ON THIS INVESTIGA-TION...
I HATE THIS PUNY BODY OF MINE!!
DON'T WORRY, CHERYL. I'LL BE BACK SOON. ♡
....
HERE'S A COUNTERFEIT POLICE BADGE.
PLEASE, BE CAREFUL. I'VE CRAFTED THE BEST FAKE THAT I COULD, BUT IT'S STILL A FAKE.
EVERYTHING WILL BE RIDING ON YOUR PERFORMANCE.
NO SWEAT. I USED TO BE A CONMAN WHO ATE CONMEN FOR BREAKFAST.
THIS ABSURDLY SEXY COSPLAY OUTFIT IS ALL I NEED.
WELL, GOOD LUCK. I'LL PRAY FOR YOU.
OH, ONE MORE THING.
I'M BORROWING THESE.

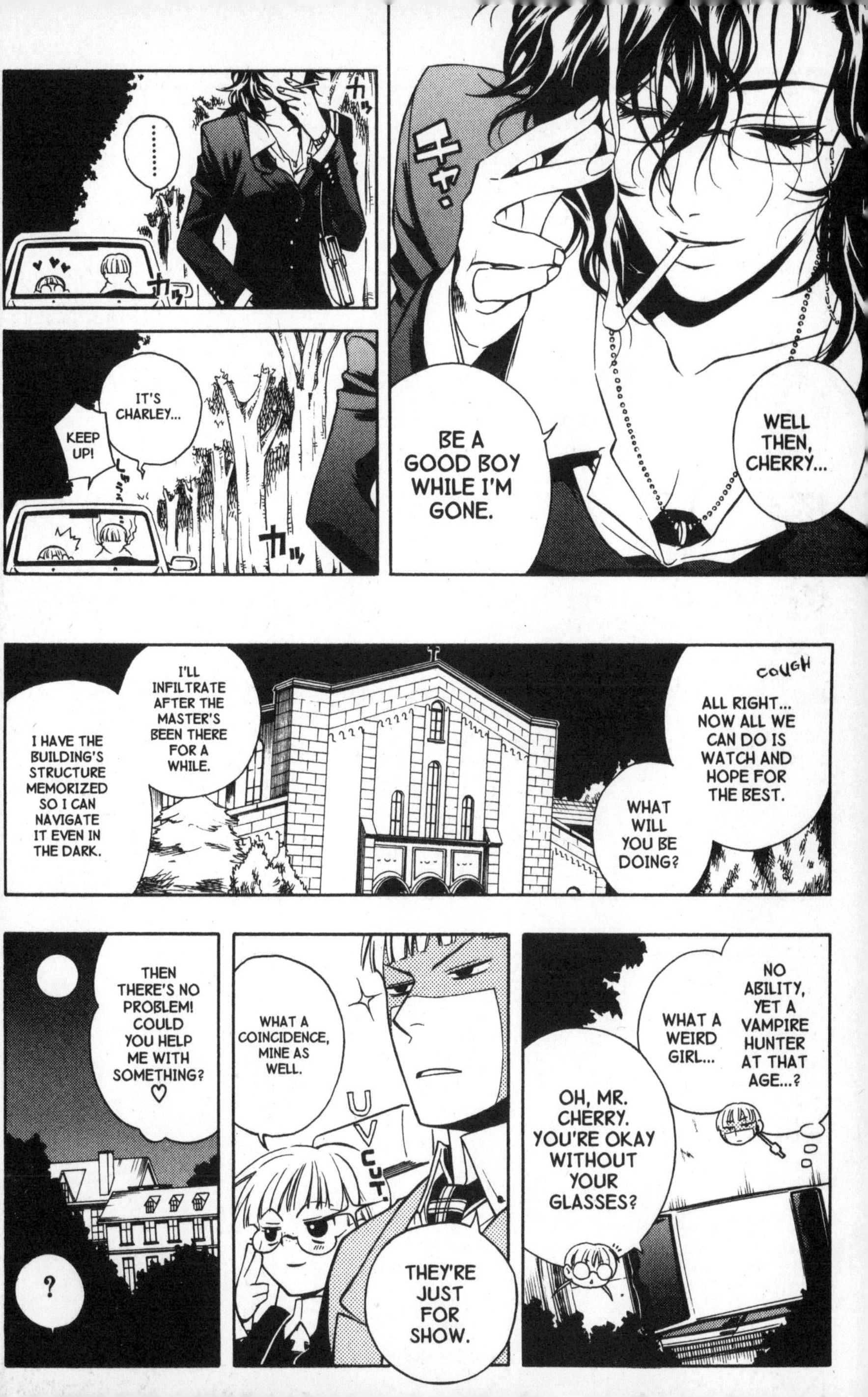
WELL THEN, CHERRY...
BE A GOOD BOY WHILE I'M GONE.
......
IT'S CHARLEY...
KEEP UP!
COUGH
ALL RIGHT... NOW ALL WE CAN DO IS WATCH AND HOPE FOR THE BEST.
WHAT WILL YOU BE DOING?
I'LL INFILTRATE AFTER THE MASTER'S BEEN THERE FOR A WHILE.
I HAVE THE BUILDING'S STRUCTURE MEMORIZED SO I CAN NAVIGATE IT EVEN IN THE DARK.
NO ABILITY, YET A VAMPIRE HUNTER AT THAT AGE...?
WHAT A WEIRD GIRL...
OH, MR. CHERRY. YOU'RE OKAY WITHOUT YOUR GLASSES?
THEY'RE JUST FOR SHOW.
UV CUT
WHAT A COINCIDENCE, MINE AS WELL.
THEN THERE'S NO PROBLEM! COULD YOU HELP ME WITH SOMETHING? ♡
?

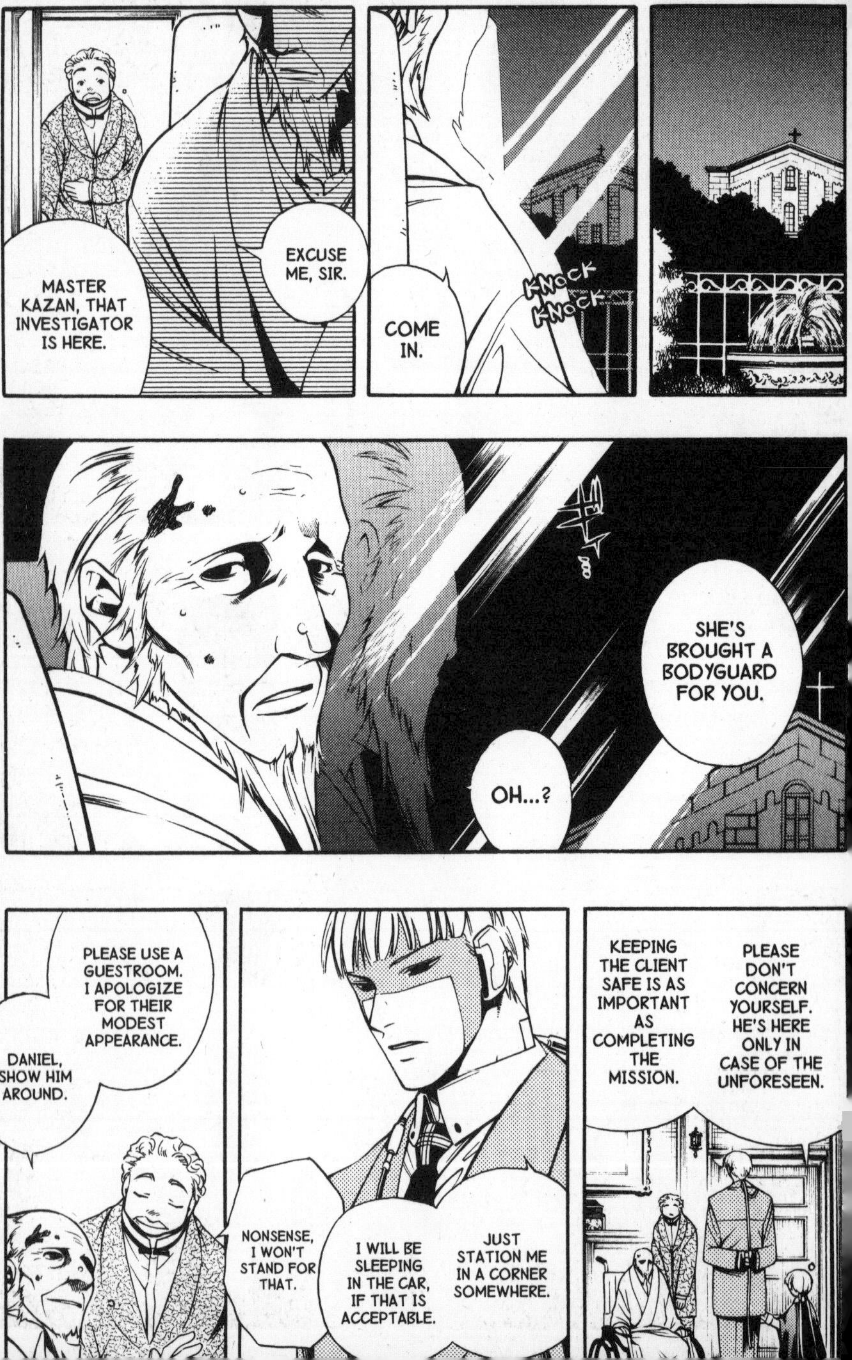
KNOCK KNOCK
COME IN.
EXCUSE ME, SIR.
MASTER KAZAN, THAT INVESTIGATOR IS HERE.
SHE'S BROUGHT A BODYGUARD FOR YOU.
OH...?
PLEASE DON'T CONCERN YOURSELF. HE'S HERE ONLY IN CASE OF THE UNFORESEEN.
KEEPING THE CLIENT SAFE IS AS IMPORTANT AS COMPLETING THE MISSION.
JUST STATION ME IN A CORNER SOMEWHERE.
I WILL BE SLEEPING IN THE CAR, IF THAT IS ACCEPTABLE.
NONSENSE, I WON'T STAND FOR THAT.
PLEASE USE A GUESTROOM. I APOLOGIZE FOR THEIR MODEST APPEARANCE.
DANIEL, SHOW HIM AROUND.

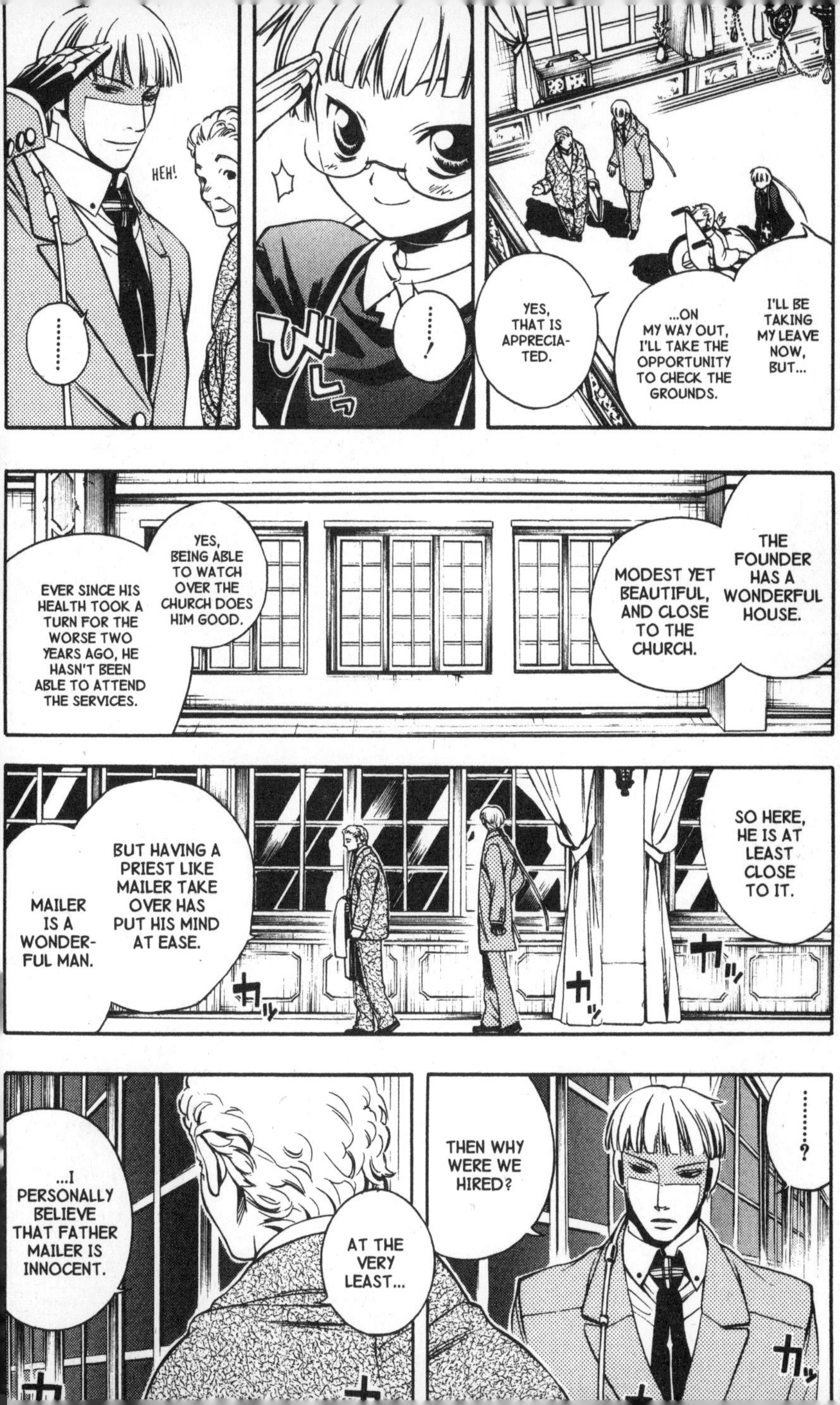
I'LL BE TAKING MY LEAVE NOW, BUT...
...ON MY WAY OUT, I'LL TAKE THE OPPORTUNITY TO CHECK THE GROUNDS.
YES, THAT IS APPRECIA-TED.
......!
HEH!
......
THE FOUNDER HAS A WONDERFUL HOUSE.
MODEST YET BEAUTIFUL, AND CLOSE TO THE CHURCH.
YES, BEING ABLE TO WATCH OVER THE CHURCH DOES HIM GOOD.
EVER SINCE HIS HEALTH TOOK A TURN FOR THE WORSE TWO YEARS AGO, HE HASN'T BEEN ABLE TO ATTEND THE SERVICES.
SO HERE, HE IS AT LEAST CLOSE TO IT.
BUT HAVING A PRIEST LIKE MAILER TAKE OVER HAS PUT HIS MIND AT EASE.
MAILER IS A WONDER-FUL MAN.
......?
THEN WHY WERE WE HIRED?
AT THE VERY LEAST...
...I PERSONALLY BELIEVE THAT FATHER MAILER IS INNOCENT.

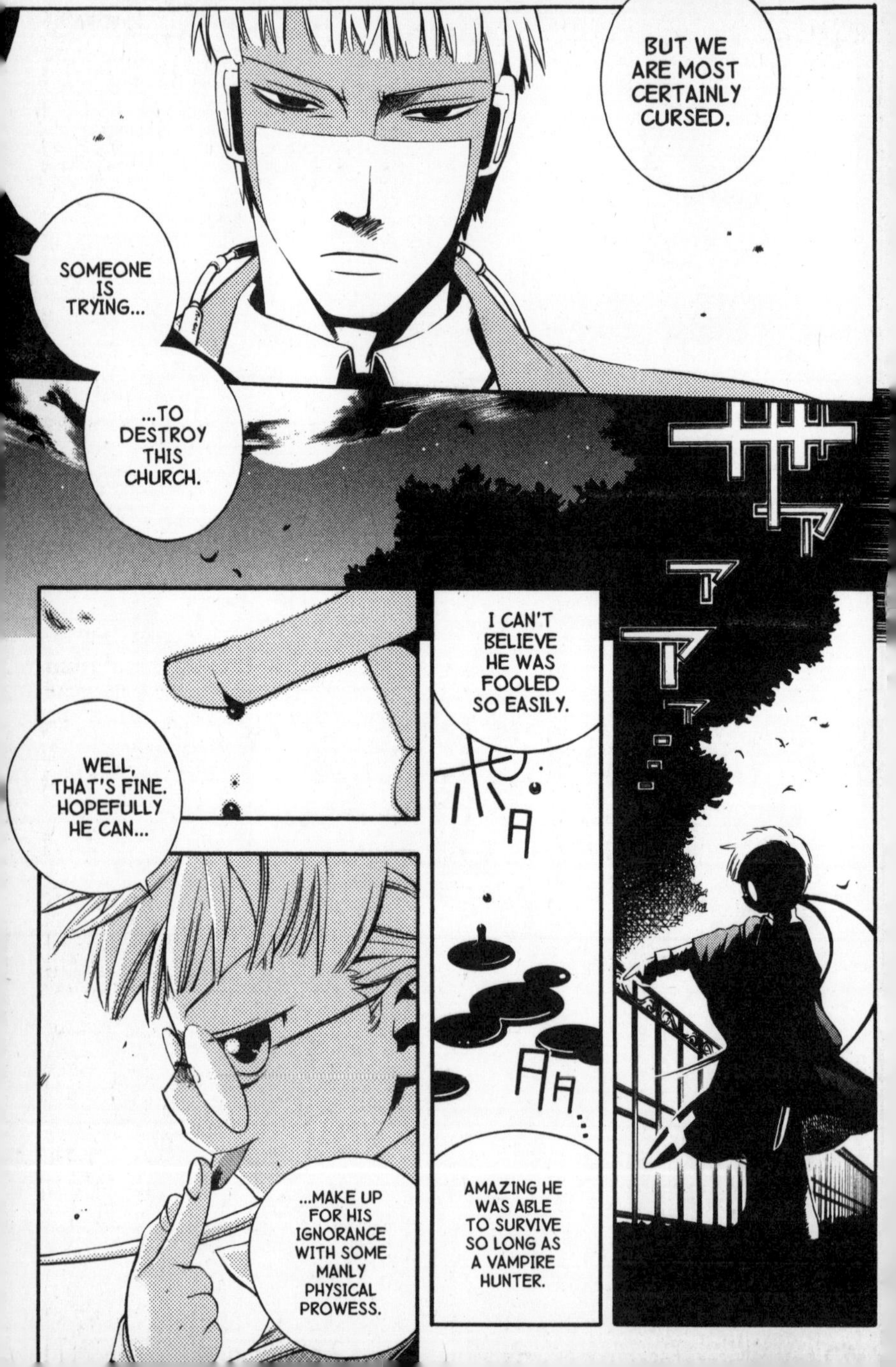
BUT WE ARE MOST CERTAINLY CURSED.
SOMEONE IS TRYING...
...TO DESTROY THIS CHURCH.
I CAN'T BELIEVE HE WAS FOOLED SO EASILY.
AMAZING HE WAS ABLE TO SURVIVE SO LONG AS A VAMPIRE HUNTER.
WELL, THAT'S FINE. HOPEFULLY HE CAN...
...MAKE UP FOR HIS IGNORANCE WITH SOME MANLY PHYSICAL PROWESS.

LET'S SEE WHAT YOU CAN DO...

...MR. CHERRY.

Heh heh heh!

THREE DAYS LATER

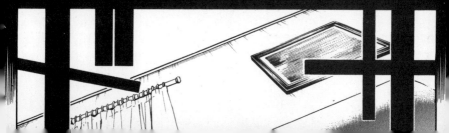

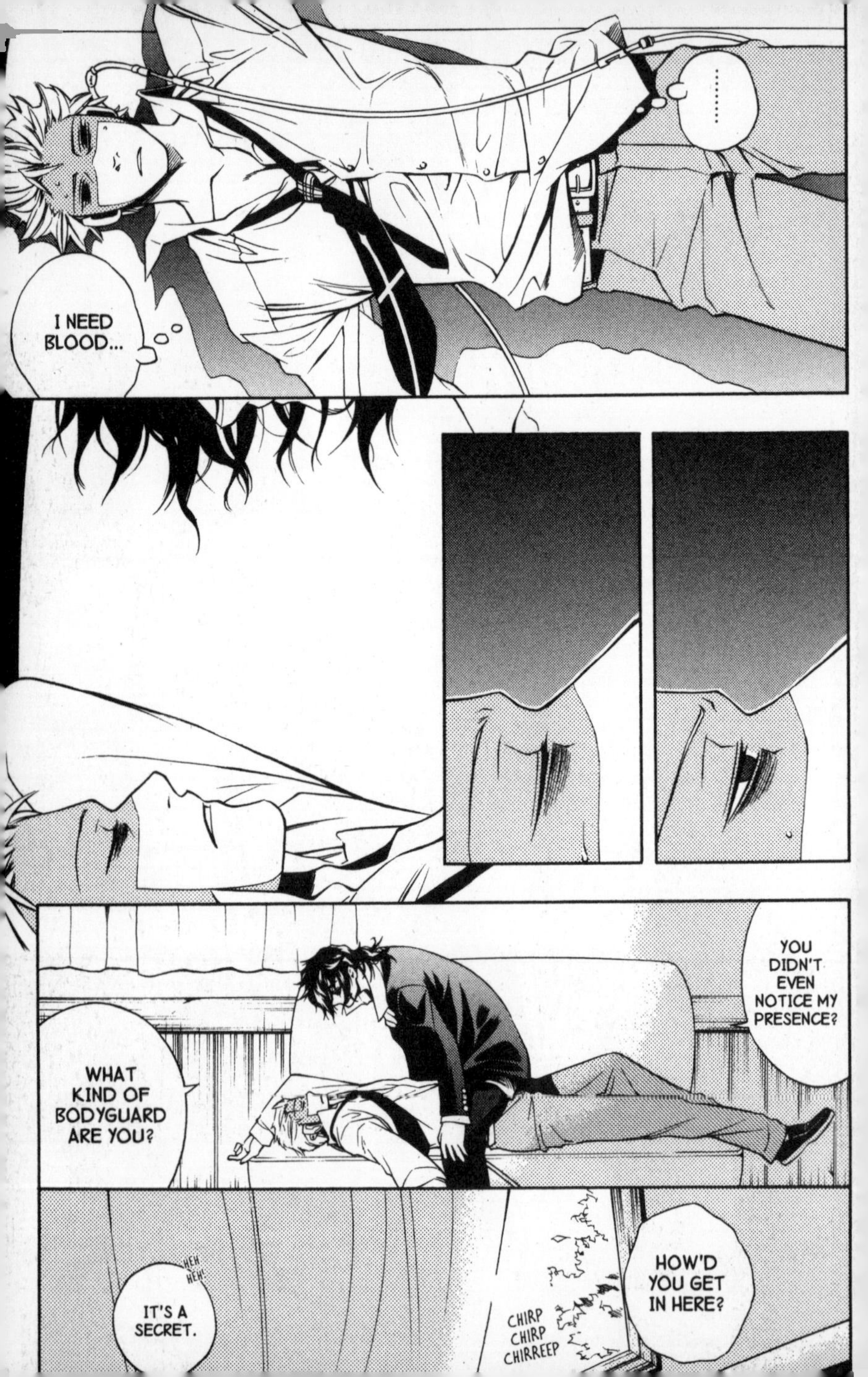
......
I NEED BLOOD...
YOU DIDN'T EVEN NOTICE MY PRESENCE?
WHAT KIND OF BODYGUARD ARE YOU?
HOW'D YOU GET IN HERE?
CHIRP CHIRP CHIRREEP
HEH HEH!
IT'S A SECRET.

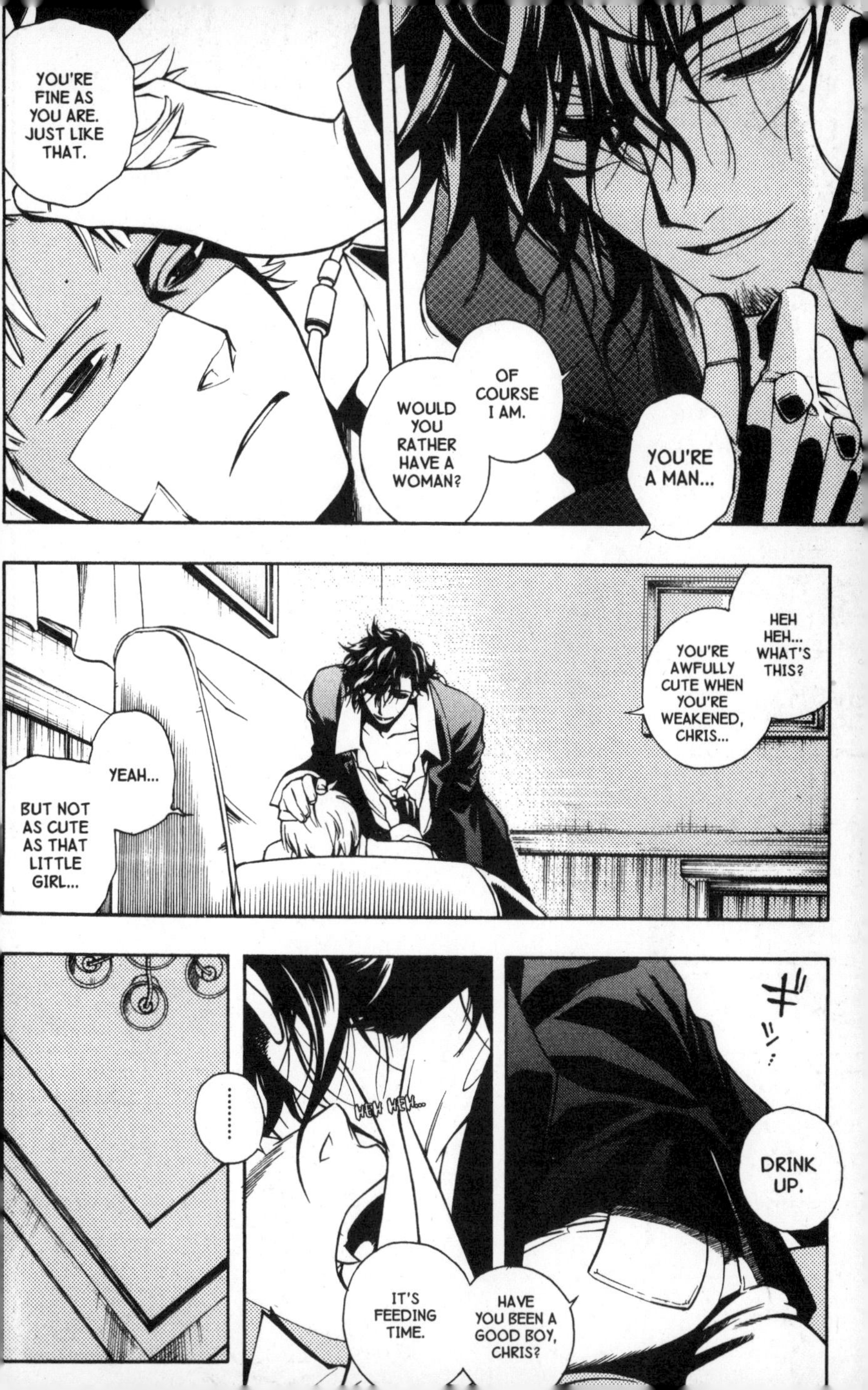
YOU'RE A MAN...
OF COURSE I AM.
WOULD YOU RATHER HAVE A WOMAN?
YOU'RE FINE AS YOU ARE. JUST LIKE THAT.
HEH HEH... WHAT'S THIS?
YOU'RE AWFULLY CUTE WHEN YOU'RE WEAKENED, CHRIS...
YEAH...
BUT NOT AS CUTE AS THAT LITTLE GIRL...
ギッ
DRINK UP.
HEH HEH...
HAVE YOU BEEN A GOOD BOY, CHRIS?
IT'S FEEDING TIME.
......

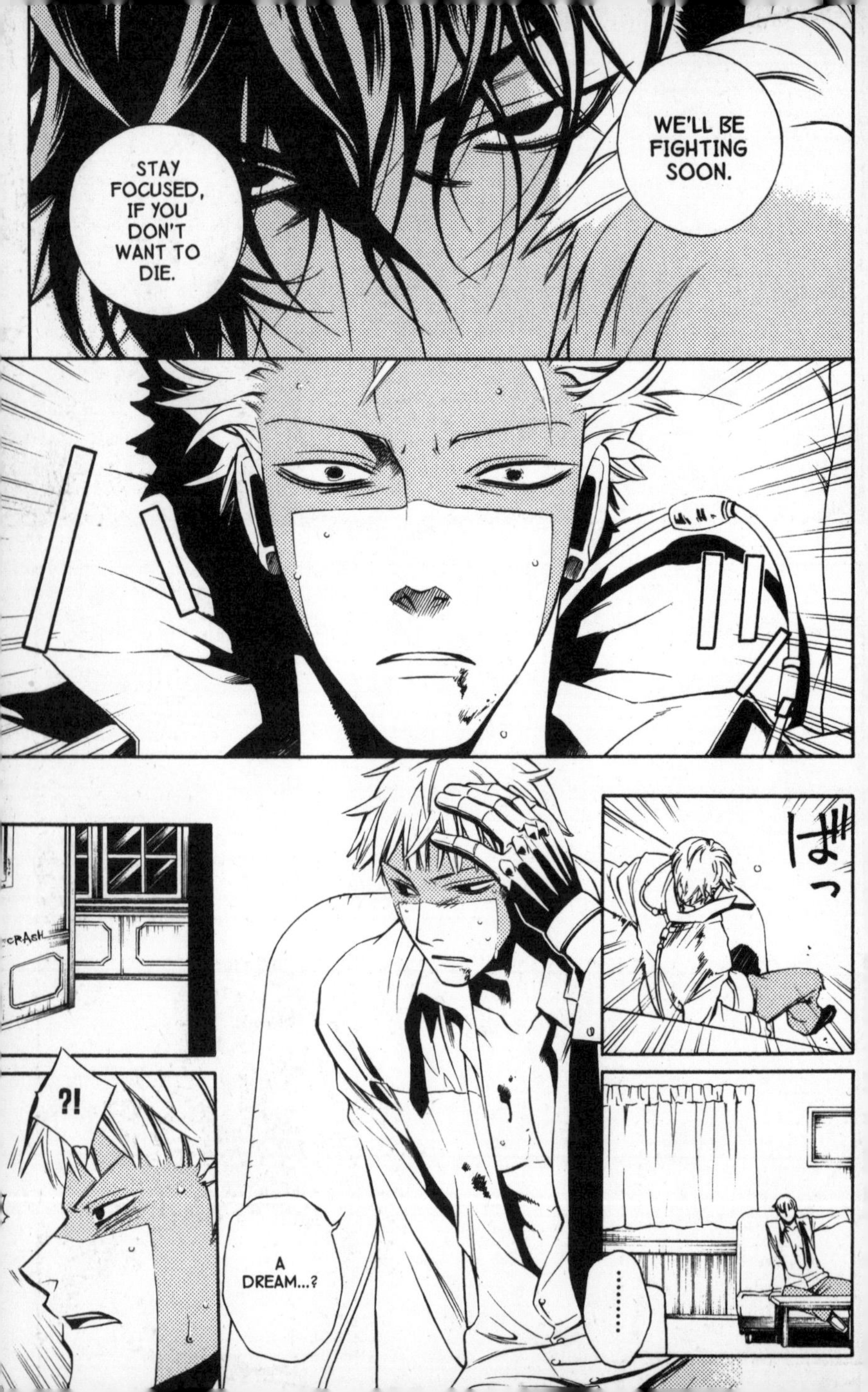
WE'LL BE FIGHTING SOON.
STAY FOCUSED, IF YOU DON'T WANT TO DIE.
ばっ
......
A DREAM...?
CRASH
?!

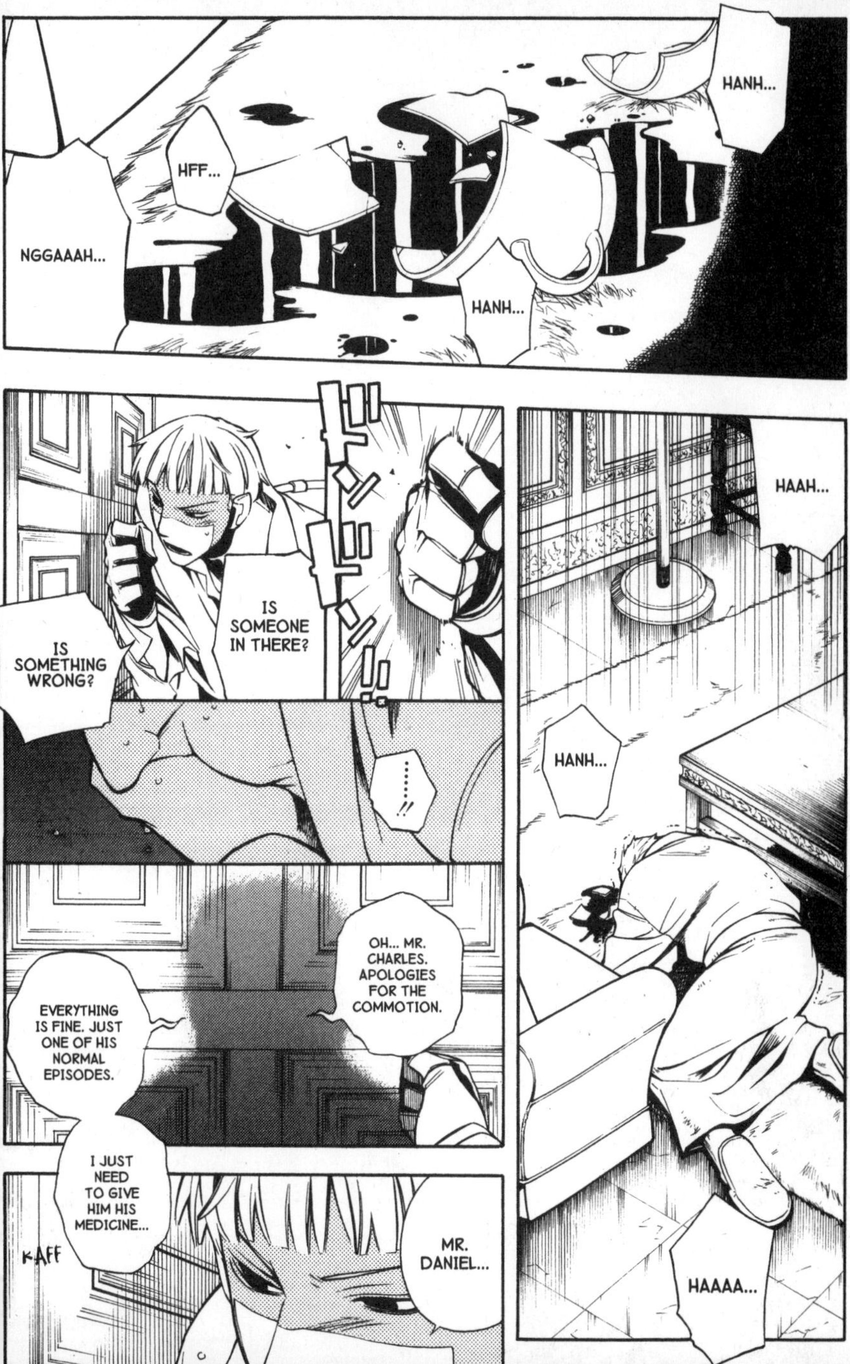
HANH...
HFF...
HANH...
NGGAAAH...
HAAH...
HANH...
HAAAA...
IS SOMEONE IN THERE?
IS SOMETHING WRONG?
......!!
OH... MR. CHARLES. APOLOGIES FOR THE COMMOTION.
EVERYTHING IS FINE. JUST ONE OF HIS NORMAL EPISODES.
I JUST NEED TO GIVE HIM HIS MEDICINE...
MR. DANIEL...
KAFF

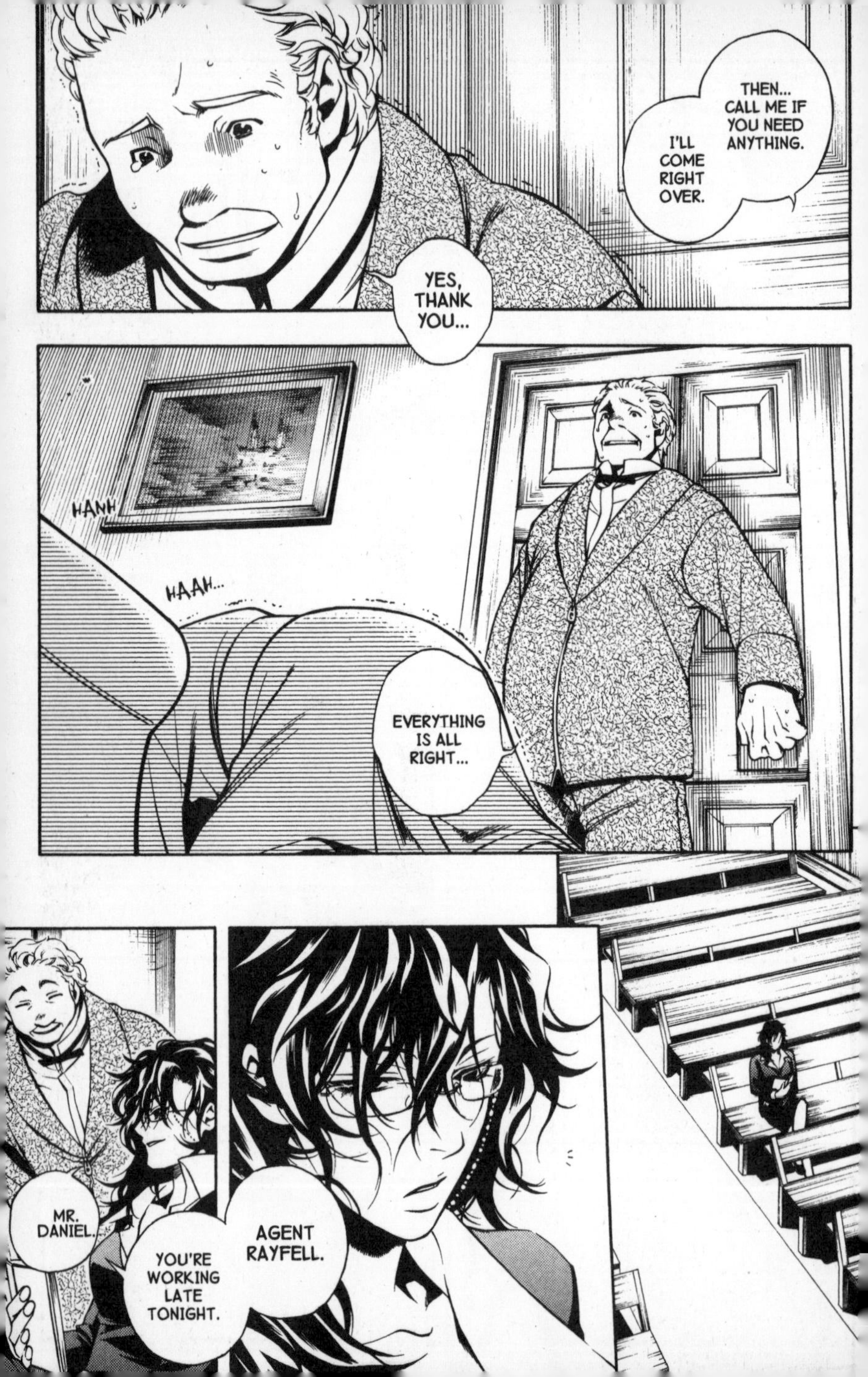
THEN... CALL ME IF YOU NEED ANYTHING.
I'LL COME RIGHT OVER.
YES, THANK YOU...
HANH
HAAH...
EVERYTHING IS ALL RIGHT...
AGENT RAYFELL.
MR. DANIEL.
YOU'RE WORKING LATE TONIGHT.

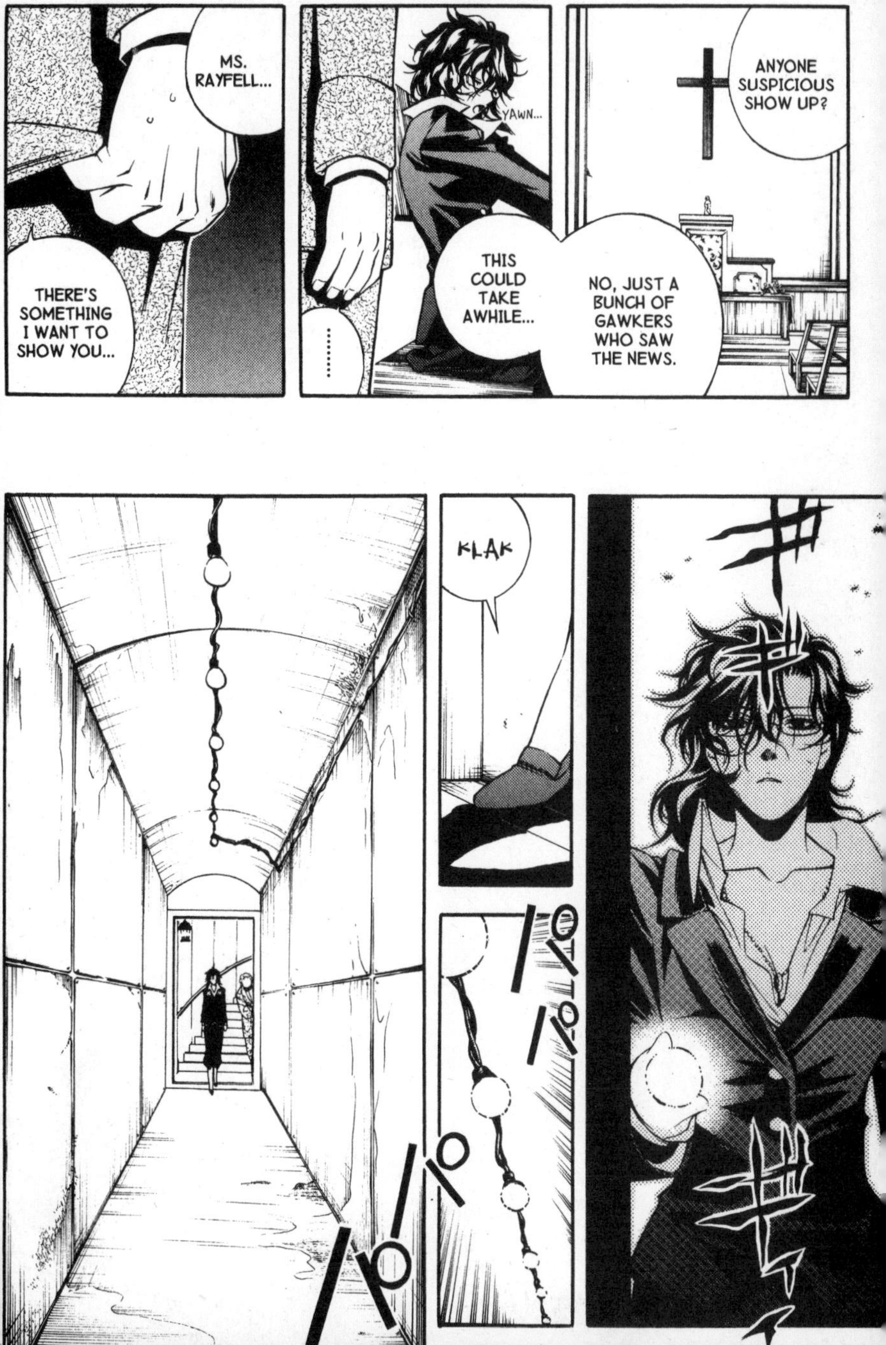
ANYONE SUSPICIOUS SHOW UP?
NO, JUST A BUNCH OF GAWKERS WHO SAW THE NEWS.
YAWN...
THIS COULD TAKE AWHILE...
....
MS. RAYFELL...
THERE'S SOMETHING I WANT TO SHOW YOU...
KLAK

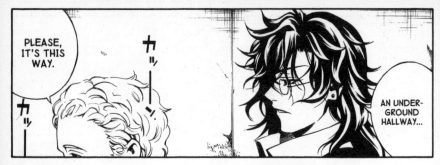

AN UNDER-GROUND HALLWAY...
カッーン
PLEASE, IT'S THIS WAY.
カッ
カッーン
WE'RE NORTH OF THE CHURCH NOW...
カッーン
I'M POSITIVE THIS DIRECTION IS...
DANIEL--
MASTER KAZAN...
HE HAS A STRONG, STRONG SPIRIT.
EVEN WHEN HE'S HAVING AN EPISODE BROUGHT ON BY HIS ILLNESS...
...HE FIGHTS HARD JUST TO RETAIN HIS SANITY.
ALL SO THAT HE DOESN'T HAVE TO TAKE THE MEDICINE...
...OR THAT HE CAN PERHAPS LOWER THE DOSAGE.

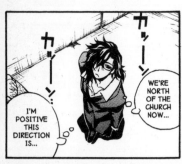

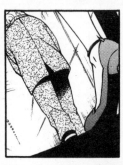

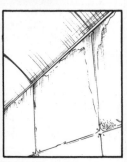

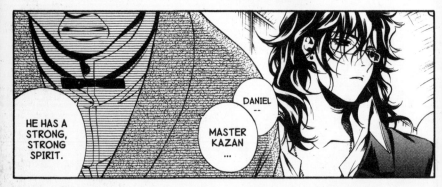

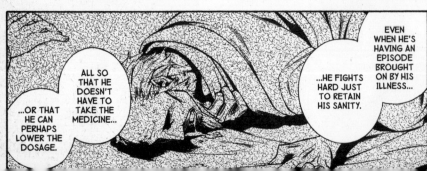

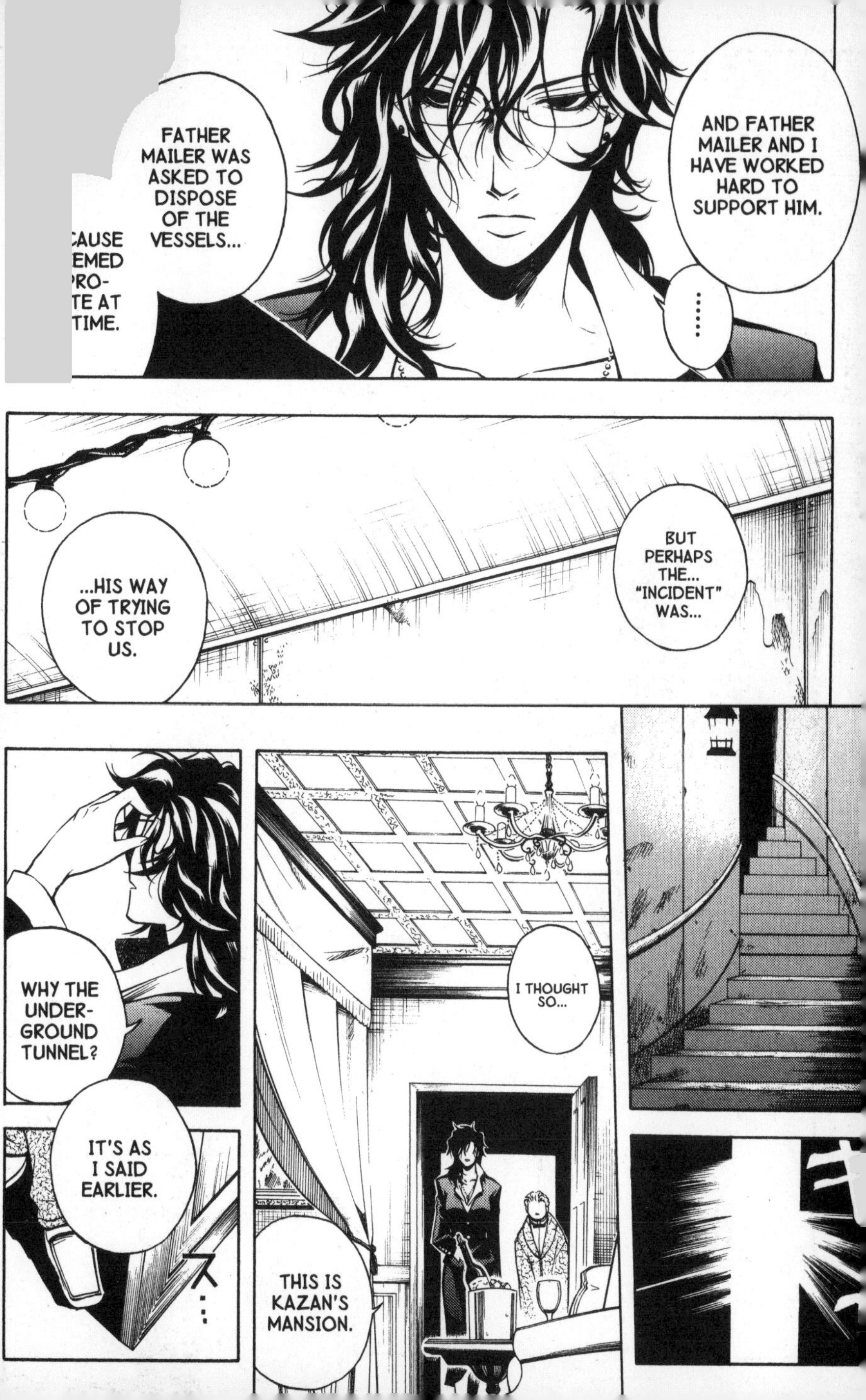
AND FATHER MAILER AND I HAVE WORKED HARD TO SUPPORT HIM.
......
FATHER MAILER WAS ASKED TO DISPOSE OF THE VESSELS...
CAUSE EMED PRO- TE AT TIME.
BUT PERHAPS THE... "INCIDENT" WAS...
...HIS WAY OF TRYING TO STOP US.
キ
I THOUGHT SO...
THIS IS KAZAN'S MANSION.
WHY THE UNDER-GROUND TUNNEL?
IT'S AS I SAID EARLIER.
ス...

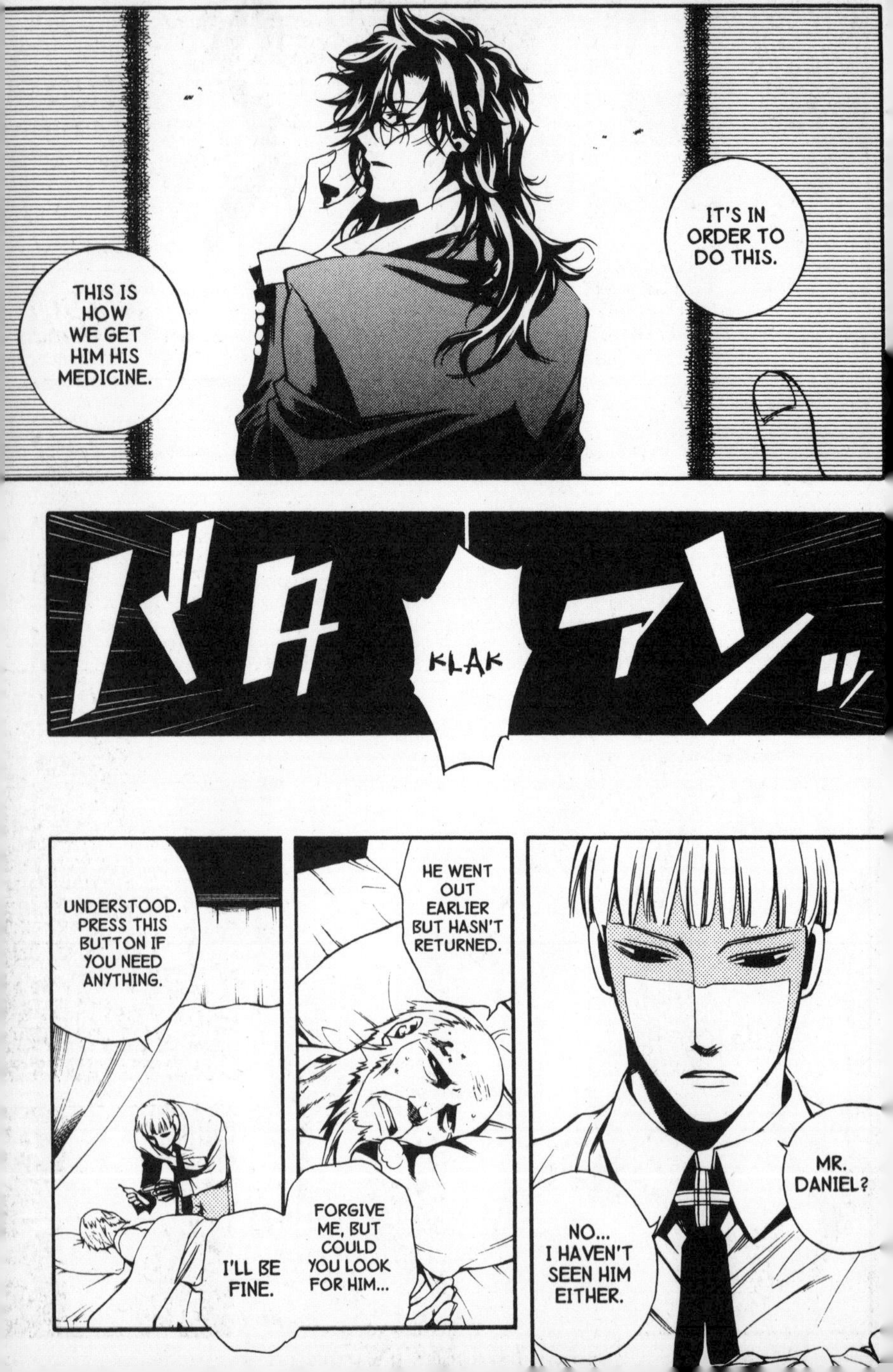
IT'S IN ORDER TO DO THIS.
THIS IS HOW WE GET HIM HIS MEDICINE.
バタアンッ
KLAK
MR. DANIEL?
NO... I HAVEN'T SEEN HIM EITHER.
HE WENT OUT EARLIER BUT HASN'T RETURNED.
FORGIVE ME, BUT COULD YOU LOOK FOR HIM...
UNDERSTOOD. PRESS THIS BUTTON IF YOU NEED ANYTHING.
I'LL BE FINE.

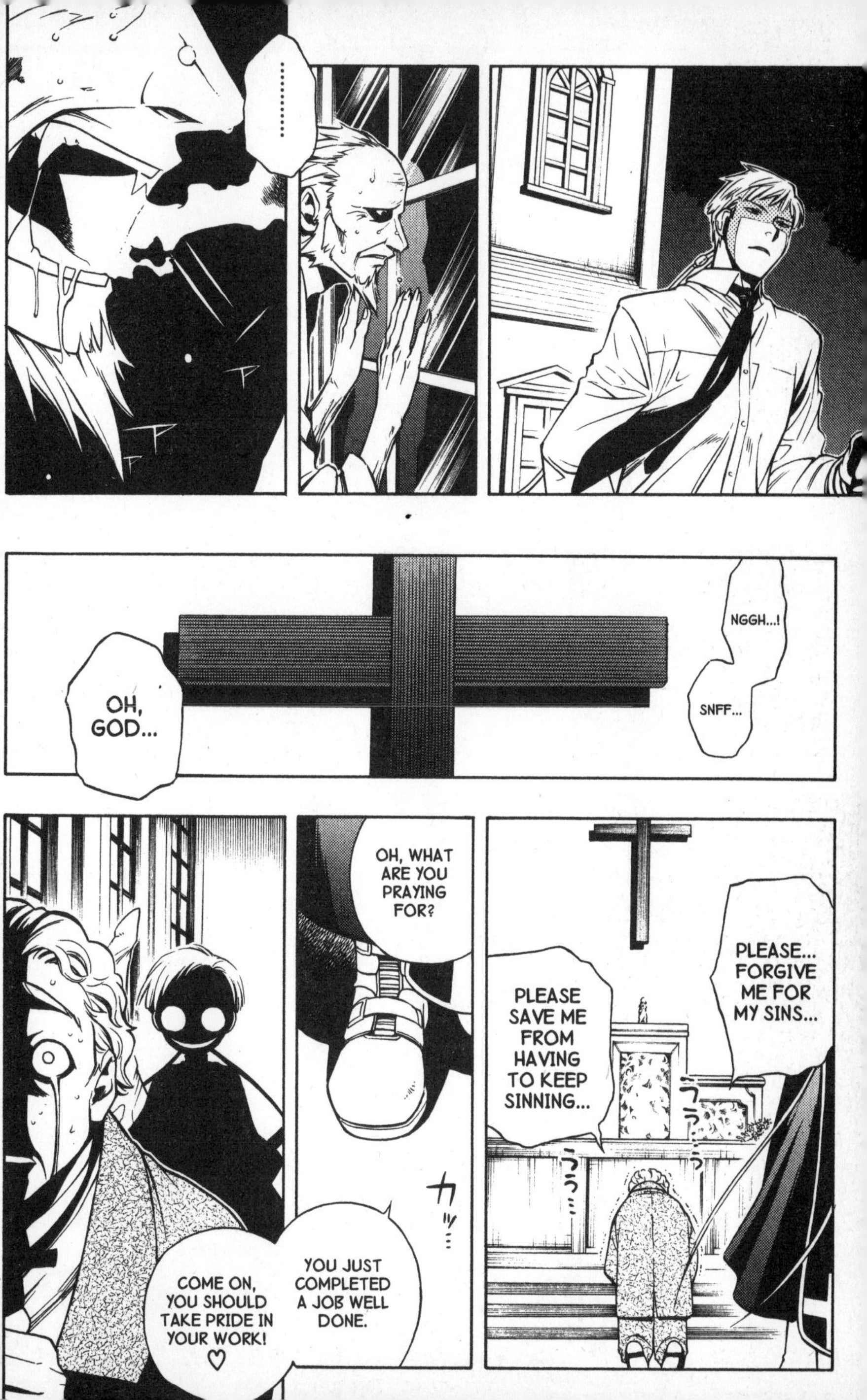
......
NGGH...!
SNFF...
OH, GOD...
PLEASE... FORGIVE ME FOR MY SINS...
PLEASE SAVE ME FROM HAVING TO KEEP SINNING...
OH, WHAT ARE YOU PRAYING FOR?
カッ
YOU JUST COMPLETED A JOB WELL DONE.
COME ON, YOU SHOULD TAKE PRIDE IN YOUR WORK! ♡

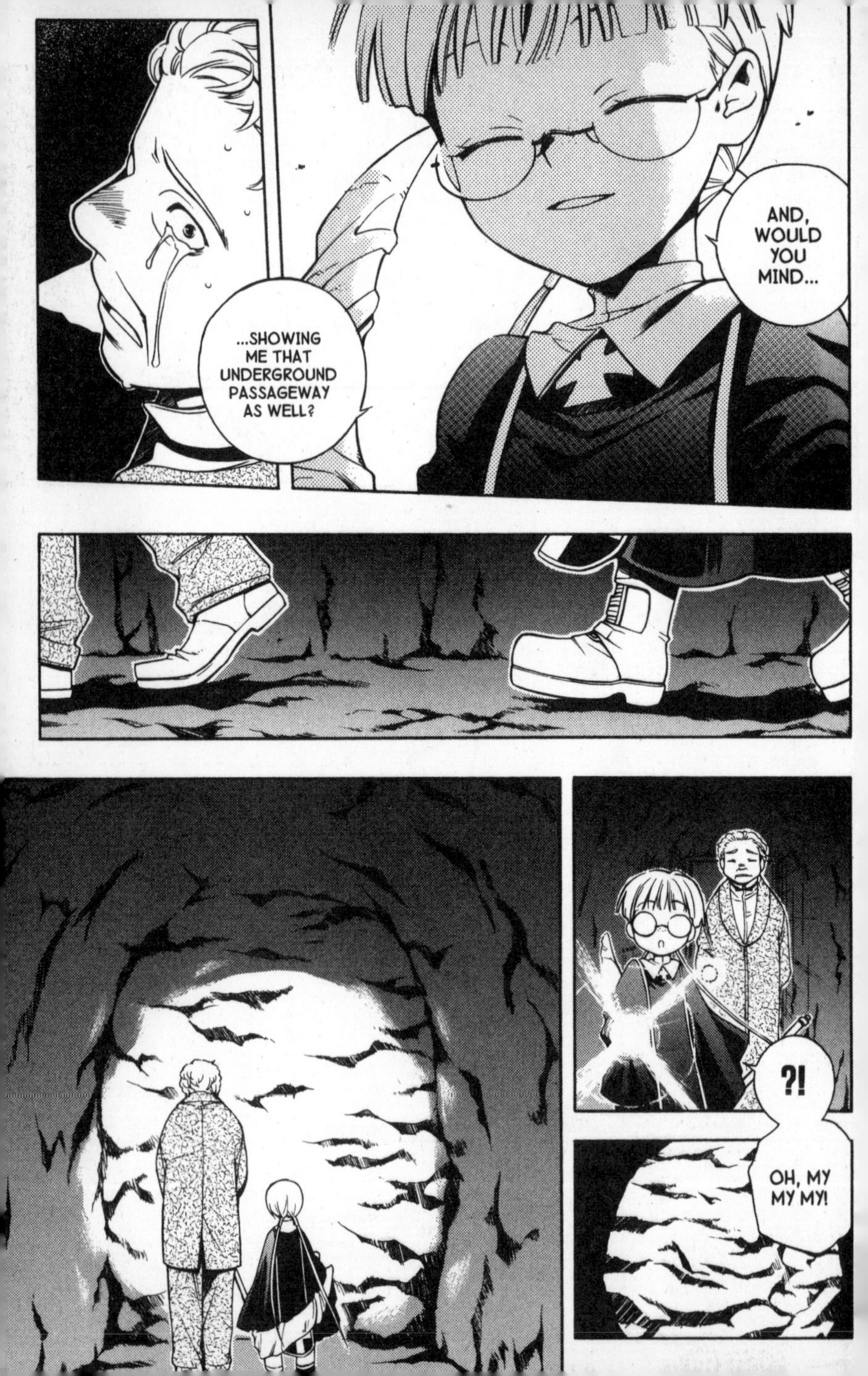
AND, WOULD YOU MIND...
...SHOWING ME THAT UNDERGROUND PASSAGEWAY AS WELL?
?!
OH, MY MY MY!

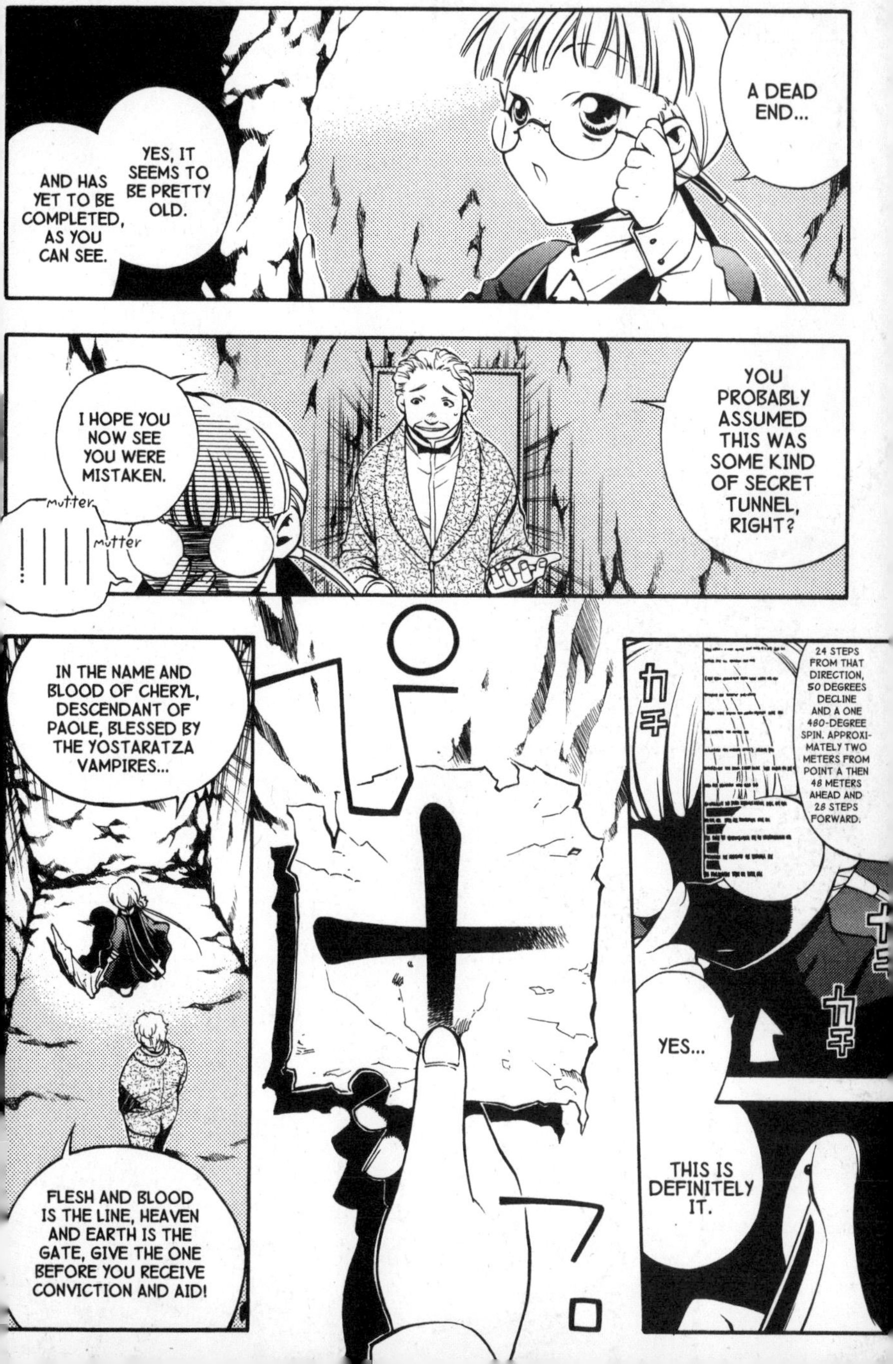
A DEAD END...
YES, IT SEEMS TO BE PRETTY OLD.
AND HAS YET TO BE COMPLETED, AS YOU CAN SEE.
YOU PROBABLY ASSUMED THIS WAS SOME KIND OF SECRET TUNNEL, RIGHT?
I HOPE YOU NOW SEE YOU WERE MISTAKEN.
mutter
mutter
24 STEPS FROM THAT DIRECTION, 50 DEGREES DECLINE AND A ONE 480-DEGREE SPIN. APPROXIMATELY TWO METERS FROM POINT A THEN 48 METERS AHEAD AND 28 STEPS FORWARD.
カチ
カチ
カチ
YES...
THIS IS DEFINITELY IT.
?!
IN THE NAME AND BLOOD OF CHERYL, DESCENDANT OF PAOLE, BLESSED BY THE YOSTARATZA VAMPIRES...
FLESH AND BLOOD IS THE LINE, HEAVEN AND EARTH IS THE GATE, GIVE THE ONE BEFORE YOU RECEIVE CONVICTION AND AID!

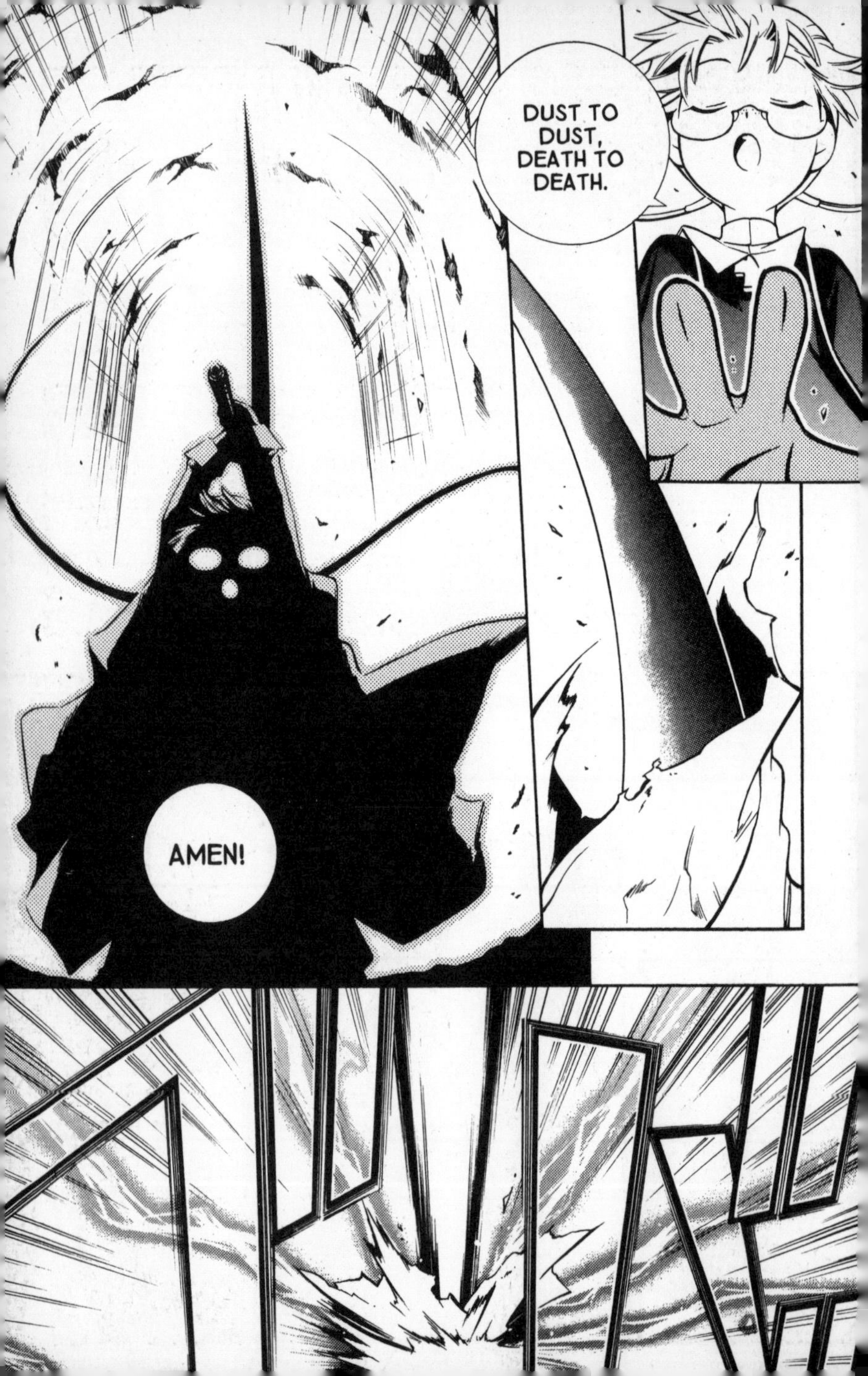
DUST TO DUST, DEATH TO DEATH.
AMEN!

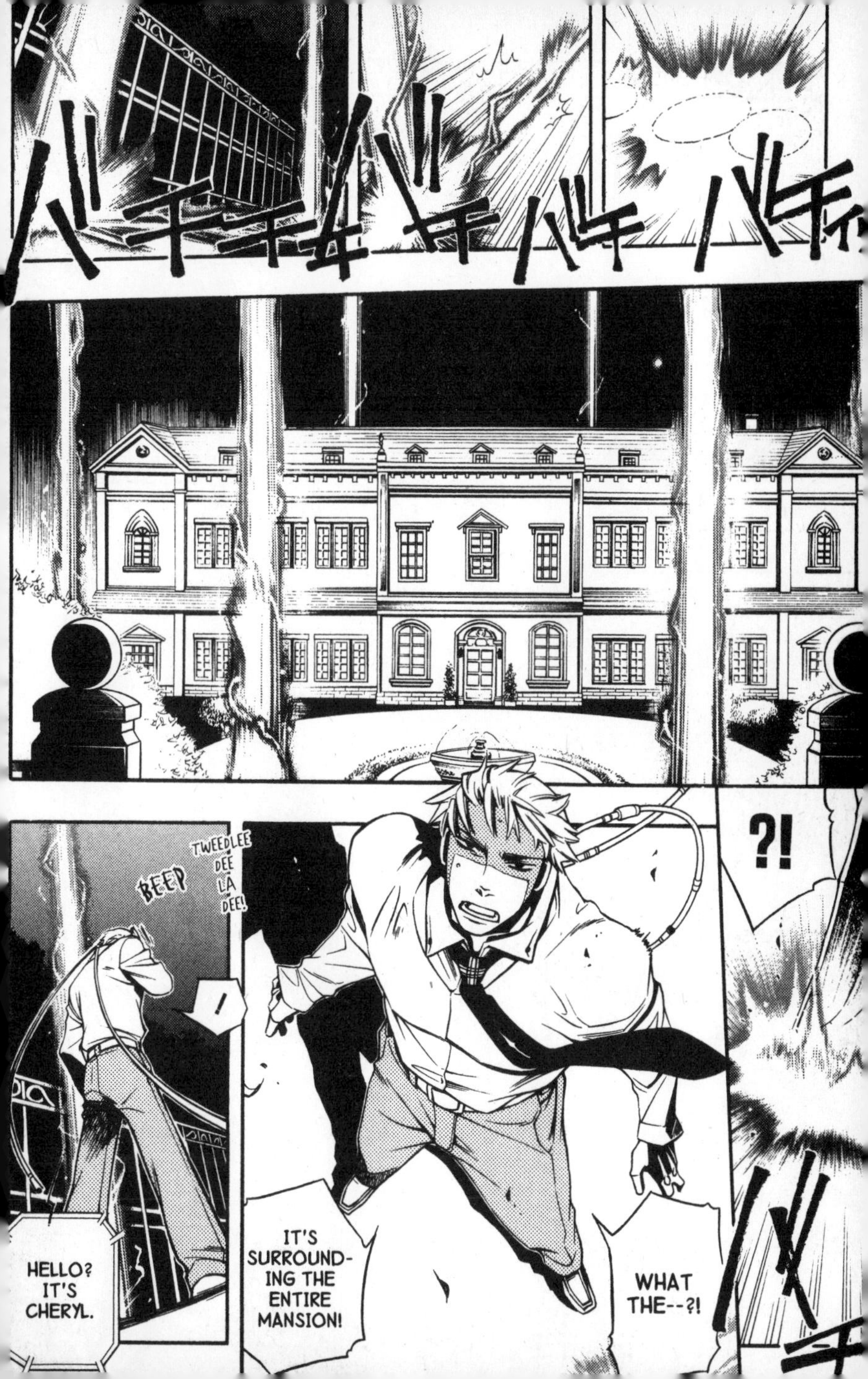
?!
WHAT THE--?!
IT'S SURROUND-ING THE ENTIRE MANSION!
TWEEDLEE DEE LA DEE!
BEEP
!
HELLO? IT'S CHERYL.

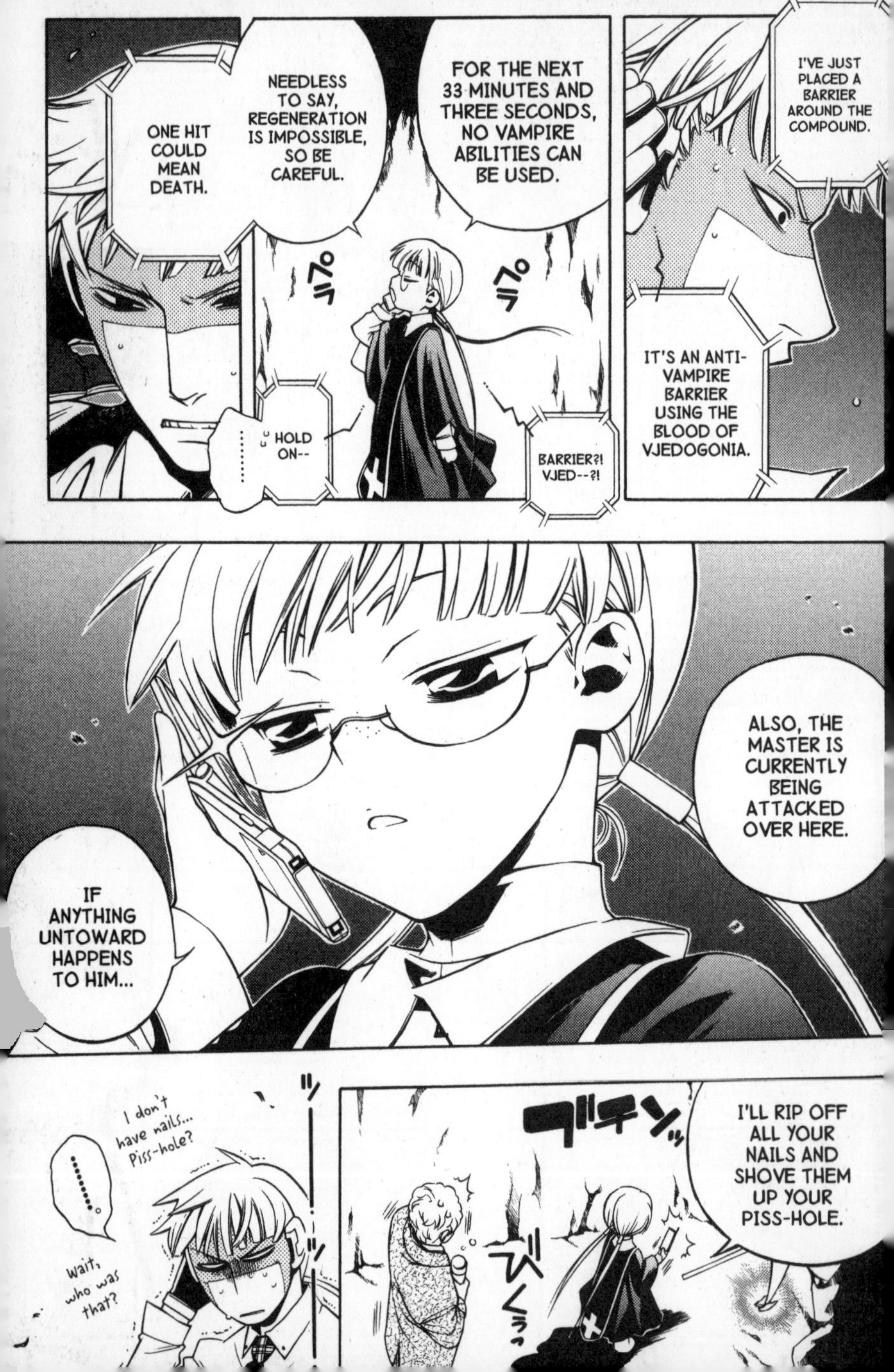
I'VE JUST PLACED A BARRIER AROUND THE COMPOUND.
IT'S AN ANTI-VAMPIRE BARRIER USING THE BLOOD OF VJEDOGONIA.
FOR THE NEXT 33 MINUTES AND THREE SECONDS, NO VAMPIRE ABILITIES CAN BE USED.
NEEDLESS TO SAY, REGENERATION IS IMPOSSIBLE, SO BE CAREFUL.
ONE HIT COULD MEAN DEATH.
BARRIER?! VJED--?!
HOLD ON--
......
ALSO, THE MASTER IS CURRENTLY BEING ATTACKED OVER HERE.
IF ANYTHING UNTOWARD HAPPENS TO HIM...
I'LL RIP OFF ALL YOUR NAILS AND SHOVE THEM UP YOUR PISS-HOLE.
I don't have nails... Piss-hole?
....
Wait, who was that?

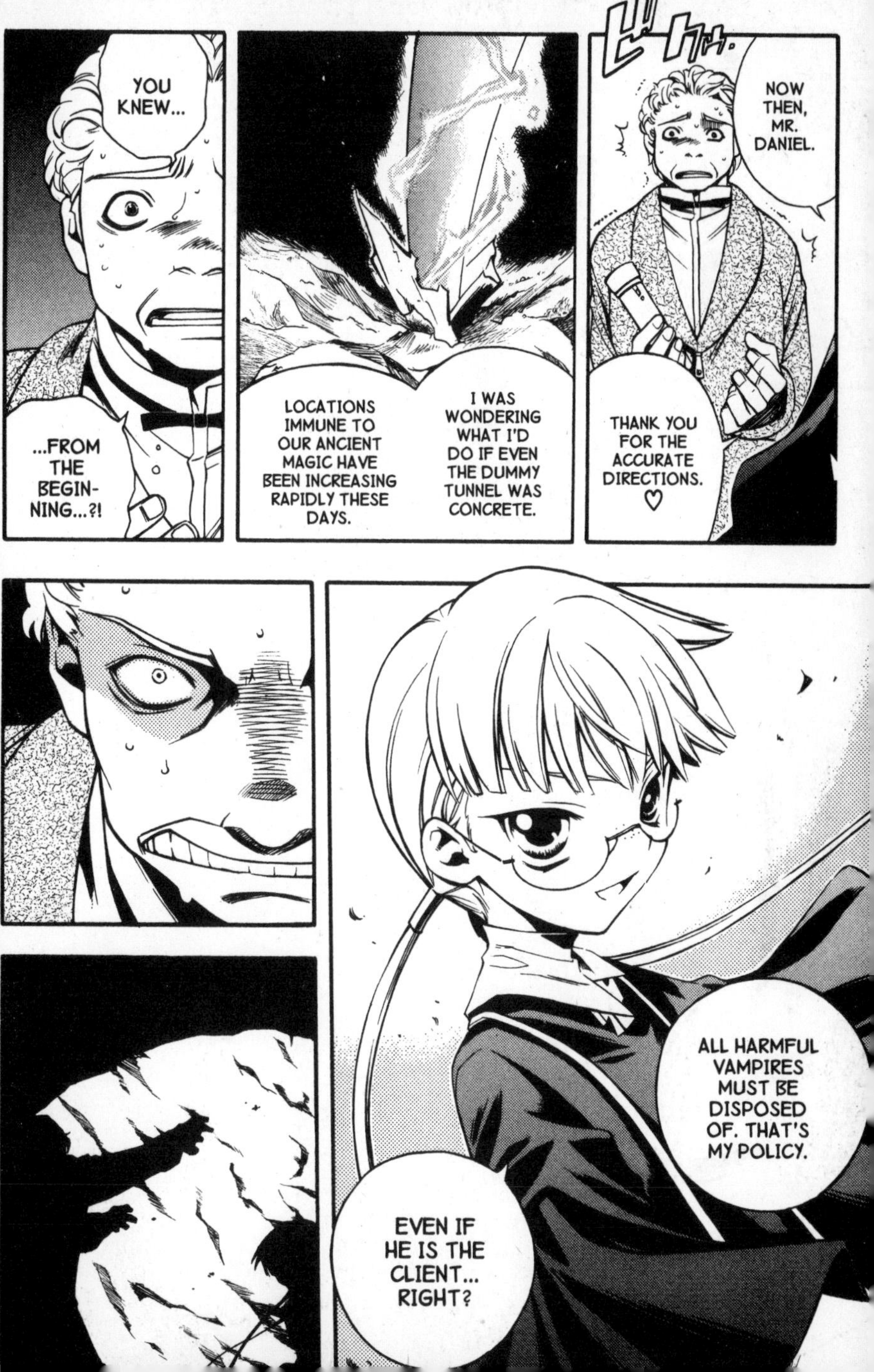
NOW THEN, MR. DANIEL.
THANK YOU FOR THE ACCURATE DIRECTIONS. ♡
I WAS WONDERING WHAT I'D DO IF EVEN THE DUMMY TUNNEL WAS CONCRETE.
LOCATIONS IMMUNE TO OUR ANCIENT MAGIC HAVE BEEN INCREASING RAPIDLY THESE DAYS.
YOU KNEW...
...FROM THE BEGIN-NING...?!
ALL HARMFUL VAMPIRES MUST BE DISPOSED OF. THAT'S MY POLICY.
EVEN IF HE IS THE CLIENT... RIGHT?

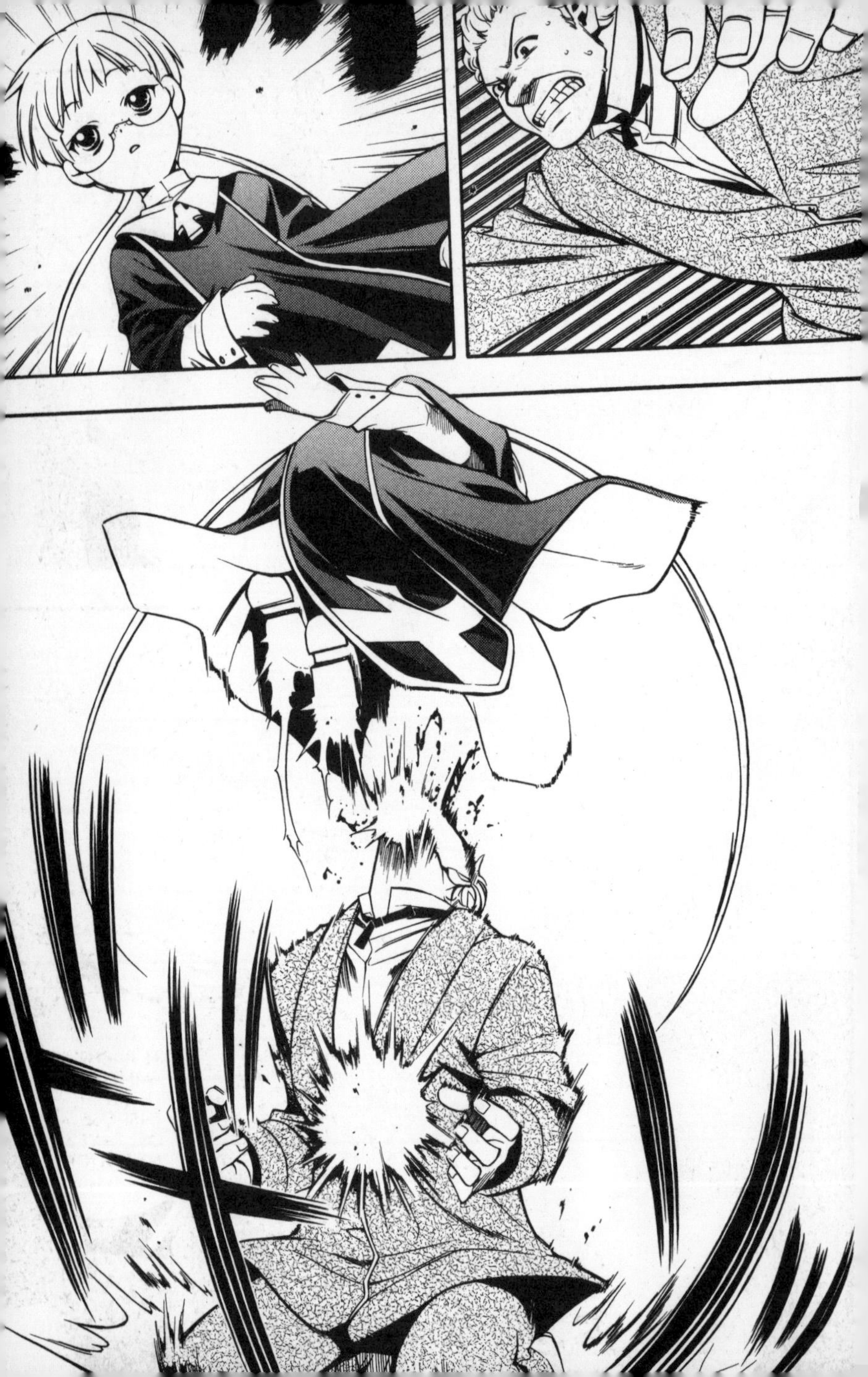

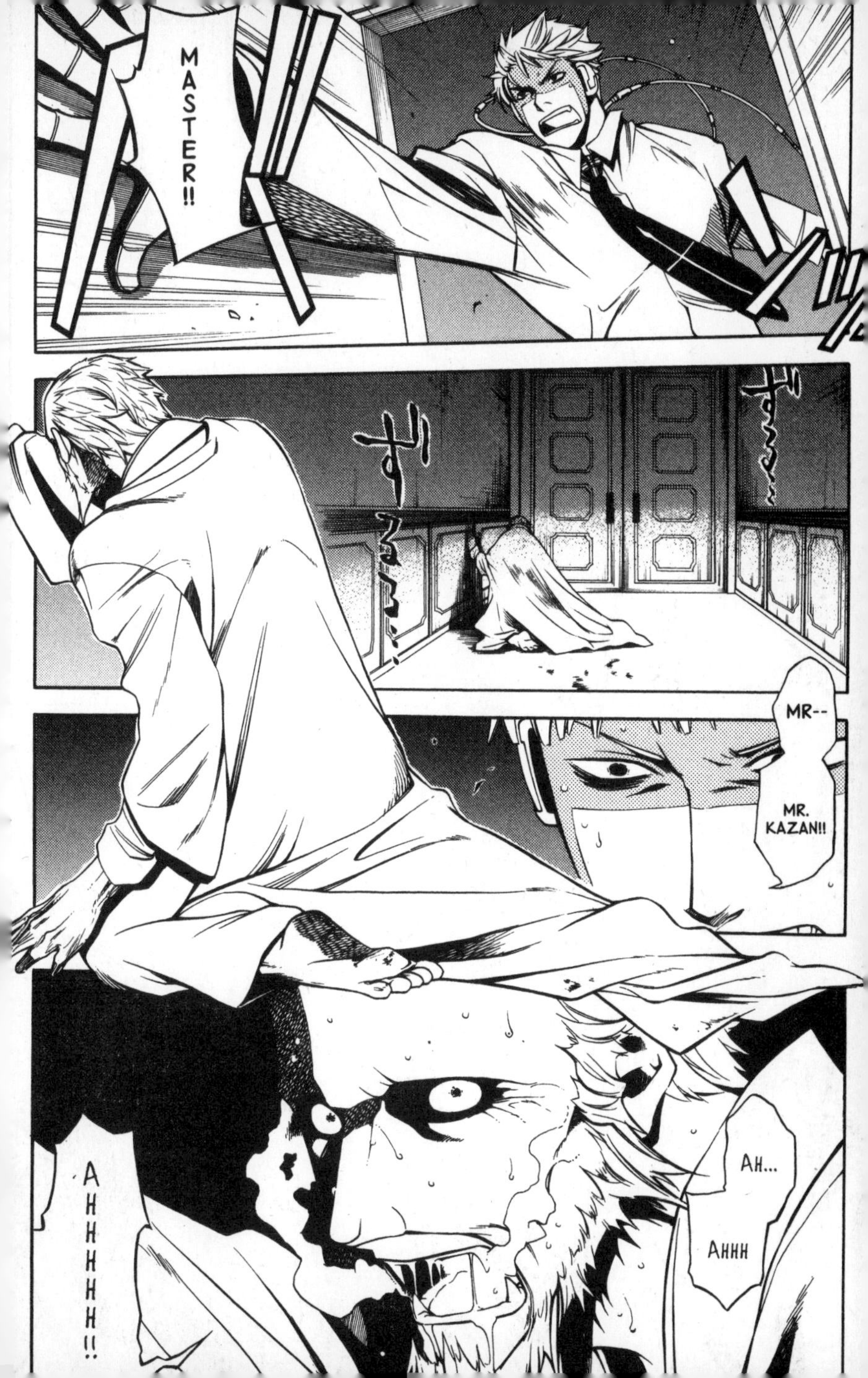
MASTER!!
MR--
MR. KAZAN!!
AH...
AHHH
AHHHHH!!

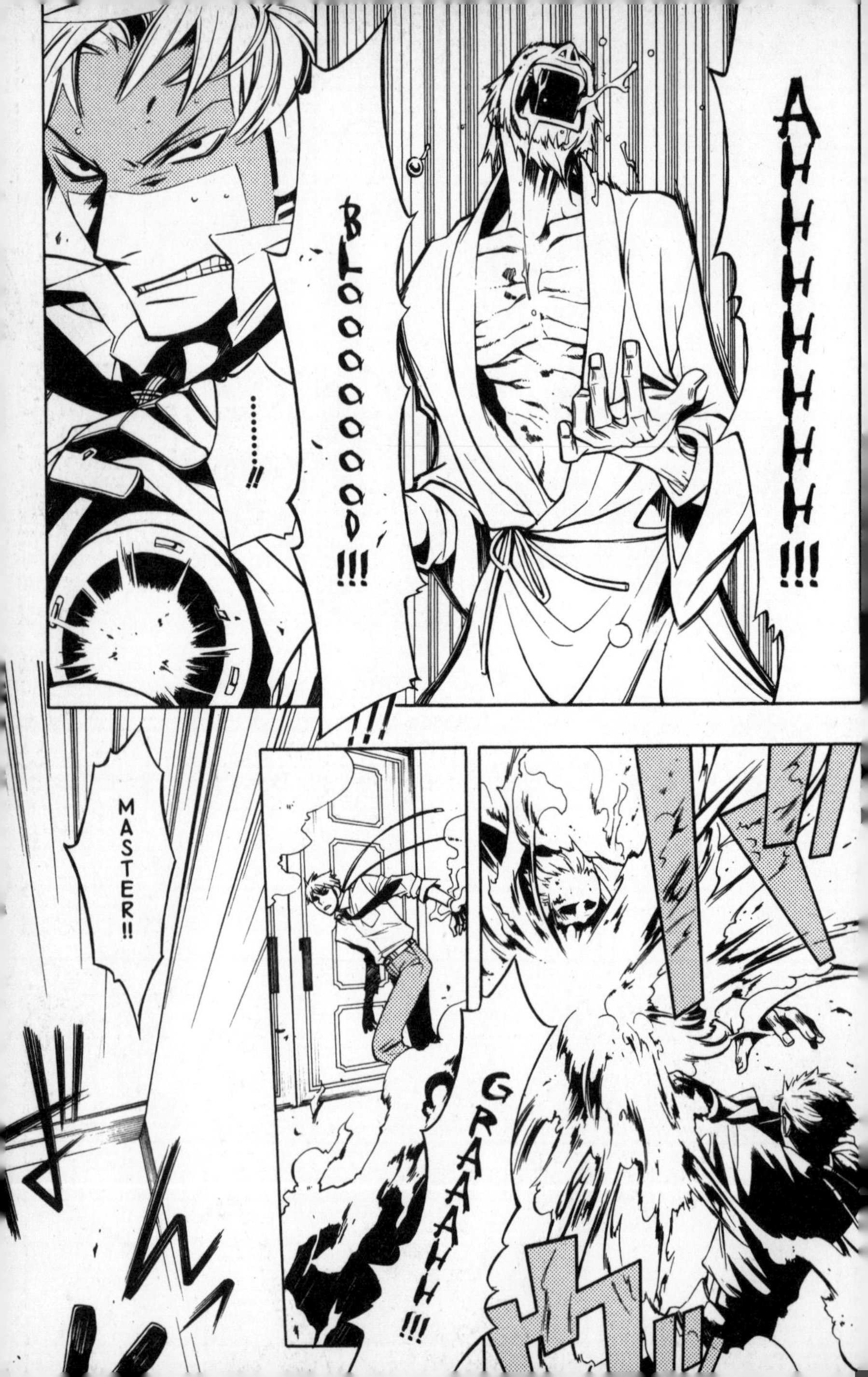
AHHHHHHHH!!!
BLOOOOOOOOD!!!
......!!
GRAAAHHH!!!
MASTER!!

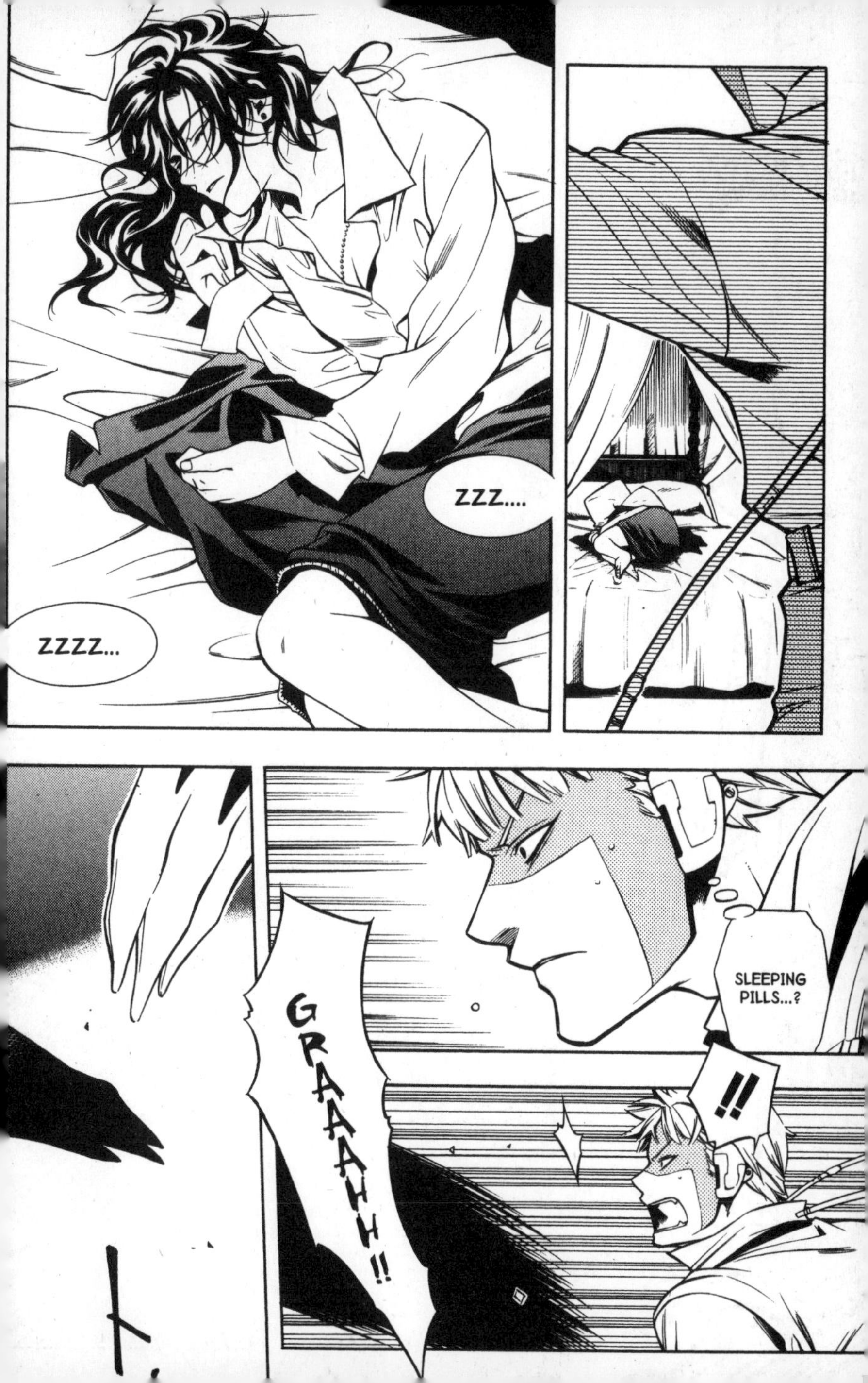
ZZZ....
ZZZZ...
SLEEPING PILLS...?
!!
GRAAAHH!!

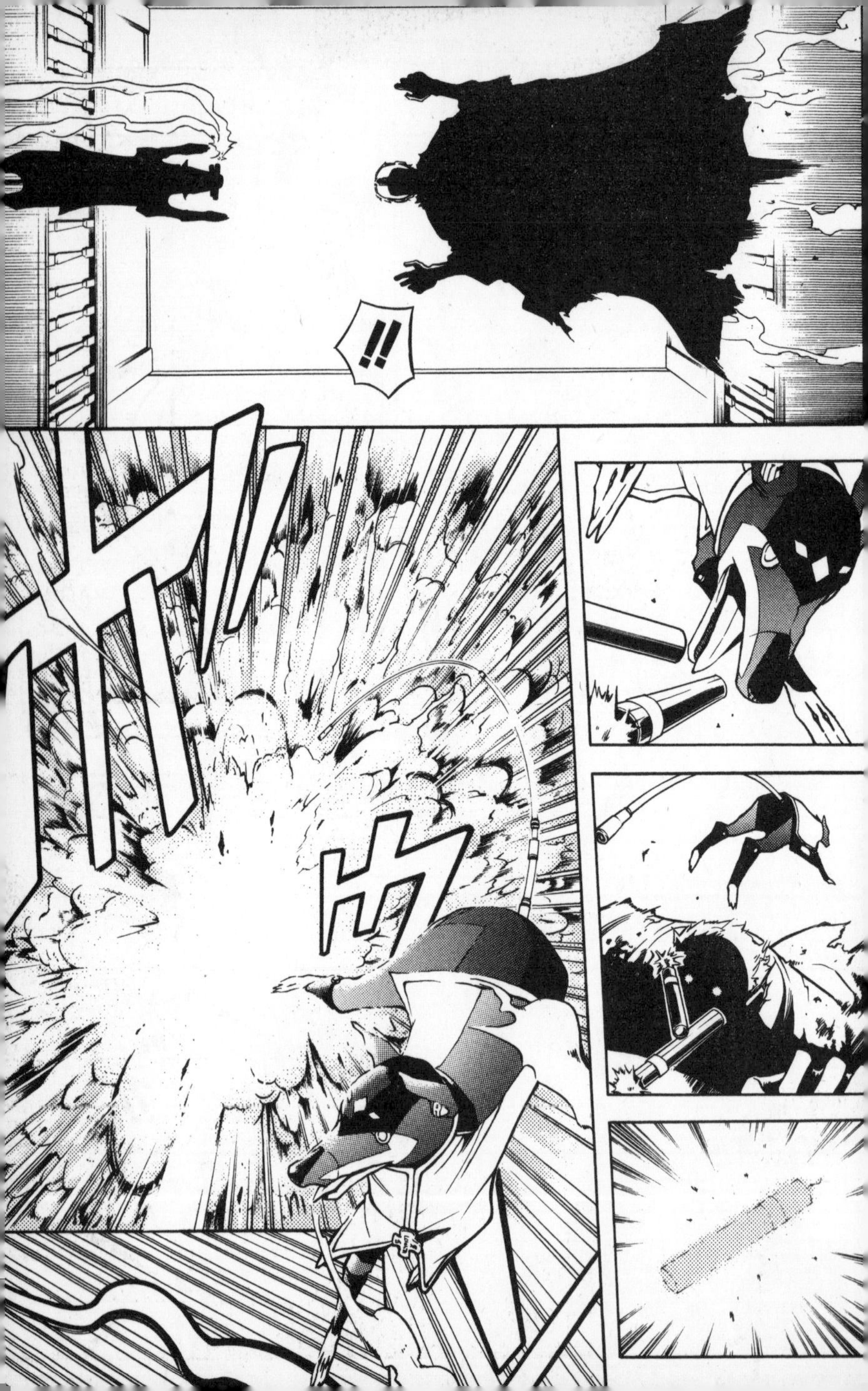
!!

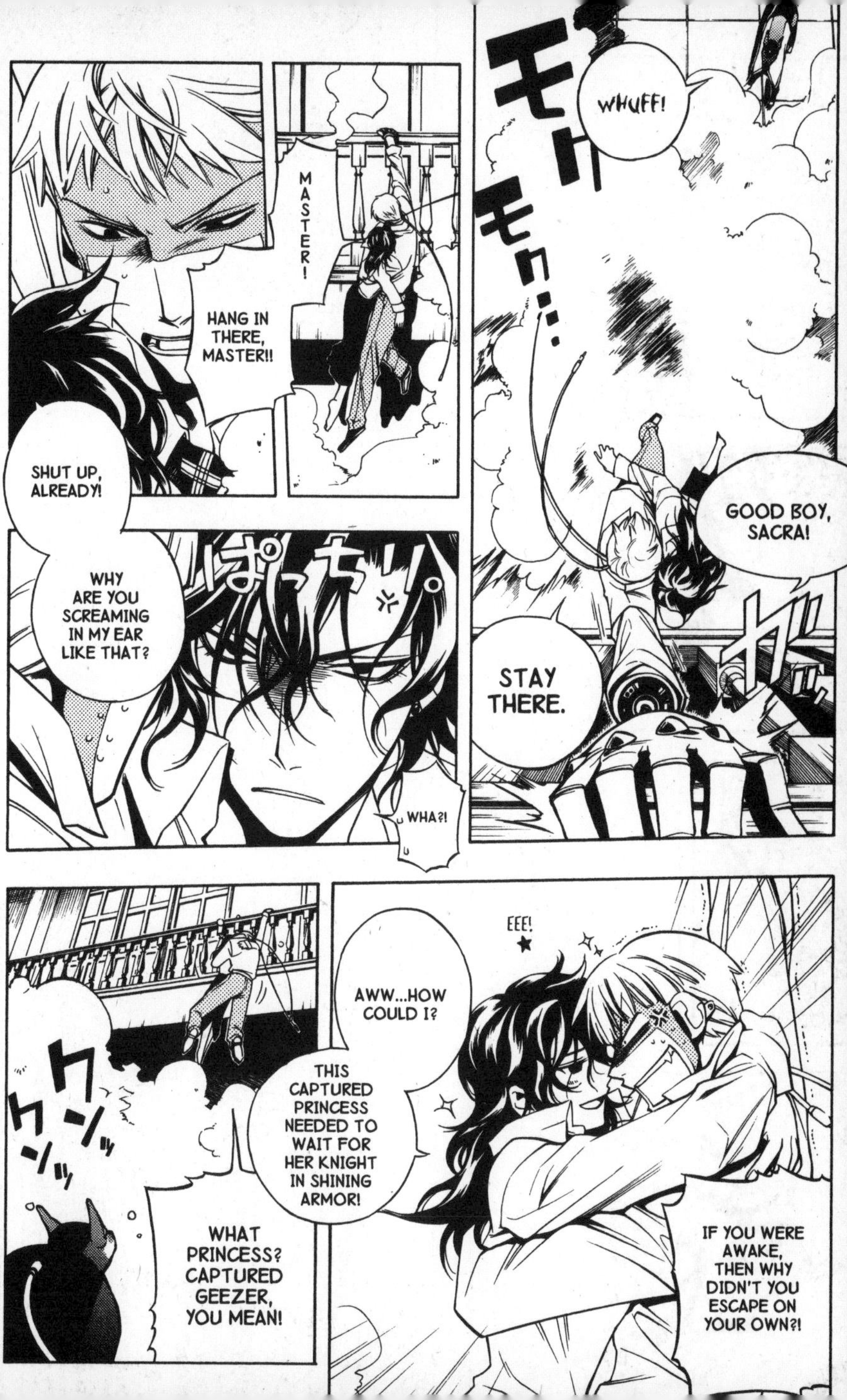
WHUFF!
GOOD BOY, SACRA!
STAY THERE.
MASTER!
HANG IN THERE, MASTER!!
SHUT UP, ALREADY!
ぱっちり
WHY ARE YOU SCREAMING IN MY EAR LIKE THAT?
WHA?!
EEE!
IF YOU WERE AWAKE, THEN WHY DIDN'T YOU ESCAPE ON YOUR OWN?!
AWW...HOW COULD I?
THIS CAPTURED PRINCESS NEEDED TO WAIT FOR HER KNIGHT IN SHINING ARMOR!
WHAT PRINCESS? CAPTURED GEEZER, YOU MEAN!

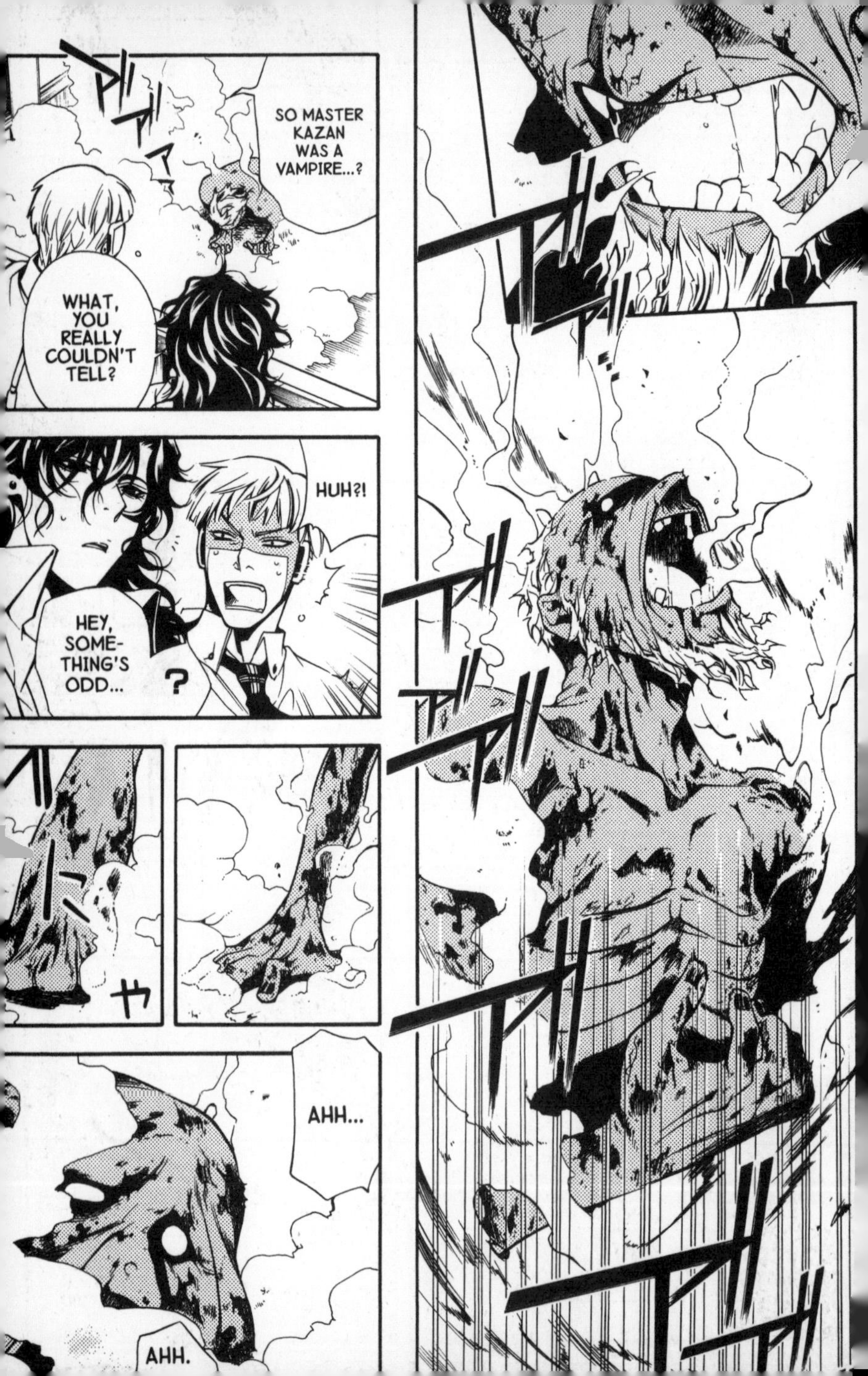
SO MASTER KAZAN WAS A VAMPIRE...?
WHAT, YOU REALLY COULDN'T TELL?
HUH?!
HEY, SOME-THING'S ODD...
?
AHH...
AHH.

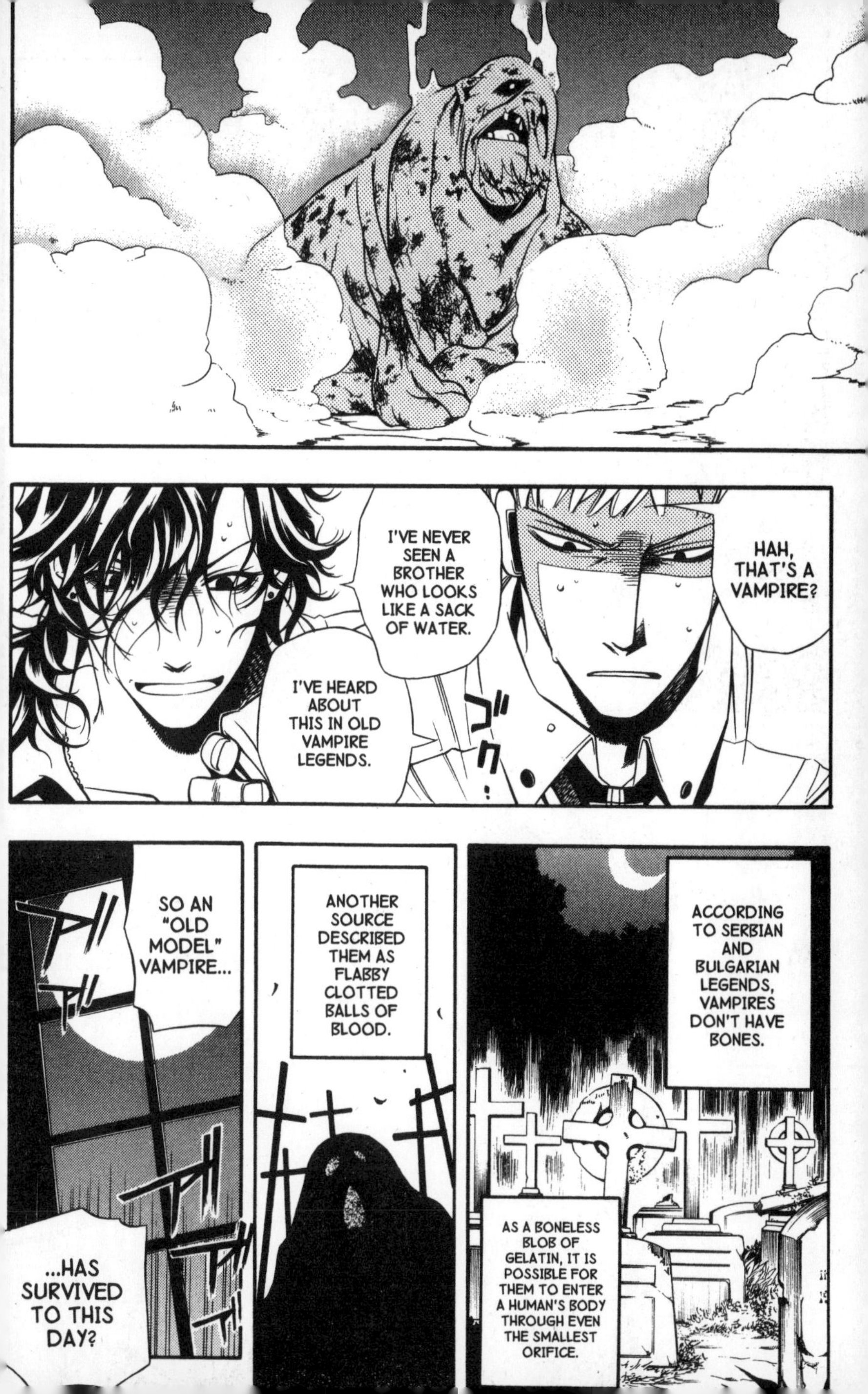

HAH, THAT'S A VAMPIRE?
I'VE NEVER SEEN A BROTHER WHO LOOKS LIKE A SACK OF WATER.
I'VE HEARD ABOUT THIS IN OLD VAMPIRE LEGENDS.
ACCORDING TO SERBIAN AND BULGARIAN LEGENDS, VAMPIRES DON'T HAVE BONES.
AS A BONELESS BLOB OF GELATIN, IT IS POSSIBLE FOR THEM TO ENTER A HUMAN'S BODY THROUGH EVEN THE SMALLEST ORIFICE.
ANOTHER SOURCE DESCRIBED THEM AS FLABBY CLOTTED BALLS OF BLOOD.
SO AN "OLD MODEL" VAMPIRE...
...HAS SURVIVED TO THIS DAY?

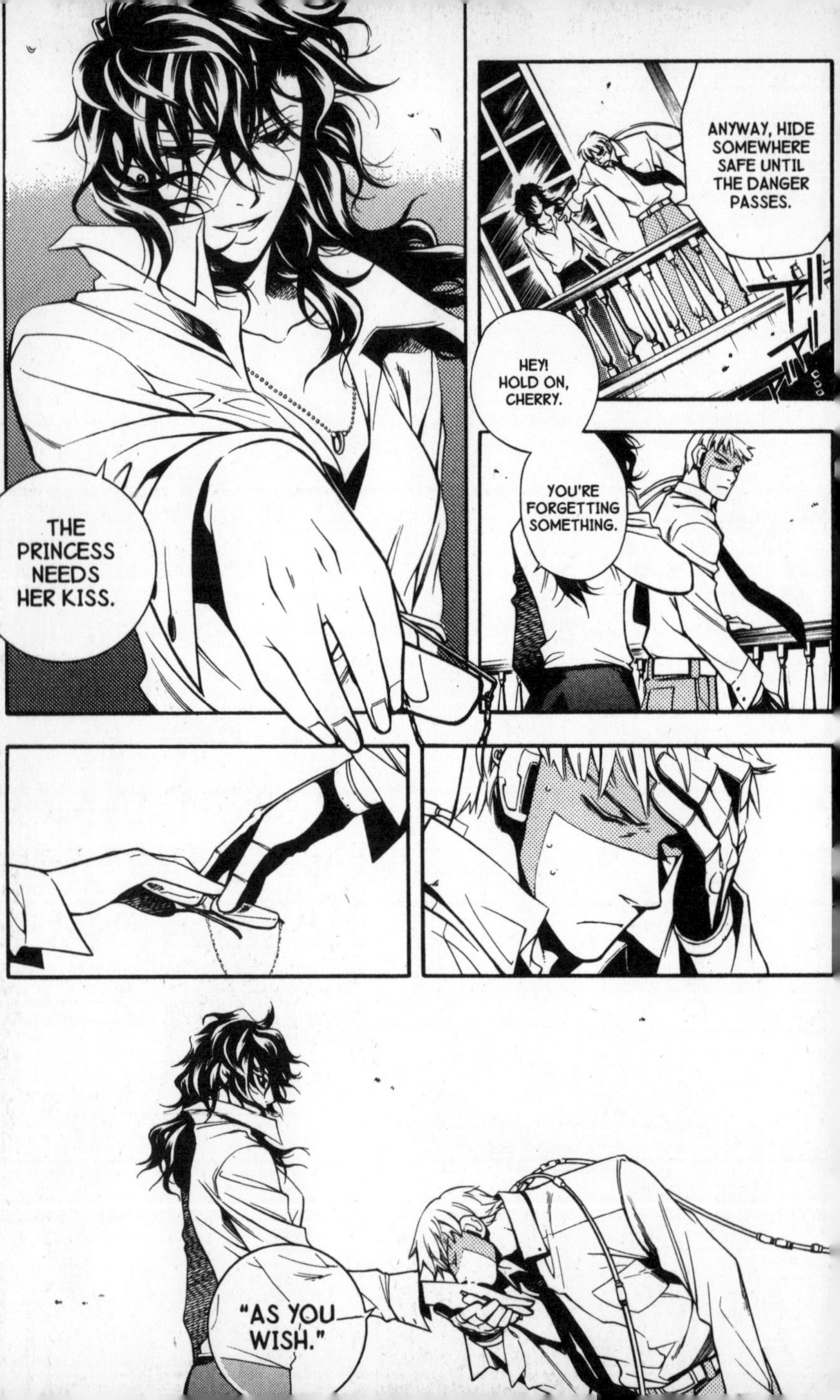
ANYWAY, HIDE SOMEWHERE SAFE UNTIL THE DANGER PASSES.
HEY! HOLD ON, CHERRY.
YOU'RE FORGETTING SOMETHING.
THE PRINCESS NEEDS HER KISS.
"AS YOU WISH."

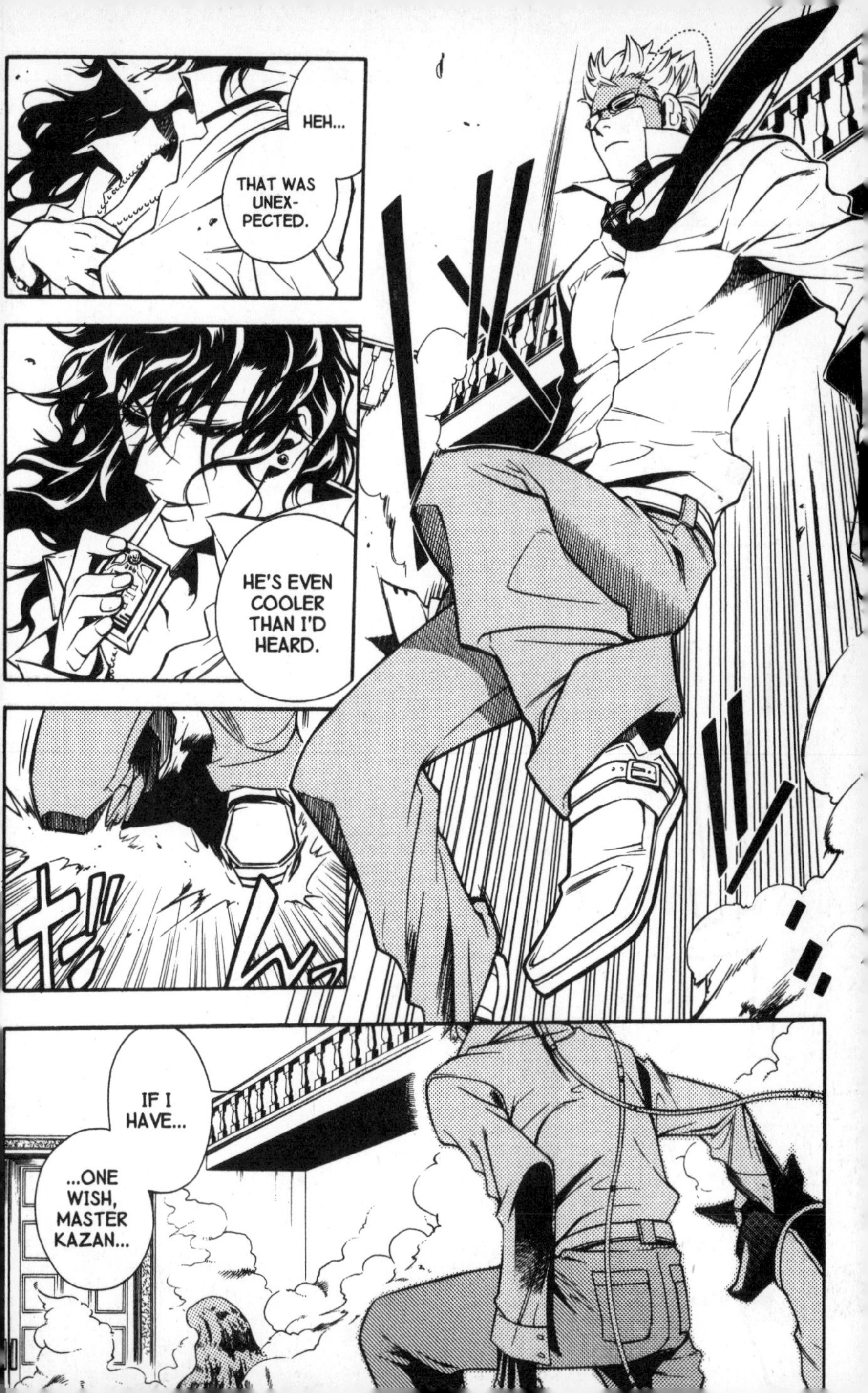
HEH...
THAT WAS UNEX-PECTED.
HE'S EVEN COOLER THAN I'D HEARD.
IF I HAVE...
...ONE WISH, MASTER KAZAN...

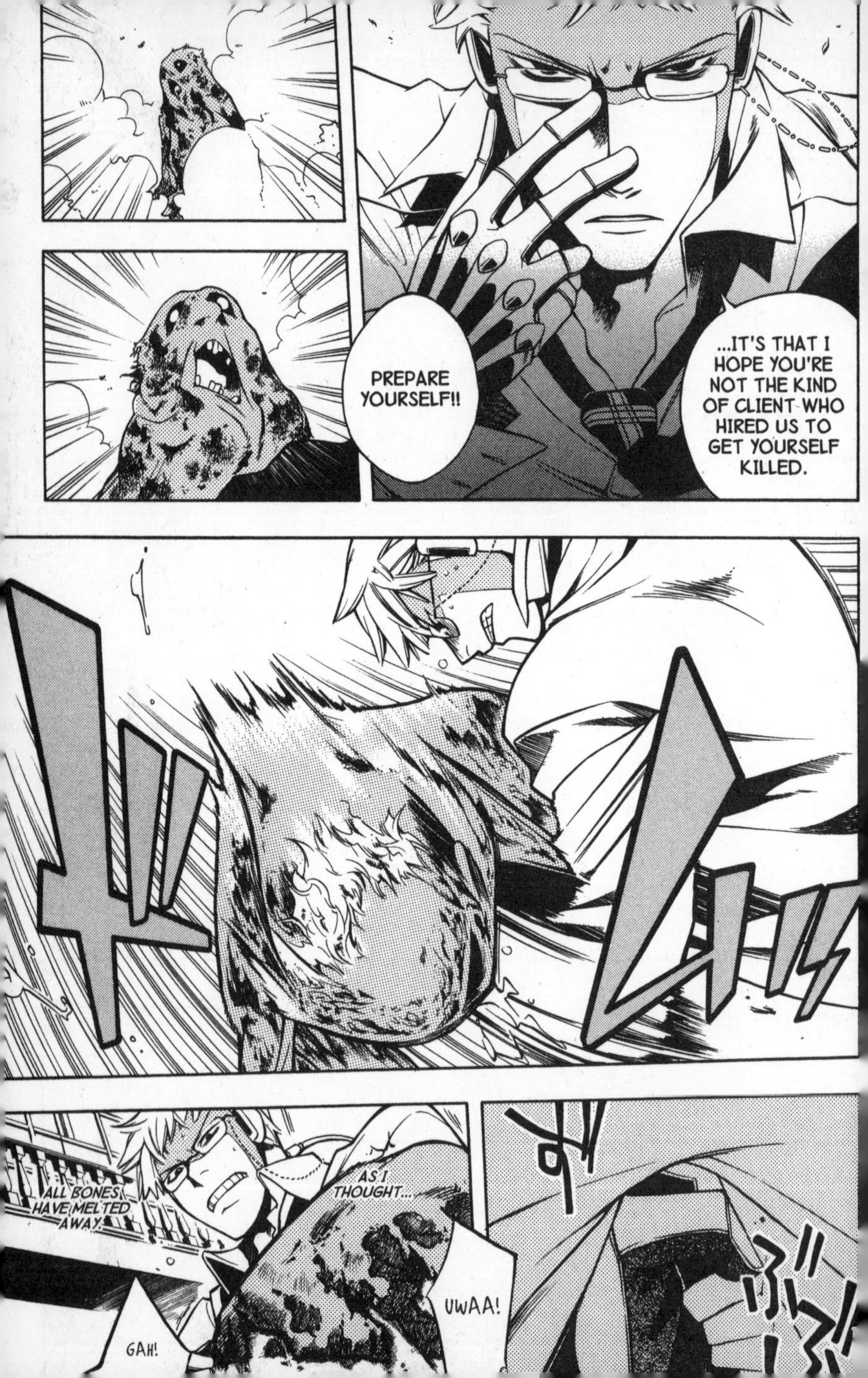
...IT'S THAT I HOPE YOU'RE NOT THE KIND OF CLIENT WHO HIRED US TO GET YOURSELF KILLED.
PREPARE YOURSELF!!
AS I THOUGHT...
ALL BONES HAVE MELTED AWAY.
UWAA!
GAH!

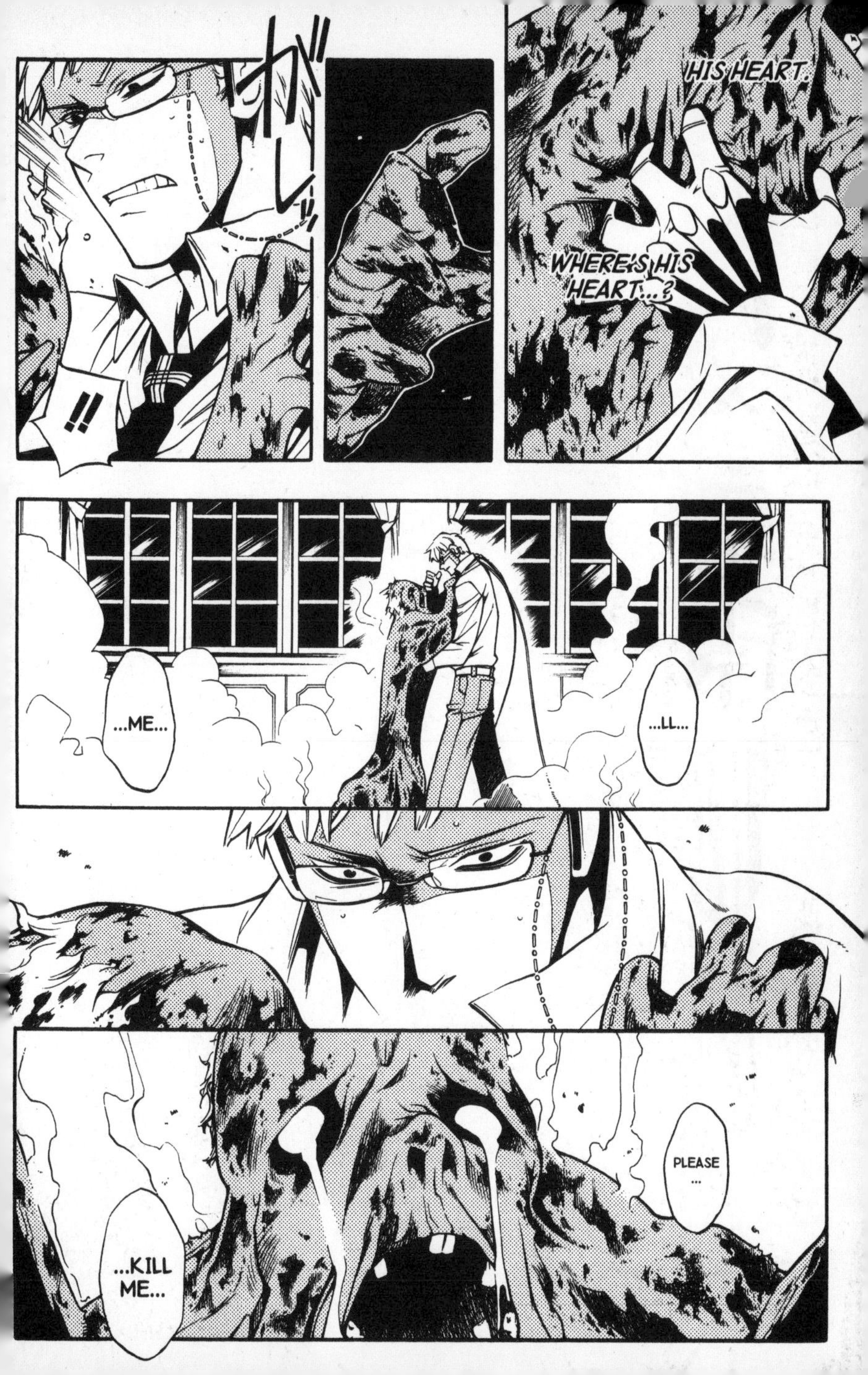
HIS HEART.
WHERE'S HIS HEART...?
!!
...LL...
...ME...
PLEASE ...
...KILL ME...

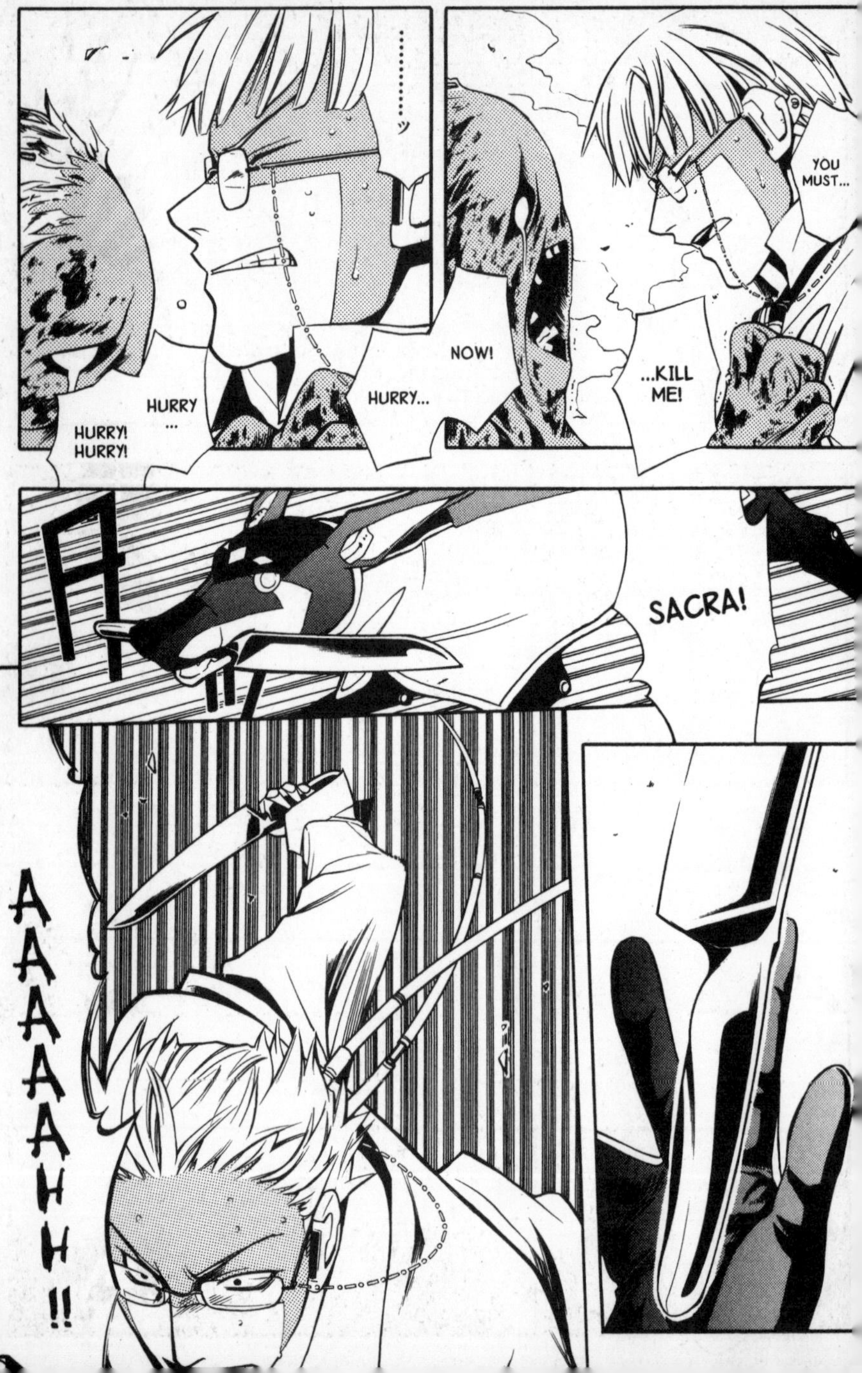
YOU MUST...
...KILL ME!
NOW!
HURRY...
......ッ
HURRY ...
HURRY! HURRY!
SACRA!
AAAAAHH!!

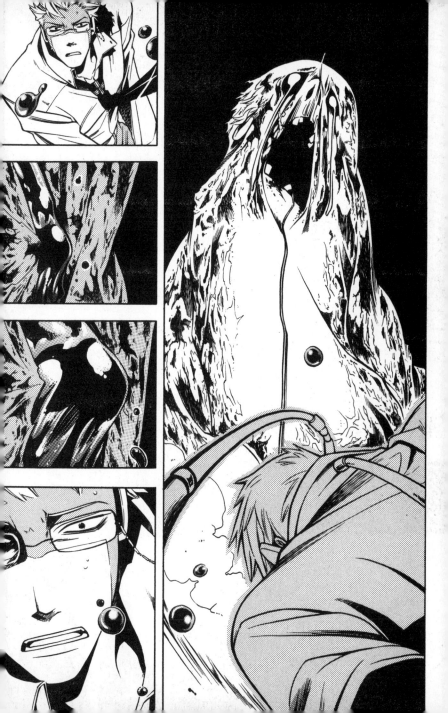

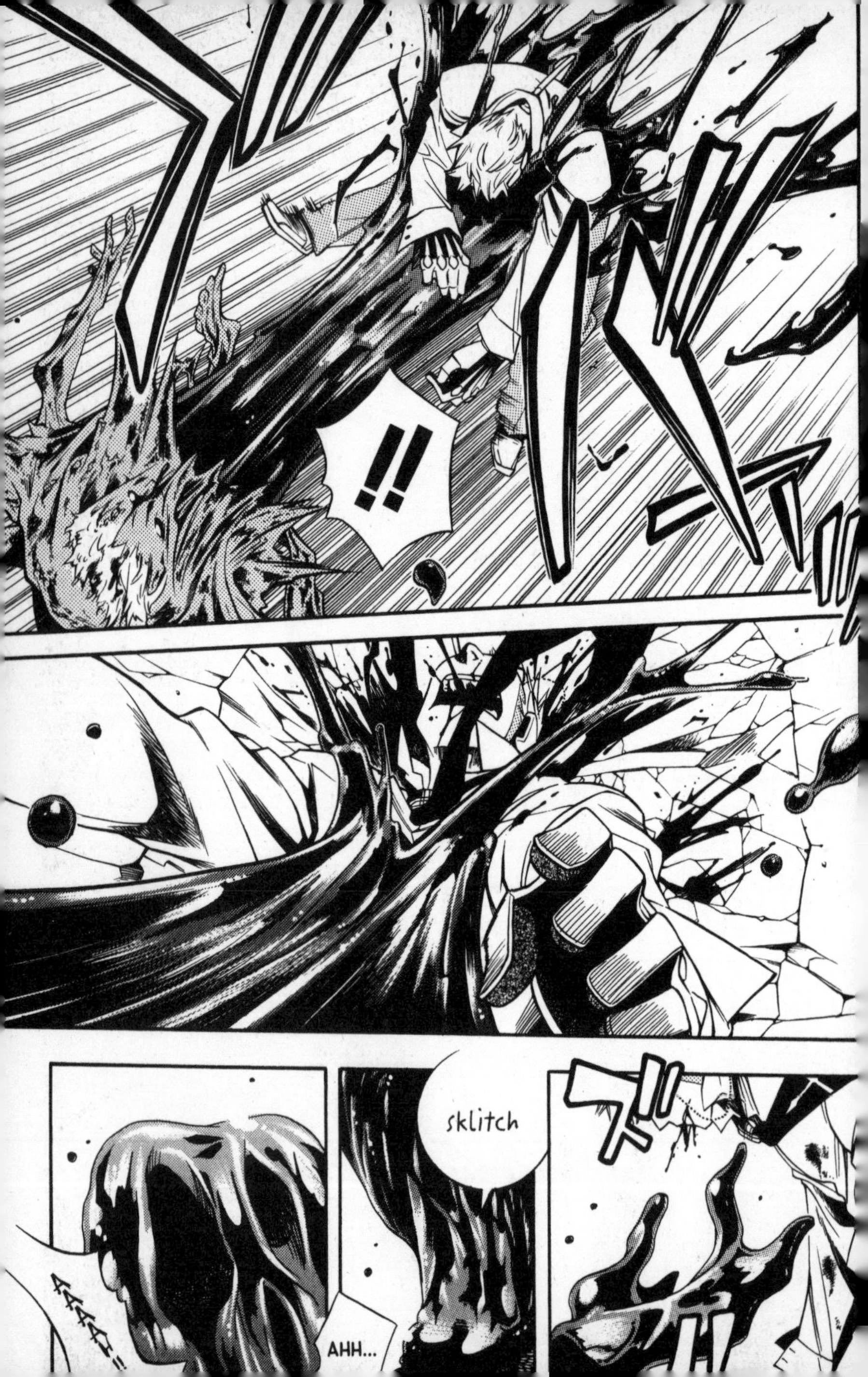
!!
sklitch
AHH...
AAAAH!!

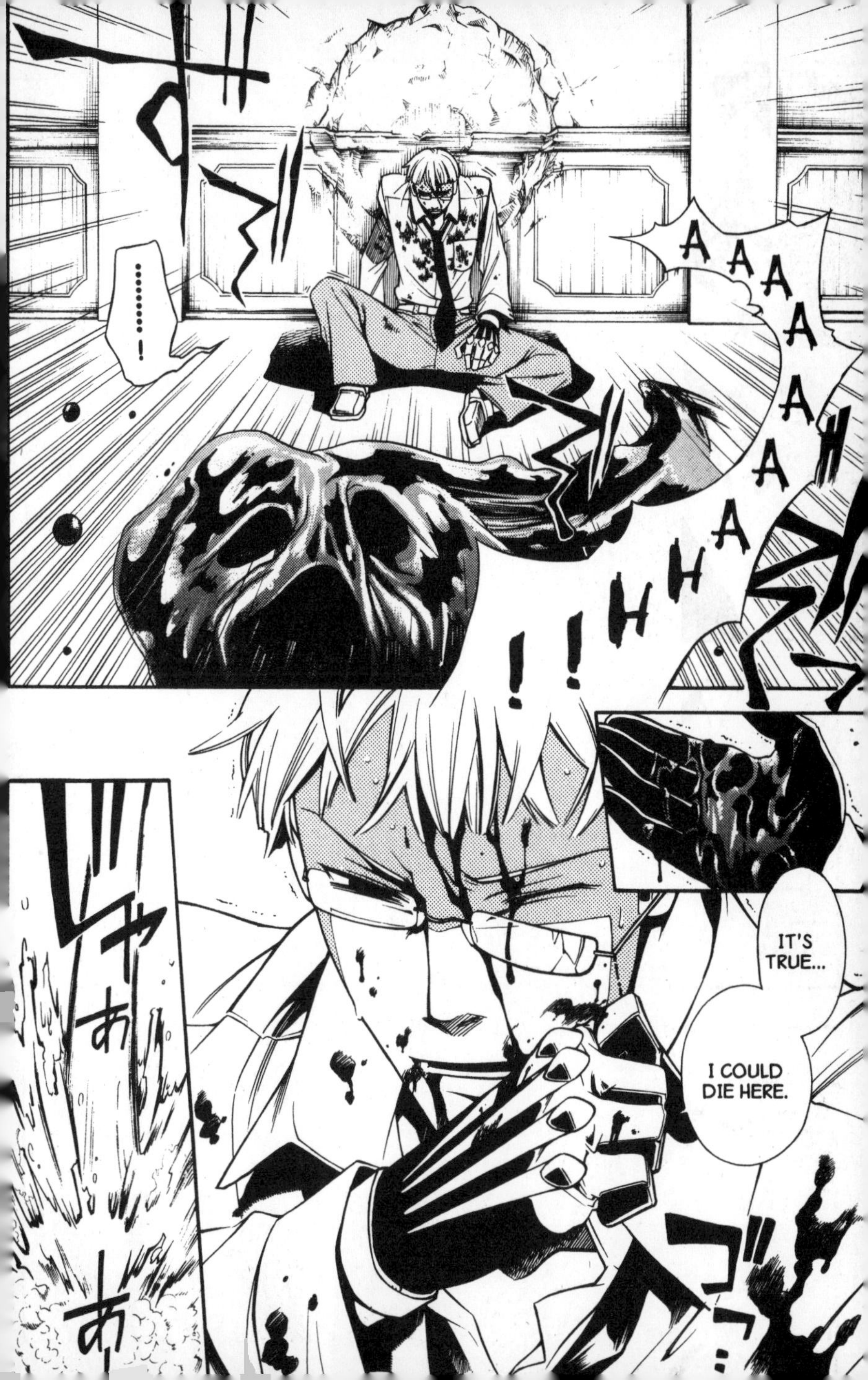
AAAAAHAAHH
.........!
!!
IT'S TRUE...
I COULD DIE HERE.

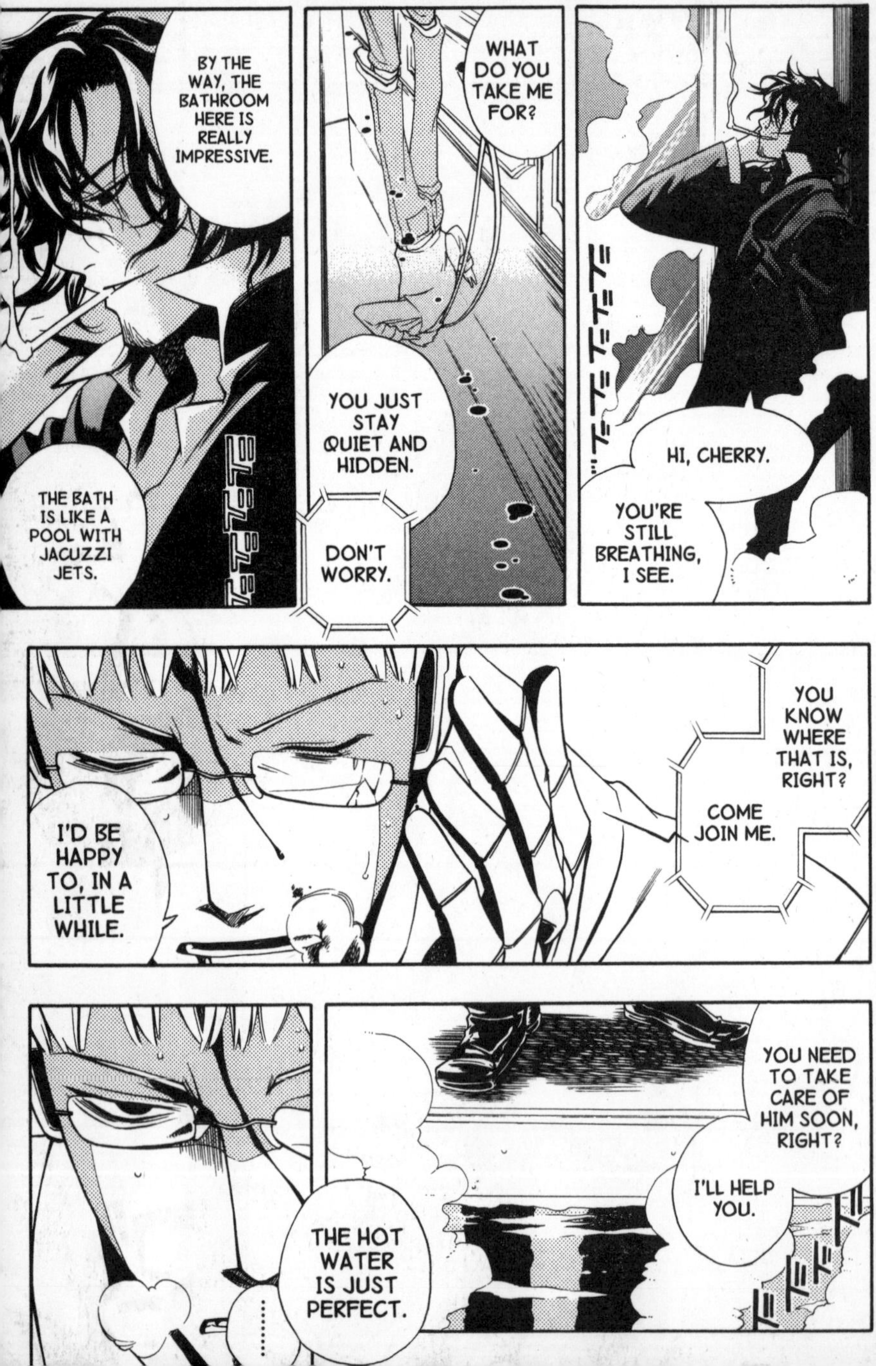
HI, CHERRY.
YOU'RE STILL BREATHING, I SEE.
WHAT DO YOU TAKE ME FOR?
YOU JUST STAY QUIET AND HIDDEN.
DON'T WORRY.
BY THE WAY, THE BATHROOM HERE IS REALLY IMPRESSIVE.
THE BATH IS LIKE A POOL WITH JACUZZI JETS.
YOU KNOW WHERE THAT IS, RIGHT?
COME JOIN ME.
I'D BE HAPPY TO, IN A LITTLE WHILE.
YOU NEED TO TAKE CARE OF HIM SOON, RIGHT?
I'LL HELP YOU.
THE HOT WATER IS JUST PERFECT.
......

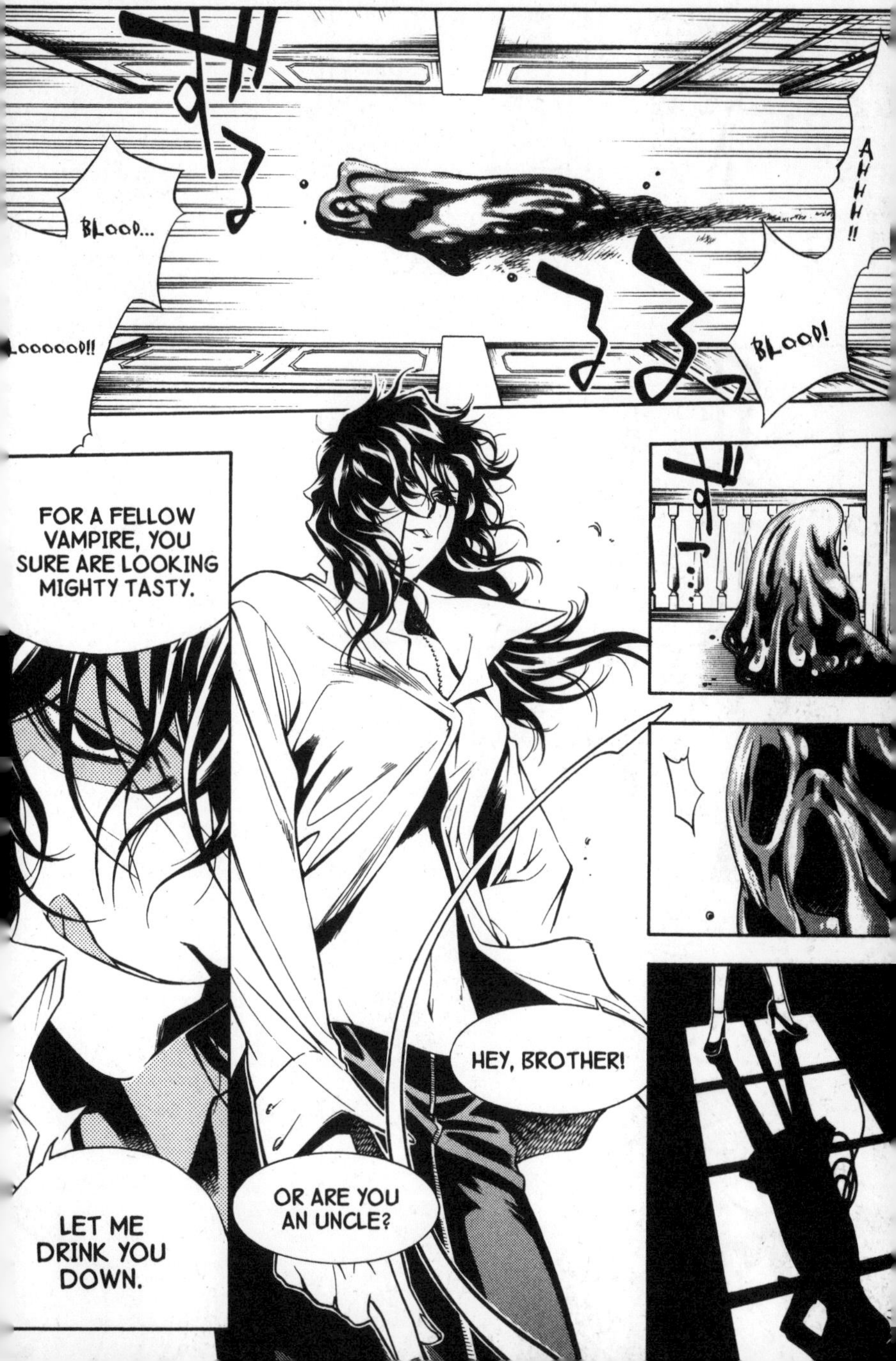
AHHHH!!
BLOOD!
BLOOD...
LOOOOOOD!!
HEY, BROTHER!
OR ARE YOU AN UNCLE?
FOR A FELLOW VAMPIRE, YOU SURE ARE LOOKING MIGHTY TASTY.
LET ME DRINK YOU DOWN.

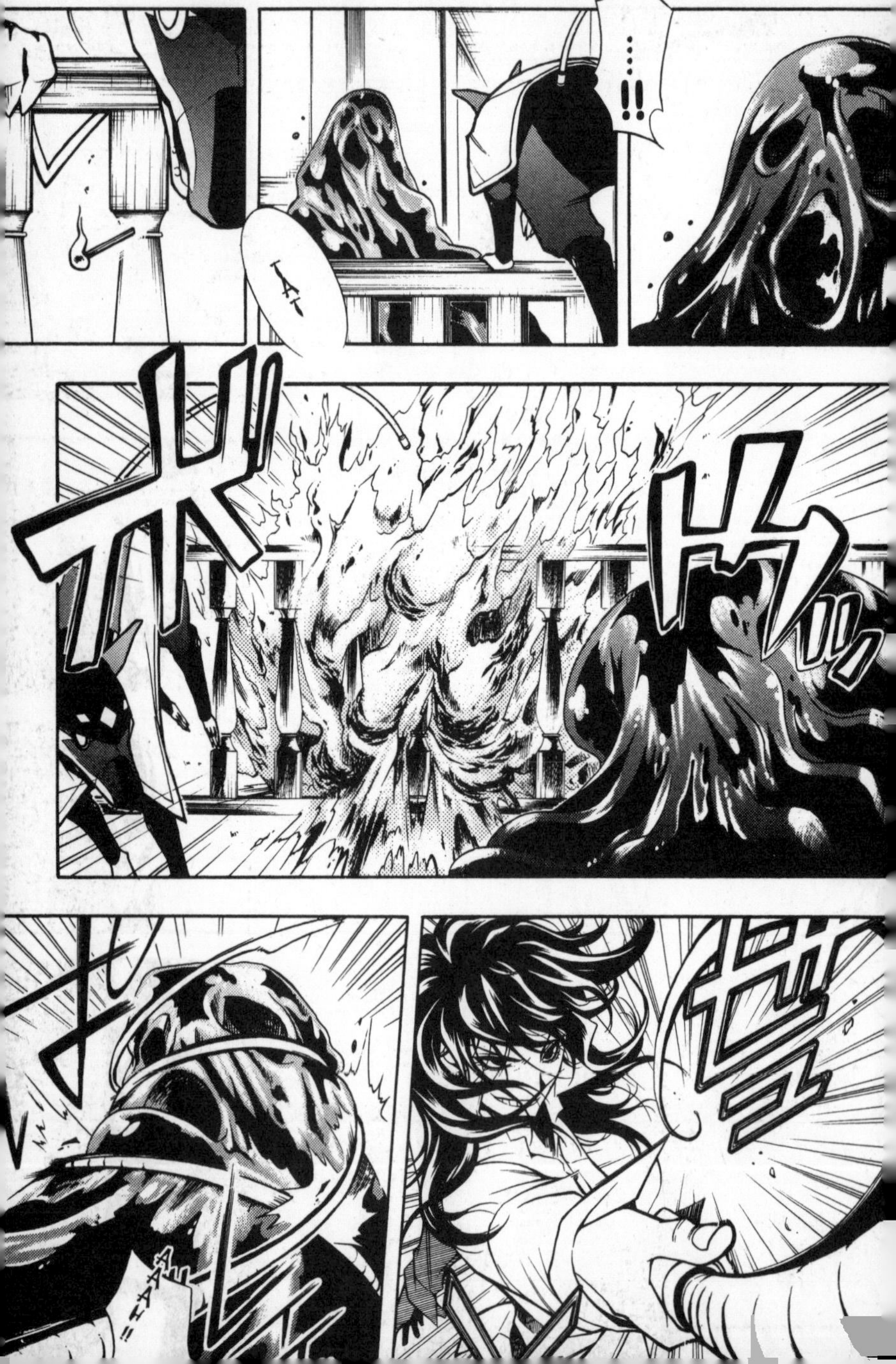

......!!
TAT
AAAAH!!

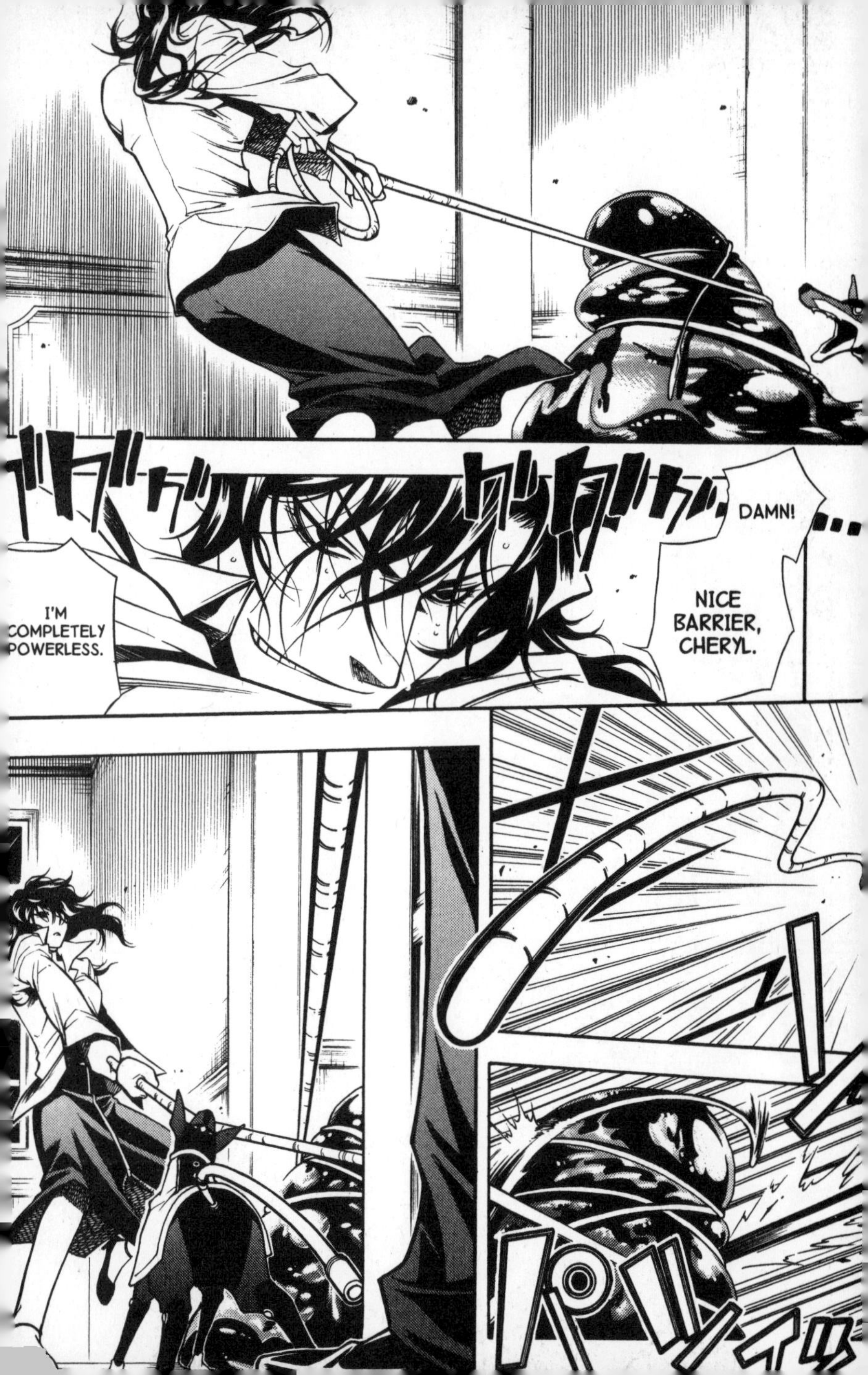
DAMN!
NICE BARRIER, CHERYL.
I'M COMPLETELY POWERLESS.

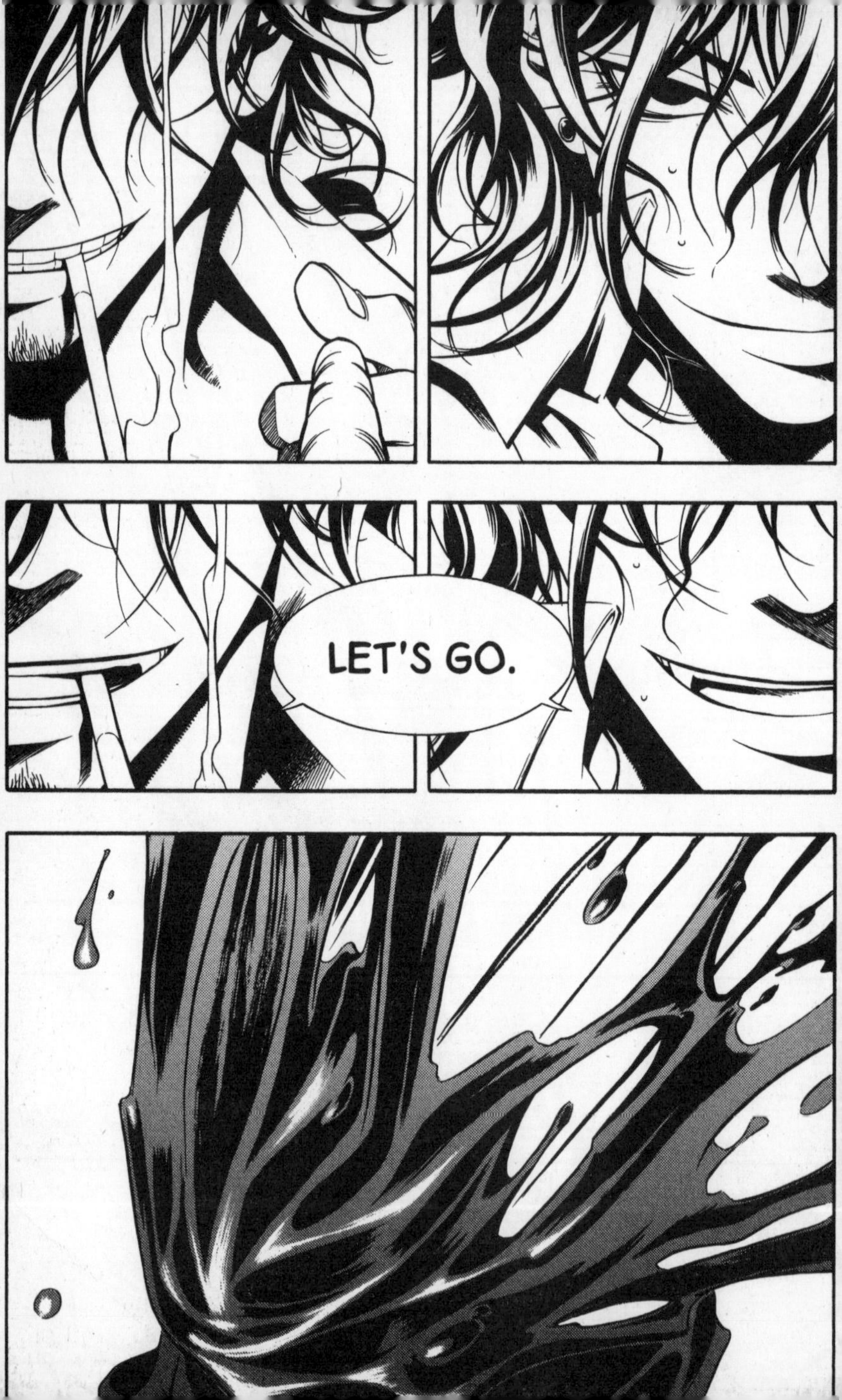
LET'S GO.

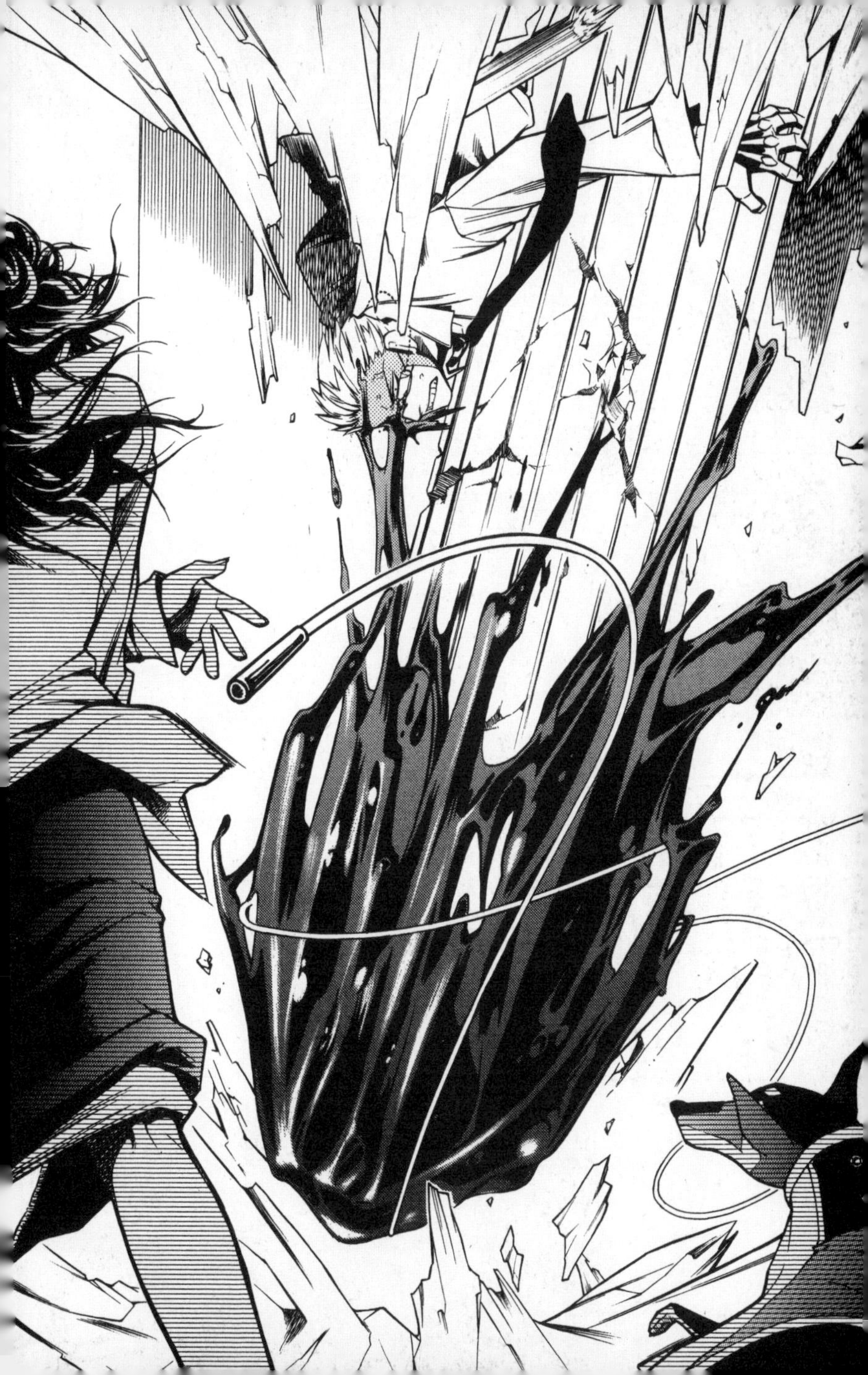

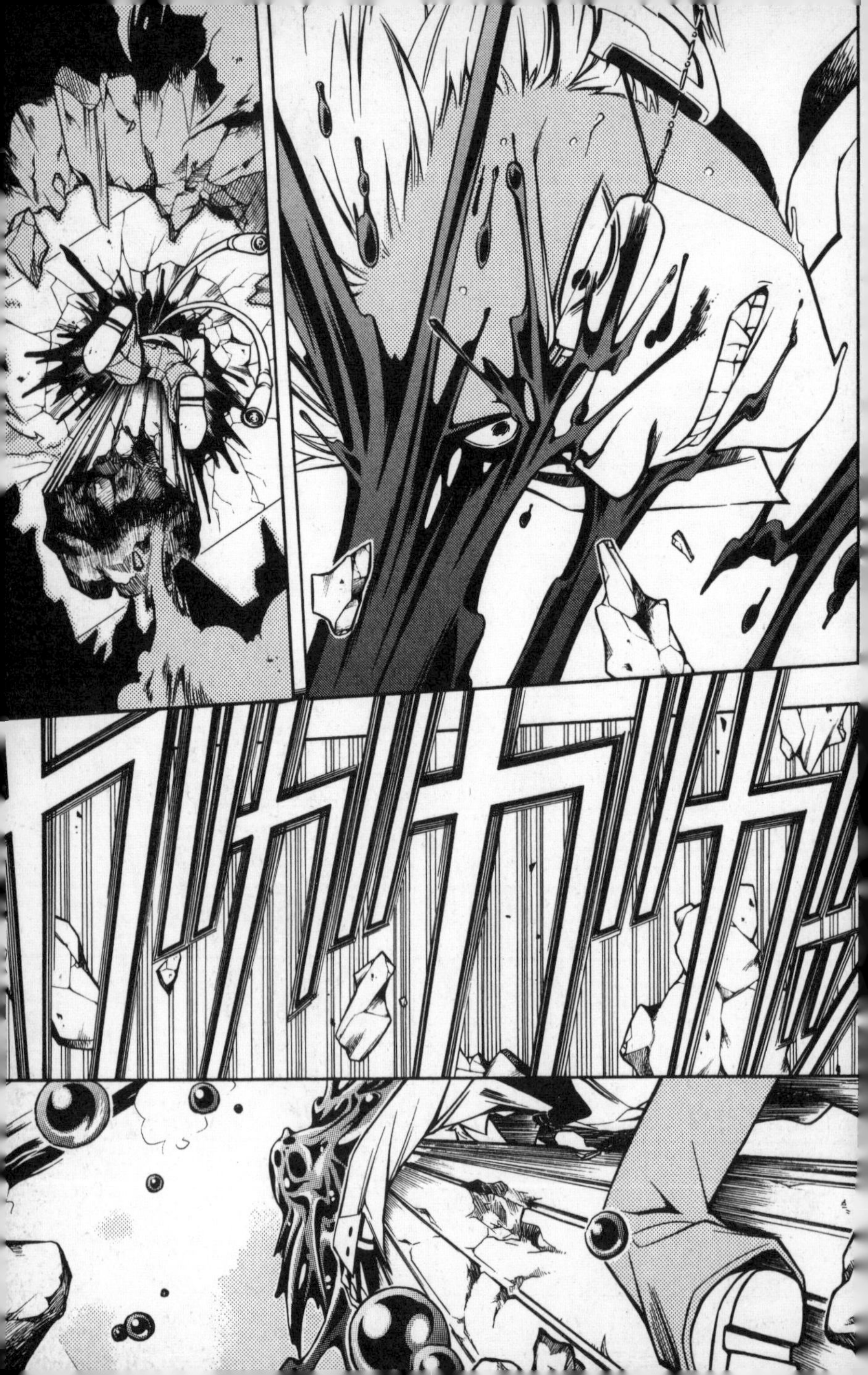

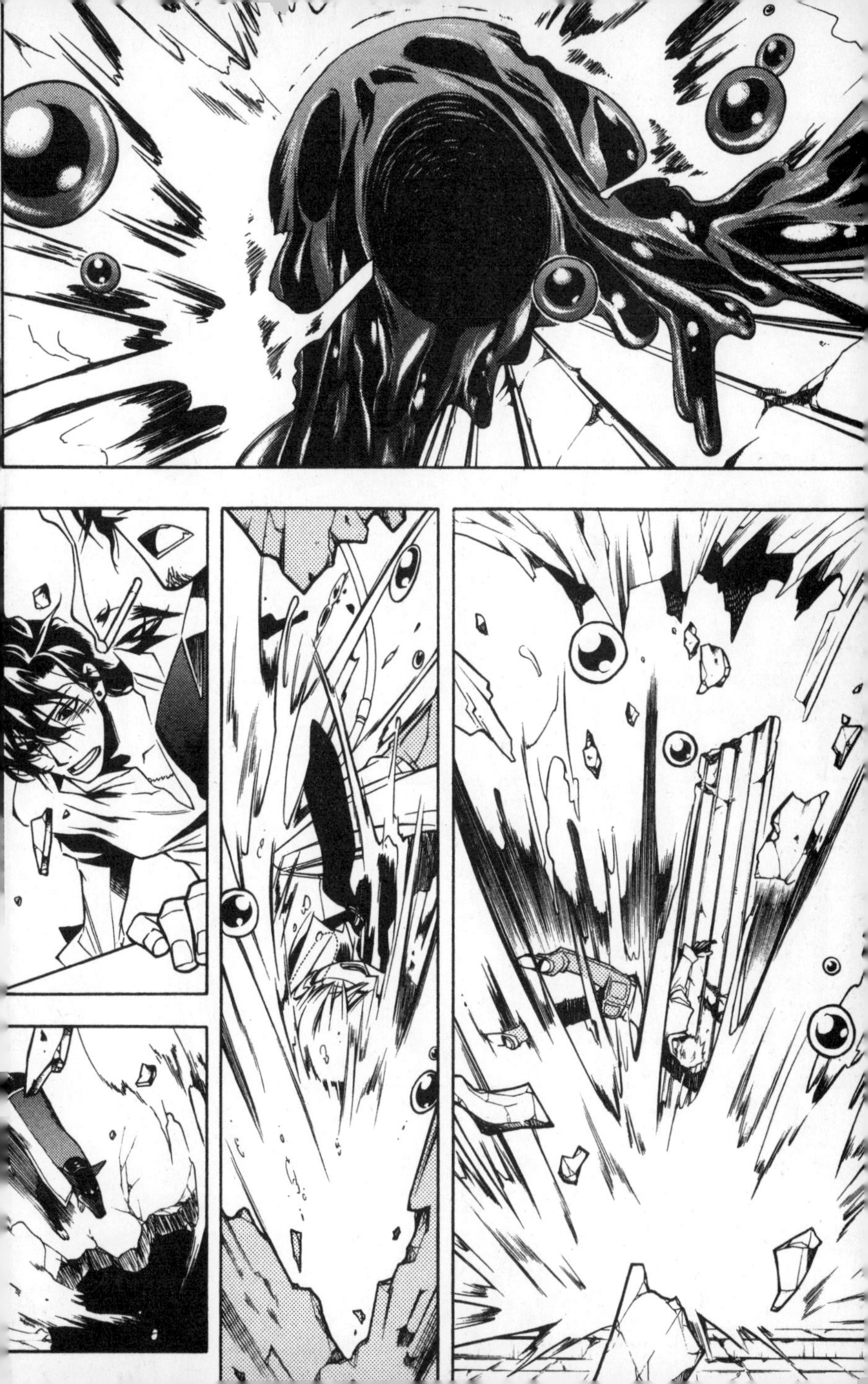

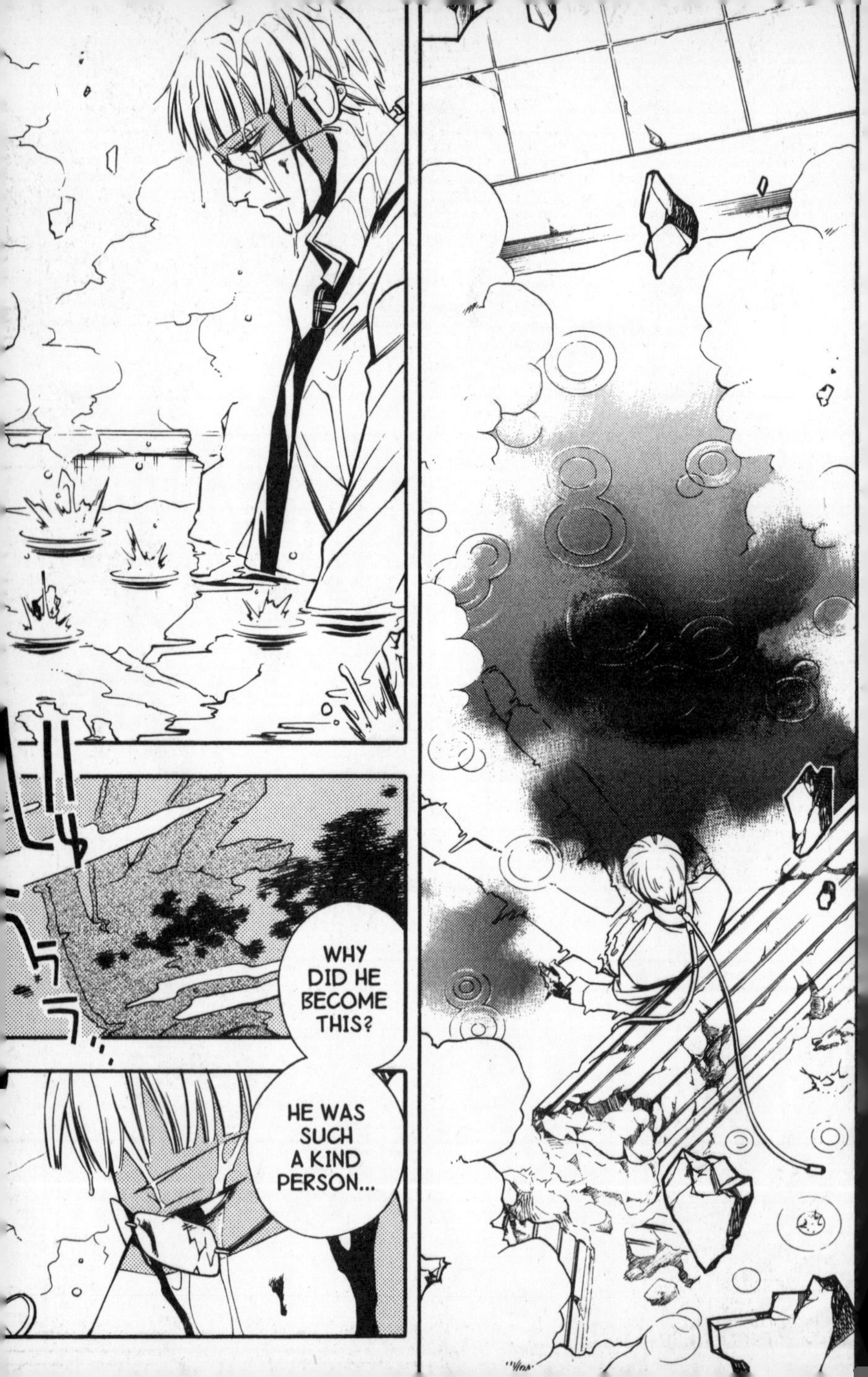
WHY DID HE BECOME THIS?
HE WAS SUCH A KIND PERSON...

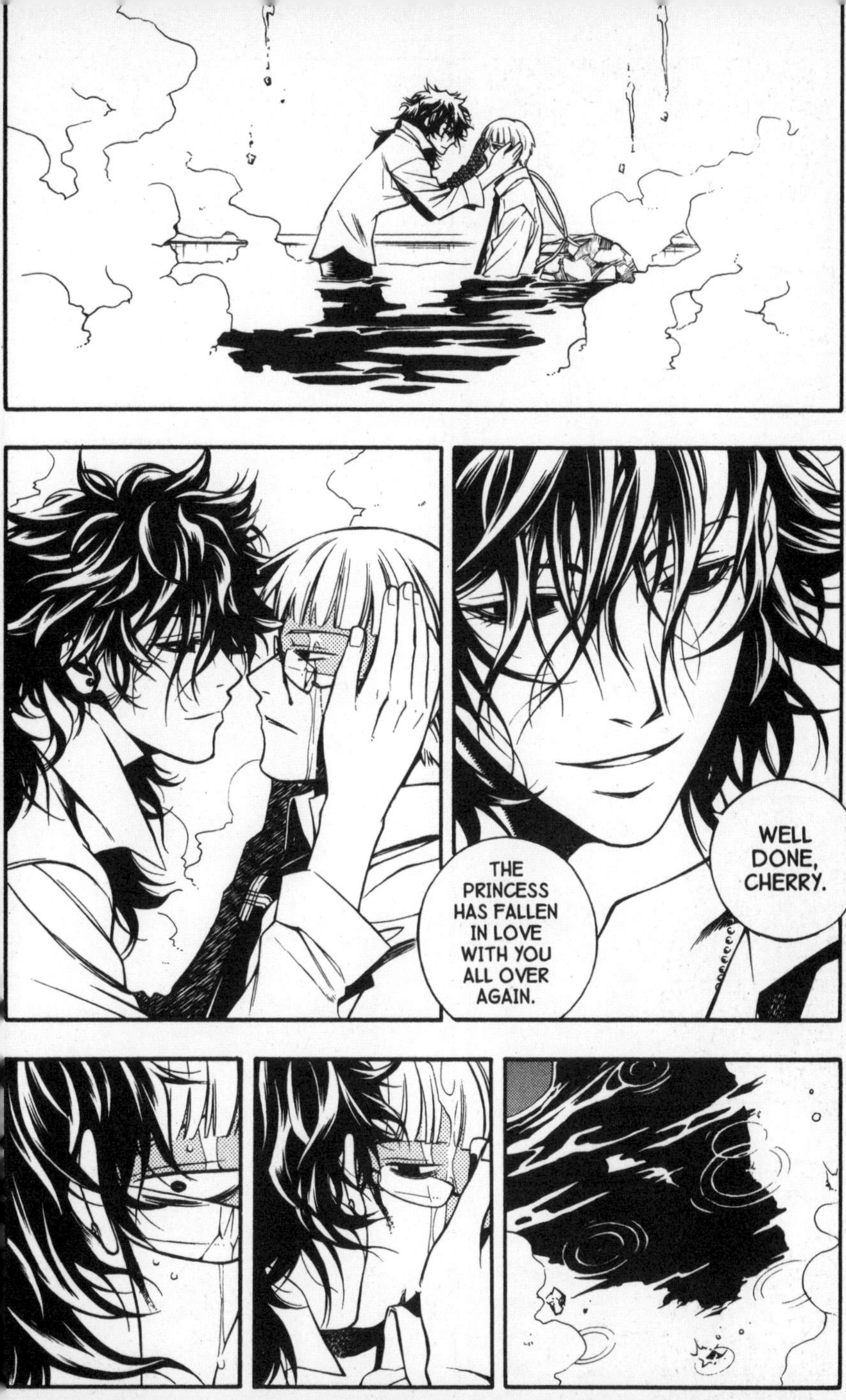
WELL DONE, CHERRY.
THE PRINCESS HAS FALLEN IN LOVE WITH YOU ALL OVER AGAIN.

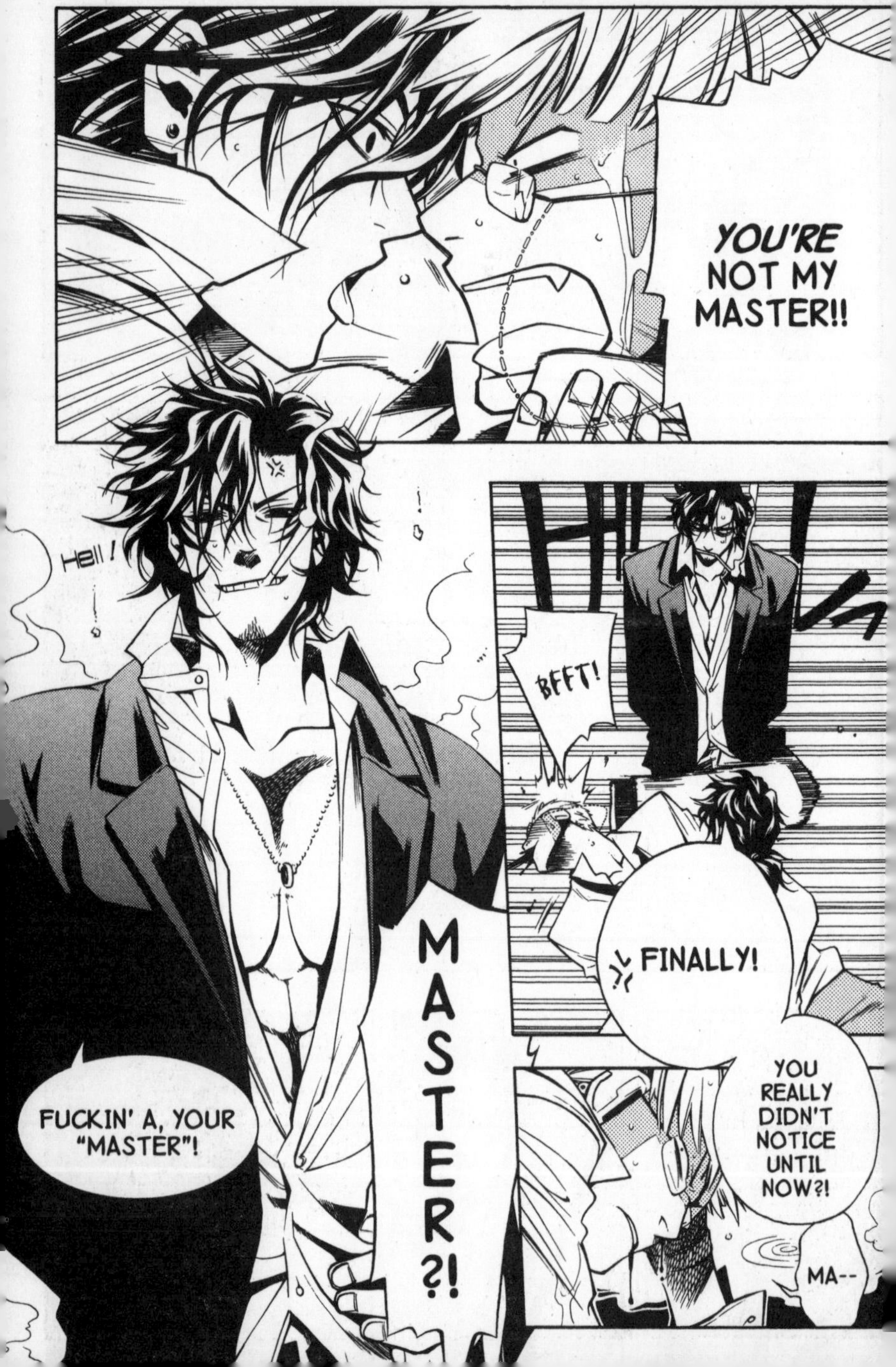
YOU'RE NOT MY MASTER!!
BFFT!
FINALLY!
YOU REALLY DIDN'T NOTICE UNTIL NOW?!
MA--
Hell!
MASTER?!
FUCKIN' A, YOUR "MASTER"!

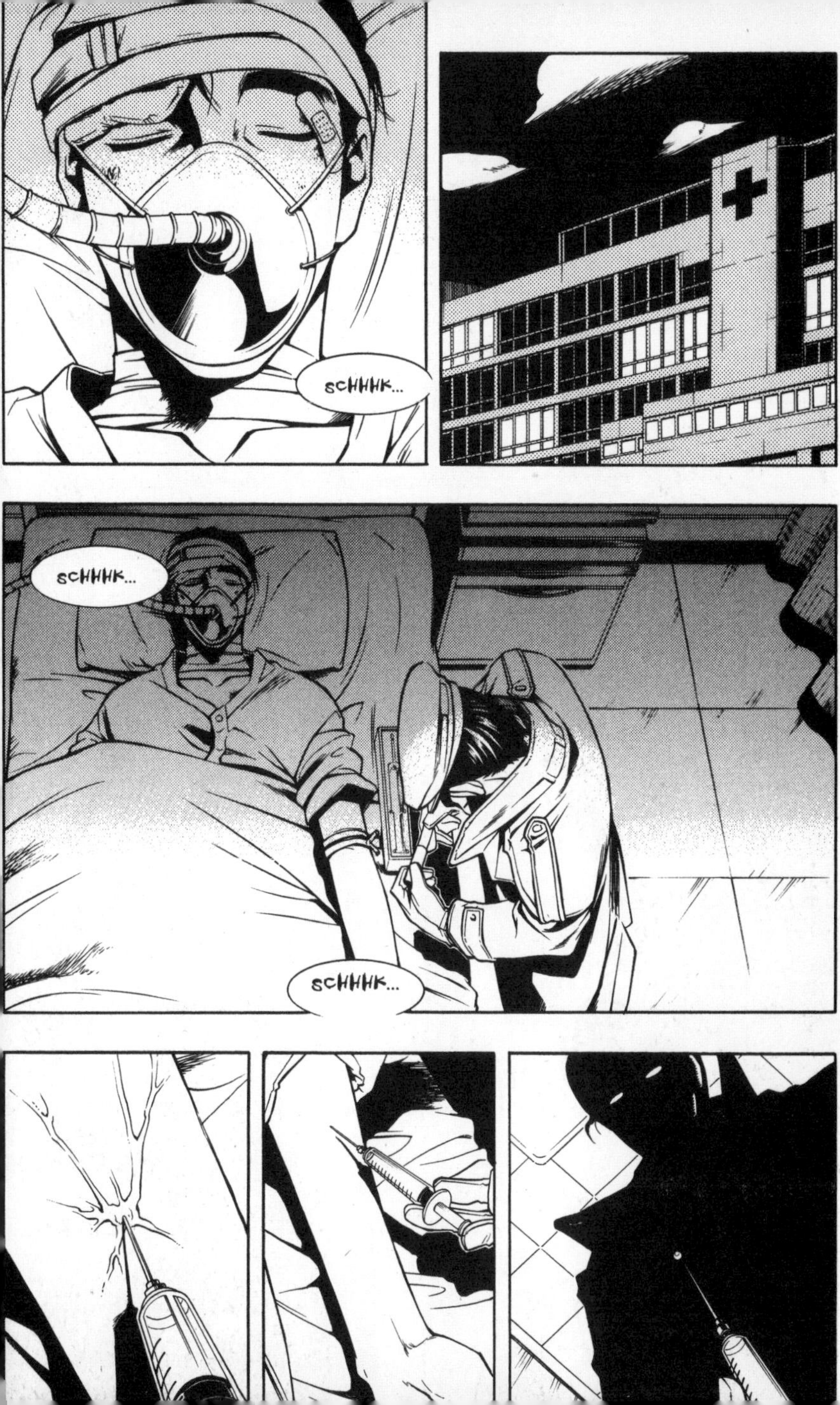
SCHHHK...
SCHHHK...
SCHHHK...

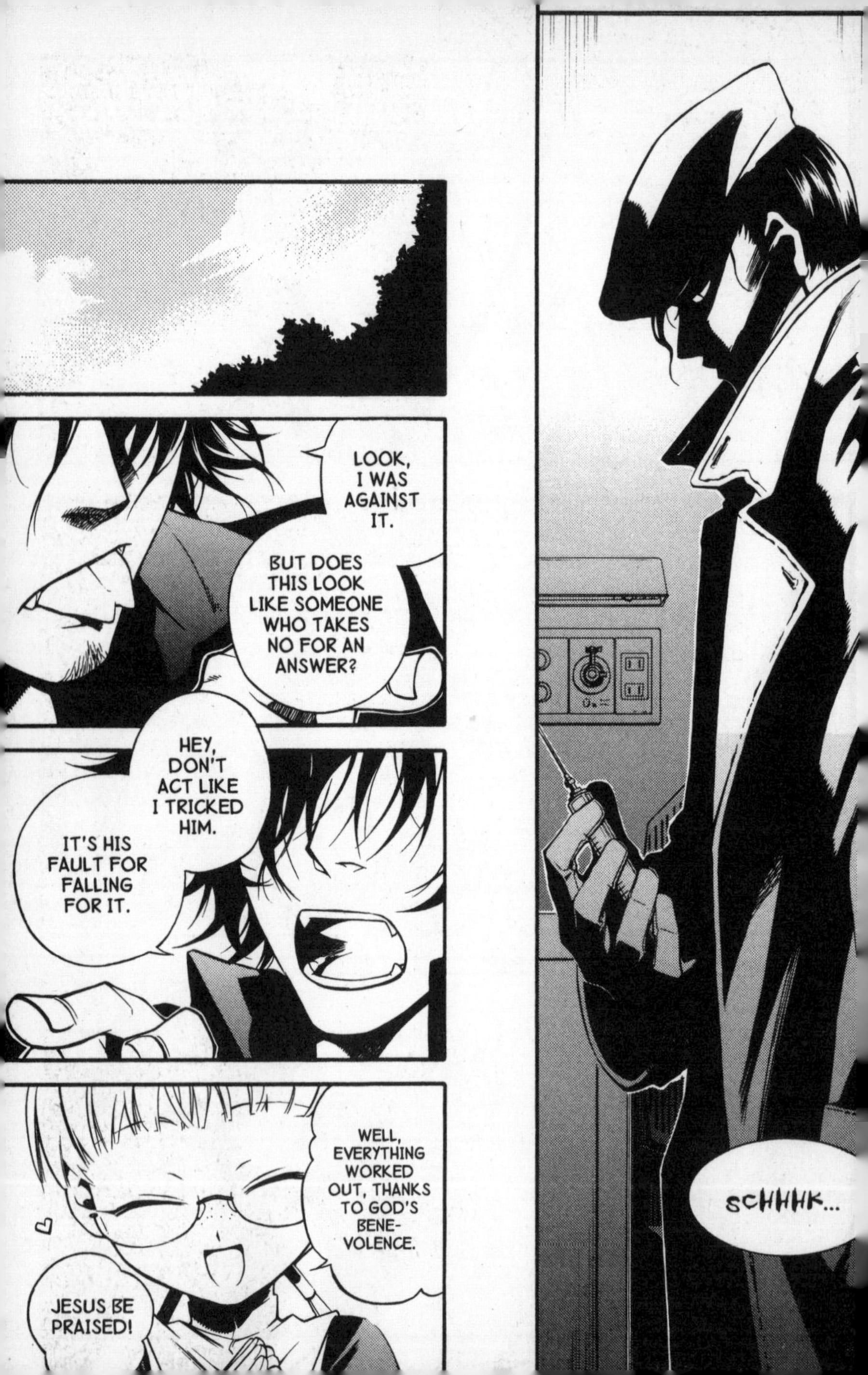
SCHHHK...
LOOK, I WAS AGAINST IT.
BUT DOES THIS LOOK LIKE SOMEONE WHO TAKES NO FOR AN ANSWER?
HEY, DON'T ACT LIKE I TRICKED HIM.
IT'S HIS FAULT FOR FALLING FOR IT.
WELL, EVERYTHING WORKED OUT, THANKS TO GOD'S BENE-VOLENCE.
JESUS BE PRAISED!

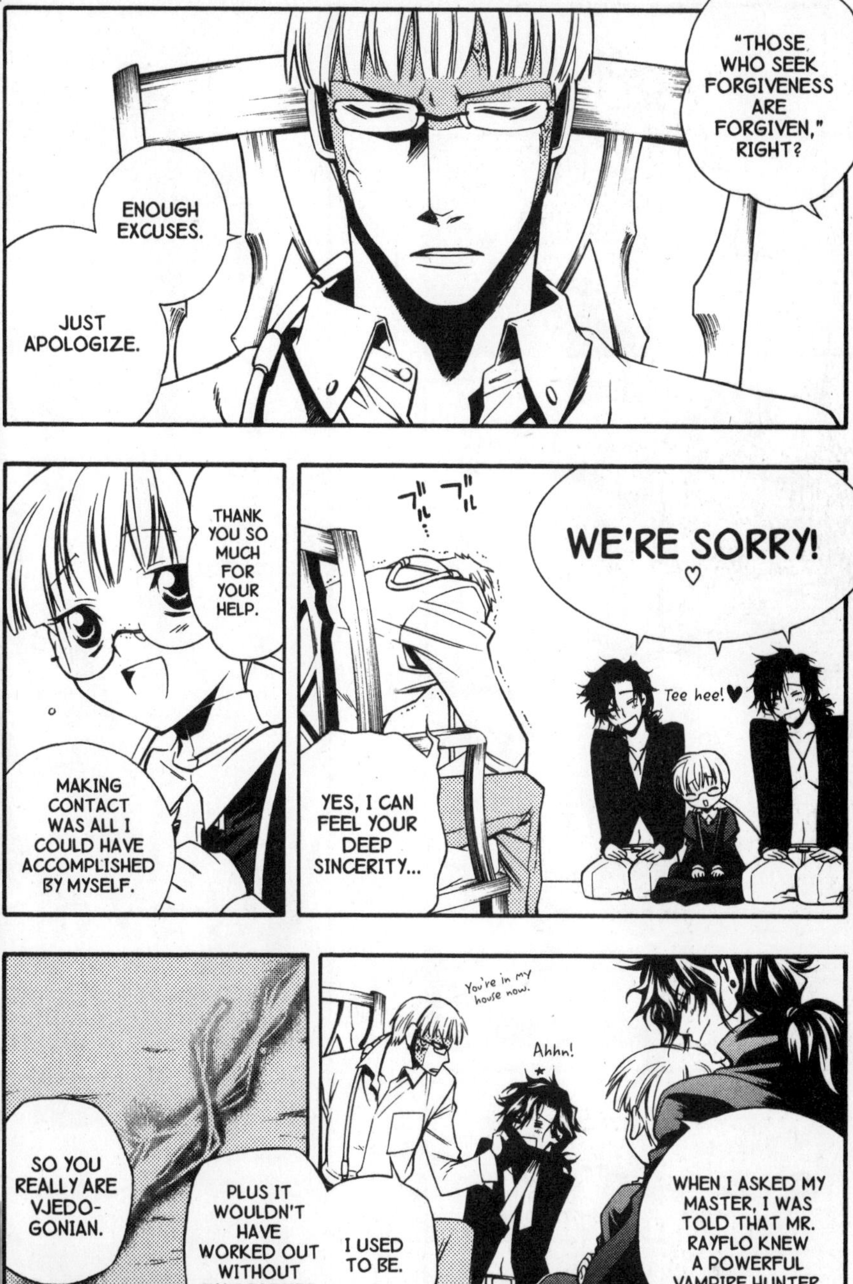
"THOSE WHO SEEK FORGIVENESS ARE FORGIVEN," RIGHT?
ENOUGH EXCUSES.
JUST APOLOGIZE.
WE'RE SORRY! ♡
Tee hee! ♥
ブルブル
YES, I CAN FEEL YOUR DEEP SINCERITY...
THANK YOU SO MUCH FOR YOUR HELP.
MAKING CONTACT WAS ALL I COULD HAVE ACCOMPLISHED BY MYSELF.
You're in my house now.
Ahhh!
WHEN I ASKED MY MASTER, I WAS TOLD THAT MR. RAYFLO KNEW A POWERFUL VAMPIRE HUNTER.
I USED TO BE.
PLUS IT WOULDN'T HAVE WORKED OUT WITHOUT THAT BARRIER.
SO YOU REALLY ARE VJEDO-GONIAN.

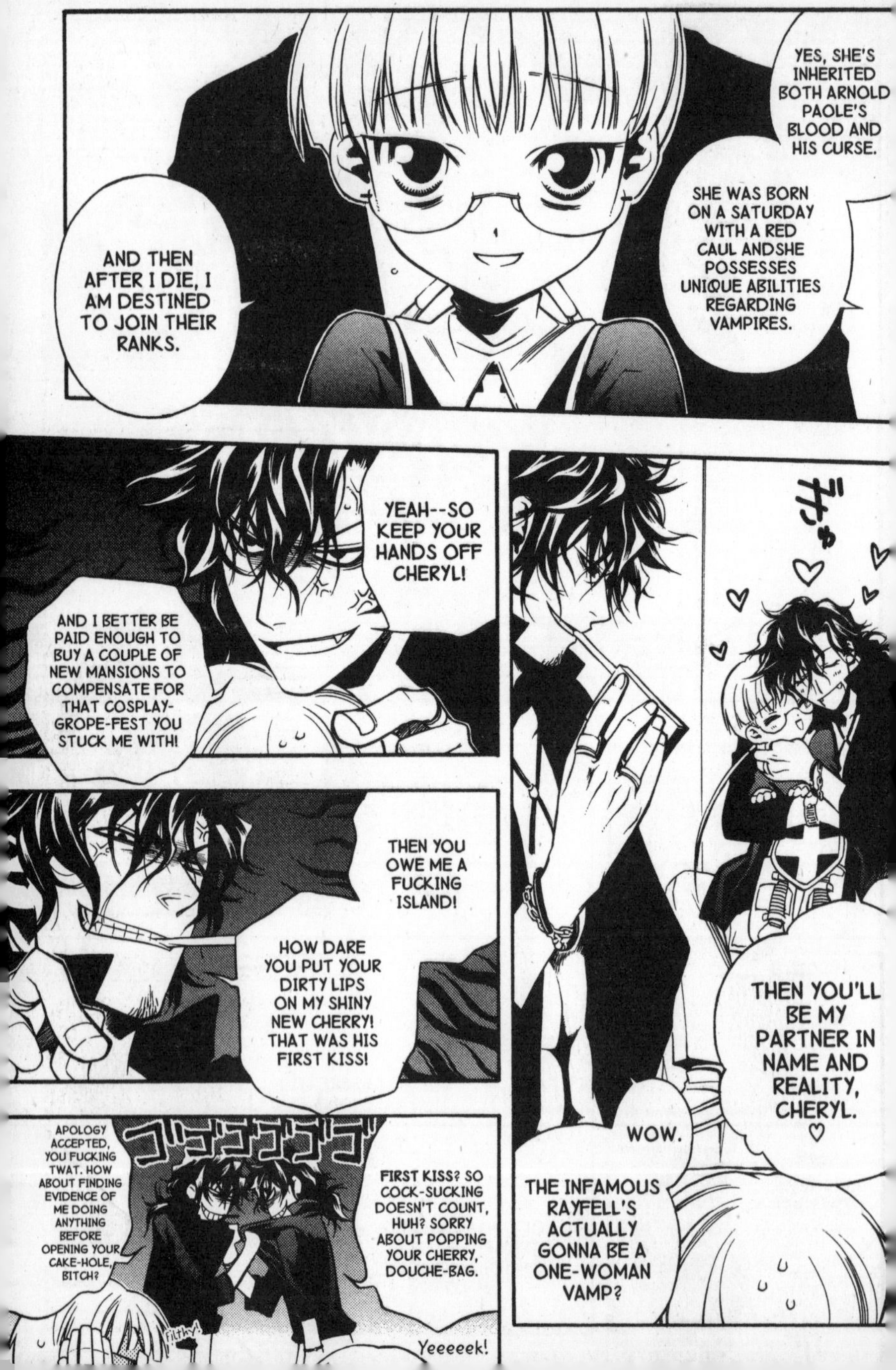
YES, SHE'S INHERITED BOTH ARNOLD PAOLE'S BLOOD AND HIS CURSE.
SHE WAS BORN ON A SATURDAY WITH A RED CAUL ANDSHE POSSESSES UNIQUE ABILITIES REGARDING VAMPIRES.
AND THEN AFTER I DIE, I AM DESTINED TO JOIN THEIR RANKS.
ぎゅ
THEN YOU'LL BE MY PARTNER IN NAME AND REALITY, CHERYL. ♡
WOW.
THE INFAMOUS RAYFELL'S ACTUALLY GONNA BE A ONE-WOMAN VAMP?
YEAH--SO KEEP YOUR HANDS OFF CHERYL!
AND I BETTER BE PAID ENOUGH TO BUY A COUPLE OF NEW MANSIONS TO COMPENSATE FOR THAT COSPLAY-GROPE-FEST YOU STUCK ME WITH!
THEN YOU OWE ME A FUCKING ISLAND!
HOW DARE YOU PUT YOUR DIRTY LIPS ON MY SHINY NEW CHERRY! THAT WAS HIS FIRST KISS!
FIRST KISS? SO COCK-SUCKING DOESN'T COUNT, HUH? SORRY ABOUT POPPING YOUR CHERRY, DOUCHE-BAG.
APOLOGY ACCEPTED, YOU FUCKING TWAT. HOW ABOUT FINDING EVIDENCE OF ME DOING ANYTHING BEFORE OPENING YOUR CAKE-HOLE, BITCH?
Filthy!
Yeeeeek!

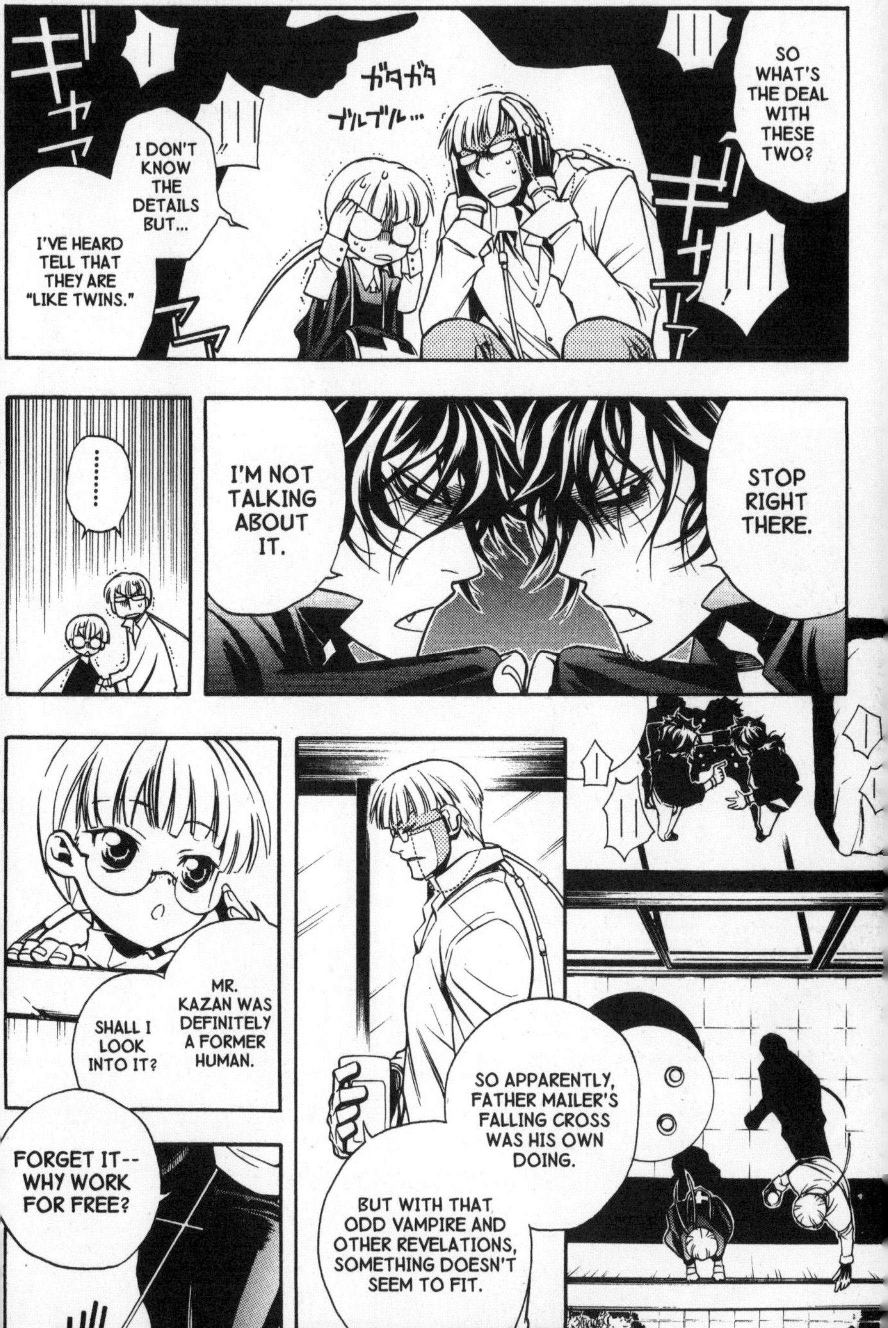
ギャァ
ギャァ
SO WHAT'S THE DEAL WITH THESE TWO?
ガタガタ
ブルブル…
I DON'T KNOW THE DETAILS BUT...
I'VE HEARD TELL THAT THEY ARE "LIKE TWINS."
STOP RIGHT THERE.
I'M NOT TALKING ABOUT IT.
....
SO APPARENTLY, FATHER MAILER'S FALLING CROSS WAS HIS OWN DOING.
BUT WITH THAT ODD VAMPIRE AND OTHER REVELATIONS, SOMETHING DOESN'T SEEM TO FIT.
MR. KAZAN WAS DEFINITELY A FORMER HUMAN.
SHALL I LOOK INTO IT?
FORGET IT-- WHY WORK FOR FREE?

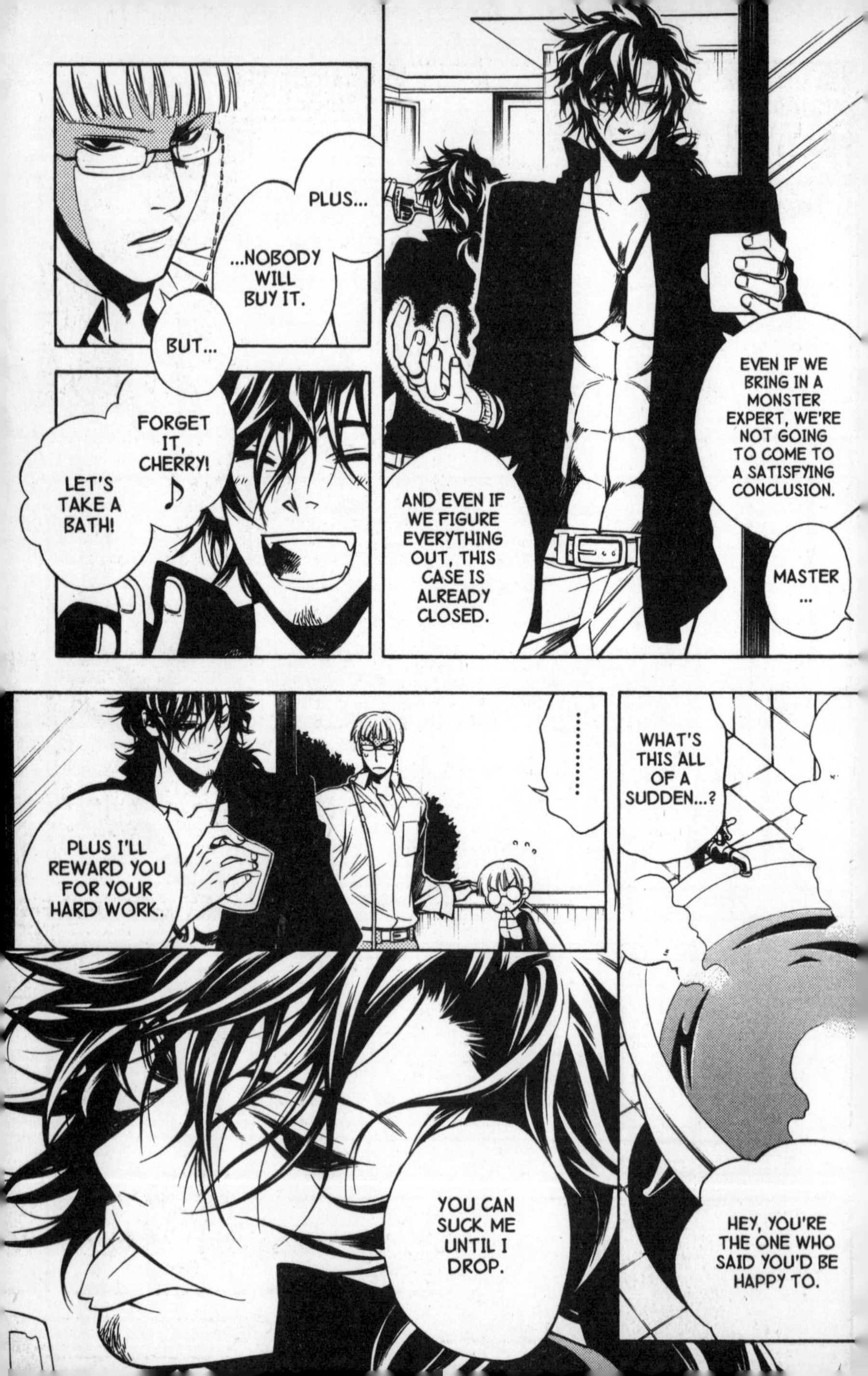
EVEN IF WE BRING IN A MONSTER EXPERT, WE'RE NOT GOING TO COME TO A SATISFYING CONCLUSION.
MASTER ...
AND EVEN IF WE FIGURE EVERYTHING OUT, THIS CASE IS ALREADY CLOSED.
PLUS...
...NOBODY WILL BUY IT.
BUT...
FORGET IT, CHERRY! ♪
LET'S TAKE A BATH!
WHAT'S THIS ALL OF A SUDDEN...?
HEY, YOU'RE THE ONE WHO SAID YOU'D BE HAPPY TO.
....
PLUS I'LL REWARD YOU FOR YOUR HARD WORK.
YOU CAN SUCK ME UNTIL I DROP.

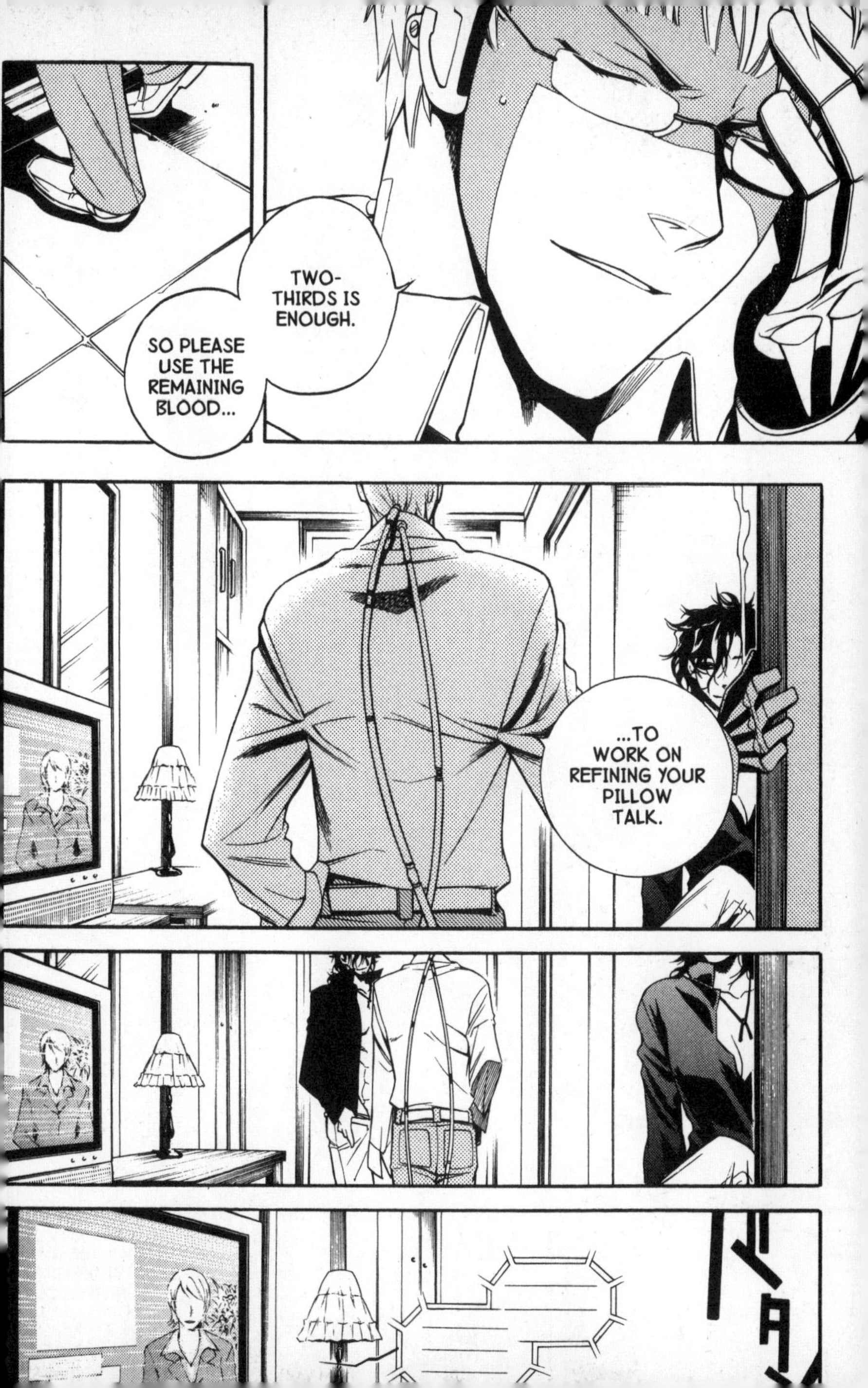
TWO-THIRDS IS ENOUGH.
SO PLEASE USE THE REMAINING BLOOD...
...TO WORK ON REFINING YOUR PILLOW TALK.

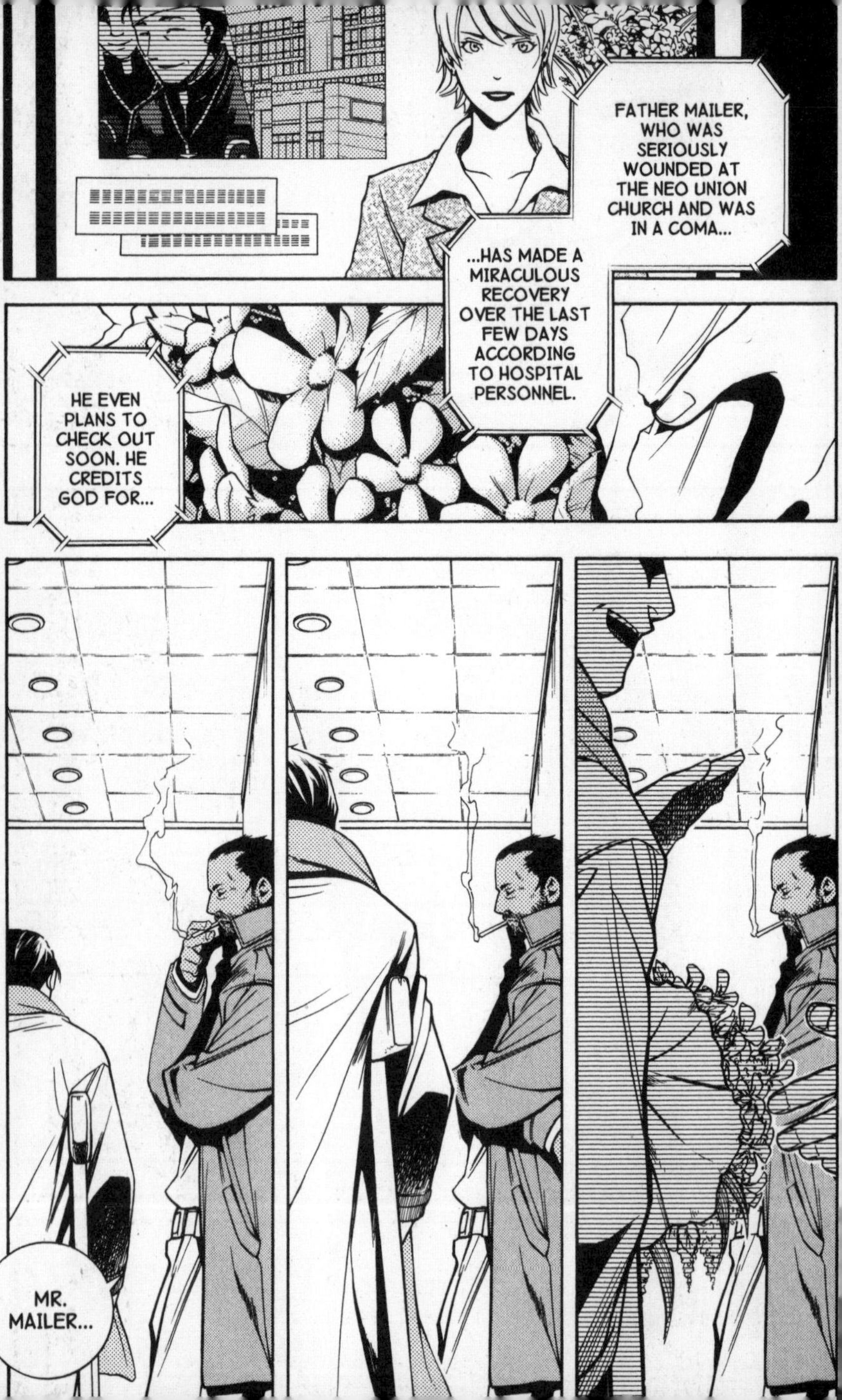
FATHER MAILER, WHO WAS SERIOUSLY WOUNDED AT THE NEO UNION CHURCH AND WAS IN A COMA...
...HAS MADE A MIRACULOUS RECOVERY OVER THE LAST FEW DAYS ACCORDING TO HOSPITAL PERSONNEL.
HE EVEN PLANS TO CHECK OUT SOON. HE CREDITS GOD FOR...
MR. MAILER...

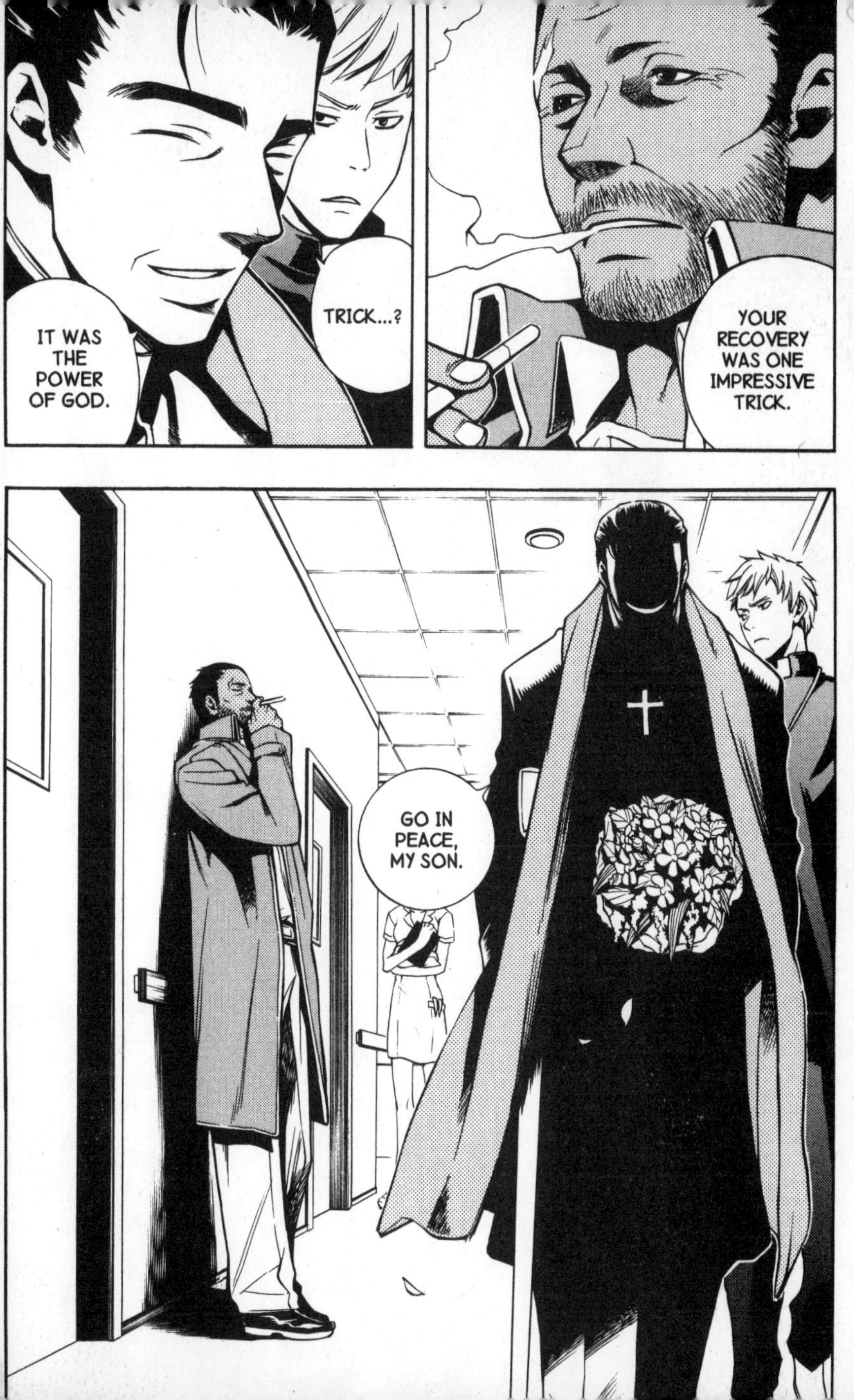
YOUR RECOVERY WAS ONE IMPRESSIVE TRICK.
TRICK...?
IT WAS THE POWER OF GOD.
GO IN PEACE, MY SON.

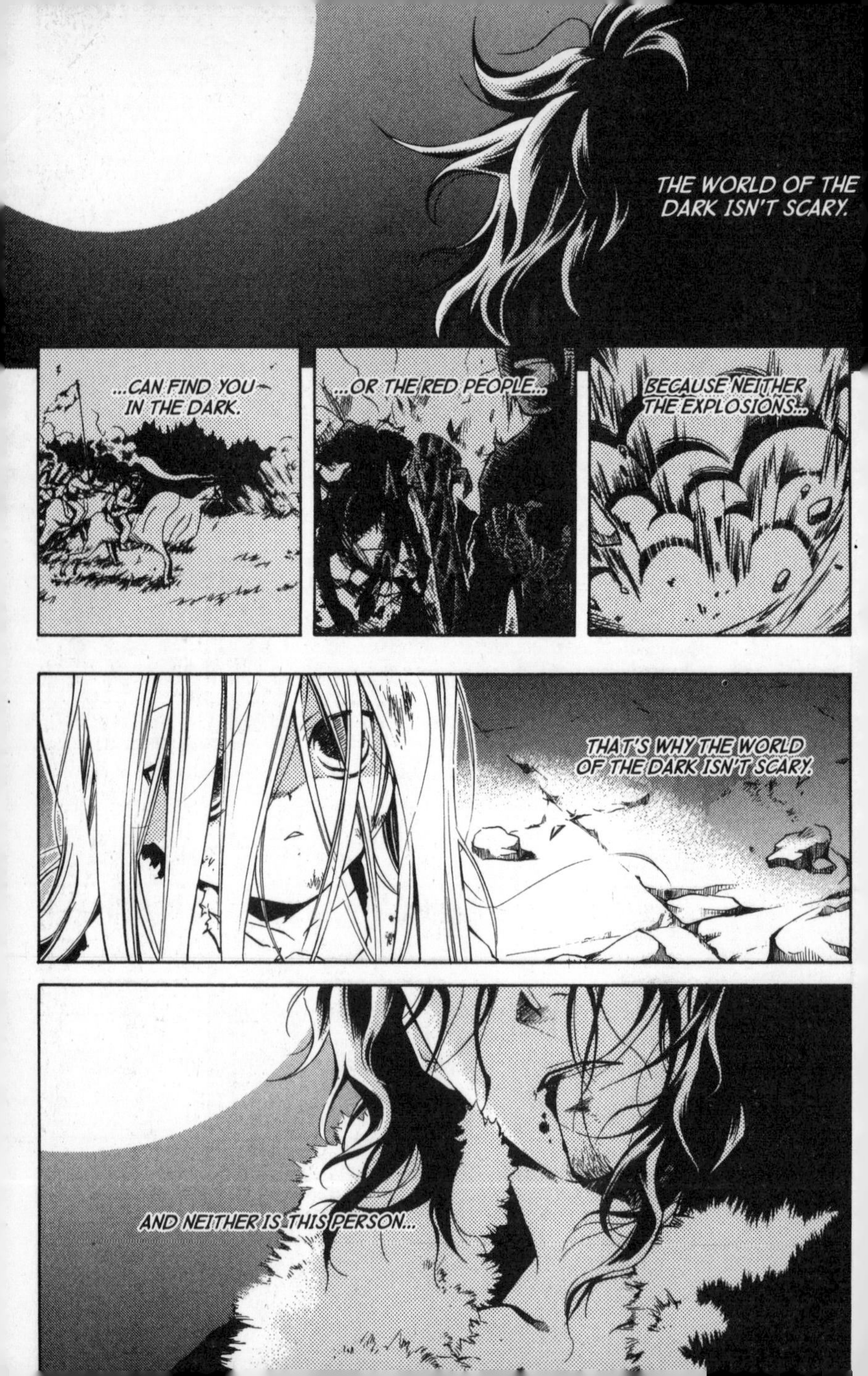
THE WORLD OF THE DARK ISN'T SCARY.
BECAUSE NEITHER THE EXPLOSIONS...
...OR THE RED PEOPLE...
...CAN FIND YOU IN THE DARK.
THAT'S WHY THE WORLD OF THE DARK ISN'T SCARY.
AND NEITHER IS THIS PERSON...

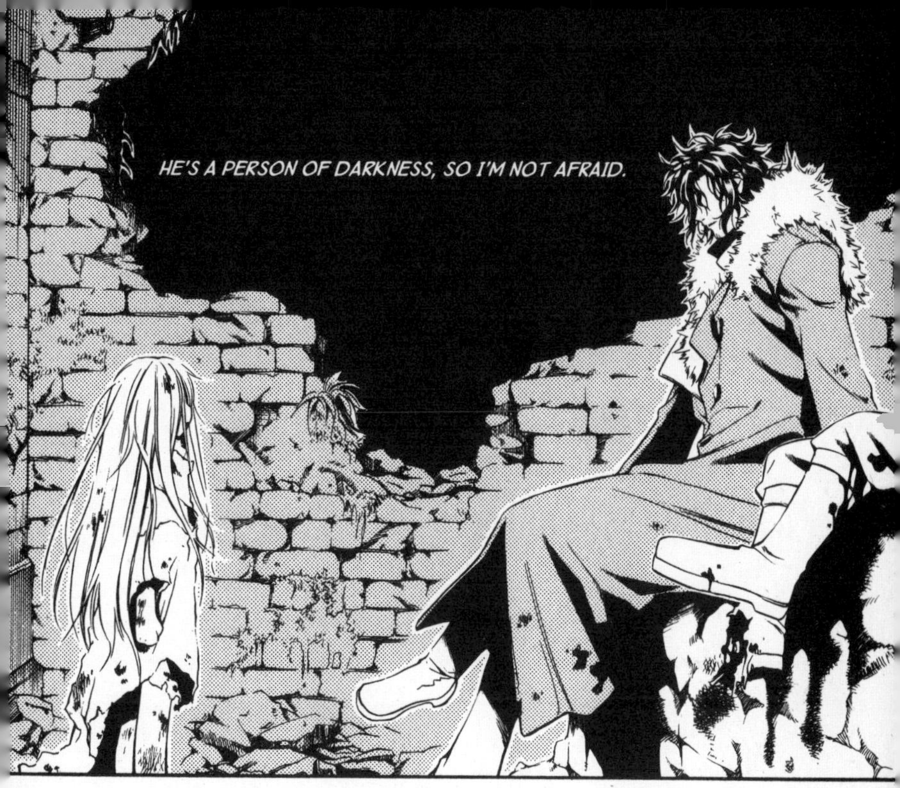
HE'S A PERSON OF DARKNESS, SO I'M NOT AFRAID.

CHAPTER 3
FLEETING DARK ABBA

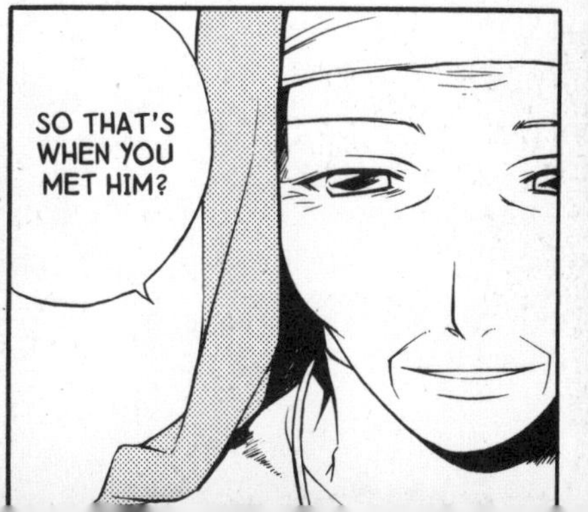
SO THAT'S WHEN YOU MET HIM?

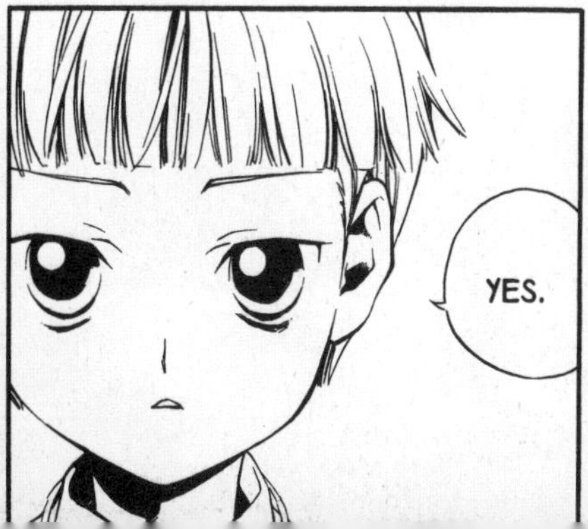
YES.

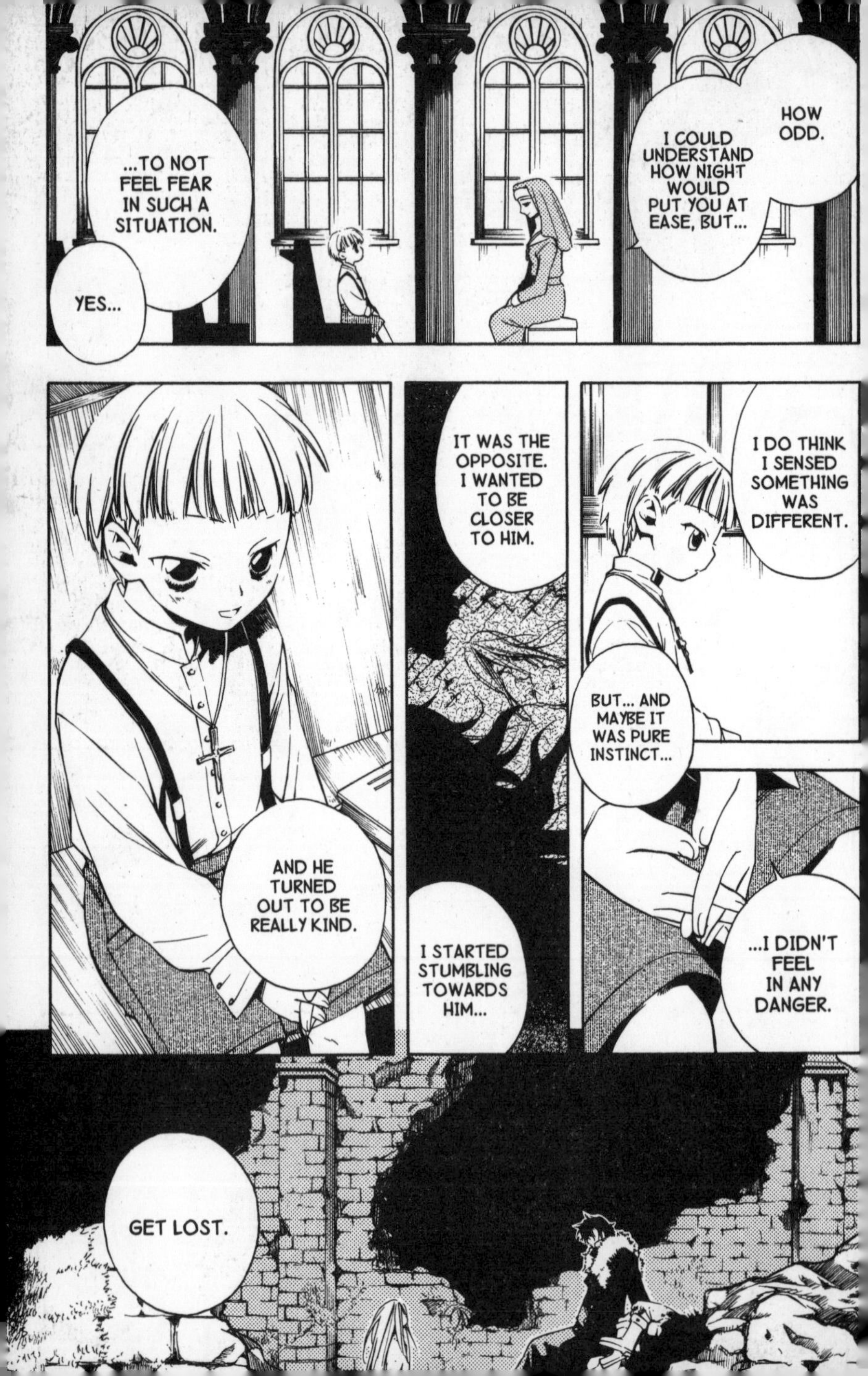
HOW ODD.
I COULD UNDERSTAND HOW NIGHT WOULD PUT YOU AT EASE, BUT...
...TO NOT FEEL FEAR IN SUCH A SITUATION.
YES...
I DO THINK I SENSED SOMETHING WAS DIFFERENT.
BUT... AND MAYBE IT WAS PURE INSTINCT...
...I DIDN'T FEEL IN ANY DANGER.
IT WAS THE OPPOSITE. I WANTED TO BE CLOSER TO HIM.
I STARTED STUMBLING TOWARDS HIM...
AND HE TURNED OUT TO BE REALLY KIND.
GET LOST.

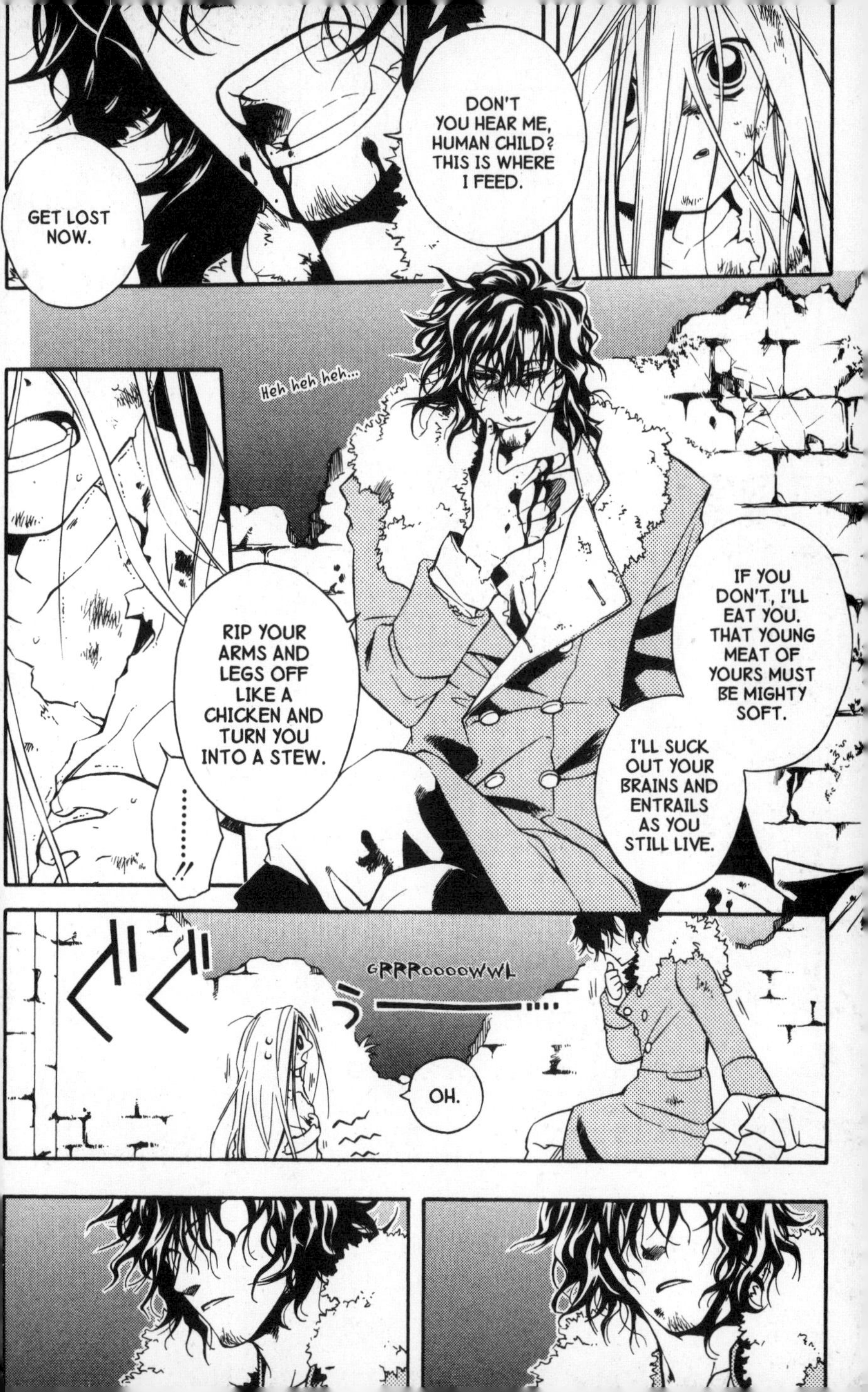
DON'T YOU HEAR ME, HUMAN CHILD? THIS IS WHERE I FEED.
GET LOST NOW.
Heh heh heh...
IF YOU DON'T, I'LL EAT YOU. THAT YOUNG MEAT OF YOURS MUST BE MIGHTY SOFT.
I'LL SUCK OUT YOUR BRAINS AND ENTRAILS AS YOU STILL LIVE.
RIP YOUR ARMS AND LEGS OFF LIKE A CHICKEN AND TURN YOU INTO A STEW.
......!!
GRRRooooWWL
ぐぐう——....
OH.

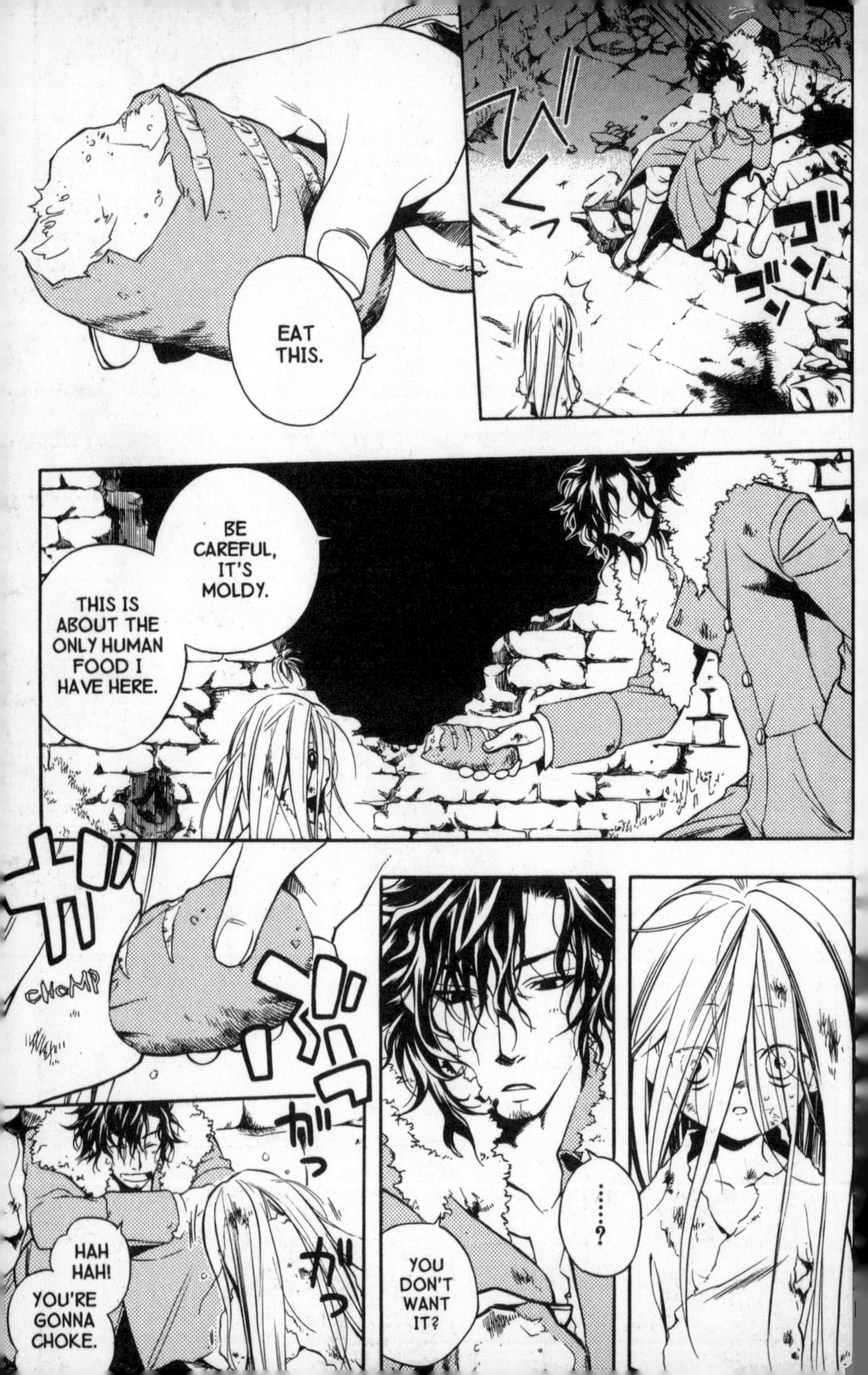
EAT THIS.
BE CAREFUL, IT'S MOLDY.
THIS IS ABOUT THE ONLY HUMAN FOOD I HAVE HERE.
......?
YOU DON'T WANT IT?
CHOMP
HAH HAH! YOU'RE GONNA CHOKE.

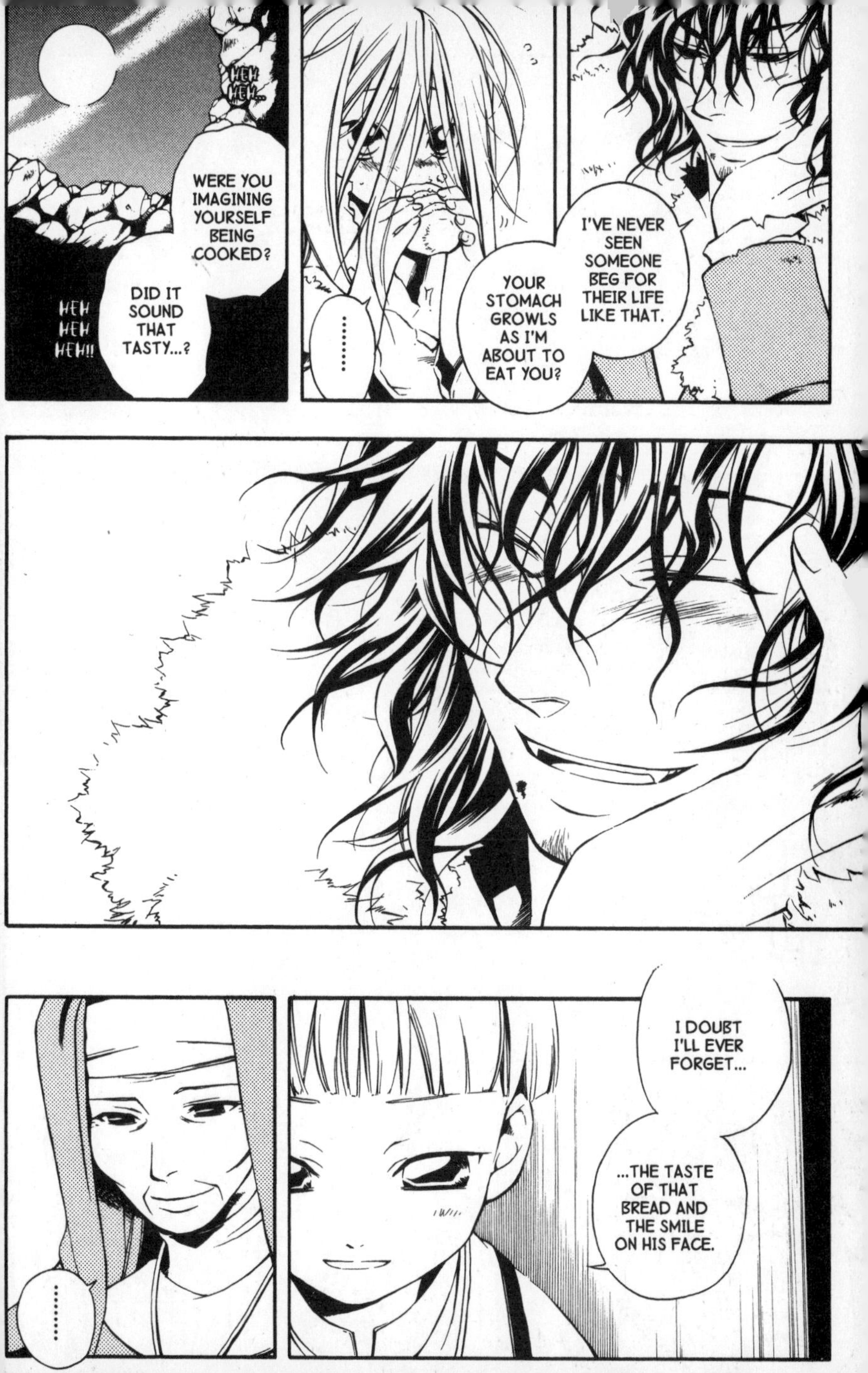
I'VE NEVER SEEN SOMEONE BEG FOR THEIR LIFE LIKE THAT.
YOUR STOMACH GROWLS AS I'M ABOUT TO EAT YOU?
....
HEH HEH...
WERE YOU IMAGINING YOURSELF BEING COOKED?
DID IT SOUND THAT TASTY...?
HEH HEH HEH!!
I DOUBT I'LL EVER FORGET...
...THE TASTE OF THAT BREAD AND THE SMILE ON HIS FACE.
....

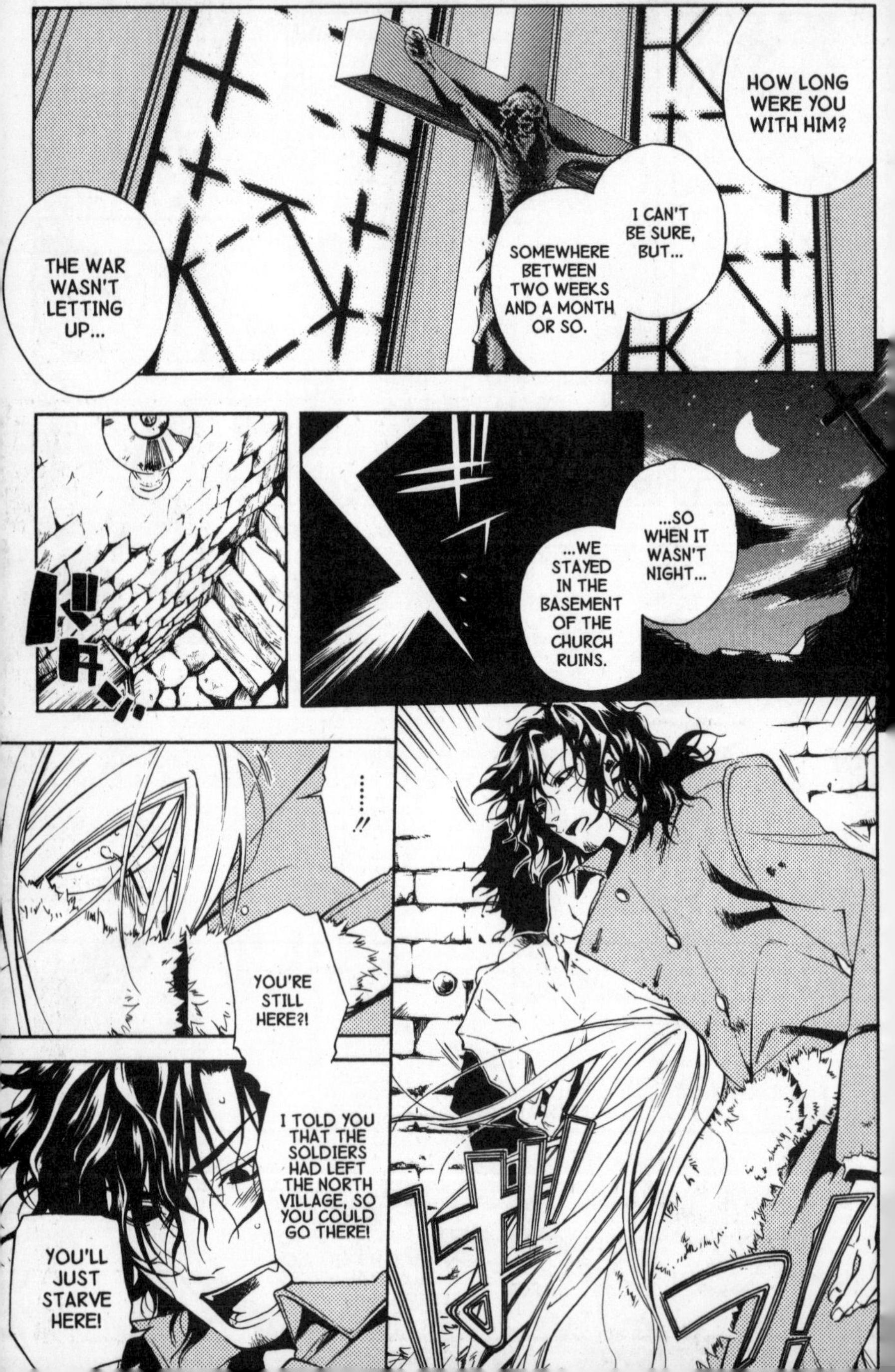
HOW LONG WERE YOU WITH HIM?
I CAN'T BE SURE, BUT...
SOMEWHERE BETWEEN TWO WEEKS AND A MONTH OR SO.
THE WAR WASN'T LETTING UP...
...SO WHEN IT WASN'T NIGHT...
...WE STAYED IN THE BASEMENT OF THE CHURCH RUINS.
......!!
YOU'RE STILL HERE?!
I TOLD YOU THAT THE SOLDIERS HAD LEFT THE NORTH VILLAGE, SO YOU COULD GO THERE!
YOU'LL JUST STARVE HERE!

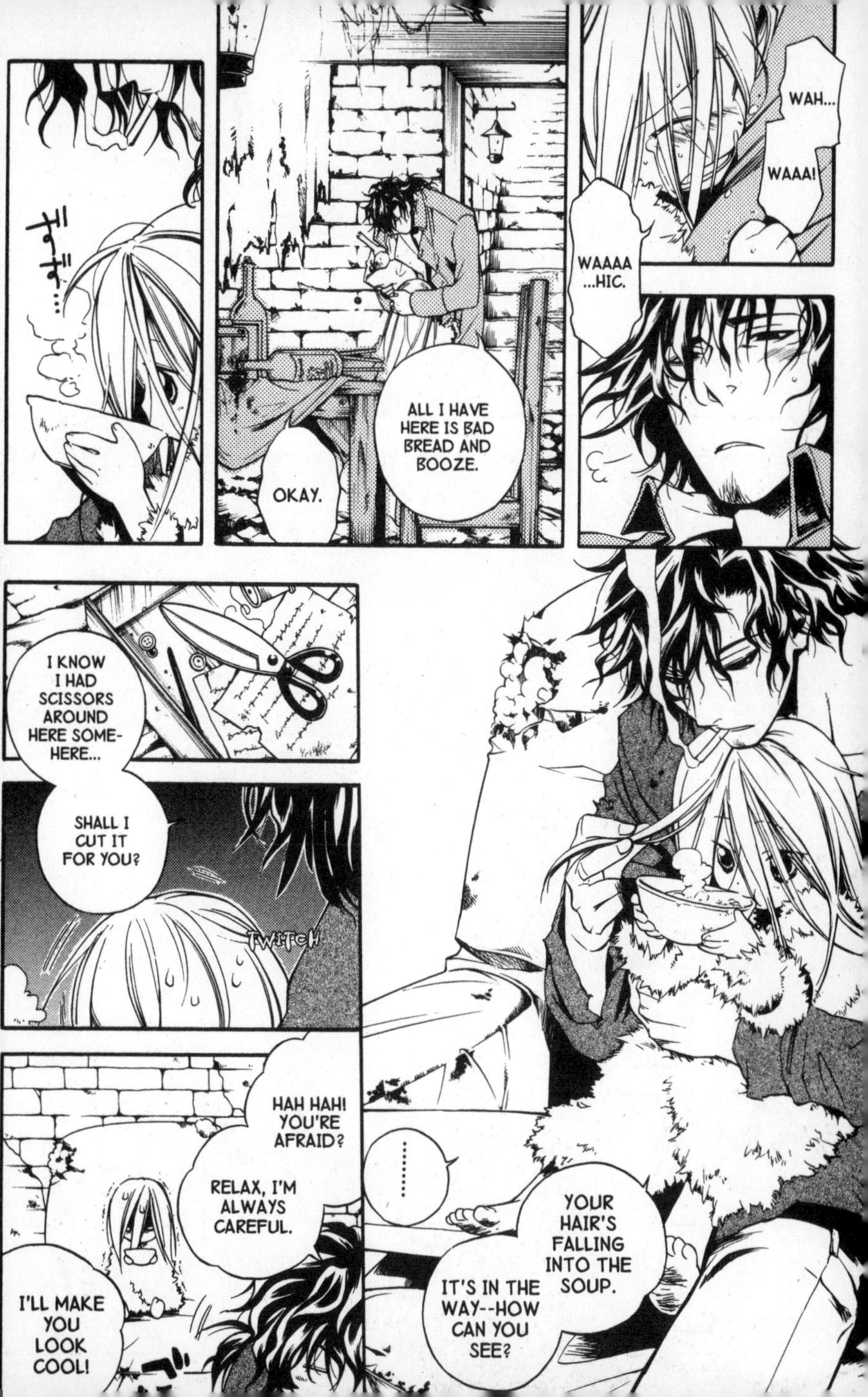
WAH...
WAAA!
WAAAA ...HIC.
ALL I HAVE HERE IS BAD BREAD AND BOOZE.
OKAY.
ずず…
YOUR HAIR'S FALLING INTO THE SOUP.
IT'S IN THE WAY--HOW CAN YOU SEE?
......
I KNOW I HAD SCISSORS AROUND HERE SOME-HERE...
SHALL I CUT IT FOR YOU?
TWITCH
HAH HAH! YOU'RE AFRAID?
RELAX, I'M ALWAYS CAREFUL.
I'LL MAKE YOU LOOK COOL!

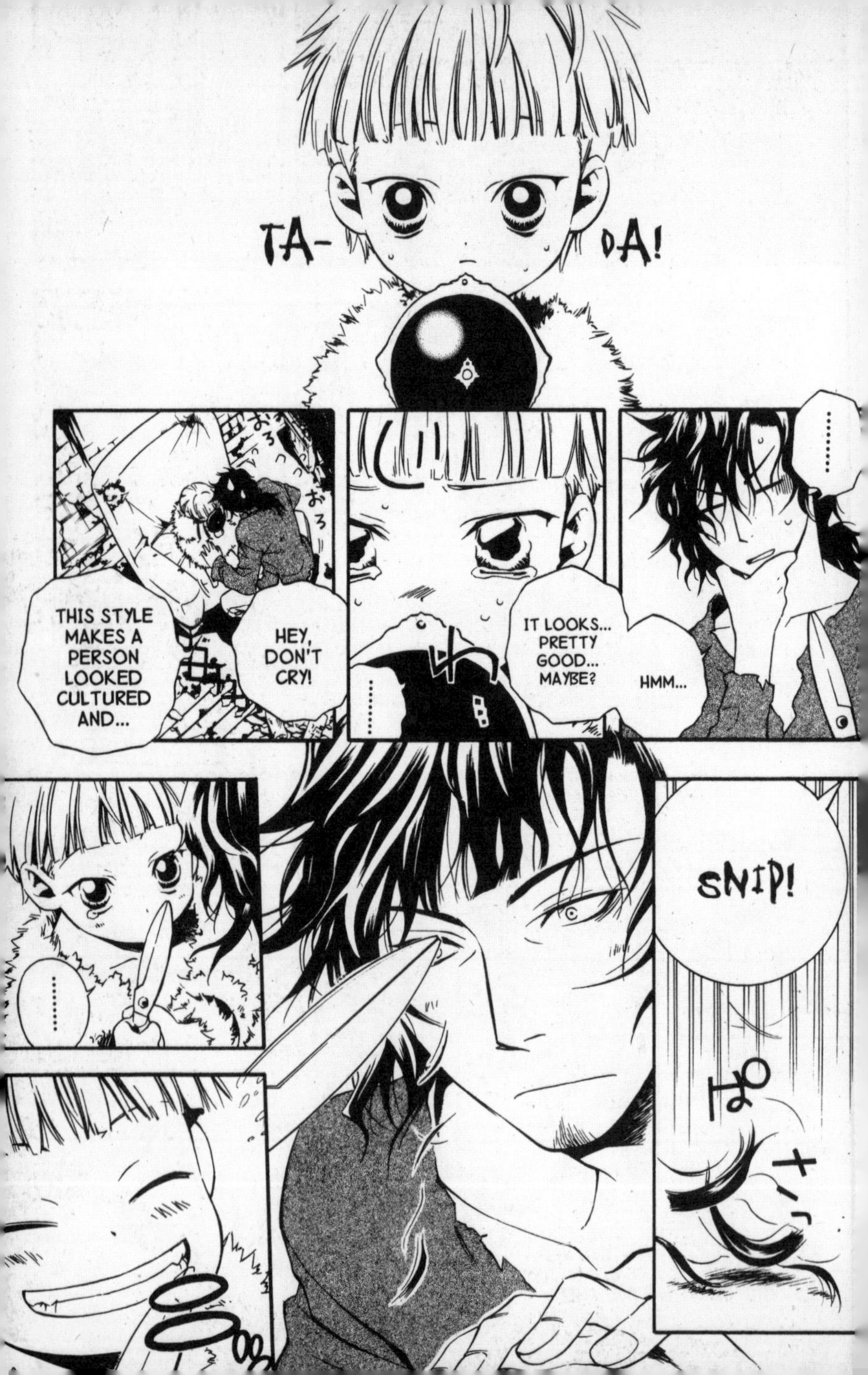
TA-
DA!
......
HMM...
IT LOOKS... PRETTY GOOD... MAYBE?
......
HEY, DON'T CRY!
THIS STYLE MAKES A PERSON LOOKED CULTURED AND...
SNIP!
......

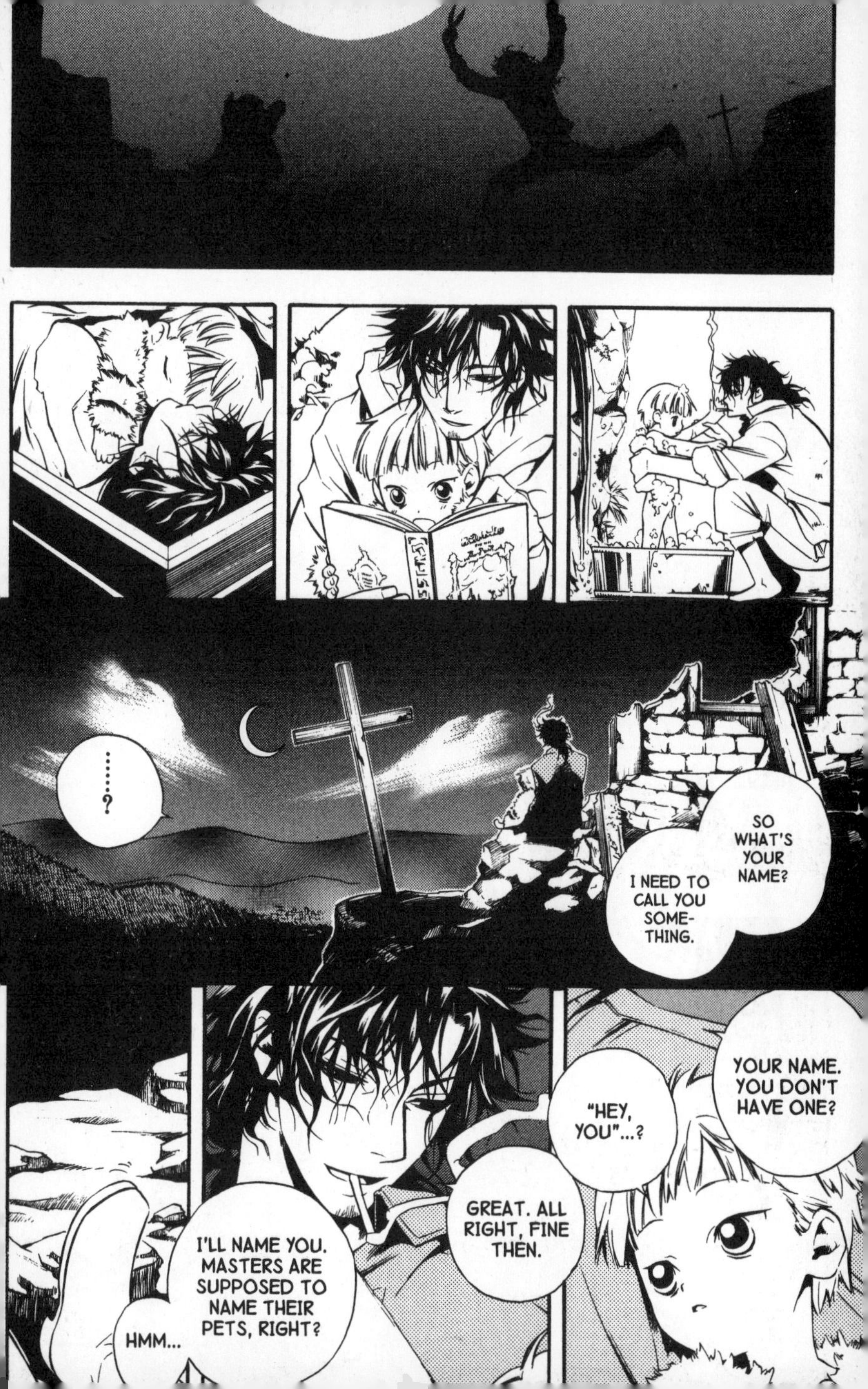
SO WHAT'S YOUR NAME?
I NEED TO CALL YOU SOME-THING.
......?
YOUR NAME. YOU DON'T HAVE ONE?
"HEY, YOU"...?
GREAT. ALL RIGHT, FINE THEN.
I'LL NAME YOU. MASTERS ARE SUPPOSED TO NAME THEIR PETS, RIGHT?
HMM...

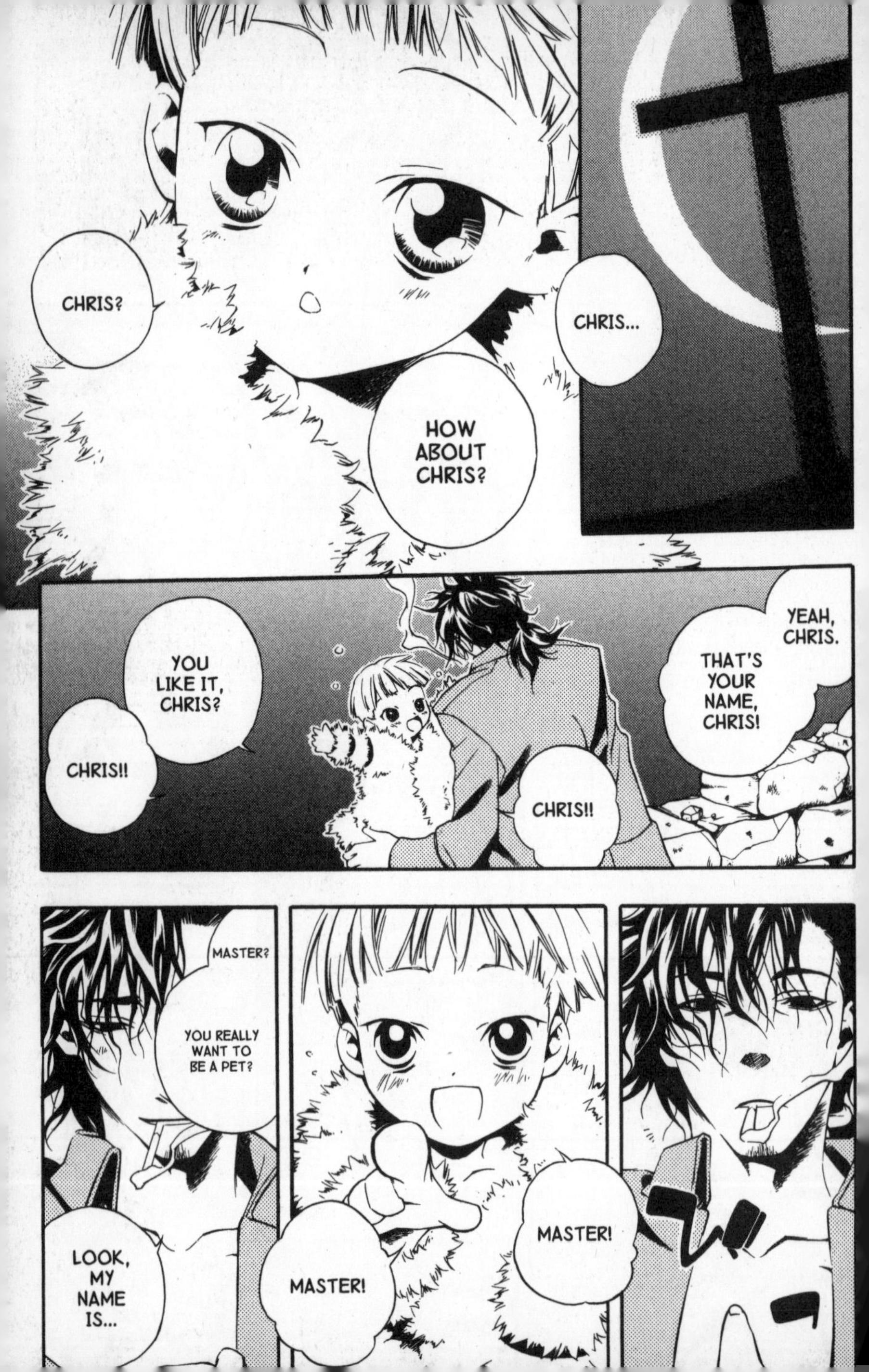
CHRIS...
HOW ABOUT CHRIS?
CHRIS?
YEAH, CHRIS.
THAT'S YOUR NAME, CHRIS!
CHRIS!!
YOU LIKE IT, CHRIS?
CHRIS!!
MASTER!
MASTER!
MASTER?
YOU REALLY WANT TO BE A PET?
LOOK, MY NAME IS...

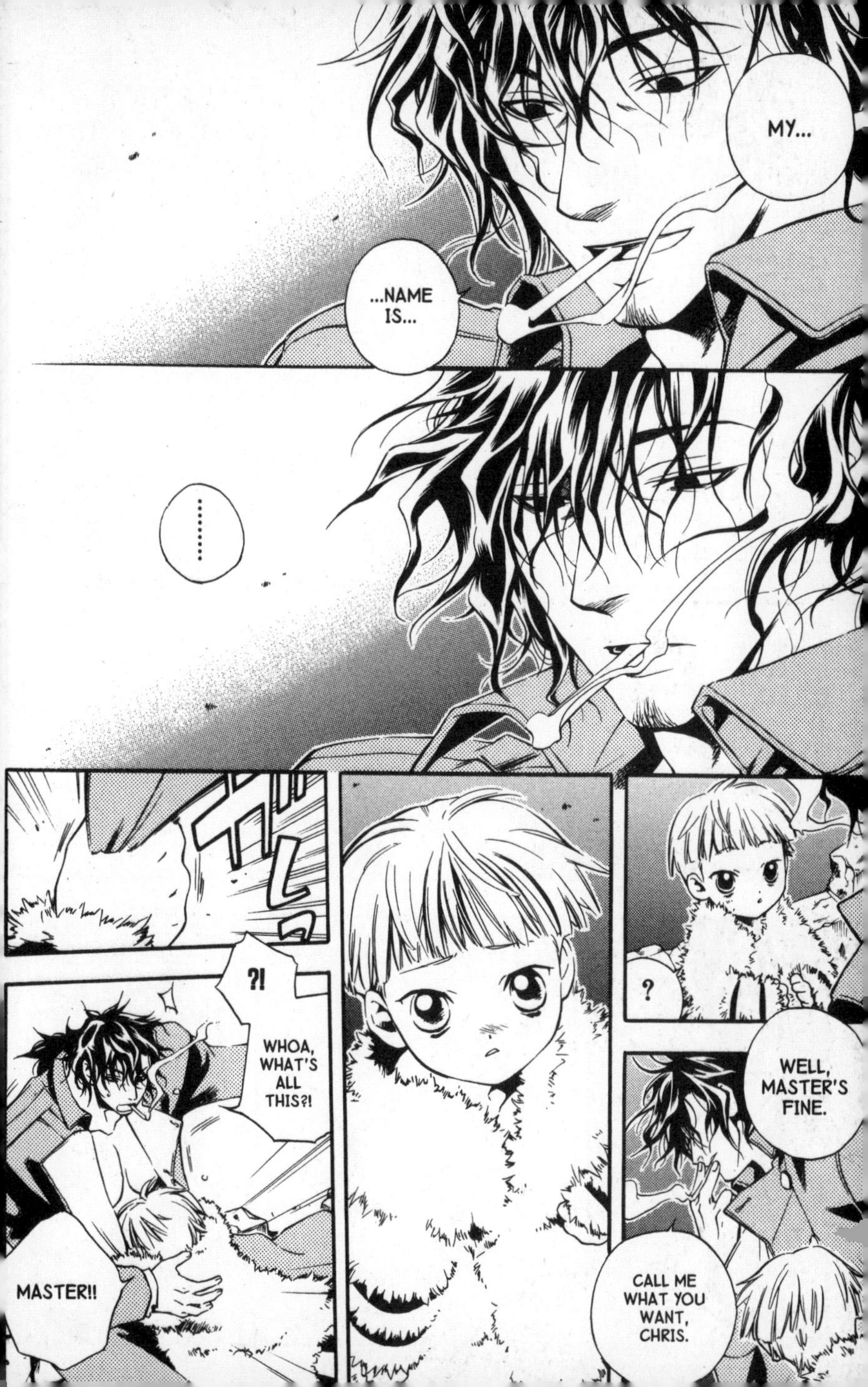
MY...
...NAME IS...
......
?
WELL, MASTER'S FINE.
CALL ME WHAT YOU WANT, CHRIS.
?!
WHOA, WHAT'S ALL THIS?!
MASTER!!

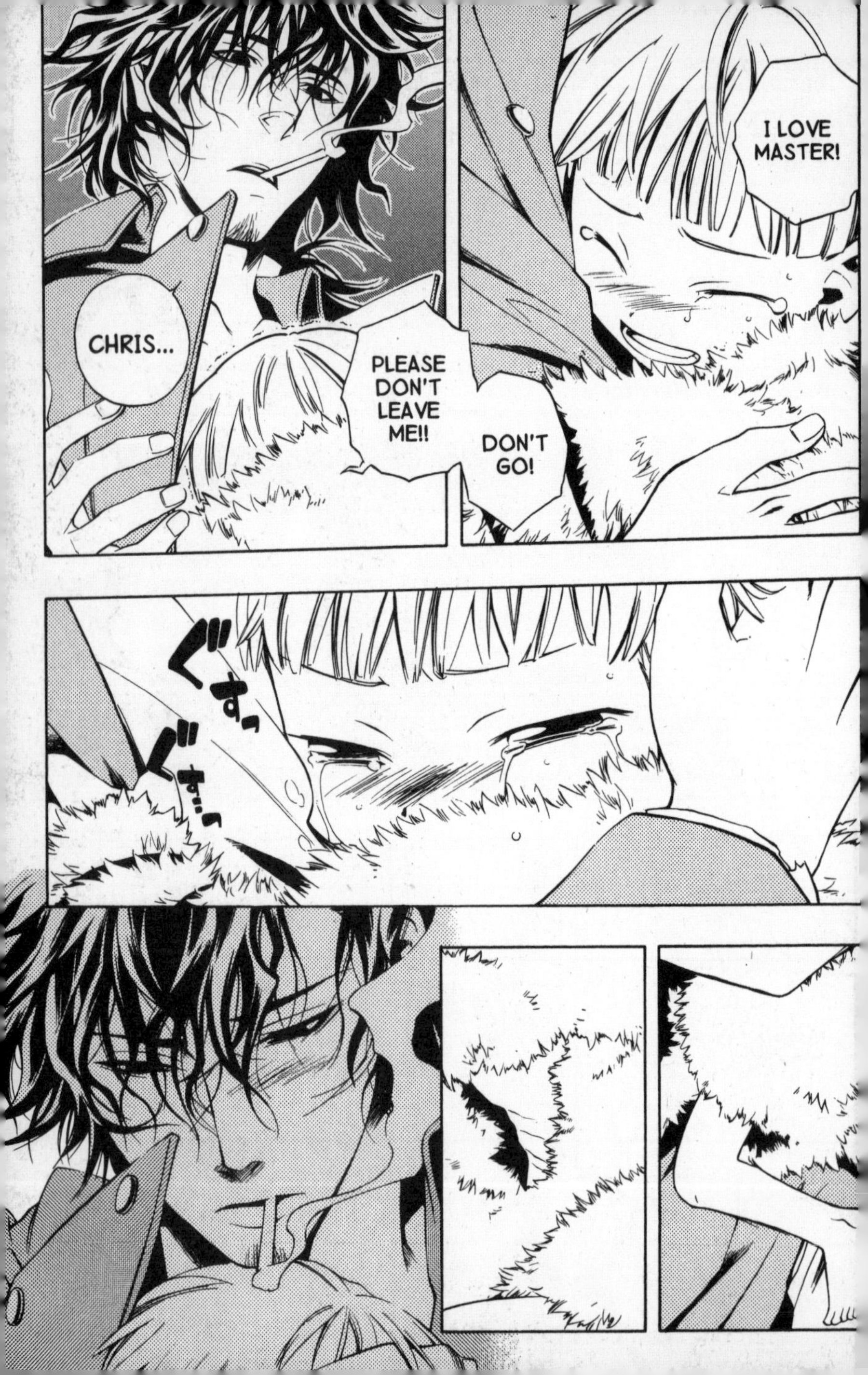
I LOVE MASTER!
DON'T GO!
PLEASE DON'T LEAVE ME!!
CHRIS...

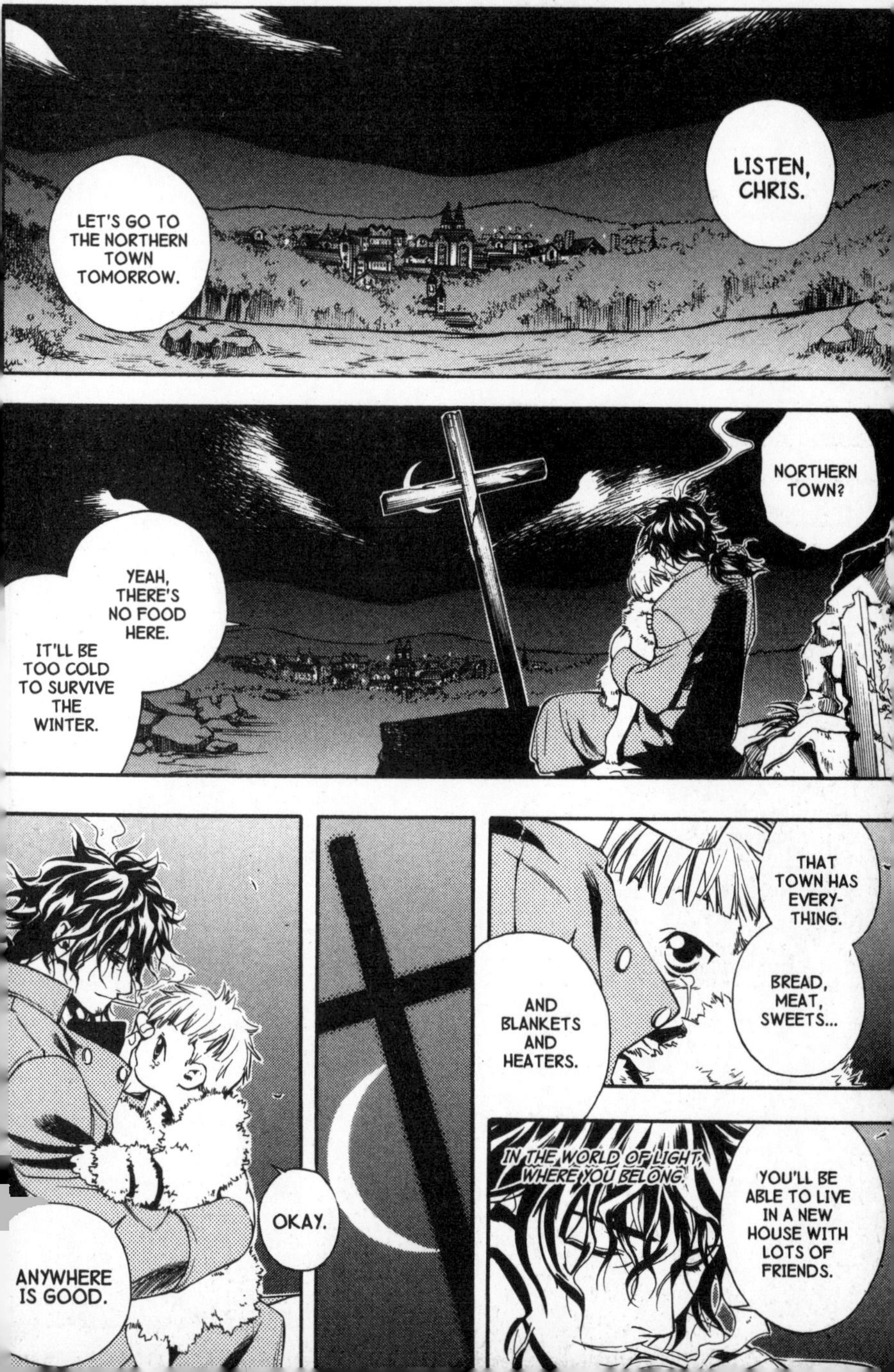
LISTEN, CHRIS.
LET'S GO TO THE NORTHERN TOWN TOMORROW.
NORTHERN TOWN?
YEAH, THERE'S NO FOOD HERE.
IT'LL BE TOO COLD TO SURVIVE THE WINTER.
THAT TOWN HAS EVERY-THING.
BREAD, MEAT, SWEETS...
AND BLANKETS AND HEATERS.
YOU'LL BE ABLE TO LIVE IN A NEW HOUSE WITH LOTS OF FRIENDS.
IN THE WORLD OF LIGHT, WHERE YOU BELONG.
OKAY.
ANYWHERE IS GOOD.

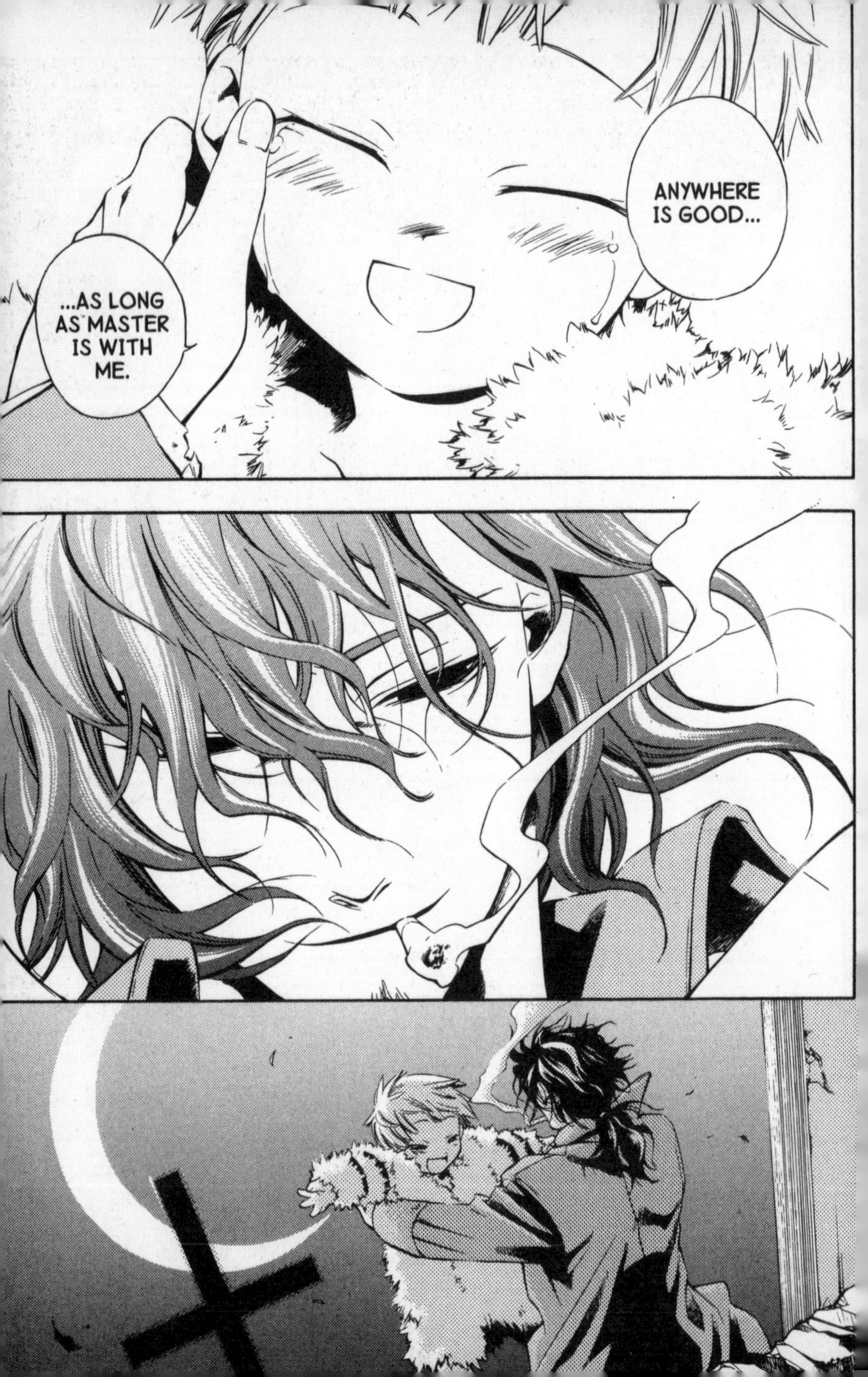
ANYWHERE IS GOOD...
...AS LONG AS MASTER IS WITH ME.

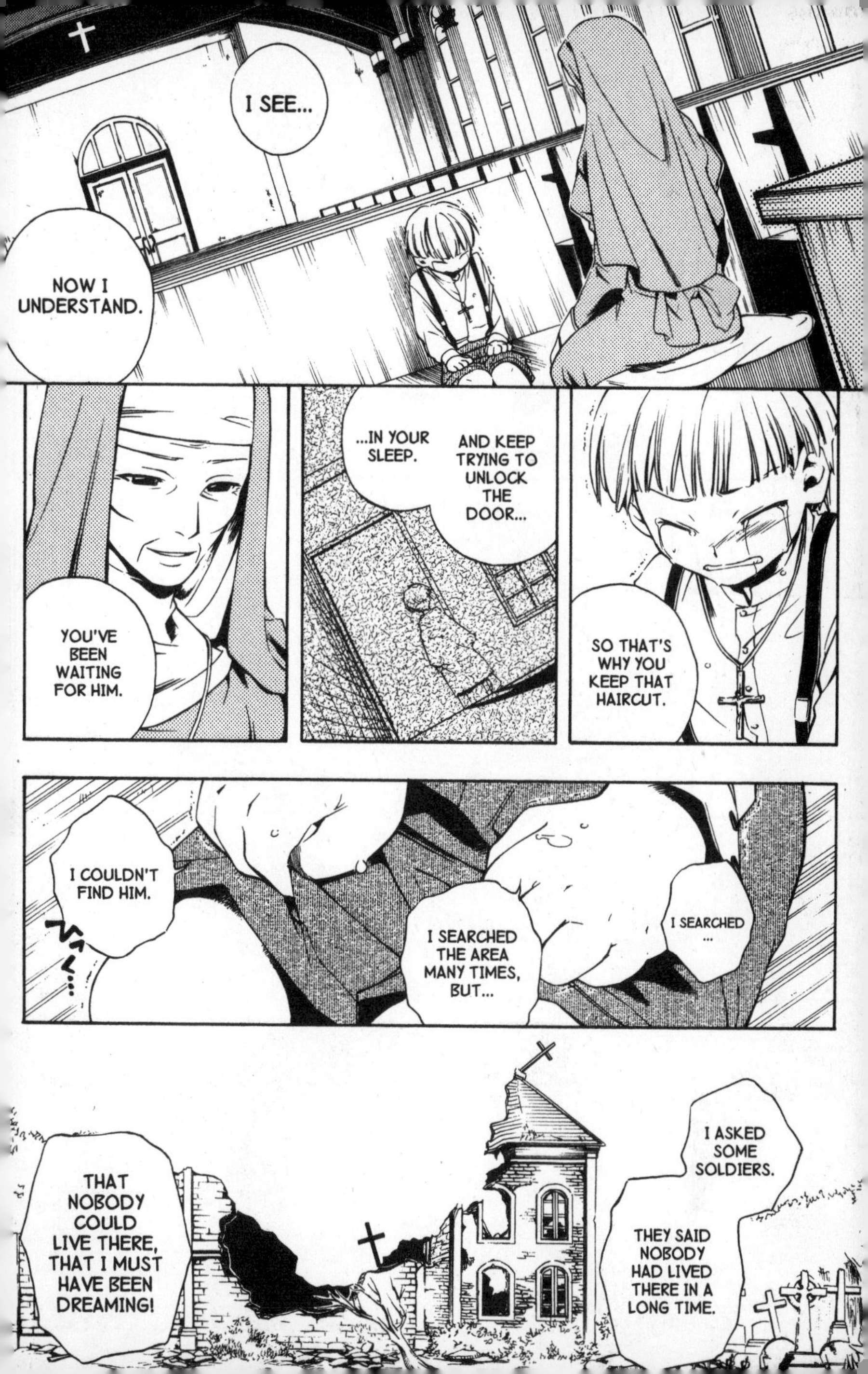
I SEE...
NOW I UNDERSTAND.
SO THAT'S WHY YOU KEEP THAT HAIRCUT.
AND KEEP TRYING TO UNLOCK THE DOOR...
...IN YOUR SLEEP.
YOU'VE BEEN WAITING FOR HIM.
I SEARCHED ...
I SEARCHED THE AREA MANY TIMES, BUT...
I COULDN'T FIND HIM.
I ASKED SOME SOLDIERS.
THEY SAID NOBODY HAD LIVED THERE IN A LONG TIME.
THAT NOBODY COULD LIVE THERE, THAT I MUST HAVE BEEN DREAMING!

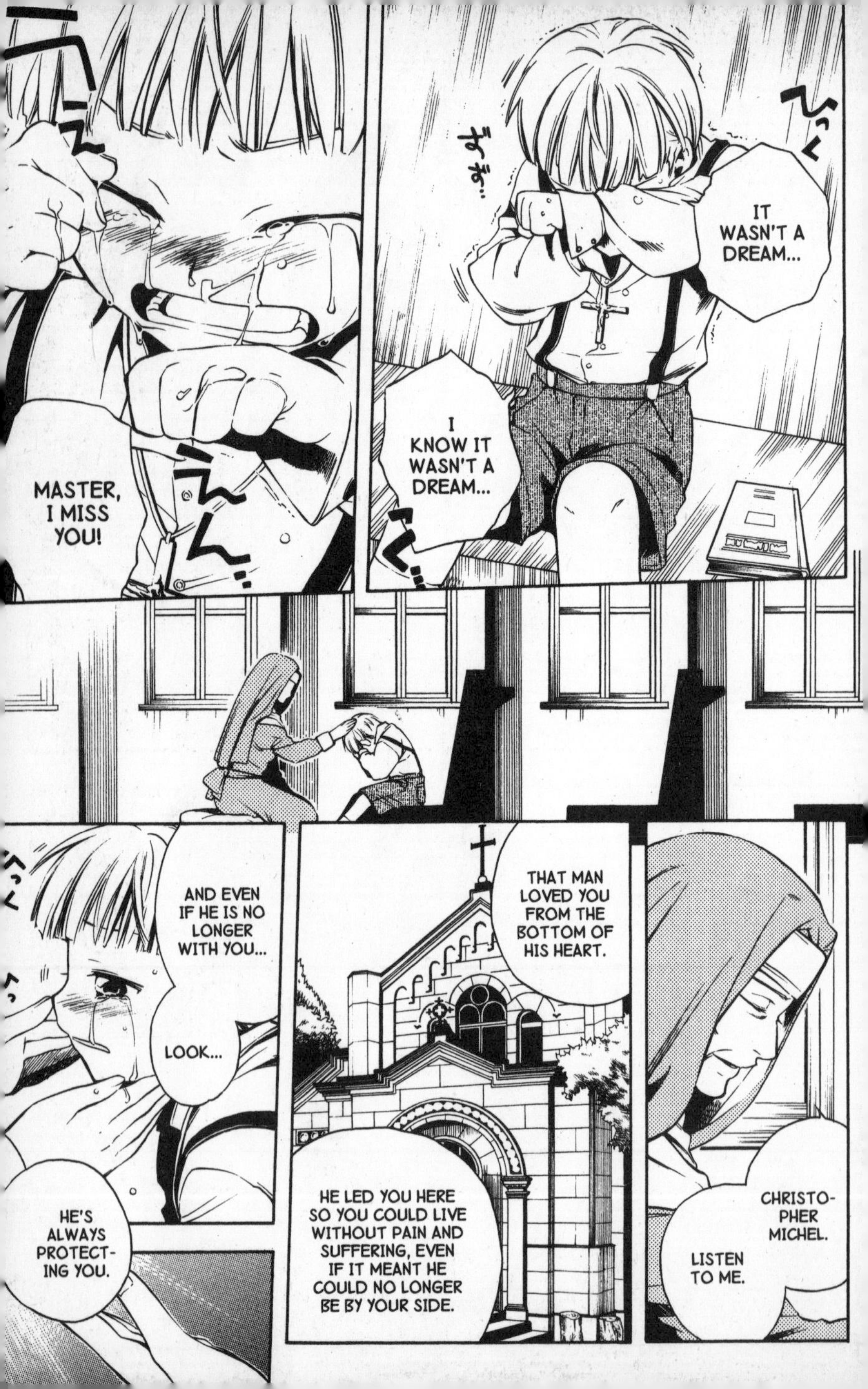
IT WASN'T A DREAM...
I KNOW IT WASN'T A DREAM...
MASTER, I MISS YOU!
CHRISTOPHER MICHEL.
LISTEN TO ME.
THAT MAN LOVED YOU FROM THE BOTTOM OF HIS HEART.
HE LED YOU HERE SO YOU COULD LIVE WITHOUT PAIN AND SUFFERING, EVEN IF IT MEANT HE COULD NO LONGER BE BY YOUR SIDE.
AND EVEN IF HE IS NO LONGER WITH YOU...
LOOK...
HE'S ALWAYS PROTECTING YOU.

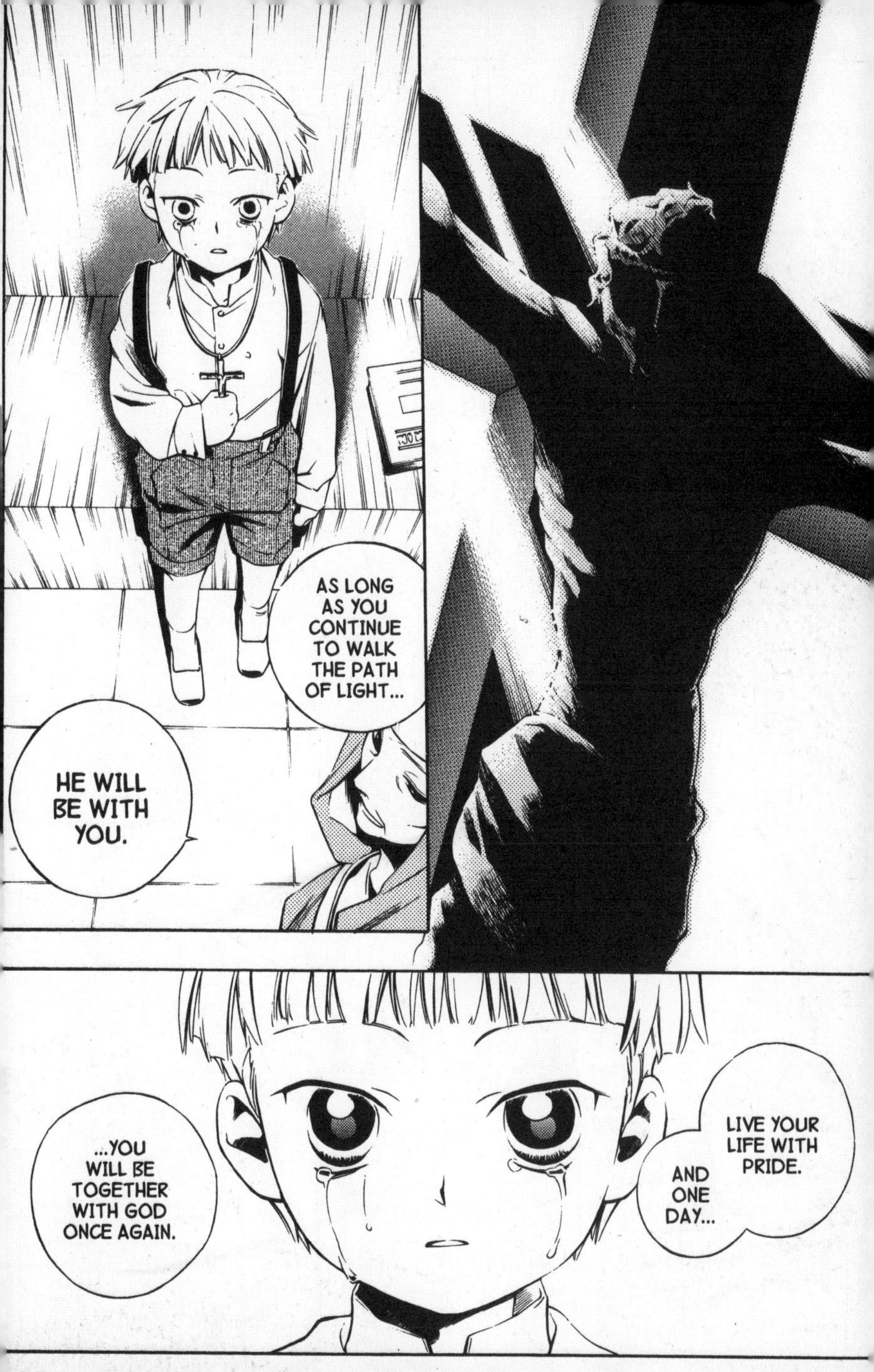
AS LONG AS YOU CONTINUE TO WALK THE PATH OF LIGHT...
HE WILL BE WITH YOU.
LIVE YOUR LIFE WITH PRIDE.
AND ONE DAY...
...YOU WILL BE TOGETHER WITH GOD ONCE AGAIN.

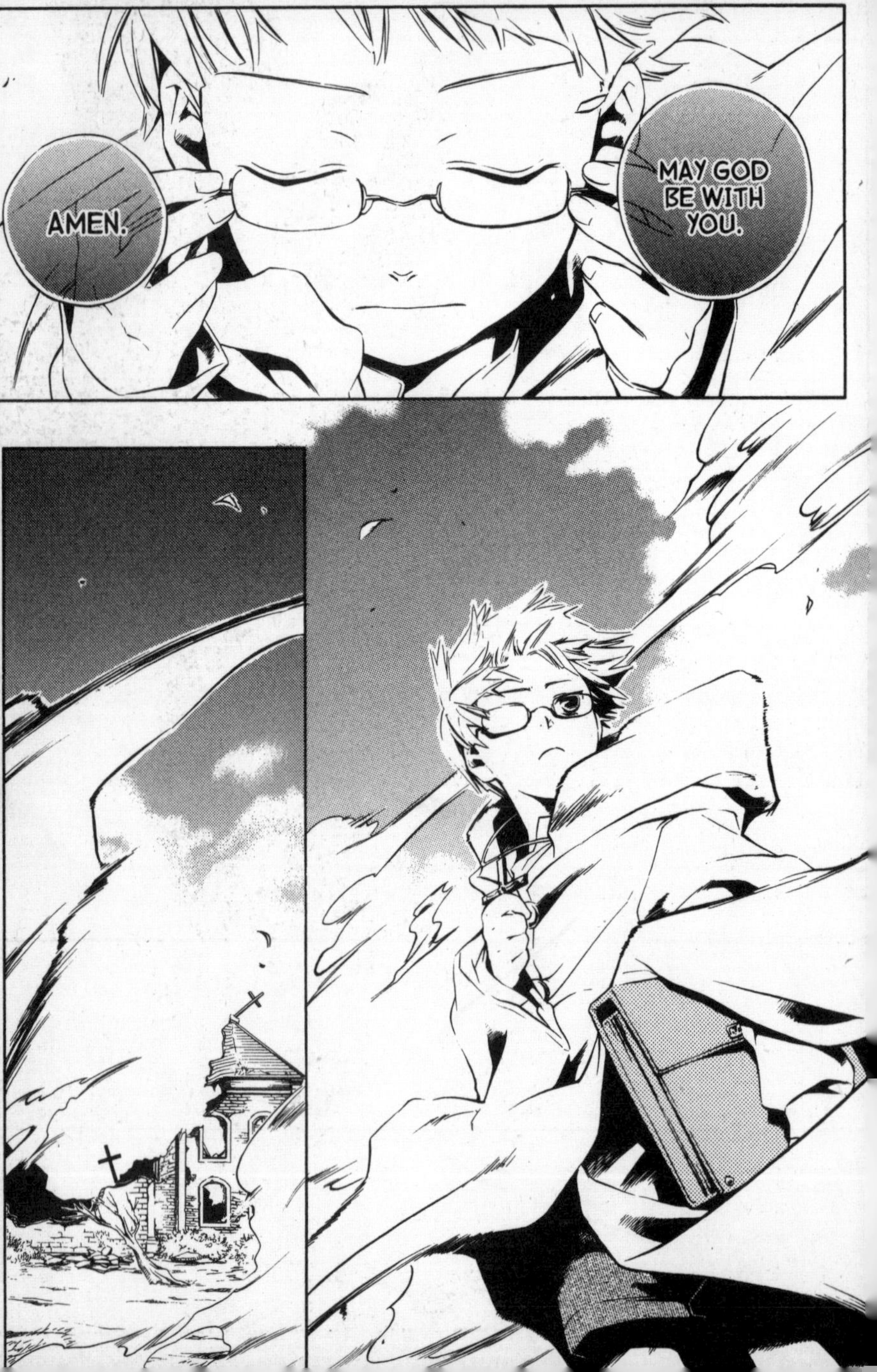
MAY GOD BE WITH YOU.
AMEN.

FAREWELL, MY BELOVED WORLD OF DARKNESS.

Vassalord. 1 **END**

a glossary of Vassalord.

ARNOLD PAOLE
A YOUNG MAN AT THE CENTER OF A VAMPIRE CONTROVERSY IN A YUGOSLAVIAN VILLAGE AROUND 1730. LOOK FOR MORE DETAILS IN CHAPTER 4.

ABBA
AN ARAMAIC WORD USED BY CHILDREN TO MEAN "FATHER." IN THE BIBLE, JESUS CHRIST USES THIS WORD TO CALL UPON GOD.

VJEDOGONIAN
PEOPLE BORN WITH A RED CAUL WHO HAVE THE ABILITY TO KILL VAMPIRES. THEY ARE IN DANGER OF BECOMING VAMPIRES AFTER THEY DIE.

THE ROMAN CATHOLIC CHURCH
LED BY THE POPE, IT IS THE WORLD'S LARGEST SINGLE RELIGIOUS BODY. CLERGY ARE REFERRED TO AS 'FATHER' OR 'SISTER.'

CRUSNIK
PEOPLE BORN WITH A WHITE CAUL WHO HAVE THE ABILITY TO KILL VAMPIRES. THEY CAN ONLY USE THEIR POWERS WHILE WEARING A PIECE OF THE AMNION.

COMMUNION
A CATHOLIC CEREMONY. BREAD AND WINE REPRESENTING JESUS CHRIST'S BODY AND BLOOD ARE CONSUMED.

SODOM
A CITY OF SIN THAT APPEARS IN THE BIBLE. IT WAS DESTROYED BY FIRES FROM THE HEAVENS. IT'S NOT CLEAR WHAT SINS WERE COMMITTED THERE BUT MANY BELIEVE HOMOSEXUALITY WAS AMONG THEM.

HIEROCLES
A FORMER SLAVE AND CHARIOTEER WHO BECAME ELAGABALUS'S FAVORITE AND "HUSBAND."

SACRAMENT
CEREMONIES OF THE CATHOLIC CHURCH, LIKE BAPTISMS, THAT BRING PEOPLE CLOSER TO GOD. THESE ARE CEREMONIES THAT GIVE PEOPLE GOD'S BLESSING AND SYMBOLIZE ONE'S BELIEF.

PROTESTANTS
A CHRISTIAN SECT THAT SPLIT OFF OF CATHOLICISM. THERE ARE SEVERAL BRANCHES AND EACH HAS ITS OWN TEACHINGS. SOME EVEN ALLOW HOMOSEXUALITY AND FEMALE PRIESTS.

ELAGABALUS
ROMAN EMPEROR, ALSO KNOWN AS HELIOGABALUS, WHO TOOK THE THRONE IN 218 A.D. A MAN OF BOTH MANY PERVERSIONS AND WIVES. HE ALSO DRESSED UP AS A FEMALE PROSTITUTE AND WAS INVOLVED IN A NUMBER OF HOMOSEXUAL RELATIONSHIPS.

UNITARIAN UNIVERSALISM

A THEOLOGICALLY LIBERAL CHRISTIAN ORGANIZATION FOUNDED IN 1961. THEY RETAIN SOME CHRISTIAN TRADITIONS BUT DO NOT STRICTLY FOLLOW EVERY RULE.

AFTERWORD!

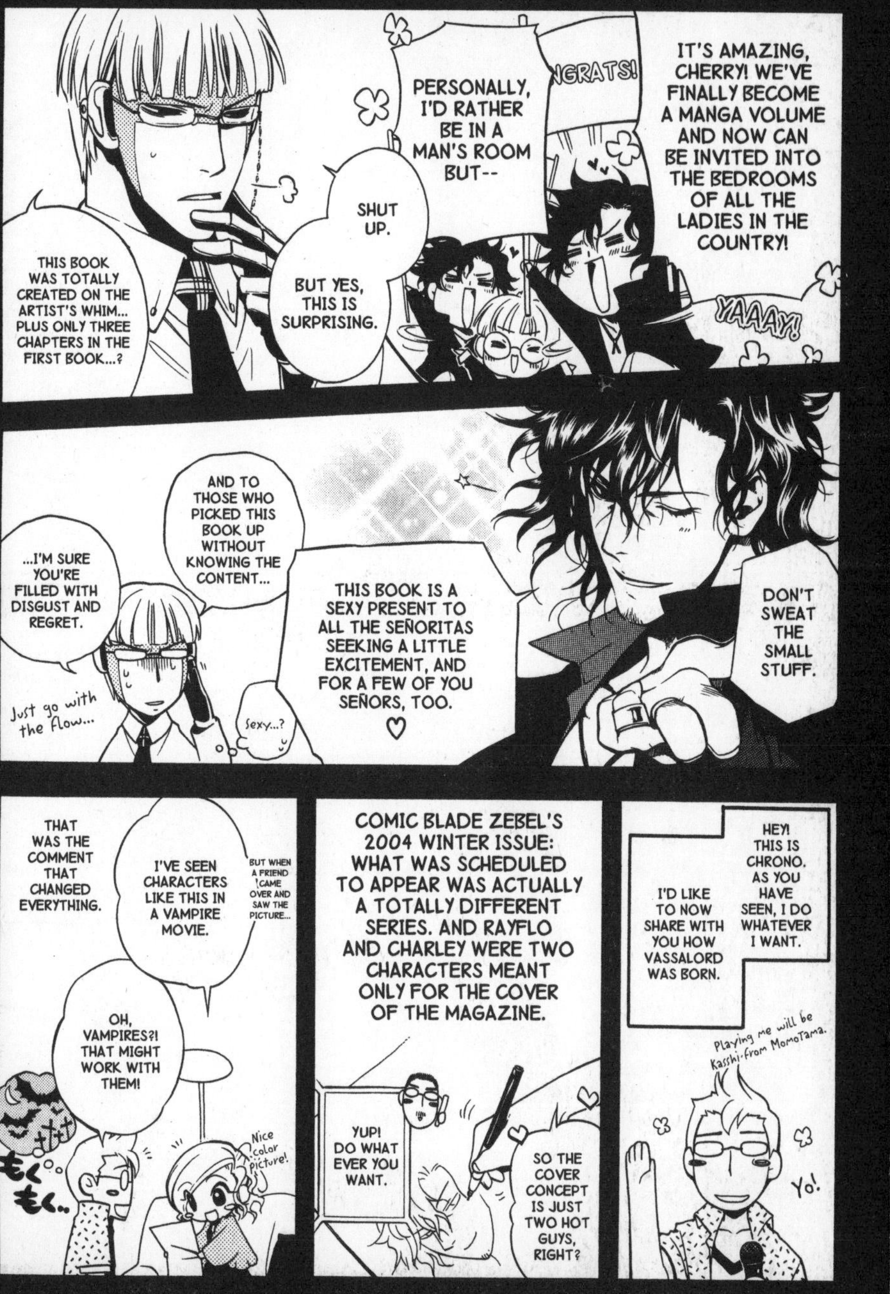
IT'S AMAZING, CHERRY! WE'VE FINALLY BECOME A MANGA VOLUME AND NOW CAN BE INVITED INTO THE BEDROOMS OF ALL THE LADIES IN THE COUNTRY!
NGRATS!
PERSONALLY, I'D RATHER BE IN A MAN'S ROOM BUT--
SHUT UP.
BUT YES, THIS IS SURPRISING.
YAAAY!
THIS BOOK WAS TOTALLY CREATED ON THE ARTIST'S WHIM... PLUS ONLY THREE CHAPTERS IN THE FIRST BOOK...?
DON'T SWEAT THE SMALL STUFF.
THIS BOOK IS A SEXY PRESENT TO ALL THE SEÑORITAS SEEKING A LITTLE EXCITEMENT, AND FOR A FEW OF YOU SEÑORS, TOO. ♡
AND TO THOSE WHO PICKED THIS BOOK UP WITHOUT KNOWING THE CONTENT...
...I'M SURE YOU'RE FILLED WITH DISGUST AND REGRET.
Sexy...?
Just go with the flow...
HEY! THIS IS CHRONO. AS YOU HAVE SEEN, I DO WHATEVER I WANT.
I'D LIKE TO NOW SHARE WITH YOU HOW VASSALORD WAS BORN.
Playing me will be Kasshi from MomoTama.
Yo!
COMIC BLADE ZEBEL'S 2004 WINTER ISSUE: WHAT WAS SCHEDULED TO APPEAR WAS ACTUALLY A TOTALLY DIFFERENT SERIES. AND RAYFLO AND CHARLEY WERE TWO CHARACTERS MEANT ONLY FOR THE COVER OF THE MAGAZINE.
SO THE COVER CONCEPT IS JUST TWO HOT GUYS, RIGHT?
YUP! DO WHAT EVER YOU WANT.
BUT WHEN A FRIEND CAME OVER AND SAW THE PICTURE...
I'VE SEEN CHARACTERS LIKE THIS IN A VAMPIRE MOVIE.
THAT WAS THE COMMENT THAT CHANGED EVERYTHING.
OH, VAMPIRES?! THAT MIGHT WORK WITH THEM!
Nice color picture!
もく もく..

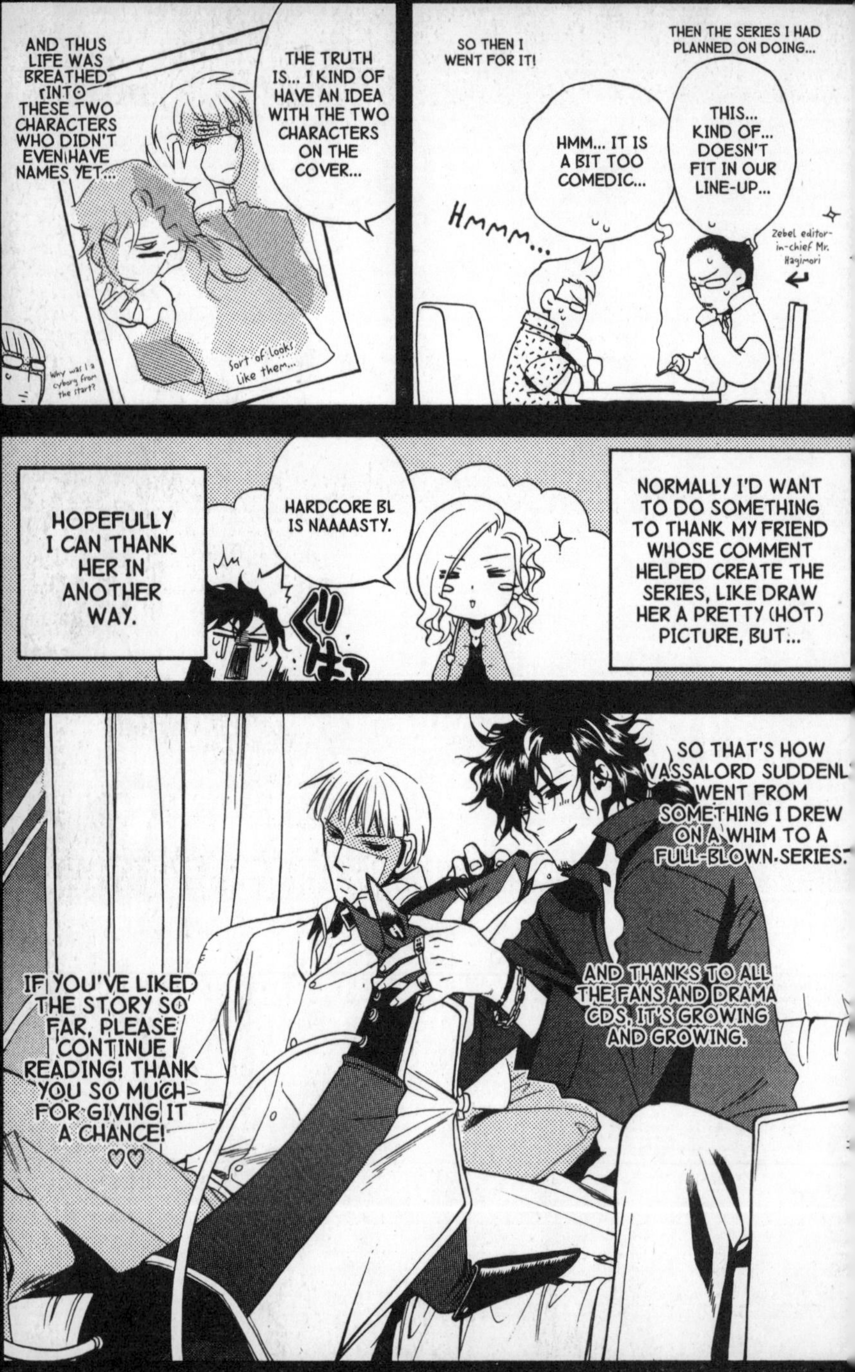
THEN THE SERIES I HAD PLANNED ON DOING...
SO THEN I WENT FOR IT!
THIS... KIND OF... DOESN'T FIT IN OUR LINE-UP...
HMM... IT IS A BIT TOO COMEDIC...
HMMM...
Zebel editor-in-chief Mr. Hagimori
THE TRUTH IS... I KIND OF HAVE AN IDEA WITH THE TWO CHARACTERS ON THE COVER...
AND THUS LIFE WAS BREATHED INTO THESE TWO CHARACTERS WHO DIDN'T EVEN HAVE NAMES YET...
Sort of looks like them...
Why was I a cyborg from the start?
NORMALLY I'D WANT TO DO SOMETHING TO THANK MY FRIEND WHOSE COMMENT HELPED CREATE THE SERIES, LIKE DRAW HER A PRETTY (HOT) PICTURE, BUT...
HARDCORE BL IS NAAAASTY.
HOPEFULLY I CAN THANK HER IN ANOTHER WAY.
SO THAT'S HOW VASSALORD SUDDENLY WENT FROM SOMETHING I DREW ON A WHIM TO A FULL-BLOWN SERIES.
AND THANKS TO ALL THE FANS AND DRAMA CDS, IT'S GROWING AND GROWING.
IF YOU'VE LIKED THE STORY SO FAR, PLEASE CONTINUE READING! THANK YOU SO MUCH FOR GIVING IT A CHANCE! ♡♡

IN THE NEXT

vassalord

ヴァッサロード

THE PLOT THICKENS AND THE HIJINKS
CONTINUE AS OUR HANDSOME DUO
PUT THEIR OWN SEXY SPIN ON THE
MILE-HIGH CLUB. AN AIRPLANE RIDE
YIELDS SEVERAL SURPRISES FOR
RAYFLO AND CHARLEY, INCLUDING
A RUN-IN WITH AN ACTRESS WITH
A DARK SECRET AND A MYSTERIOUS
SABOTEUR. BUT AS CHARLEY BEGINS
AN INVESTIGATION OF HIS OWN, HIS
FEELINGS FOR RAYFLO SEEM TO
GET IN THE WAY AT EVERY TURN...

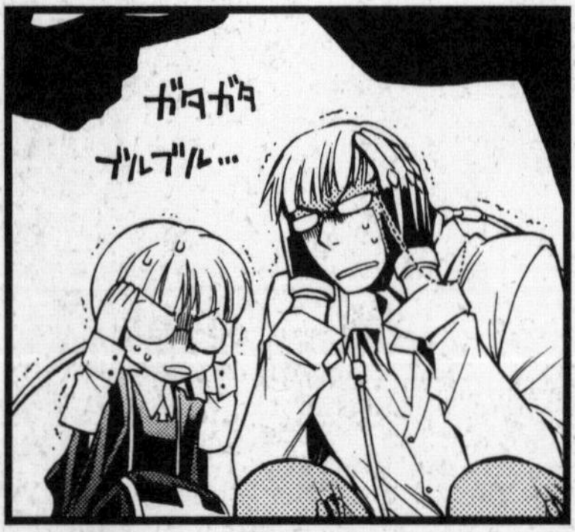
ガタガタ
ブルブル…

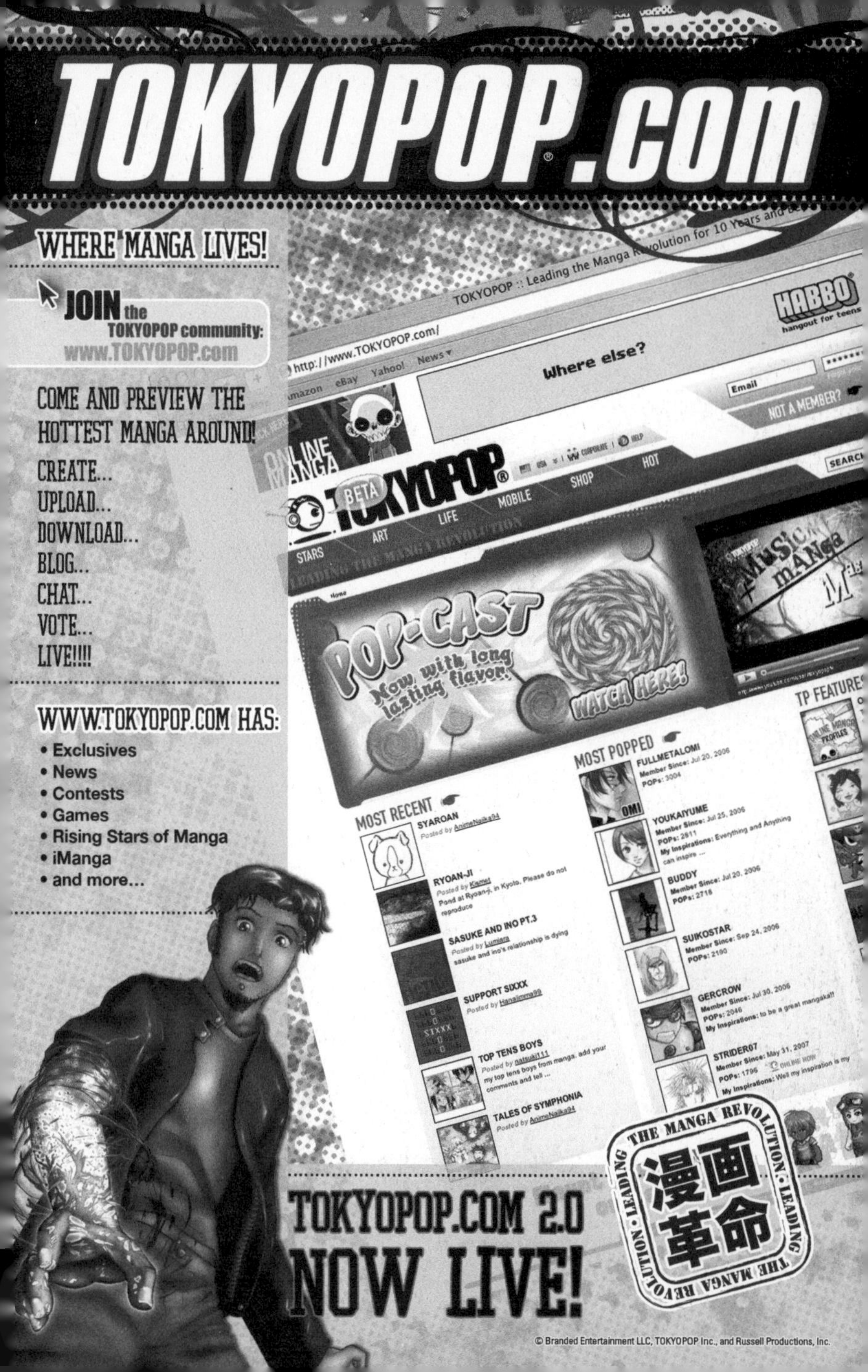
TOKYOPOP.com
WHERE MANGA LIVES!
JOIN the TOKYOPOP community: www.TOKYOPOP.com
COME AND PREVIEW THE HOTTEST MANGA AROUND!
CREATE...
UPLOAD...
DOWNLOAD...
BLOG...
CHAT...
VOTE...
LIVE!!!!
WWW.TOKYOPOP.COM HAS:
• Exclusives
• News
• Contests
• Games
• Rising Stars of Manga
• iManga
• and more...
TOKYOPOP :: Leading the Manga Revolution for 10 Years and
http://www.TOKYOPOP.com/
Where else?
NOT A MEMBER?
TOKYOPOP
STARS
ART
LIFE
MOBILE
SHOP
HOT
POP-CAST
Now with long lasting flavor
WATCH HERE!
MOST RECENT
MOST POPPED
TP FEATURES
TOKYOPOP.COM 2.0 NOW LIVE!
LEADING THE MANGA REVOLUTION
漫画革命
© Branded Entertainment LLC, TOKYOPOP Inc., and Russell Productions, Inc.

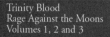

Hotel AFRICA™

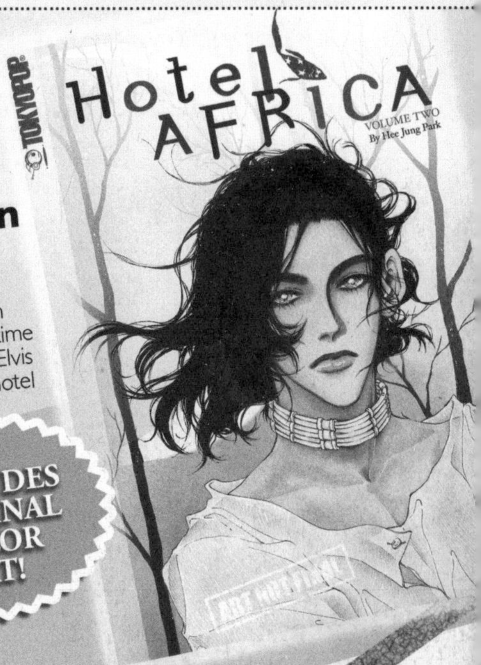
TOKYOPOP
Hotel AFRICA
VOLUME TWO
By Hee Jung Park

Anything can happen at the Hotel Africa

Tales of heartbreak, irony, and redemption are in store when you check in a second time to the Hotel Africa. Continue along with Elvis as he reveals more tales of the desolate hotel and its strange guests.

INCLUDES ORIGINAL COLOR ART!

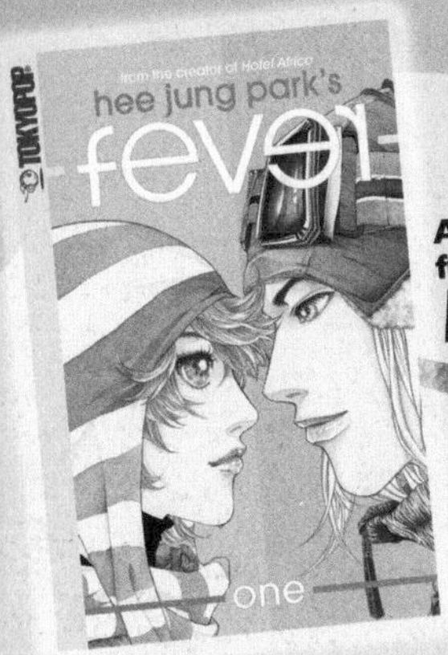
TOKYOPOP
from the creator of Hotel Africa
hee jung park's
fever
one

Also available from Hee Jung Park

Fever

Once you go to Fever, you will never be the same...

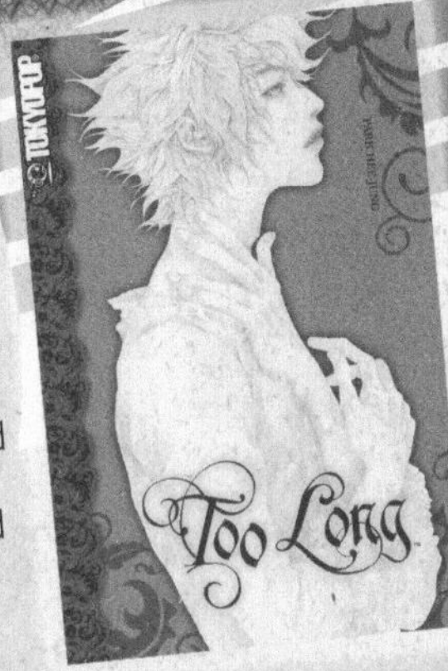
TOKYOPOP
Too Long

Too Long

A girl who attracts suicide victims, a shy record store customer, and the star of a rock band... what could these three have in common? Find out in this moving collection of short stories.

FOR MORE INFORMATION VISIT: WWW.TOKYOPOP.COM

This is the back of the book.
You wouldn't want to spoil a great ending!

This book is printed "manga-style," in the authentic Jap_____ ft
format. Since none of the artwork has been flipped or a_____
get to experience the story just as the creator intended._____
asking for it, so TOKYOPOP® delivered: authentic, hot-_____
and far more fun!

DIRECT

If this is your first time
reading manga-style, here's a
quick guide to help you
understand how it works.

It's easy... just start in the top
right panel and follow the
numbers. Have fun, and look for
more 100% authentic manga
from TOKYOPOP®!

Vassalord.

1

CONTENTS

Vassalord.

ヴァッサロード

1

黒乃

絵

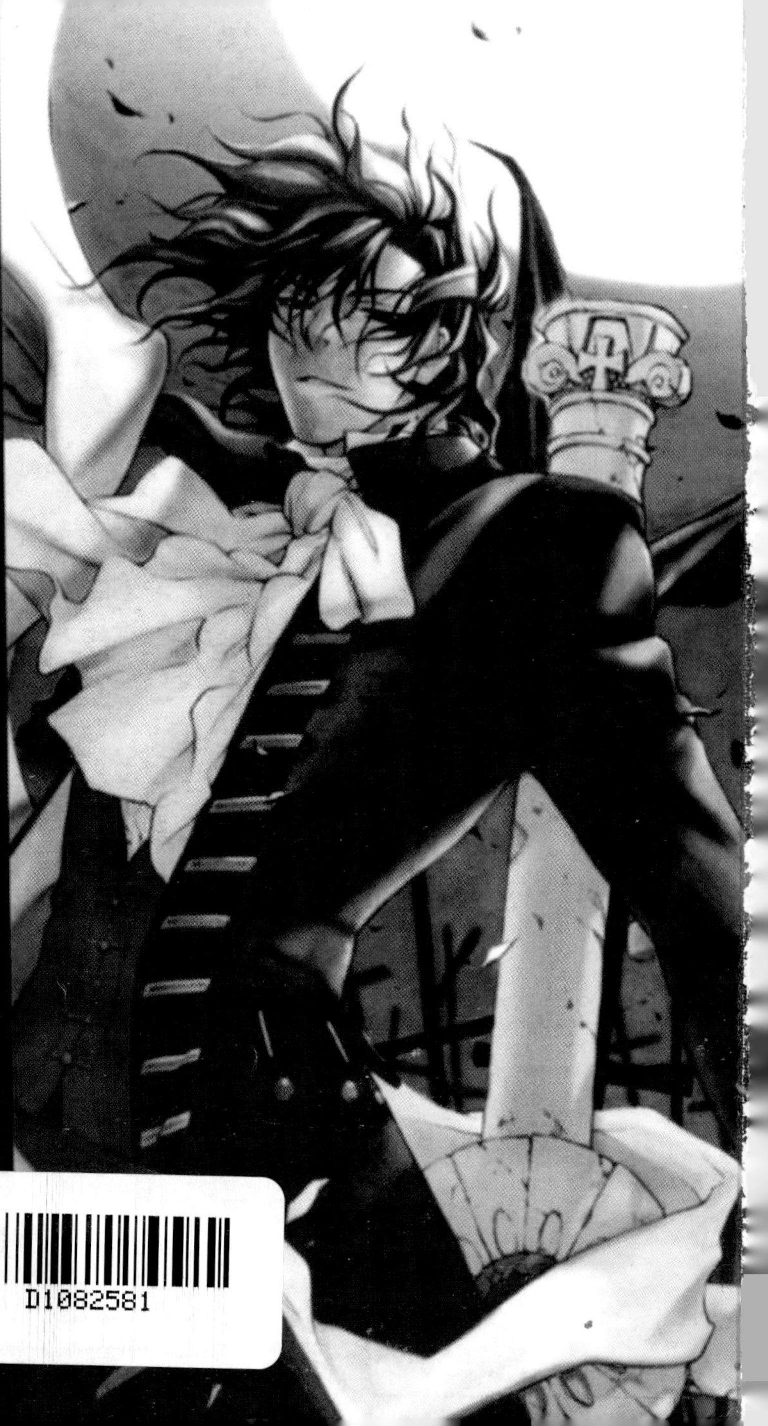